IGNITION TO SANCTUM

Book 3, The Dragon Age Prophecy

N. A. HYDES

Cover Art by Neal Hopkins: Elerfine - Etsy

Original Edits by Vicki Greer www.vickiedits.com

Developmental and Line Edits by Jennia Herold D'Lima https://jenniaedits.com/

Proofreading by Roxana Coumans https://proofreadebooks.com

N. A. Hydes can be reached at https://nahdes.com or on discord at https://discord.gg/nnSETXPbtH

�֎ Created with Vellum

NOTE TO READER

Sometimes I wish the characters in this book were real. I have a lot I'd like to ask them. But, alas, this is a work of fiction. The story is based on several mythologies and folklore from around the world. It's not meant to insult or belittle cultural beliefs or history, but rather to entertain for a few hours.

If you are curious as to what questions I would ask, have questions you would like to ask, or how I think they would respond, I can be reached at nahydes@nahydes.com.

Yours truly,

N. A. Hydes

For my dad, Jerry. You taught me more about life than any other person.

PROLOGUE: ANCIENT PROPHECY

An abandoned prophecy sat in a turret designed to resemble a ziggurat, built at the end of a lava tube off the main cavern of the dragon city of Dernogard. Instead of parchment, it was recorded on whalebone and written in the language of dragons. The document's creator was the earth elemental dragon Yangdi, the firstborn son of the first dragon, MiFeng.

MiFeng, the king of dragons, placed the prophecy there long before the birth of his other children, Spring and River. Though many had heard of the prophecy, few had seen it. Fewer still remembered it. The prediction read:

Father,

I had a vision of the future of dragons.

In the vision, I was above a map of the world. The dragons' territories were marked in blue, and the Earth was filled with dragonkind.

An ancient serpent rose from the ocean and urged humans to kill dragons. As it talked, blood filled the water, and a red wave rose, killing all the dragons it touched from shore to shore.

A green dragon, who looked similar to Mother, stood in the sea of blood. In his hands, he held a basket. He gave it to a human just as the red water touched him. The green dragon shriveled and disappeared.

The human carried the green dragon's gift away through the sea of blood to another land. A wyvern sniffed the basket, licked it, then was blotted out by the sea of blood. The basket grew and expanded.

As it floated, dragonkind vanished, and the ocean turned blue and calm once more.

Eventually, the woven cradle opened as if it was hatching. A human the color of crimson, the lifeblood of all those who had died, stepped out, and when his foot touched the earth, it shook as a mighty earthquake grabbed the corners of the world.

The human dragon spoke to me in the voice of many angels. "I am the Mark of Redemption, the return of dragons to this world," he said.

As he breathed fire on the water, the sea bubbled and boiled. The bubbles reached the surface and popped, leaving many human dragons to fill the sea and land.

He ordered me to write down what I witnessed and to share it with you—as a warning. My magic will block most of these words from your memory and from your thoughts. When the vision is to come to pass, you will remember all I have written in this letter. Only then, will dragons remember these words. They are secrets to protect the red human dragon, lest he be killed.

When the Mark walks our world, I will return to Dernogard and teach the new human dragons. Until then, I will be preparing.

Encourage the young dragons to read this prophecy when they visit you. When they do, they will see and remember only three things.

The Age of Dragons has ended. A human-looking dragon who commands fire marks the redemption when dragons will repopulate the Earth. Soon after, a new Dragon Age will begin.

Yangdi

Except Yangdi was wrong. The Mark of Redemption wasn't a man, but a woman.

CHAPTER 1

SHANNA

WEEKEND BEFORE THANKSGIVING

NOTHING IN SHANNA WHITE'S LIFE HAD GONE ACCORDING TO plan.

That included today, the Friday before Thanksgiving, but at least she had the apartment to herself.

She had settled on her bed with a bowl of popcorn propped on her knees and grabbed the remote to stream whatever looked good when a loud blast vibrated through the dorm room. The sound entered every cell of Shanna's body, forcing her to turn into an ice-blue, seven-foot-tall dragon. Her sudden shift shoved the furniture into the walls, shattering the flat-screen TV, and she almost lost her balance on the carpeted floor.

The noise disappeared as quickly as it started.

She immediately took control and resumed her human shape. What had happened? Trying to catch her breath, her chest rapidly rose and fell. Nothing had forced her dragon form her first shift over thirty years ago.

The memory barged its way to the forefront of her mind. At sixteen, she had thought herself wholly human. The night of her first change, she stormed out of her parents' home over something meaningless. The exact subject eluded her now—

smoking, maybe. But she remembered her feelings—wanting freedom and to escape their overbearing rules.

She could almost hear how the front door creaked and banged shut when she angrily ran out.

With nowhere to go, she had walked aimlessly along a forest road. Her eyes blurry from tears, she didn't see the car until seconds before it hit her. Instead of dying, like she expected to, a high-pitched sound brought her to her knees, and to her surprise, she morphed into a sea serpent, similar to the ones drawn on the edges of old maps.

Few details remained in her memory from that night, but if she concentrated hard enough, she could remember the taste of human flesh.

Days later, the local news articles blamed Dan Smith's disappearance on drinking, driving fast, and an animal. The damaged Pontiac suggested the driver sustained head injuries and left the scene of the accident. Searchers in the area hunted for the man, but, of course, they never found him.

Back then, she feared everything, lived on adrenaline, and made poor choices, all in hopes of controlling her destiny.

Now... Now she knew she had no freedom—she was a caged dragon. But what was done was done.

Control your shock and fear. It's over, and you're safe. Assess the damage, she thought.

She glanced at the window. Luckily, the blinds were shut, and the lights were off. No one saw her transformation, so she wouldn't have to kill today.

Shattered glass stretched from one side of the room to the other. Two televisions, her computer, and multiple picture frames all lay in devastation. Having shredded her clothing when morphing into a large reptile, she stood naked. She had never minded the breeze on her bare skin, but with sharp objects scattered about, she'd prefer having shoes on—dragon feet might not get cut easily by glass, but human soles split easily.

After she got dressed, she'd have a few hours of work ahead of her to clean up and replace everything that had been broken. At least she didn't cave in a wall or bust out a window. She counted the destruction as minimal since only objects were broken and no one died.

What happened? she thought.

"Gourdy!" she screamed to her dragon guide, thankful her roommate went home for Thanksgiving. It made her free to speak out loud to a creature only she could see. And, if Chloe had been there, Shanna would have had to kill her since she couldn't allow witnesses to her shift.

"I hate that name," Gourdy said. He appeared near the window. Tall, at least six-foot-two, skinny, and with pale blond hair, he resembled the very alive human version of the dragon shifter Jormungant. Not that she had met him, but she'd seen pictures of him. Unlike the modern version of Jormungant, her dragon guide wore a beard and kept his locks unevenly cut, as if he used the sword he held in a scabbard over his shoulder to trim any growth.

"I know you hate it," she thought, smiling.

The nickname *Gourdy* came to her the first fall after she'd finished the Family's training. Seeing the carved pumpkins and with the story of the headless horseman fresh in her mind, she thought of how her dragon guide reminded her of a dark spirit or force that wanted to be the actual person it represented. But Jormungant lived, and Gourdy was only a fake version of the breathing dragon. Just like the pumpkin would never be the horseman's missing head, Gourdy would never be Jormungant. And since a pumpkin was a type of gourd, the pseudonym Gourdy matched her dragon guide perfectly.

She thought to Gourdy, *"But it separates you from the real Jormungant... Anyway, what was that noise? Why did I change?"*

"An awakening. A human just got their dragon wings," he said.

3

She knew the word awakening from her dragon classes. It meant a human who descended from a dragon just became a dragon for the first time. She remembered her own period of awakening, right after her first shift. She'd spent her nights living her ancestors' lives backward until she dreamed of Jormungant.

It had been horrible waking up as a different person, trying to remember her name. Some days, she forgot how to turn on lights, brush her teeth, and even speak English. But because she was lost and confused, at least she didn't remember the truth of her reality and the taste of human flesh. None of her ancestors had tasted human flesh.

In her last ancestorial dream, she was Jormungant. His memory started surveying a magnificent horizon—neither day nor night, stretches of blue sky and white snow. She had no idea that her worst nightmares were only just beginning.

Gourdy tortured Shanna. As an imprinted memory of her dragon ancestor, Jormungant, Gourdy had dominion over her mind, causing her to see and hear things that weren't there. He could even inflict pain.

"It's amazing the control I have over you just by making a single twitch," Gourdy said, holding up his pinky. At the same time, a pain exploded in her upper temple.

The pain ebbed away. *"It doesn't change that Jormungant is real and alive, and you aren't."*

Only she could see and interact with Gourdy. His control over her brain seemed absolute. She thought of him as a computer virus implanted in her DNA, coded to activate the second she went all dragon.

She and Gourdy had discussed his predominance repeatedly, but the presence of a new dragon shifter left her with different questions. *"Will I turn into a dragon every time I hear an awakening?"*

He stood up straighter, dressed like a Renaissance fair knight with his sword hilt jutting over his shoulder. "How would I know? I hatched as a dragon. I'm not controlled by anyone or anything."

"You're not real," she reminded him, but somewhere, another person existed like her. Would the new dragon shifter find themselves in a similar predicament to hers—a vicious dragon guide and involved in an unescapable cult-like group?

As a descendant from the sea serpent Jormungant, she'd been ensnared in a cult that called themselves the Family. A few days after she turned seventeen, a car picked her up and whisked her away to a remote training facility. At the time, she willingly took the opportunity to escape. Once there, she studied alone and was trained directly by her supervisor, Roland.

The evil organization even had a public persona—a pharmaceutical company named Wing It Laboratories. Its CEO was none other than the living and breathing version of her dragon guide, Jormungant. Of course, he'd modernized his name, calling himself Tom Johnson.

But she had to call him Father—because cults required their leader to have a revered term of endearment…and the figurehead of the Family, Jormungant, was… *"Is crazy."*

"Crazy, do you mean genius?" Gourdy asked.

"No. I meant demented," she thought to Gourdy.

Shanna avoided the glass on the floor and dressed swiftly. Then she climbed over her bed to where her nightstand was shoved against the wall to retrieve her cell. She dialed Roland's number.

"Hello, Amy," he said, using her spy name—the name she chose for this job.

She huffed. "No one is here. You can call me Shanna."

"Amy, it's unsafe for you to think of yourself as anyone but the character you're playing. Do you understand, *Amy*?"

She'd heard it a hundred times: *stay in character*. She rolled her eyes. "Yes. I understand, Roland. I'm Amy... Listen, did you hear the awakening?"

Roland never had a smell, not of emotions or of what special abilities he might have, so she was unsure if he had dragon hearing. Around everyone else, she used her gift of smell to determine the meaning behind their words. With him, she relied on his body language. But during a phone call, she couldn't use either smell or his posture to determine the thoughts behind his words.

"Yes," he said.

From what he said, she knew he had dragon hearing or another way to detect the first transformation.

He continued. "I'm sending you a present. *Ode de Dragonne*. A perfume designed by Wing It Laboratories to block the scent of dragon. If anyone who has the gift of dragon smelling is near you, say, for instance, a Nose"—she knew that meant a person capable of detecting odors that equaled a dragon's ability—"or a dragon, this will block their ability to tell you are a shifter. You'll have to set an alarm. When it arrives, you must spray it over your whole body every twenty-four hours. If you take a shower, you must reapply it. Do you understand?"

"Yes. I understand."

"Good. It will block any dragons from being able to smell you."

Would it mask her odor, like Roland's? Was that what he used? The answers to her questions could wait. She needed to focus on the immediate threat of another dragon being so close to her. She asked, "Roland, it forced a shift. If I hadn't been alone, I would have... I'd have loose ends. Will I turn into a dragon every time a human becomes a dragon?"

He paused, and she imagined him searching through his files for the answers. Finally, he said, "I don't know." A few seconds later, he added, "Listen, Amy, I told Father about the professor who ate a dragon's heart. He's sent an operative to handle the situation. Stay away from the man, don't take his classes, and do not engage. Do you understand?"

The college professor was oblivious of her. She'd passed him several times without him reacting. He had no clue what she was. Plus, Shanna aced her smelling exam at Wing It. She could accurately identify the different gifts Dr. Smith received from eating dragon, so she wasn't worried about him. "Yes. The only gift he has is dragon hearing. I'm sure of—"

"Do. Not. Engage. Repeat what I just said," Roland demanded.

"Fine. I will not engage with the professor." She sighed. "How long will I be at South Holt?"

"I'm not sure of that. When I have more details, I'll let you know."

"Are you sending in a team to determine who the dragon is?"

In the background, on the other end, she heard a tapping noise. "We already have operatives in the area. No Noses yet. We won't send them until we know you are protected. That's why it's important that when you get *Ode de Dragonne* that you spray it generously all over yourself... Amy?"

"Yes?"

"I want you to be aware that as soon as the delivery company says the package has arrived, Father will assign Noses to South Holt. We haven't told many other operatives about Father's treasured daughter, and I'm not ready to let everyone know about you... Please repeat your orders."

"When the perfume arrives, spray generously once a day or whenever I have a shower."

Never before had she been this close to an active operation. All her previous jobs involved nothing more than surveillance of some of Father's entirely human descendants. Roland made sure she stayed miles away from anyone who might mark her as a dragon shifter.

"Good."

"How will I know it works?"

"We've tested the perfume with Noses. Father even volunteered. It covered up Father's dragon scent. It will cover yours. It will keep you safe. I'll talk to you soon… *Amy*."

"Yes, sir." She turned off the screen and put it back on the bed. Kicking the TV's broken frame, she noticed her roommate's family photo was part of the carnage. She grabbed the image, carefully removed it from the sharp edges, dusted it, and inspected the picture of her roommate's two younger brothers.

Shanna had many found brothers, even if they didn't know about her. They were tied to her through the Family. They were wicked and caged animals... Just like her.

When the Family swept Shanna away so long ago, they told her she was special and that they could help her. They left off their insane *take-over-the-world* ideology. If they had told her the truth, she might not have ever gotten into the car. Like boiling a frog, they slowly introduced their purpose, turning up the heat until she could no longer jump out of the water. She didn't buy into their beliefs. But she had done a myriad of evil things. She had no one who wanted to save her. The only ones who saw any value in her, she hated, but they gave her a purpose.

Trapped by her actions, years later, she realized they needed her. Now over forty but stuck in a sixteen-year-old girl's body, she made a perfect spy.

How many secret agents did the Family have? How many other ensnared and tortured souls like hers? How many others who had killed willingly for freedom?

The question haunted her thoughts. Could her found family be the jailors who'd blocked her escape? More than once, Roland knew about her day without her mentioning a word to him. How could he know so many details if someone wasn't watching her?

For instance, one time, she stopped for something sweet. He called and asked if she liked the strawberry ice cream she picked up. Another time, he requested her to slow down when she was driving over the speed limit on some obscure street. Still another time, he asked if she enjoyed the book she had just finished.

Shanna got the message. She was being watched. Roland had people following her, informants scattered here and there. The Family watched everything and everyone.

Even if she had a savior or a way out, she concluded it was pointless to try to unshackle from the Family—they'd find her—leaving her no choice but to comply with their demands.

How many other people were lured into the organization that called themselves the Family? Last fall, Shanna calculated an estimate. If Jormungant was ten thousand years old, he had approximately two hundred family lines. He kept the boys and trained them to recognize, kill, and harvest dragons. The girls were married without knowledge of the dragon world, their children tracked for generations. If half were girls, that left one hundred family lines that could be operatives.

If all one hundred lines were still around, and the men who ate a dragon's heart married every fifty years, then conceivably, fifty more lines could be added. That was because descendants of dragons typically couldn't have more than one child. Multiple children were rare but possible. She minimized the math and didn't include families with more than one kid or cases where the bloodline stopped. So, that brought the number to approximately two hundred fifty members.

If half of the two-hundred-fifty descendants were girls, that left only one-hundred-twenty-five. The number of descendants was too small to pull off the size of the spy network she knew was in place. Plus, she knew the family lines were being watched. With each of the ten assignments she had before watching Jennifer, she had replaced another operative. When she left, a new operative replaced her. The only way the Family could do that was with external help. Perhaps a branch of Tom Johnson's pharmaceutical company that did all the research for each bloodline?

Grabbing the broom, she thought about how this job had changed in the few months she'd been at South Holt University. As with any assignment, Roland debriefed Shanna on her target, her newest target being Jennifer Wright, providing information about her life and notes from the last operative who watched her.

As one of the oddball families with two children, the Wrights were blessed. Shanna postulated they had assigned other operatives to Jennifer's brother, Randy, but assignments were only shared on a *need-to-know basis*.

The tall, blond Jennifer was beautiful and had a friendly smile. According to the documents, she made honor roll in high school and didn't go out much. Making assumptions about how to integrate into Jennifer's life, Shanna predicted she had overbearing parents. Like any caged bird, Shanna expected Jennifer's college days to be full of parties. Catering to her expectations, Shanna created Amy, attempting to personify a friend for Jennifer. Someone to join the same sorority, hold Jennifer's hair back when she puked, and encourage outrageous adventures.

"Well, you know what they say about people who assume," Gourdy said, reading her thoughts.

Frowning, Shanna remembered the many times Jennifer studied in the library on the boring green couch and the cute way she flirted with the boy she obviously liked, Matt. It was like watching *Leave It to Beaver*. "Gosh golly, Gourdy. How was I to know she was a square?"

Gourdy smirked.

As she swept, she realized at least this mess was something she could clean and straighten back into like new conditions, unlike her life.

CHAPTER 2

SHANNA

SATURDAY MORNING BEFORE THANKSGIVING

SHANNA COULDN'T SLEEP EVEN THOUGH SHE TRIED SEVERAL times. Sometimes, after she closed her eyes, she felt a phantom wind brush the hair on her neck, and she imagined a dragon inches from her skin. Instantly, she'd sit up, checking the room. Or she'd hear a noise outside that sounded like the low roar of a dragon. Standing, she'd peek between a slit in the blinds, finding nothing.

This pattern repeated, causing her to wonder where this mysterious dragon lurked. Were they close? How close? Could they find her? Smell her out? Cameras were everywhere. Would the new dragon shifter be caught on tape in their dragon form? Instead of having Big Foot hunters, would people be snooping around for a mythical monster?

Would they find Shanna instead?

Her imagination went wild, picturing a hunter's room. There would be a Teddy Roosevelt lookalike lounging in a thick, tan leather armchair, his feet propped up in front of a crackling fire. Above the mantel, someone had mounted her head, her red curls hanging down. The sign underneath read *Dragon*.

"*You're being ridiculous. Go to sleep,*" Gourdy said in her mind.

"I know. I'm stupid tired. But knowing it's not real isn't helping."

Gourdy appeared, sitting on her roommate's bed. "Go to a store and buy items to replace all the things you broke."

She stuffed her pillows between her and the wall, sitting up. "Too late. Stores are closed. Plus, what if the dragon is out there? I don't want to face a drag—"

"You know how to fight, and unlike most miserable humans, you aren't a wimp." Furrowing his eyebrows at her while nodding, he continued. "At least you maintain your dragon strength as a pathetic human."

"The only fight you are sure to win is the one you avoid," she stated as she wrapped her arms around her legs. She missed that, physical contact, having someone stronger who could hug her and make her nightmares stop. "I could go to a bar and pick up—"

"Greg," Gourdy said.

She remembered the night the blond boy was arrested. His angelic face turned toward her, begging her to tell the officer it was alright, that she wanted him as much as he wanted her. She couldn't return his affection. She could only play with Jared's ring on her mother's necklace, knowing the horror her desperation cost the poor innocent man. The utter loss of hope on his face was permanently etched into her soul. Her mistake. Greg probably starved himself to death in jail, not realizing that without the hormones she produced, he'd forget about the joys of life, including food, as he mourned her absence.

All she desired that night was someone to hold her and help her forget about her life. She'd lied to herself, saying one time shouldn't have been enough to cause the addiction. Yet that was all it took for him to become her stalker. Even with the police arresting him for sneaking into her house in the middle of the night, the Family thought it essential to transfer her to a new location. It was the catalyst that led to her spying on Jennifer Wright.

She never wanted a man to become addicted to her again —well, not right now.

As a comfort, she reached for Jared's ring. For this job, she didn't wear it, and it wasn't currently around her neck. She hid it in her keepsake drawer while she pretended to be Amy.

Jared, the love of her life... Another life she took.

The first act her dragon guide did was torture her and drive her crazy, until she did what he asked and killed Jared. Oh, she refused when she had all her mental abilities intact. But day and night, Gourdy haunted her. He sent her visions of things that were not there, made noises, not allowing her to sleep, and clawed at the very fabric of her morals until she couldn't take it anymore, and she snapped.

Everything shattered that week, like a tree with deep roots pulled up and thrown by a powerful storm. When the Family drove to her parents' small trailer, her parents clinging to life, she'd already been broken like a wild mustang. She'd been more than willing to ride off into the sunset with the Family. They picked up her cracked pieces and turned her life into a mosaic of hell.

She blamed Gourdy for Jared's death, but she blamed herself for submitting to Gourdy.

"It was necessary to remove Jared. Mates make one weak. Now you can have as many partners as you want," Gourdy said, like that was a boon.

Dragons mated for life. To kill one was a slow, painful death for the other. Yet Shanna lived through Jared's death with the Family's help.

Greg wasn't the only one she'd taken to bed who the Family had stepped in and removed. Not that she had loved anyone since Jared, but she didn't want anyone hurt because of her selfish desire to be touched. Even though her mate died, if a man slept with her, he became addicted to her hormones. "No, I can't... I don't want to hurt anyone else."

"Please, Shanna. All the losers you had sex with don't count. Who cares that the mortals died? You, the dragon shifter, do count. Trust me. You can have a variety of lovers when this job is done. Have a harem of male consorts if you want. It might be fun to put them in a ring and pit them against one another. Let them fight to the death to bed you every night."

She ignored him. "Do you know why I lived when Jared died?"

"For the same reason I lived when my mate died. We're stronger than the rest."

She didn't believe him. It had to have something to do with the machines the Family hooked her up to; she was sure of it. She wanted to die then. Bury herself in the ground and welcome an eternity of darkness. "Do you know why when I have sex with them, they fall in love with me and I don't with them? Or why I never age?" she asked. Not that it would do any good. She'd asked before, but this version of Jormungant didn't know. Maybe the real Jormungant, Tom Johnson, did. If Shanna ever met him, she would ask.

"No," Gourdy answered.

Nodding, she glanced around the room for something to occupy her time. She'd already cleaned until the floors shined. Under her phone, she had a list of all the damaged items she needed to replace. Grabbing her cell off the nightstand, she unlocked it to watch a drama her roommate said was hysterical. She didn't understand the comedy, perhaps too old or battle-worn to find humor in the mundane. But at least she'd be able to follow the references made when in the mist of other students.

Gourdy stood and walked to the mirror, grooming his beard and hair. For a figment, he liked the act of maintaining his appearance. She assumed to keep up the pretense of being alive.

When he finished, he moved back to her roommate's bed and propped up his feet on her comforter. "You've done nothing useful all night. Why don't you grab a shower before the sun is up?"

Glancing at her watch, she realized Gourdy was right. After a slow soak in the hot water, the stores would be open, and she could buy all the items she'd broken. When her roommate returned, she'd apologize, blame it on drinking, and offer her better, newer things. Her roommate had seen Amy/Shanna drink before and would believe it.

In truth, as a dragon, alcohol didn't affect Shanna like it did them. Not that she couldn't get drunk, but it would take a lot of liquor to even touch her metabolism.

Most of the time, Shanna didn't trust Gourdy's ideas, but keeping busy sounded like a great one. Gathering her toiletries, she took a step into the hall.

The scent of a dragon, a smokey rosemary smell, overwhelmed her senses. Breathing deeply to calm her heart, she searched the long, narrow corridor for the lizard. The only person who occupied the hallway was Jennifer Wright, her charge. She appeared disheveled, wrapped in a sleeping bag and barefoot.

Had Jennifer been camping? If so, where were her shoes?

She headed in Shanna's direction. As Jennifer moved, the zippered blanket opened, revealing Jennifer's white legs.

Wearing shorts in fall? She needed a coat and pants, not a blanket.

Unless she and Matt had become more than friends last night.

The cooking rosemary scent increased when Jennifer passed her, and Shanna almost missed a step. The puzzle pieces fell into place.

No shoes, possibly naked underneath, smelling like a dragon, and a recent awakening…

"Jennifer Wright is the dragon!" Gourdy echoed her thoughts.

Shanna blinked rapidly while she thought about her next approach. Was she in danger? Could Jennifer attack her? Perhaps Jennifer didn't know what a dragon smelled like. After all, she wouldn't have had all the nightmares yet. It would take months of horrible dreams before she was introduced to Jormungant and recognized another dragon by its scent.

Play it calm. If she attacks me, I can defend myself.

As Shanna passed, Jennifer dipped her head in acknowledgment, her face appearing a little green.

Would Jennifer's dragon guide, her Samarbied, notice and tell her later that Amy was a dragon—that is when Jennifer finished all the nightmares?

It didn't matter. When Jennifer met Jormungant, the Family would swoop her away like they did Shanna.

Forcing herself not to glance Jennifer's way, she walked into the communal bathroom. The person she was sent to watch turned into a dragon. The reason she had been assigned this position, all her positions, was for this very moment.

Regardless of the Family's policy, she cared most about her own safety. How could she protect herself? Could she flee? Leave the area?

No. That wouldn't work. The Family would only find her like all the other times she tried to escape. If they let her live, they would torture her with their propaganda, breaking her mind again to persuade her to continue doing what they wanted. At least now she was allowed to pretend to be normal.

"If you were sent to watch Jennifer, it only makes sense you need to tell Roland that Jennifer is a dragon shifter. Then he will remove you and put someone capable of capturing Jennifer in your place," Gourdy said.

Capable? Shanna was more than able. But he was right about letting Roland know. She needed to tell Roland. *"This is so not like you. Useful twice in one day,"* Shanna thought.

Instead of taking a leisurely shower, Shanna peeked out the door to find Jennifer's door shut and no one in the hall. Walking as fast as she could, she returned to her room, locking the door.

Calming her breathing and deciding what to tell Roland, she opened the blinds. She recognized Matt's truck, puffs of vapor coming out of the exhaust, parked near the small turn-around park.

"Poor guy," she said, grabbing her phone. She sat on her bed, facing the window. *"You'll make Jennifer kill him, won't you, Gourdy?"* she thought, remembering how Gourdy pressured her until she snapped.

"Of course. She'll be free, just like you... Cheer up, Shanna. Killing your partner opens up all kinds of possibilities. When we rule the world and you can have any man you want, you will thank me," he thought.

"The only man I will ever want is Jared."

When Jennifer killed Matt, there would be the sickness. Dragons mated for life, not out of desire, but some strange chemical reaction. Partners became addicted to each other's touch, and without the love drug from physical contact, they died. The only reason Shanna lived after the death of her mate was due to the Family's intervention. Hours and days of being hooked into a machine that provided her with the nutrients to stay alive, and the whole time, she wanted nothing more than death.

She imagined the golden-blond athletic girl hooked up to a machine to stay alive. Sarcastically, she thought to Gourdy, *"But hey, Jennifer will be able to take on as many lovers as she wants."*

Shanna dialed Roland's number. He didn't answer, so she tried again.

"Come on," she said. It went straight to voicemail. On the third attempt, she glanced outside. The truck still waited.

"Amy? What's wrong?" Roland answered. When she heard his voice, it felt like a weight fell off her shoulders.

Whispering, she said, "It's happened."

"Why are you whispering?"

"It's happened," she said a little louder.

"What's happened?"

"Jennifer. Jennifer Wright is a dragon." Her words came out rushed.

"Are you sure?" he asked.

She rolled her eyes, though she knew he couldn't see it. "Of course, I'm sure. Should I confront her? When are you coming to get her?"

On the other end, she heard his chair creak and pictured him leaning against its back, deep in thought. "Let me talk to Father." He sighed. "Hold on."

She focused on the exhaust exiting the back of Matt's truck like a chimney. If Matt was waiting, perhaps it was for Jennifer, and she wasn't staying. Shanna scooted closer to the window.

Think, Shanna, think. The dragon wouldn't break down the door to get to her. If Jennifer wanted to attack her, she would have done so by now. Besides, it wasn't until Shanna met Gourdy that she went all psycho. It took days of having dreams of her ancestors before she met Gourdy. If Jennifer's awakening happened last night, it would be weeks before she was driven psycho by her version of Gourdy, unless Jennifer was a direct descendant—which Shanna knew she wasn't from reviewing her files.

Wanting to make sure Jennifer left with Matt, she kept her eyes glued to Matt's vehicle and didn't so much as blink. *Come on, Jennifer, leave the dorm already.*

If Jennifer left, Shanna would be safe from a dragon attack. The Family could pick her up at Matt's or her parents, or wherever Jennifer went. Shanna could rest easier knowing the dragon wasn't around her.

Interrupting her thoughts, Roland said, "The perfume will be delivered today. Keep it sprayed on you. It will protect you from anyone, dragon or Nose, from knowing you are a dragon shifter. Do you understand?"

"Yes. Spray generously." Like she would forget that.

"Amy," he said.

"Yes."

"Congratulations. You are now an operative."

"Thanks. What did I graduate from?" she asked. She wondered what she was before now if she wasn't an operative.

"A noob, fresh, not yet ready. I'll call you with more directions when I hear from Father. Do you understand?"

"Yes."

On the road below, Jennifer strolled out toward Matt's vehicle, carrying a green duffle bag. She got in, and he drove off.

Closing her eyes, Shanna leaned against the chair, and more release washed over her. For now, the other dragon shifter had left. Not only did she know who the dragon was, but she knew for a fact that the dragon shifter wasn't in her building or searching for her.

"Did you hear me, Amy?" Roland asked.

"No," she said. Now that the danger had passed, she wanted to crawl into a little ball and sleep for a day.

"When I hear something back from Father, I'll call you. Until then, stay in your roo—"

"Jennifer left. She's not here. She drove off with her boyfriend."

"The Matt character in your reports?" So, he *did* read her reports.

After sending him report after report without him ever asking a question, she assumed he didn't read them. She'd even tested him once. When she was assigned to a boy named Andy, she changed his name to Christian in one of the reports to see if Roland noticed. If he did, he never mentioned it.

"Yes, sir," she answered.

"Stay there. I'll call you when you can leave. Do you understand?"

"Actually…I broke almost everything in this room. I was going to go to the store and grab a few items and replace them before my roommate—"

"I said no. Stay in the room. I'll call you when I hear back from Father. Repeat your orders."

"Stay in my room until you call me back."

"Exactly. I'll call soon."

Constantly being told what to do irritated her, but she couldn't escape. Gourdy would lock her mind down until she didn't know what was real and what wasn't. It's how he broke her in the first place. Just like the FBI did to those souls in Waco, Texas.

Hopeless but at least safe, she leaned back in the chair and went to sleep in her cage.

CHAPTER 3

SHANNA

A WEEK AFTER THANKSGIVING

BEFORE SHANNA WAS A DRAGON SHIFTER, SHE NEVER CONSIDERED herself the go-to-college type. Yet now that she was at South Holt, she found she liked her psychology classes. Perhaps this was for her after all.

"Get your head back in the game, soldier," Gourdy said, appearing beside her.

Her foot missed a step, and she rearranged her arms to balance her stack of books. A few students at the nearby library desks glanced at her. She smiled at them as an apology.

"I'm in the game. My job is to be a college student, and I'm pretty good at that. I've already reported to Roland this week. I told him Jennifer is still having the nightmares. When I went to the restroom this morning, she was playing with the toilet's handle like she'd never seen indoor plumbing."

"And the spray?"

"I always keep it on. I'm not sure how anyone can smell anything over that stuff."

She kept the softball-sized crystal perfume bottle with its pink puffer spritz nozzle on her nightstand. All it took was three squirts and walking into the mist to cover her from head to foot all day. The overpowering fragrance held hints of cinnamon, cloves, and allspice, with a touch of vanilla and jasmine. At first, it reminded her of a dark, cold winter night filled with possibilities.

Now, she hated it.

"And—"

"No. You know all this. You live in my head. We don't need to talk about it anymore."

"You need to practice, Shanna. You will be the best operative out there since I am your guide. As my soldier, you shall always train and be aware."

She rolled her eyes.

In retaliation, her head started hurting in the same spot Gourdy always first caused the pain—above her left eye on her temple.

"Okay," she said out loud. *"Jerk! I'll obey."*

Her phone rang with the kids' song "Three Blind Mice." Roland. She hunted for a place to stack her books, found a nearby half wall, and placed them on top. Rolling her shoulders, she repositioned the bookbag to pull the device from her side pocket. The gosh darn study material inside weighed as much as her, tipping her off balance.

Before answering, she smiled. That small act helped Shanna become Amy. "Hello," she said.

"Amy." Roland had this way of saying her name in a flat tone without inflection. It meant he was calling to give her orders.

"Yes," she said, moving to a bench near the half wall and dumping her load on the ground.

"I've talked with Father. He's sending a Nose into the field."

"Oh. Kay?" she asked.

"You are to help the opera—" Roland said before she interrupted him.

"Help collect Jen—"

"No. Let me finish. He is using the name of Johan. You are not to reveal that you are anyone other than Amy. Pretend to be his friend. Help him persuade Jennifer to date him. Do not become romantically involved with—"

"What about Matt?" she asked as she surveyed her surroundings for anyone eavesdropping.

Jennifer's boyfriend, Matt, was tall with an athletic build. He reminded her of an actor she had a crush on as a teen—dimples in his cheeks, flat chest, muscular arms. Yet Matt, so consumed with Jennifer, hadn't even noticed Amy. The character that Shanna created, Amy, liked short skirts and low-cut shirts that showed off a little cleavage while still appearing guarded. A majority of the men she met as Amy gave her the slow check out. She thought Matt's lack of interest had to do with the hormones that accompanied having sex with a dragon.

"What about Matt?" Roland asked.

"If Jennifer is, um…you know…romantically involved with Matt, she's not going to have anything to do with Johan, no matter how golden his dingleberry is."

"Dingleberry?"

"Yes. It means she won't want to have a relationship with this operative, regardless of what he offers her."

"She might not. Then again, if Jennifer is as naïve as your reports say she is, Johan will be able to sway her."

She sat back and glanced around the area. Finding no one close by, she continued. "You think Jennifer is innocent? That she hasn't tasted Matt's finer details?" Then why didn't Matt ever glance at Amy? All straight men liked to look, whether they had a partner or not. Heck, Shanna spent hours to make Amy attractive for that very reason, so men's eyes would drift her way with appreciation.

"Father has only ordered him to engage with Jennifer. The plans to pursue a relationship with Jennifer will be revealed to him next semester."

At least she wasn't the only one the Family kept in the dark. Did he feel as hopeless as her? Was he also trapped by the crazies?

Gourdy straightened his sword over his shoulder. "If you embraced our ways, you wouldn't feel trapped."

She ignored Gourdy. "Why not let this operative…Johan, did you say…Why doesn't he start now?" she asked.

"Amy, Father wants you to woo Matt. You are to steal Matt away first before Johan makes a move on Jennifer. And Father has ordered you to begin your seduction over Christmas. Not that you need to know any of this, but Father sits on the board of Matt's father's company and has arranged everything. This year, they're having an annual winter retreat in the Bahamas. Matt will be going, and you, my dear Amy, will join him."

She swallowed. "What about Jennifer? Wouldn't Matt rather she went?"

"That's not for you to worry about. I'll send you the details, and you can come up with a story to explain why you're there."

She glanced in both directions. Classes had started, and the library was nearly empty. The surrounding area was clear of eavesdroppers. "What do you mean? A vacation with the intention of breaking them up?"

"Your orders are to make moves on Matt. Luckily, at this time, I don't have any commands for you to bed him, so no sex."

"You can order me to have sex? You've told me I can't so much as look at a male, and I got in trouble over Greg. When and why will I be allowed to copulate?"

"Listen. I neglected this part of your education. I realize having Jormungant as your avatar—"

"Dragon guide. He lives in my head. He can control what I see, feel, and hear."

"I know, and I'm sorry. Look, I've been fighting for you

not to have to marry like the rest of us. And, for the most part, Father wants to protect you, his dragon child. He let what you did with Greg and all the others slip, but he specifically told me to tell you other operatives are not allowed. Don't mess with Johan." He sighed. "Unfortunately, Shanna"—since he used her real name, she listened—"you are like all of us. Father will tell you when you can wed, and he will need to approve of the candidate."

"What!"

"Calm down. It's not as bad as you think. He's never told me no to my choice when he has insisted I join someone in wedlock."

"But you've had to marry because he demanded you get married?"

"Yes. And I would say he will do the same to you, but for now, I've talked him out of it. He wanted you to settle down with a politician and gain some favor in Congress. I suggested we wait until your biological family—the ones who knew you—pass away before we make any strategic alliances."

Gourdy sat on the bench beside her. He wore a smug expression, his lip curled up like Elvis Presley's when he sang "You Ain't Nothing but a Hound Dog." "You should have known, Shanna. It's the only smart thing to do."

"What is the smart thing to do?" she thought.

"Apply the tools we have to our advantage. If you make a strategic alliance, we can use that person. If you marry someone else handpicked by me, you can ensure your offspring will have strong dragon genetics," Gourdy answered.

"Did you hear me?" Roland asked.

"What?" she replied, her voice coming out more hateful than she meant it to. She should be accustomed to having her free will stripped from her.

"Don't borrow trouble from tomorrow, okay? Wait it out. All Father is asking you to do now is help Johan obtain his target by separating Jennifer and Matt. Johan will not know about you, so keep Amy's true identity to yourself."

"I'm not trying to borrow trouble." She closed her eyes. "If I'm refused the right to marry or have sex when I want, I want details. Who is Johan? Why is he important to the Family? It sounds like I'll be more involved with him than just giving him a reason to hang out at the dorm. Since I can't smell his gifts, what all did he receive from eating a dragon's heart?"

She guessed about Johan's credentials, since Jennifer, both a dragon and descended from Jormungant, would only have the most seasoned operative collect her. That meant Johan had to be old. She knew of only three ways to have a long life: be a dragon, mate with a dragon, or eat a dragon. Roland told her stories of a fourth way, but as a kid she'd seen that movie he'd apparently confused with reality. Shangri-La, the fountain of youth, wasn't real.

"Good question. He has all the gifts that eating a dragon can give someone. He is old—"

"As old as you?"

He paused before answering. "No." She filed that away for later. She didn't have any memories of Roland, but she was sure Roland was Father's son. She even reasoned he was one of his oldest kids, making him *very* old. Come to think of it, he didn't resemble Gourdy. His face reminded her of a mouse with his brown hair cut into a mullet, the skinny nose that protruded to a point, and his thin lips. Thus, the mouse ringtone for his calls.

"If he has eaten dragon heart, Jennifer will smell it. A dragon's natural inclination is to flee from someone who has killed other dragons. The survival instinct will be especially strong in a young dragon," she said.

"Thank you, but this is not your concern," Roland answered.

Did that mean Jennifer would trust him because her ancestor would have known Johan, therefore making the likelihood of her accepting Johan's advances higher? Could they give him cologne to cover up his scent, like they did her perfume?

Instead of questioning Roland, she asked, "Is he living on campus?"

"I doubt it." He sighed on the other side of the line. "Father has allowed him to pick where he resides. He will be taking a few classes in the spring, but not many. Next semester, his focus is to earn Jennifer's trust, make her fall in love with him, and collect her. Your job is to help him do so. I've sent you pictures of him."

Curious, she said, "Hold on." How very unlike the Family to send pictures of an ancient operative. She'd always been told that if you could live forever, pictures could become evidence of someone that shouldn't exist. Some operatives got away with saying they looked a lot like their great-great-grandparents, but that wouldn't always work, especially with new technologies. She wasn't sure how Father would pull off being incognito for the next hundred years... Maybe his pharmaceutical company would invent a very expensive bottle of immortality?

Then the image came through, and she stared at it. He had that rough and tough appearance, like James Dean. Yet his eyes gave off innocence—pale blue like an arctic winter sky. He wore a black leather jacket with a T-shirt underneath.

"Handsome," she said, bringing the phone to her ear.

"You can't have him."

"Why?" she asked. "We can collect the package"—meaning Jennifer—"together."

"Follow your orders," Gourdy said, raising his arm. A full-on migraine, complete with light sensitivity, started in her left temple. Her stomach rolled with the onset of nausea.

"Amy?" Roland asked.

She closed her eyes and rubbed her head. "Yes, Roland. I'll do it."

But inside, she thought, *How can I get free?*

CHAPTER 4

SHANNA

CHRISTMAS DAY, BAHAMAS

SHANNA GLANCED OVER TOWARD MATT; HE SAT ACROSS FROM her, a deck of cards in his hands. He winked at her, and she smiled, as required by her woo-Matt job. He sacrificed the window view overlooking the ocean.

So very chivalrous of him, she thought sarcastically.

So far, he and Jennifer seemed well suited for each other. He might look chiseled from stone, a lifelike statue of a Greek god, but he was boring—so incredibly, tediously dull. For instance, he stayed in the boat, when they went parasailing, letting her take to the skies. He said it was so she could have an adventure. If she wasn't wearing dragon perfume, she knew she'd smell the bitter barbeque of fear.

Why couldn't he be the bad boy type? The kind who said he didn't want to kiss, then swept her off her feet in the next second—the one who promised her a rocky whirlwind romance and left her wondering what happened when it was over?

What good was it to be built for sin and then... nothing? It was like buying a book with a picture of a couple on the cover, wind messing up their hair, expecting a historical romance, and finding out it was an action-packed adventure set in Italy in the nineteen seventies.

"I liked that book," Gourdy said, interrupting her thoughts.

Instead of rolling her eyes, she inhaled and glanced at her cards again. So far, she had successfully laid down some terrible hands. By the glances Matt's parents gave her, she knew they assumed she didn't know how to play Spades, but that wasn't it. It reminded her of her real home, her parents, her family. They also bonded behind heated games using kings, queens, and jacks. She didn't want to remember in front of others. By throwing each round, she could detach from those forgotten moments.

Her typical Christmas day was spent alone, and she'd have her yearly cry while missing her past, her lost childhood. She'd never had to act like someone else on this holiday. But this year, she faked jolly when they had opened Christmas presents earlier. They even gave her a small necklace they bought on the island to make her feel included.

She didn't come empty-handed to their vacation suite. After doing her research and wanting it to seem natural, she selected a present for each of them, hoping to make a more personal connection. For Matt, she picked a day trip to visit the glass bridge with her. For Andrew, Matt's dad, she purchased a new Rolex watch she located in an island shop— of course, charged on her company credit card. Before she left, she made sure the shops had what she thought would make the biggest impact with him—a well-thought-out gift that seemed to be acquired while on vacation.

His mother's present needed to be special. She was the center of the family, the rock that held them together. Her gift could be the key to winning over both Matt and his dad. It had to be something that could endear Amy to his parents. During her research, she discovered Maria was only a year and two months older than her. That knowledge helped Shanna understand Maria better.

Shanna uncovered several controversial articles on child brides written by Maria's mother. The news stories caught the negative attention of a militant cult. At seven, Maria watched her mother be tortured, then murdered because of the pieces she wrote.

Shanna placed herself in Maria's position. What item would mean something to her? She'd found a family picture in front of the Taj Mahal's famous pool. In it, Maria's mother wore an elegant ruby and gold choker with delicate designs. Shanna located a similar one online and had it mailed to the Bahamas. Stores around the resort stocked expensive pieces, so Maria would hopefully believe Shanna had happened upon it and that any resemblance to her mother's necklace was a coincidence.

If she didn't find the symbolism as Shanna hoped, she knew Maria would at least like the gift. Her studies revealed the Davises were impressed with money. Before she saw this room, she guessed the hotel room would be impressive. They, or their company, she wasn't sure which, paid for a presidential suite, while Matt roomed on the fourth floor a few doors down from her.

She wished now that he would have stayed with his parents; then, maybe the Family would have put her in a similar room.

When Matt led her into his parents' hotel apartment, she didn't ask for a tour. It would have been rude to request one. Besides, it would show that she wasn't accustomed to something this nice. Instead, she acted like she grew up in luxury because Amy did. She'd beheld enough just passing through the oversized fancy living room into the dining room to know this was definitely the best the island had to offer.

Growing up in a trailer, Shanna had never celebrated Christmas in paradise. Then again, since joining the Family, she hadn't enjoyed Christmas at all. And she would enjoy this one a little more if she had a different leading man.

Matt gave her a half grin and tapped the deck on the table. She'd bet he practiced that expression and thought it was sexy.

If it weren't for Matt and his cheesy grin, she'd slip out of character, though. Playing cards reminded her of too many past holidays. Her mom was like most dragon lines, with families only having single births back to Jormungant, but her father came from a large family of Southern farmers who ran moonshine for fun and rebuilt cars on the lawn. Every chance they had, they gathered and spent hours sitting at card tables. She'd play with her aunts and uncles, engaging in different kinds of poker. She missed it... and them.

Blinking several times, she reached up to her eyes, rubbing to hide the tears forming in the corners.

"Amy, how do you like South Holt?" Maria asked.

Shanna welcomed the change of thought. "I like it. Just small enough to feel cozy and set in a large city. Plenty to do, and it has a feeling of community." She left off the *ma'am*. That was a mistake a lot of kids made. They assumed it was a sign of respect, but really, it was a reminder that the person was getting old, and she knew that Maria wouldn't like it.

"And what are you studying?" Maria asked, laying down the final card. She played the Ace of Spades, taking the last hand and winning the game.

On campus, Matt was known for being a card shark. Apparently, he'd learned from the best.

"Psychology," Shanna answered.

While Maria had smiled at her earlier, this was the first time that her smile touched her eyes. "That's what my degree is in," Maria said.

"Oh. Do you work as a psychologist?" she asked.

"No. I run an auction house for charities," Maria said, gathering up the deck.

"She does more than that. She's the president of our HOA, as well as collecting donations for three other charities," Andrew said as he stood from the table.

Maria blushed as she handed him the cards. "Such flattery. You know how it embarrasses me."

"But you deserve it." He looked at his watch. "The light show will start soon. Shall we relocate to the living room, my love?" he asked.

"We shall," she said.

"Can I get you something more to drink?" Andrew asked.

"A glass of champagne would be wonderful," Maria said, offering her empty flute to her husband.

Standing from the table, Matt said, "Amy, would you like another glass?"

"Of course," she answered. "Please," she added.

Once Matt took her crystalware, he followed his dad out of the room.

"I think we should move to the living room," Maria said. "We can watch the Christmas boat parade that should start within the next hour from there."

Shanna watched the taller woman stand up. She wore a simple red jumper with bright coordinating lipstick. Despite the humidity and wind, her black, wavey hair had appeared controlled and manageable all day while Shanna fought with her kinky curls, trying to give off romantic fifties vibes and failing.

What would have happened had Shanna never turned into a dragon, if she had aged like a normal human? Would she be as elegant as Maria? Would she have taken care of her figure, or would she have grown a belly?

Gracefully, like a silent film star, Maria glanced over her shoulder at Shanna. "We should be able to see the boats from the living room just fine. When the boys return, we can have them turn off the lights." She waved her hand in the air, appearing nonchalant. "If we can't, we'll relocate outside."

"I'd like that. I'd rather watch from inside too," she confessed.

A wall of windows allowed them to see past the glass guard rails. Its design kept the view of the ocean from being obscured. Maria sat on the furthest sofa from the dining room. Shanna took the other couch.

Andrew placed his hand on his wife's shoulder and tenderly rubbed.

How long had it been since someone looked at Shanna like she was precious? His sweet tenderness caused a pain of regret in her stomach, and she forced her eyes away and toward the water.

"We've run out of champagne. Matt and I are going downstairs to pick some more up. Do you need anything else?" Andrew asked.

"I'm fine… Amy, do you need anything?" Maria asked.

"No," she answered, but it came out as more of a whisper.

The two men left the suite, discussing golfing.

Once the door closed, there was a heavy, awkward pause. Shanna attributed it to being alone with someone her age who thought she was thirty years younger. She didn't know what to say. The only other parents she had met were Jared's, and they despised her. She imagined that Amy would be delicate around parents, like Shanna had witnessed so many other students behave. So she sat there quietly, waiting for Maria to speak first.

"Matt has told me you live in his girlfriend's dorm. Do you know Matt's girlfriend?" Maria asked.

"Jennifer." Shanna said it more like a question, but it wasn't, and Maria didn't respond. "Only a little. She's in my art history class."

"Oh," she said. Another long pause followed, and Shanna stared out the window.

"I can see that you like my son, but I doubt he notices," Maria stated.

Shanna sat up a little straighter. She was such an excellent actress that his mom actually believed she was attracted to him. But Shanna's reaction could be attributed to being found out and feeling guilty—she hoped. How his mother stated Amy's attraction was very direct, catching Shanna off guard. Why would Maria confront her about it? What good would it do?

If Shanna had a son, would she behave the same way with a girl who clearly liked him? Honestly, Shanna might, but Amy wouldn't.

How could Shanna use this to her benefit? And how would Amy respond?

She glanced over her shoulder back toward the door where Matt had just left through, something she thought Amy would do. "I do like him," she said. "I don't know Jennifer well. She's smart, makes good grades, seems to be dedicated."

"Yes," Maria said, looking out the windows. She smiled one of her fake smiles.

Shanna inhaled, but with the perfume that blocked dragons, she couldn't smell anything that might give her a clue about Maria's feelings. Maria's expression alone made her think she didn't like Jennifer. But why? Jennifer came across as amicable enough. For those who didn't know she was a dragon shifter destined to be the Family's pawn, she would pass as a great future daughter-in-law.

How could Shanna word what she said next to get Maria to explain her reasons? She couldn't be direct. That wasn't Amy's style. After thinking it through, she said, "She's very focused and seems to have her head on straight. She makes Matt happy."

"You think so?" Maria asked sarcastically.

What if Shanna could suggest something negative about Jennifer's personality—something that would encourage Maria to bond with Shanna? A little truth to add to the big lie? Plant the seed for some doubt and build Amy's relationship with Maria. Then maybe Maria would help Amy woo Matt?

"Sure. I do. But," Shanna said and pressed her lips together, opening her eyes wider. She hoped Maria understood the look as *I almost said something I shouldn't.*

"Oh, you have reservations about whether Jennifer is good for my son?" Maria asked as if she picked up on Shanna's expression.

"Well…" She looked up at the ceiling for a second and wrinkled her forehead. "I think they will be great together one day… They'll just have a lot to overcome."

"What do you mean?" Maria asked.

"Everyone has baggage that they bring into a relationship, but some have more than others. To me, Jennifer is too naïve. She hasn't had anything hard happen in her life. I mean, Jennifer's parents are still married. She has a scholarship to fully pay for college. She's just never experienced a life event that creates depth of character," Shanna said. She paused, hoping the Maria-fish took the bait. Her father told her when you felt the nibble, jerk, and the hook would catch the fish. Reeling in, she added, "I'm sorry. I shouldn't have said that. It was unfair. When I was taken away from my parents—"

"I thought your parents abandoned you here on this trip," Maria interrupted.

"They did. But they aren't my birth parents. My mom had cancer and passed away. After her loss, my father couldn't handle me. The other family, the one I have now, then took me under their wings." She wanted to add, as in, Wing It Laboratories, as in, the company the Family owned.

"Oh," Maria said, but Shanna didn't detect any sympathy. Maria only nodded while staring out the window. "I'm sorry you lost your parents… I'll let you tell Matt in your own time. Things like that should be shared by the people who experienced them."

"It was a long time ago, and… it made me a better person. Not that I wished for the experience, but it taught me so many different life lessons… Anyway, being abandoned like that hurt more than"—she raised her arms in the air, looking around the room—"more than being left in paradise."

The Family did take her away from her parents. Yet she had a great idea of where her parents were. They divorced after she disappeared. Her father remarried and gave her half-siblings she would never meet. Her mother wed again as well and now lived somewhere in lower Alabama.

Maria stared out the window for a few minutes. "You will find, Amy, that there is always chaos, even in paradise."

"From losing my parents so young, I learned more than I would have had I focused on school. I have scars from living a hard life lesson." And boy had she. As she aged, she realized her parents set rules because they loved her. That she was better off living in a trailer than sitting in this fancy hotel with Matt's mother.

Continuing with the Amy story, Shanna added, "That's why I made that comment about Jennifer. When Jennifer experiences more life events and overcomes some things… When she's more well-rounded, she'll be a better fit for Matt."

"You think so?" Maria asked. "I have my doubts."

The truth was that Matt and Jennifer suffered the same lack of experience issue. He had his innocent baggage, too. What would he do the first time something didn't go right for him? She glanced at Maria and couldn't tell if Maria hadn't noticed Matt's naivete or just didn't acknowledge it out loud. But Shanna's job wasn't to help Matt. Her assignment was only to break up his relationship with Jennifer.

Shanna smiled. "What doubts do you have about Jennifer?"

This time, Maria turned her body toward Shanna. "Would you use that information against Jennifer if I told you? Would you end his relationship with her so you could date him?"

Once again, she asked a straightforward question. Time for a new approach and to tweak Amy's personality by adding a little of a strategic, driven angle. "Your son is honest, puts his friends first, and is faithful... I would use any trick I know to make him mine. I want him to have what is best for him, and I'm it," she lied. She would never make a suitable partner for Matt.

Maria nodded and studied her. "You've entertained my son. I love your fashion sense. You even threw the card game tonight. I take it you didn't want to play Spades?"

How did Maria notice that? Shanna was careful. Her cheeks warmed with a flush. "It brought up too many memories. I would hide under my parents' card table when they played. It made me miss them," she said, telling the truth.

"You're obviously smart. Very few people your age can answer trivia questions from my generation," Maria observed, recalling a bar game they all played the previous night.

It helped that Shanna was close to Maria's age and was alive during those events, but she couldn't say that.

"Have you ever heard the story of the three daughters and the broom?" Maria asked.

"No," Shanna confessed.

"Can you keep a few of my secrets?" Maria asked, raising her eyebrows and crossing her legs.

"Yes," Shanna answered, curious as to how this related back to Jennifer.

"Well, the broom story is something my mother told me before she was murdered in front of my eyes."

Based on the multitude of articles Shanna had read, she knew the kidnapping was very publicized and that Maria had witnessed the event unfold. Still, Shanna drew her hand to cover her open mouth and opened her eyes wide as if she was shocked.

Maria continued, looking slightly pleased, as if she got the desired reaction. "A king wanted a wife, so he devised a test. He went to a farmer who had many daughters of renowned character. When he arrived, he asked the farmer where his daughters were. When he confirmed they were upstairs, he laid a broom at the foot of the staircase. One by one, the farmer presented each of them to the king. The first daughter's beauty took his breath away. Daintily, she picked up her skirt and stepped over the broom. The farmer pointed out his daughter's beauty and how envious all the people who gazed upon her face. But no, not her.

"The second came down singing with the voice of an angel. She danced and twisted over the broom. She will fill your home with music, the farmer said. But no, not her.

"The third came down in a plain brown dress. When she saw the broom, she picked it up and put it away. The farmer looked displeased and apologized. I want her, the king said. The king didn't need a beautiful woman or one who could sing while there was work to do. He wanted someone who would serve alongside him.

"I see you as someone who would do the work necessary to make my son happy. Jennifer is like the first two sisters, pretty on the outside but with no substance. I want my future daughter-in-law to be like—"

"Listen, I like Matt, and it would be nice if it went to marriage, but—" Shanna interjected.

"I know. You aren't here trying to woo my son to matrimony. But if Jennifer wasn't dating my son... Dating leads to marriage. If they weren't dating, he would never marry her. What I'm telling you are secrets. Matt doesn't know that my mother was murdered in front of me... He could look it up, but who would even think of doing an internet search on their parents? He doesn't know I was married to someone else before his father. And I will never tell him. I'm telling you because I see myself in you. You're calculating, smart, intelligent, and know how to keep a secret."

She caught all that from a card game? The woman was brilliant if she deducted that from barely knowing Amy. Shanna liked the woman.

"My wonderful Andrew. He was like you. He wanted me and followed me around even after I married Jack, my first husband. But Jennifer reminds me of Jack." Her beautiful features twisted into a hideous grimace for a second. "Innocent, loving, made great grades in college. He landed a great job after."

"What happened?"

"I caught him in bed with my best friend," she said.

"And you think Jennifer will cheat on—"

"Yes. She has all the red flags. Pretty, smart, and doesn't seem to care if Matt goes on vacation without her," Maria said, crossing her arms.

More curious than anything, Shanna said, "Matt told Jennifer couldn't come—"

"On our family vacation, no. But Matt went to the beach without her. I know because he charged the room to my credit card. When I asked, he said Jennifer doesn't want to be in a clingy relationship." She raised one eyebrow. "I think he thought that would make me like her more. It did the opposite. Jack didn't want to always be together either. He would go out with his friends. I thought it was because we had a secure, mature marriage. Turns out he just didn't love me enough to keep his pants on." She huffed. "I didn't even have enough sense to be jealous before that day."

Maria smiled and uncrossed her arms. "But that was then. I don't have to feel insecure with Andrew. He doesn't give me a reason to be. Always faithful and continually thinking about me. I can see you will be thoughtful and loyal to my son."

Shanna's phone rang. "Three blind mice" played seconds before the door opened.

"My parents," she said. She acknowledged Matt and his

father's return with a nod. Then she asked Maria, "Do you mind if I take it in another room?"

"Of course not, answer your phone," Maria said.

She answered. "Hi, Dad, let me go into another room so we can have some privacy," she said as she walked past the dining room and through the last door. She shut the door but left the lights off.

The bathroom stretched the length of the suite and included a clawfoot tub, a walk-in shower, and a window overlooking the bay. The first boat she saw was lit up to look like a Christmas tree as it crested the horizon.

"Hey, Dad," she said, doubting the Davis' could hear.

"Seeing how I took you under my wing, I called to cut off your conversation when Matt's elevator stopped at your floor," Roland said.

Did Roland have receivers in the apartment somewhere, or was the use of the word *wing* random? She stared around the room.

"Maria's right, you do dress sharp. That green dress you are wearing looks very becoming."

"I'm in the tallest building on the highest floor. How can you see me?"

"Listen, Amy, don't get too comfortable. You don't want to blow your cover. You have one job, and that is to break up Matt and Jennifer. Your orders are not to have sex or to marry. If you would like that assignment, I can ask."

"What, no... I'm—"

"I had an older brother. Not by the same mother. Father adored him. One time, he slipped up and cost Father a dragon he planned to kill. I watched Father wring his neck like a chicken."

Because she dreamed of her ancestors' lives, she could recall Jormungant holding the man off the ground and all the emotions that surrounded the event. It had been days since his son had helped the dragon shifter escape. When his neck popped, Jormungant honestly felt like he did the right thing and that he had murdered his son in love.

Roland continued. "He killed him days later after he'd cooled down. Before his quick death, Father threw my brother outside into a small pit dug into the ground. He ensured he wouldn't escape by adding bars on top. My brother was left naked, in the elements, in winter. He gave orders for us to wake him up every fifteen minutes. He wasn't allowed food or water... *This was someone he loved*, Amy—his first flesh and blood son that dreamed of having rule beside him. You've never met Father because it's easier to dispose of you that way. If he can so easily torture and then murder his own son, his firstborn, he would have no problem ending you. Don't think because of what you are that you hold any favoritism... Father still talks about my brother like he's alive... If I know where you are and what you're doing, so does Father. Straighten up. Do your job. That way, Father won't kill you."

The phone went dead.

CHAPTER 5

JENNIFER

SPRING SEMSISER, LAST WEE OF
JANUARY, MONDAY MORNING

JENNIFER HYPER-FOCUSED ON PETR'S KNICKKNACKS DECORATING the room, recalling what they each meant to him. Maybe, if she could do that, her guilt wouldn't pull her under. The items included a piece of driftwood inside a fish tank, supported on a stand, that held no water or fish. Small plants grew around the wood like in a terrarium. A simple keepsake of the day Petr met his second wife. Jennifer no longer felt jealousy toward the long-deceased woman because Petr fully belonged to her. He didn't make comparisons between the two of them.

Near it was a partially burned purple candle—a reminder of his daughter, who passed away as a toddler. He told her he lit it in honor of her every May twelfth. In honor of her, Petr also liked to give toys to those in need, which was his way of staying connected to the ones he loved. A tradition she hoped to continue in their, Petr and Jennifer's, future.

On one side of the candle, the wax filament melted away and became close to the color of…

…Blood. It bubbled around her ankles, mixing in

*with the pale blond hair. Johan lay dead. A hole in
his chest that she had made…*

The walls felt like they were caving in again, and she slowed her breathing, closing her eyes. The aroma of cashmere and sandalwood with a touch of wrongness calmed her. The smell belonged to her mate, Petr. Not that they had completed the claiming, but he hadn't refused her either.

"You can do this, Jennifer," she whispered to herself.

"It's okay," Barry, her dragon guide, said. It was hard to believe he had lived in England in the fourteen hundreds when he sported modern clothing, like he was wearing now: a brown button-up shirt, a pair of jeans, and hiking boots. He controlled how he appeared—today, his wavy blond hair with strawberry highlights hung past his ears.

Staring into his blue eyes, she said, "I killed a man."

"Yes, Johan, and in self-defense. I'm pretty sure that's okay—even to non-wyverns."

"Barry, I don't even want to kill a rabbit for food." The scent of fall leaves and smoky fire, which belonged solely to Barry, wafted around her, comforting her as well.

Dressed in only a towel, she went to the closet. Her things were intermingled with Petr's. He'd been careful, keeping his distance from her, but everywhere she looked, she already saw them blending together. How would they make it four years without completing the claiming? She didn't think it was possible.

Last week, she'd hung up all her clothes in matching outfits—like a shirt with pants—to take up less space in Petr's closet. She randomly picked an ensemble out and walked over to the drawers to retrieve her undergarments.

She dressed, leaving her feet bare, and plopped back down on the bed.

I killed a man. Once again, she remembered the orange orb

passing through Johan's chest, a look of surprised horror on his face seconds before he collapsed.

Someone knocked on the door.

"Yes," Jennifer answered.

"It's Petr. May I come in?"

"Yes."

"I'll take that as my cue," Barry said, disappearing.

The man from her dreams opened the door but stayed in the hall, surveying her. She returned the favor, drinking him in. He was slightly taller than Jennifer, standing at six feet one. He had ear-length, wavy, auburn hair except for a white patch almost in the middle of his head. For his job, he grew an unkempt beard, which made him appear to be in his late twenties or early thirties. Despite his youthful facade, Petr was the oldest person she knew.

Eventually, he spoke up. "I came to gather something to wear today, but you..." Shaking his head, he moved to the vanity and opened the drawer below the candle.

Light reflected off Petr's watch, and she again remembered the orb of fire.

...Johan's surprised face, his eyes wide, as the ball went through his chest like slicing butter with a hot knife. It happened so quickly that he didn't have time to grab at his missing stomach. He fell headfirst into the water...

With Petr's good arm, he grabbed her hairbrush, leaving the drawer open. The other arm, the one Johan shot, rested in a sling. He sat on the bed, moaning, she assumed from the recent wound's pain. "Turn, please," he said.

She nodded, facing away from him. If she didn't have dragon hearing, she wouldn't have heard his groan of pain as the brush ran through her hair. The damage on his right side would take days to heal.

"You look beautiful, as always, but haunted," he said, lowering his voice.

Even Petr saying she was beautiful didn't send thrills down her back. "I keep seeing..." *Johan die*, her mind finished.

"I see." The brush made another stroke.

"How do you deal with the guilt?" she asked.

"Me personally, quite well. I have a wound that, had I not eaten a dragon's heart, would have put me in the hospital"—he huffed—"or ended me. It stings nicely. If I recall right, Johan gave me that injury."

She tensed, remembering Petr on the ground with the iron and copper zing of his blood tainting the air seconds before she killed Johan.

"The first man I slew was in a hunting accident," he whispered. He pulled her hair out from under her shirt collar and continued. "His name was Khan, and he was my friend. Even though I have lived many lifetimes since then, I can remember... I remember throwing up. Wanting to die myself and running out into the forest, hoping to freeze to death. It was hard, Jennifer." Another stroke down her scalp. "The second time I took a life, it was on purpose. It's easier to kill when it is someone trying to kill you... Time. Time makes it manageable. The guilt is something you have to forgive yourself for, but time covers the anguish... After about the twentieth person I kill—"

"Twenty? You've killed over twenty people?" she asked.

"I'm sure I have. I've been in a few wars, you know. Living forever... There have been times I've prayed for death. It gets bearable. If you—"

"How can it possibly get easier?"

"It just does. If you didn't feel anything, if you weren't human, if you were a monster, it wouldn't impact you. As long as you keep your mercy and search for ways not to kill, continue to grow and forgive yourself, it will get better." His deep baritone sent chills up her spine, and she shuddered. He finished running the brush through her hair.

Turning toward him, she took the hairbrush from his hand. When their fingers touched, electricity from the claiming zapped between them. "People are going to find out. I'm going to go to jail." She couldn't hide the panic from her voice.

"It will blow over." He smiled. "You'll see. Hard to blame someone when there isn't a body. Plus, Johan was old. I'd guess he was born before there were accurate records."

She assumed Johan was over the twenty years he appeared to be when she smelled the rotting poison of consumed dragon heart, and because dragons didn't roam freely anymore. She figured he had found and killed a dragon when they still prowled the earth. She speculated his age was more like four or five hundred. "I know." She glanced at the floor.

"It will improve," he said. She heard him inhale as he put his left arm around her and pulled her into a peaceful embrace.

Jennifer tried to be strong and not shed a tear, but she wanted to cry.

When he moved, he breathed in, shifting as he stood. "Now I have to get ready to teach a class, and you need to be presentable because you're riding with me," he said matter-of-factly. "I don't want you far away from one of us."

Us included Petr, Che-non—alive because of the City of the Giants' secret—and a dragon named Kamar.

He continued. "Che-non talked with Fritz this morning."

"Who's Fritz?"

"A friend of Che-non's. He will tell MiFeng and Lung"— Jennifer remembered they were the rulers of the dragon city, Dernogard— "about what happened. Remember how we agreed to stay as long as it's safe?"

"Yes."

"With everything that happened this weekend…" He trailed off.

"You're concerned that it's not safe for me to stay in Charlotte and finish my degree."

"I'm concerned there are other people who want to harm you, and your life is too important."

If they were out to hurt her, were they after her mother, father, or brother too? And in the next few years, a lot of things could change. What if there was an accident that involved someone in her family? How would she know? That's how her grandfather died: a car wreck in the middle of the night. "What about my family? I'd like to see my brother graduate."

He sighed. "I know. Kamar has already left the house and is roaming the campus to sniff out any other individuals, either a dragon or someone who has eaten a dragon's heart—"

"Or the fruit of the giants?"

"Yes, or the fruit of the giants…"

"I understand, Petr. My safety comes first." She squeezed his leg, standing.

"Apparently, Jormungant thinks he has a vested interest in you. We need to appear normal until we leave for China."

She put the brush back on the dresser, not staring at her face in the mirror, afraid she would glimpse the monster that could kill.

Petr walked to his closet, moaning as he moved. She watched his reflection as he mumbled while he searched for clothes. He held a pair of navy pants, a white button-down shirt, and a plaid sweater. Another hideous outfit that she should burn.

"Still going for the college professor look?" Jennifer asked, frowning.

Tipping his head in a sign of yes, he passed her, only stopping to kiss her cheek. "I'll be ready in about thirty minutes." He closed the door.

CHAPTER 6

MATT

Matt didn't believe the new story of a fairytale romance spreading around campus. According to rumors, Matt's recent ex-girlfriend, Jennifer, had moved on to Professor Smith. But only last week, she was having a whirlwind affair with another college boy, Johan.

Except none of what he heard or that had transpired over the last few weeks sounded like the Jennifer Wright he had dated. Her cheating on him with Johan surprised him, to say the least. He'd ended the relationship a week ago when he found out about her secret rendezvous. If she'd moved on from Johan already, maybe he didn't know her at all.

The intelligent, athletic girl he met last fall had an incredible sense of humor and laughed at herself as much as she did at his jokes. She was always determined to do her best at everything. Matt was the first person she had dated. How could someone go from not dating at all to dating three people in two weeks?

Since he sent the breakup text, Matt spent many a night trying to understand what Jennifer found attractive about Johan. At least part of Matt's negative opinions about Johan came from bitterness. In his defense, Johan smoked, gave off bad-boy vibes, and seemed materialistic. All characteristics Matt would have thought Jennifer detested.

With the new rumor hinting that Jennifer had moved on to Dr. Smith, Matt wondered what any young, beautiful girl saw in an old, accomplished, different stage of life, man. Dr. Smith wasn't really in Jennifer's age-dating bracket, let alone league.

The whole thing—the rumors, Jennifer cheating, his hurt and anger—left him feeling raw and bare to the world. Jennifer was Matt's first girlfriend, the first girl he trusted, and her cheating on him with Johan burned down his willingness to be vulnerable.

He had a new girlfriend, Amy, but something was wrong with their relationship's foundation. He couldn't identify what or put the emotion into words. His mind seemed to be on replay, stuck on Jennifer cheating, and he felt his intimacy issues Amy was a guilt reflex from the way things ended.

How could Jennifer do that to him? How could she do that to *them?* Matt had offered her a future together. When he asked her to live with him and share a bed as lovers and partners, he meant every word. How could she so easily turn down all he had to offer and then do the same thing to the next guy?

Trying to understand what happened over the past two weeks bothered him enough to cause him to toss and turn all night. The stories didn't add up with Jennifer's personality. Either he never really knew Jennifer, or someone spread fabrications. In that half-asleep state, he attempted to sort lie from truth and fact from fiction—and failed.

Eventually, he concluded he needed to take the moral high ground and apologize for breaking up with her over text. Ending what they had in such an impersonal note was done in the heat of the moment—that was crass of him. Yet, finding out the girl you thought you loved was dating someone else really hurt. The pain hadn't stopped even though he had someone else.

He needed to own up, talk about what happened, and clear up fact from fiction. In the conversation, if she admitted to cheating, he could forgive her, let go of the pain, quell the rumors—and finally sleep at night without thinking about her.

Maybe, if he'd confronted her about the rumors before ending their relationship, about her kissing another man when they were a couple, perhaps she'd have understood what she did was wrong, and they both would have moved on. But he couldn't fix the past. He could only move forward.

Smiling, he opened the door to Jennifer and Amy's dorm building and searched the common area for Jennifer. In the best-case scenario, he'd catch Jennifer preparing to leave, and he could walk her to class.

If she was with a guy? It'd hurt, but he could handle it. He needed to clear the air, find out the truth, and attempt to save their friendship, no matter what. Being able to sleep peacefully depended on it.

The inside of the dorm building was set up like a coffee shop, with chairs and couches around small tables. A brunette with her bare feet on a coffee table chatted with two other people, all three wearing pajamas. A tall desk designed almost like a check-out counter at a department store had an attendant behind it casually flipping through something on her phone.

Jennifer's roommate, Belinda, stood near the stairs, staring at the TV mounted on the wall. A man with mousy brown hair stood beside her, so close that his locks meshed into Belinda's golden blond. Whatever he said caused Belinda to turn sharply, her eyes locking with Matt's in intense anger.

Angry? Why would Belinda be mad at him?

Oh, that's right. Matt heard Belinda had taken Jennifer to reclaim Jennifer's green couch on the library's second floor. After the breakup, Matt and Amy had made out on the couch. Amy insisted as revenge for all Jennifer did to him. In his heartache, he agreed. But now, he regretted being so petty.

Of course, Belinda would know about Jennifer's study spot being spoiled by Amy and him. Belinda kept up with all the rumors.

Matt knew he pushed a limit of civility by meeting at and occupying that particular place. Admittedly, he crossed a line. But at the time, he thought Jennifer deserved it all for cheating on him with Johan in front of the entire school and destroying his trust like that.

He had expected Jennifer and Johan to go public after the breakup, especially after Matt and Amy's couch make-out session. Jennifer didn't have to hide her relationship behind Matt's back anymore. She could kiss Johan in front of anyone she wanted to. So why hadn't she?

Maintaining eye contact and clamping his jaw tight, Matt approached Belinda. After all, Jennifer had cheated on him, and not vice versa. He had no reason for not being able to approach Belinda and ask if Jennifer had left for class yet.

When trepidation grabbed his voice because of the upcoming hard conversations, he reminded himself why he was there—to clear up the rumors. He smiled while clenching his hand into a fist, determined to walk Jennifer to class. He nodded and greeted Belinda.

"Hey, Belinda. Is Jennifer still here? I need to talk to her."

Her shoulders tensed. The guy beside her seemed to notice and stepped away, but Matt focused on Belinda. What Jennifer had done was wrong. That left Matt on the side of righteousness, no matter what Belinda thought.

She huffed, not answering him, and turned to the man. "*This* is the one I told you about. The one who broke up with Jennifer over a text."

Glancing over at the man, Matt remembered seeing him at a few Pi fraternity parties, but he'd never talked to him. The name Rob rang true in his memories.

Turning back to Belinda, Matt said, "I'm here to talk with Jennifer. I admit what I did was crummy. And two wrongs doesn't make a right, but Belinda, her dating Johan behind my back was pretty lousy of her."

She snorted, sizing up Matt with her nostrils flared, like she smelled something stinky. "The stalker? Jennifer hid from him every time he was around. I miss Jennifer, but not having creepy Johan standing outside at all hours has been wonderful. Whatever gave you the idea she was dating him?"

Matt opened his mouth to refute Belinda's comments, but before he could Rob said, "Hey man, I don't know you, and I don't know what all happened, but Jennifer doesn't like Johan, not even as a friend. The rumors about Jennifer and Johan aren't true."

Impossible! The rumor that Jennifer kissed Johan came from several people, including his roommate Lauren. People he trusted and several acquaintances told him that Johan and Jennifer were acting like a couple behind his back. Belinda and Rob were wrong. He started to defend his friends and said, "No, you're—"

"He brought her a huge bouquet last week. If she liked him, she'd have kept those flowers. But she refused to greet him or acknowledge him. If she were dating him, even stringing him along, she would have called or run downstairs. Instead, I watched her curl into a ball on her bed and refuse to leave," Rob said.

"I had to force her to go to the library. She's afraid to be on campus because of him. If Dr. Smith hadn't offered her a safe house—" Belinda said, but Matt interrupted.

That answered what he had heard about Dr. Smith—he was helping Jennifer, not in a relationship with her. "But she kissed Jo—"

"Gross! No, she didn't. She thought Johan was going to kill her. That's why she told the professor about Johan and why he helped her move out." Her nose wrinkled, and she curled her lip upward like Matt stank. Turning to Rob, she said, "I wonder if that's where the cretin is? Standing outside her new apartment, or house, or wherever she's hiding." Facing Matt, she said, "Jennifer's not here. I figured her new place's location was a secret, so I didn't ask where it is." She scrunched her nose again and narrowed her eyes into slits of judgment. "Not that I would tell you if I knew."

"Why didn't she call the police?" Matt asked.

Belinda huffed as if he was crazy. "Because your girl-friend, Amy, and her friends are always with him at the fountain. All he had to do was say he was visiting his friends. I'm sure *Amy* would vouch for him. And come on, even her own boyfriend didn't believe her or try to ask her if it was true." She leaned over to Rob. "Let's go."

They left the building without another word to Matt.

Belinda was right. He hadn't asked if it was true.

As he watched them go, he pulled out his phone. Once the door shut, he dialed Lauren.

"Hey Matt, did you clean the kitchen like I asked?" Lauren said.

Shaking his head, he cleared his mind of the image of dishes sitting in the sink. "Listen, I need to know something."

"Okay. What?" she asked.

"Did you see Jennifer and Johan kissing?"

"No. I didn't. But I heard about it."

"From who?" he asked.

"Amy and I were drinking at a local bar. She let it slip then."

"My Amy told you that Jennifer kissed Johan?"

"Yep. She said not to tell you after she apologized to me several times for letting it slip—something about how it was none of her business and she shouldn't have told me, let alone how it would hurt you if you found out. Why?"

Realization crashed into him. He wrote a text to break up with Jennifer. He distanced himself from her, and all for a rumor he now realizes might not be true. Had he wanted to believe Jennifer cheated so he could date Amy? Was that why he so easily assumed that Jennifer strayed? Did Amy create the story knowing how he would respond? "I have my doubts that Jennifer kissed Johan."

"Why do you say that? Because if she didn't cheat, you, Matt, compromised one of your *I'm a faithful partner* rules," she said, ever to the point.

He had nothing to gain from being angry at Lauren. The fault stopped with him. He made the assumption that what he heard was true. He broke up with Jennifer in the most painful way possible, using a text, and announced he was dating someone else. "I know. I might have made a mistake. Thanks, Lauren. I'll talk to you and Doug tonight, okay?"

"Sure," she said, hanging up.

If Jennifer wasn't even Johan's friend, then how would they have touched, let alone kissed? If she didn't go camping with Johan, then why did she act so funny, and why did she stand him up at his bunny party? She had said she would tell him later and explain everything. But by that time, he was over defending her actions to his friends.

He could picture her studying, caught up in the latest *Architectural Digest*, but that didn't explain missing the bunny party—unless she'd had a job interview scheduled for the same time.

He perked up at that thought. He'd heard rumors that several companies approached the college looking for interns. She'd mentioned having something to show him. Maybe she interviewed for one of the coveted positions and the only night she could interview was Friday. It would be like her to be nervous and want to focus on doing her best. She wouldn't mention it until after.

Or maybe her brother came to visit and she didn't want to tell Matt because she knew Matt would ditch the party to see

Randy, and Randy was too young to be around college kids who were drinking.

But what was it she had wanted to show him?

He held his breath. Had she wanted to have sex for the first time? He'd been on his way to her bedroom for that very thing right before he left for the Bahamas.

He placed his phone in his back pocket and sat on the chair near the entrance. Focusing on staying calm, he forced himself to accept the truth. He screwed up. For the first time in his life, Matt was the bad guy. To redeem himself, he needed to unwind the rumor, apologize, and discover what had really happened.

CHAPTER 7

SHANNA

SHANNA PEEKED OUT OF HER DORM WINDOW, SEARCHING FOR Johan. Every morning, he made it a habit to stand in the small park with the other smokers while he waited for Jennifer. As soon as she stepped outside, he'd follow Jennifer to her classes. Shanna had even seen him trailing behind Jennifer after she moved out of the dorm.

Despite this being his usual arrival time, he wasn't there—instead, another college student entertained their friends around the cherub fountain.

"Do you think he finally succeeded?" she asked Gourdy.

Shanna had completed her job, stealing Matt from Jennifer, and easily planted doubt in the boy's mind. Johan had two weekends in which to secure Jennifer—take her on a date, woo her, and drive to Wing It Laboratories. Heck, in that amount of time, he should have been able to kidnap her, at least.

As a bonus, she'd made Jennifer insecure by kissing Matt in public, studying with him on Jennifer's library couch, and eating with him at the cafeteria—anything and everything to help Johan succeed.

So much for Johan being a Casanova.

Gourdy had his leg propped up on her end table, a dagger in his hands, cleaning out his nails. "Maybe he completed his one and only job. But you're right. His skills are not as good as yours, my daughter."

"Daughter?" She stared at him.

"I can be loving when you are obedient."

Nodding, she glanced back out the window. *"Mated, Jennifer would have no choice—right?"* she asked.

"She will join willingly. Why wouldn't she want to be a good soldier in the greatest army? But Johan could take her directly to Wing It Laboratories, and you wouldn't know," Gourdy said, drawing out the last part, she assumed to irritate her.

So much for being his daughter.

Any day now, she expected Roland to order her to drive to another town and change cars as she left South Holt University. The order to evacuate hadn't happened... yet.

She dialed Johan. The first call went straight to voicemail.

Not being in the know made her vulnerable, and she hated feeling exposed, like someone could pop out of a crack and shoot her dead. If Roland had given her all the information on the operations in the area, she could anticipate everyone else's next moves and plan around them.

Did this lack of communication mean that Johan had finished his directive?

She turned off the *do not disturb* mode, revealing two texts. Her heart accelerated in the hopes that Roland used a different phone number and was telling her this nightmare had ended. He'd changed numbers before when he ordered her to the fresh horror of a new job.

She ignored the first message from Matt.

Seeing Matt's name reminded her that Amy had a date with him tonight. As alluring as Matt's dark brown eyes and hair were, his personality was all wrong for Shanna. She never had an ounce of attraction for Matt, but maybe if he was a dragon.

It upset her that she instead found a strange appeal to Johan. With his blond locks and cool blue eyes, Johan reminded her somewhat of Gourdy, which should repel her. Plus, she fancied dark hair and eyes. So why did she feel a pull toward Johan and not Matt?

Arrogant Matt believed the world rotated around him. If something happened, good or bad, Matt took ownership of it. Not in a positive way, but as if his actions alone impacted the universe. Johan screamed danger and broken rules, and she liked the potential for anarchy.

On a deeper level, she envied Johan's freedom. But escaping from the Family was a pipe dream. What good would it do her to want something she could never have?

Shaking her head to clear the thoughts, she turned her attention to the second text from her private investigator.

Opening the screen, she saw a picture of Jennifer, Dr. Smith, and two other men walking into Dr. Smith's house. They all appeared to be covered in mud. Jennifer's face was red, like she'd been crying, and her hair was a mess. Underneath, the message read, *Dr. Nick Smith is @ home with two other men and a young lady.* The photo was dated around five p.m., just before dusk.

"Well, Johan didn't take her back to the labs this weekend," she said. *"I guess we have another day of pretending with Matt."*

Once she reported the information about a person who ate a dragon's heart being in the area, she expected Roland to indulge her with what he found. Especially after he went all out to tell her to avoid the professor. It scared her, and since she'd been fooled by everyone she trusted, she decided she could only rely on herself.

Using the Family's credit card, she secured a private investigator's services. Roland never questioned her charges or who she hired. Financial freedom related to benefiting whatever assigned task she worked on as a Family operative. And Gourdy didn't object to her hiring her own detective.

"Why would I? It's a wise precaution to have someone on our payroll that answers to us," he said, eavesdropping on her thoughts.

She hoped by hiring a detective, she would have the answers she needed. Was Dr. Smith a friend or foe? Was he another of the Family's prisoners? Was he working for a different organization that harvested dragons, and would he kill her?

And what was taking Johan so long?

The door to the room opened, and her roommate, Chloe, stepped into the doorframe without entering. She watched Shanna with *the stare,* Chloe's tell that she had something she wanted to share. Not for the first time, Shanna missed her gift of smell.

"Hi, Amy," Chloe said cheerily. "Do you want to grab something to eat at the cafeteria?"

Quickly, she covered her real self with a bright, over-the-top, Amy-style smile and said, "That sounds great, but I'm waiting for Matt to call me."

"Oh." Chloe's voice sounded questioning as she tilted her head to the side with a puzzled look on her face. She said, "Matt's downstairs talking to Belinda, Jennifer's roommate. Is he not here to see you?"

He didn't call like he usually did when he visited. Maybe he said something in the text she didn't read about visiting. Pulling her phone into view, Shanna switched text strings and peered at Matt's words. Blah blah… He missed her and asked how she was doing… Nothing about visiting.

That was why Chloe was waiting at the door without coming in. She was expecting drama. But why? Because Matt was talking to Belinda? Nothing in his text indicated an issue. Maybe he was changing things up, like when he surprised her by taking her to the country to watch shooting stars from the bed of his truck. It was hard to sit there and pretend his breath didn't stink. Hopefully, his surprise wouldn't be something so repulsive this time.

Stretching as she moved toward the door, Amy said cheerfully, "I better go see him."

Before she left the room, she stopped in front of the mirror. She inspected the well-painted Amy character—styled red curls, makeup flawlessly applied, adorable pink shirt with a cute matching miniskirt—a vision of perfection.

Moving out of the way to let her pass, Chloe followed close behind her.

Another romantic day with Matt, she thought. To Gourdy, she added, *"Showtime, Gourdy."*

Exiting the stairs into the common entrance, Shanna studied the area. Matt sat on the armchair. On instinct, she opened her mouth to taste the air for emotions. Overpowering cinnamon and cloves assaulted her senses but no other scents above the dragon-blocking-perfume smell.

Matt hadn't noticed her and stared at a spot near a wall to his right. Rigid, he had red blotches on his cheeks, his nails dug into the arms of the seat, and his teeth were clenched. When he detected her, not a muscle in his face moved as he stood. Eyes locked on her with a death glare, he approached her.

Something was wrong.

She smiled, trying to take away some of the bite from the anger she swore radiated in the air. "Hi, baby," she said. Standing on her tippy toes, she pecked his chin.

Still stiff, he didn't return her affection, his hands balled into fists at his sides. He said, "Amy, did you tell Lauren that Jennifer kissed Johan?"

So, he had heard the truth. That took longer than she predicted it would. Earlier last week, she would have pinned it all on Johan, saying she was innocent. Today, she was over the charade. She wanted this fake relationship over with. Still, without knowing where Johan stood with Jennifer, should she lie or clear the rumor mill?

"Johan has had enough time," Gourdy echoed her thoughts.

"Yes," she said. Trying to seem natural, like a young girl desiring her first love—in case she had to stay in the area longer as Amy—she pleaded with her eyes. "Johan told me Jennifer kissed him."

"You lied to me," he said through locked-together teeth in a cold, detached voice.

Over the years, Shanna had developed the ability to act on demand. Pulling from past experiences, she made Amy cry. Her voice cracking, she said, "Why are you being so mean?" She touched his arm with two fingers. "I love you, Matt."

In her peripheral vision, she perceived those in the common room, including her roommate, rubberneck at the carnage and whispering to each other with hushed voices so they could still overhear the conversation.

Matt stepped out of her reach. "I heard the rumor while playing cards at the Pi house. I called them this morning. After I confirmed they didn't witness it for themselves, I asked my poker buddies who they heard it from. They all pointed a finger at you. No one I talked with actually saw Jennifer and Johan together."

"Johan told me he was dating her. And he was always here," she begged him to understand. Now, enough tears formed to create trails down her cheeks.

"No," he said, pausing and searching her face. "When I asked you, you told me they kissed. You indicated you saw it with your own eyes. But Belinda says Jennifer avoided Johan to the point she moved out of the dorm."

"I, I..." Amy hyperventilated. Only years of practice allowed her to insert this fine artistic masterpiece into the drama she was weaving. Pretending to be one of the stalkers she inadvertently created, she controlled the Amy character.

"Johan told me. But you're right, I didn't see it," she admitted between deep throaty sobs. "I told other people because I love you. Can't you feel it? Can't you see it? We belong together! We're right for each other!"

"Amy," he said calmly and firmly. "It's over. I hate being lied to." Stiffly, he turned toward the entrance. She grabbed his jacket sleeve. He jerked, and she used the momentum to collapse to the floor, bawling. Her sight blurred from the tears she produced for the show she was putting on. Despite everyone appearing as blobs of color, she could pick out Matt flinging the doors open as he left.

Raising the volume of her crying, she drew in a crowd.

Supporters gathered around her.

The girl from the first floor said, "You can do better."

The bulky girl, who always studied in the basement, patted her head and said, "He doesn't deserve you."

The other redheaded girl on the third floor shook her head as she headed toward the stairs and said, "I never liked him."

Fake mourning while plotting, she took a napkin someone handed her and blew her nose.

"Matt still cares for Jennifer. Knowing his sense of righteous nobility, he's probably more worried about how he looks to others and that other people will see that he caused Jennifer grief that she didn't deserve... Arrogant Matt probably thinks he has a chance to get Jennifer back," she thought to Gourdy. *"Matt should be thanking me he's alive. Had he stayed with Jennifer, she'd have killed him after her dreams finished and her Jormungant drove her crazy."*

Killing her beloved Jared was one of Gourdy's first acts, but it didn't happen overnight. His control over her started with her headaches on the first day of her life with a dragon guide. Whenever Shanna attempted to sleep, banging noises or the sounds of people screaming kept her awake. The visions of being chased by dragons began a week later. And then, her skin hummed with pain, like tiny fire ants climbed over her arms, stinging every inch of her epidermis.

Shanna had hunted for missing patches of hair or red, painful scratches or scabs on Jennifer, signs she tried to scrape off her flesh. She had even looked for dark circles under her eyes that indicated Jennifer suffered at the hands of her version of Gourdy. So far, Shanna had found no indication Jennifer had met her tormentor yet.

"All you have to do is to be obedient, and I will reward you with peace. Perhaps Jennifer is doing everything her Jormungant is commanding her to do. What I did to you was done to help you. I made you better," Gourdy said.

"Breaking me mentally was helping me?" she asked. Yet that wasn't what bothered Shanna. *"But why hasn't Jennifer lost her mind?"*

Why hadn't Jennifer's own Gourdy driven her mad?

Almost two months had passed since Thanksgiving. If she dreamed of an ancestor up to conception each of those nights, she should be around sixty or seventy generations back in time. If each succeeding ancestor was conceived when their parents were around twenty, just to make the math easy, that would be about one thousand two hundred years ago.

Jormungant was old. Shanna guessed around ten thousand. So Jennifer could still be having the dreams that led back to meeting him.

Yet she seemed sane this semester.

Well, not in the photo the investigator sent her. Crying in that picture could mean the change had finally happened.

But then another thought came at her, and like a brick of insight, it slammed her upside the head, and she jolted alert.

"Are you okay?" Chloe asked.

Regaining the Amy character, she mumbled, "I'll be alright."

But Shanna's mind whirled as she realized there was a detail she'd missed. Would Jennifer have moved in with someone who had eaten dragon heart if she didn't know them? A dragon's natural instinct was to avoid danger, and nothing screamed danger more than someone who smelled of consumed dragon.

Shanna assumed the Family picked Johan because Jennifer's ancestor knew him. Having someone she recognized and felt comfortable with would have helped Jennifer shift from a college student to a pawn for the Family. The Family kept track of the lineages of all potential dragon lines, tracked them like priced stallions. They'd know if Johan knew Jennifer's ancestor. That would mean Jennifer dreamed of Johan, and from those memories, felt she could trust him.

And was it possible that Dr. Smith approached *her*? But how would Dr. Smith know Jennifer was a dragon? Before using the perfume, Shanna had a good whiff of Dr. Smith. She confirmed he didn't receive the gift of dragon smelling when he consumed a dragon heart; he wasn't a Nose.

Was it possible there was another person who could smell dragons—maybe one of the other men in the photograph? She'd text her investigator later and ask him to find out more information about the other two men. If she had more knowledge, she'd be able to answer that question.

But thinking back to Dr. Smith and his role in all this, Jennifer could have approached him for help. Did that suggest that Jennifer knew him from an ancestor, had dreamed of him too?

It seemed random and not probable for one of her ancestors to have come across Dr. Smith and not be involved in the dragon world. If he knew Jormungant, then why didn't Roland just say so? Why did Roland give caution to avoid Dr. Smith? She'd never been told to avoid other operatives. Her directive was to interact with Johan.

She ruled out Dr. Smith as a friend of the Family. What other possible reasons would Jennifer's ancestor know Dr. Smith?

Who knows? Jennifer's such a strange dragon, having a brother and all, she could have multiple dragon lines. She breathed deeply, turning it into a heave to keep up the ruse of crying.

Then the idea settled more into her consciousness, and it had some merit. Could a human-born dragon have multiple dragon ancestors? Could Jennifer have descended from more than one dragon? Was that even possible? *"Can someone have multiple dragon guides?"*

While she waited for Gourdy's answer, she continued with her Amy charade. Slowly picking herself off the floor and using her sleeves to clean the snot, she addressed her well-wishers. "Thank you." She glanced at the faces around her, keeping the sadness in her eyes. "I'll be all right."

A long mirror hung on the wall across from her. In her reflection, she observed mascara smudges marking the tears' trail. Her face was almost the same red as her hair.

Chloe tapped her on the shoulder. "Are you all right? Can I help you?"

She tried to fake an insincere smile. "I think I'll eat the chocolate ice cream in our freezer and watch sad movies," she said, including the crowd gathered around her.

"Once again, I'm a hatchling. How would I know?" Gourdy said, finally answering her.

"But I bet that's it. That must be the reason she's not crazy. Jennifer has multiple guides and several dragon lines. You aren't her only one. That's why Jennifer hasn't gone crazy."

Shanna was wrecked, trapped, and controlled while Jennifer remained free. So much for her being the sister she never had and the friend she always wanted.

Yet, as Shanna thought about it, she might be able to use Jennifer to gain her freedom.

CHAPTER 8

JENNIFER

NUMB AND TIRED OF THE CONSTANT REMINDERS OF THE WEEKEND, Jennifer stared at a brown smudge on the otherwise empty eggshell-white wall perpendicular to Dr. Smith's desk. Who knew killing someone, even if they threatened you harm, came at such a large mental cost? Yet that imperfection in front of her kept her mind grounded. To her right, out of the corner of her eye, she barely noticed Petr rummaging through a gray file cabinet behind his desk. He raised a folder in the air with his good hand and swiveled around, placing the document on the desk's surface.

"What's up?" he asked.

She didn't face him as she leaned her head against the other wall, the back of the chair shoved against the painted cinderblock. "I find that if I hyper-focus on something unimportant, I have fewer visions of..."

...Johan stood a few feet before her, a look of horror twisting his features, a hole in his chest, as he collapsed into the water...

"Jennifer," he whispered.

"Yes." She lowered her voice, again finding the brown

spot on the wall. She thought the imperfection was a leftover from a previous paint color, like perhaps this room was darker at one time, and they didn't do a thorough job of repainting the office.

"Have you ever heard the phrase *fake it until you make it*?" Petr asked.

She glanced at him, and he leaned back in his chair, grimacing from the pain.

"Yes," she answered.

"Do you understand what it means?" he asked.

"Yes."

"Please apply it. When we get home, you can act all down. But here, you need to appear to be a normal college student." He opened the folder, pulling out papers from inside. He reached into his drawer, grabbing sticky notes. In her mind, she separated him from the man she claimed as a mate and the man he was now, the professor.

"Is your homework caught up?" he asked.

She couldn't remember anything beyond this weekend without reliving what happened in the forest. Did she even have homework?

...Blond hair floated in the water, tainted with red blood. His heart visible, bobbed in the middle of the wound she created, a reminder of the dragon's heart he had eaten...

"I don't know," she answered.

"Instead of focusing on unimportant things, I suggest reviewing last week's notes and seeing what you can figure out. When you finish that, start considering what we will say to your parents."

That caught her attention, and she turned the chair toward his desk. "What?"

He glanced up. "Remember our agreement, that your safety comes first?"

"Yes, but I'm saf—"

"You agreed. If your safety is at risk—"

"But I'm safe, Petr." She put her elbows on his desk and brought her hands together like she was praying. "Please."

"I'm thinking of your parents. After this past weekend, I'm not sure when we'll need to leave, and I want your family to feel like you will be protected. I have every intention of meeting your parents this weekend or next. If they know you're with a responsible adult, with other people they can reach out to, and have a face to go along with that person, it will help them feel more secure when you are no longer in the same country." He returned to the papers on his desk.

"What are you going to tell them? Are you going to say you're my friend, a college professor, or that you're the guy who hopes to be my lover?" she asked.

She could tell by how his left hand ran through his hair that he was contemplating her words, but he didn't glance at her. Petr pulled out a single sheet of paper from the recently retrieved folder and laid it down. After seconds of glaring intensely at the page, his eyes met hers again, and he said, "I don't think we're at the point where we need to tell them I'm your college professor or that we're dating. How about a friend?"

This soon after Matt, it was probably what her parents would expect: a friend, not a boyfriend. Besides, well, other than weekly dates, they hadn't established a term for what they were to each other, and mating, well, that didn't sound human, and claiming sounded too sci-fi.

"Friends it is," she said. She could tell her parents about Matt at the same time she introduced Petr.

While Petr returned to grading papers, Jennifer reached down to grab her work planner. Barry appeared on top of the backpack she had placed on the ugly industrial tile. Smaller than a Barbie doll, he was sporting a green button-down shirt, brown pants, short hair, and a pair of reading glasses.

"What he said makes sense. I've kept a tally of your classes, and you're caught up in everything but AutoCAD. Currently, the computers in the lab are fair game, open hours and all. We could finish your project. Your next class starts in..." Barry looked down at his black wristwatch. "Almost an hour."

"*Okay.*" Jennifer slung her bookbag over her back swiftly as she stood, ignoring that Barry was still on the bag. The momentum threw mini-Barry through the air. Like a rubber ball in a racquetball court, a smashing noise echoed in Jennifer's mind when he hit the cinderblock wall, close to the brown spot she found so fascinating. As an extra layer of goofiness, he included in pink neon writing, reminding her of a comic book, the word *SPLAT!* above his head. Jennifer faced the hall, not in the mood to laugh, but not before the word melted off the wall in front of her. Barry hmphed when she didn't respond.

"And where are you going?" Petr sounded more like a parent than a friend or the guy she had had a date with last week. She again questioned her attraction to someone so old.

Assuming innocence, she ignored the inflection and blamed it on his worry for her. "I'm going to the lab to finish some work there. I have class right after, but I'll return when I'm out, *Dr. Smith.*"

Maybe she didn't ignore his calling her a friend or the tone as much as she thought she had.

When they locked eyes, she forced an over-the-top zealot smile to her lips. She pictured her grin with red lips and sharp teeth, not happy or go-lucky at all. It was irrational to be hurt by him using the term *friends*, but she wanted him to claim her with the same passion she had claimed him.

She left the room and headed for the lab. She knew Petr desired her; she could smell his pheromones, though they were lighter than last week. Ever since she killed a man, he acted almost indifferent or like he was too busy for romance.

But she desired more. She craved the chemistry he had for her on their date before...

...The fireball sliced through Johan's chest. She smelled sizzling flesh, like burning hair...

Materializing beside her, Barry touched her back. She hadn't even noticed she had stopped walking. "I hate to say this, but something is happening around here."

Picking up her pace, she confirmed no one was close enough to overhear her. "What do you mean?" she asked.

"All the people are stopping as you walk by," Barry said.

Leaving the biology building, she spotted several clusters of students. Very few weren't gawking at her.

"Hi," she said to some girls who had been in her art class last year as they passed her. They glanced in the other direction and didn't respond, like she was a pariah.

Panic swirled in her thoughts as she pictured Johan falling into a puddle of water. *"They know. They all know."*

"Keep walking. You've inspired a lot of rumors lately. Matt breaking up with you. You dating Johan. Oh, yes, I forgot one. You're living with Dr. Smith."

"Are you reading other people's minds?" she asked. She missed a step as she peeked at him and had to take two steps to catch up.

"No. I can hear their conversations. Can't you?" he asked.

Listening more closely, she opened the door to the lab. In the distance and getting louder, she heard students talking. The closer she came to the stairs, the clearer the voices became. True to Barry's words, three individuals quieted when they saw her, but after she passed, someone said, "That's her. The one who was dating Matt, then Johan, and now I hear she's having sex with a professor."

I wish, she thought as she rolled her eyes—*friend zoned.* "So I'm the talk of the school. Yippee!"

The lab door was open, and she peered inside. Ben, the only one in the room, sat in the dark, his screen reflecting on his round wire-rimmed glasses. When she walked into the room, the motion-sensor lights popped on. He stopped working and glanced up at her, waving enthusiastically. "Hey, Jennifer! Did you have an enjoyable weekend?"

If those words came from anyone else, she would have thought he was playing along with the rumors, asking her if she spent the weekend having wild sex. But Ben, with his unwashed hair, laughed at his own corny jokes and didn't seem like the type to participate in spreading stories—he spent all his free time studying. She'd witnessed him shoo off gossipers, explaining he didn't want to know. Plus, he always greeted her by asking if she enjoyed her day. She paused anyway, taking deep breaths, forcing the memories away.

Barry touched her back in comfort. "Lie," he whispered in her ear.

"Yep," she said as she dropped her book bag in the chair to Ben's left. "Do you mind if I sit here? Or is this seat taken?" She indicated the spot two computers down from him.

"Sure, there's no one here but me, and I can't use this many PCs."

She placed her books down and asked, "Did you have a great weekend?"

"I spent it here. My mom told me not to take nineteen hours, and I hate this lab. I'm two projects behind, but it's not my fault the computer crashed before I saved my progress. I was completely done! Seriously, the department needs to invest in new tech here..." He sighed. "I asked my parents to buy me a copy of AutoCAD, but they said it cost too much money, and that they doubted I would use it much when I was out of college, so here I am."

"Wow," she said, sitting down. "I'm only one project behind, but it would be nice to be done with the course. I wonder if we asked the lab tech...What's his name?"

He smiled. "Carlos."

"You think he would give us a copy of the rest of the labs?" she asked. If he would, she'd have less to do and could focus on training.

"I doubt it." Ben's attention moved back to the screen, and he started trying to connect a line.

Jennifer hit her computer's *on* button. While waiting for the computer to warm up, she hyper-focused on Ben, moving lines and zooming in and out.

Once she typed in her university ID and password, she used all her energy on her work, forgetting everything else.

CHAPTER 9

SHANNA

THE CHOCOLATE ICE CREAM BUCKET WAS ALMOST EMPTY. THE movie finished. Shanna stared at her roommate. Chloe didn't budge, not making eye contact, her knees pressed into her chest.

They'd moved the furniture out of the way and constructed a makeshift seat out of blankets. Above them, a laser skylight machine made waves of red, blue, and green. After pulling the blinds closed, blocking the light from coming into the room, they started a black-and-white love story. Chloe called it movies under the stars and said it was the perfect solution to a bad day with Matt.

Allowing fresh tears to fall down her cheeks, Shanna said, "Chloe, I'll be fine. Don't miss the rest of your classes on account of me." With a sharp intake of air, she grabbed a tissue. It was the last one in her third box.

Finally, Chloe looked. "Sweet girl, I'm here for you. That's what roommates are for."

Once again, Shanna wished she didn't have on the dragon masking perfume and had access to that extra sensory detail. Then she would know how to motivate her roommate to leave. Somehow, Shanna needed to convince her to go so she could update Roland. Supposedly mourning Matt, Shanna had to remain in her apartment the rest of the day to make the breakup pain seem believable.

Did Chloe want to support Amy or gather juicy gossip to spread on campus? The answer to that question determined how she would respond.

She guessed. "And I love you for it," Shanna said, embracing her roommate. "But I don't need to feel any guiltier. Please don't stay on my account."

Sighing, Chloe stood. "Honestly, it's fine. I don't mind staying. Misery loves company and all."

Sniffling, Shanna said, "We only dated for a little over a week. I'll be fine. I promise. But I'll call if I need you."

Moving over to her bed, Chloe stuffed her bags full of clothes. "Well, if it's all right…"

"Absolutely. I don't want you to feel trapped here by me," Shanna responded.

"I'm sorry, Amy. I already had plans tonight… To see a concert. I'll grab my books and spend the night with Jim." Jim was Chloe's boyfriend. "I'll drop everything and head back if you call."

Shanna nodded as she snuggled an opened tissue box, cuddling it close.

Chloe's heart thundered while she moved around the room, grabbing things and packing. The woman wanted to leave. Shanna didn't blame her and tried not to smile at her discomfort.

With her hand on the doorknob, Chloe said, "I'll see you." She cracked open the door. With the blinds shut, the room had been dark, and although Shanna could see with or without light, she faked discomfort at the change, throwing her hands over her eyes, pretending to be blinded.

"Thank you," Shanna said.

Once the door closed and locked, she waited and listened in case Chloe returned. Confident she was alone, she turned the new television on to some cartoon and increased the volume. Then she pulled out her phone and dialed Roland.

Gourdy appeared, sitting on her bed. "I think it's a good plan," he said, nodding in approval.

"I'll still need permission. We'll see if I can sell it to Roland."

In case anyone came back in, she had her cover story ready and moved back to the floor amongst the dirty tissues she had haphazardly thrown around.

"Hello," Roland said.

"Matt broke up with Amy," she whispered.

"Television's on, and you're whispering. You must be playing a mourner."

"I am," she agreed.

"You thought he might break up with Amy soon," Roland said.

"Have you heard from Johan? Did he acquire the subject?" Of course, she knew Johan had failed, and that Jennifer still roamed the campus. And yes, the Family paid for the private investigator, but she wouldn't give away what she knew or that she had a person watching Dr. Smith's house. Roland could read her credit card statement and draw his own conclusions or ask.

"Interesting question. I understand that Johan didn't report in last night as required."

"Is that common? For him not to report in?" she asked. Johan gave off rebel vibes. It wouldn't surprise her if he avoided deadlines and slacked on orders. She envied his freedom.

"I'm not the person he answers to, so I don't know. But Father doesn't seem concerned."

"I know how to bring Jennifer into the fold."

"The job belongs to Joh—"

"But I know I can do it. I know I can get Jennifer to willingly join the Family."

"Interesting. How do you plan on doing that?" he asked.

Glancing up at Gourdy, she thought about how to sell the plot without divulging the details. She'd have to keep her strategies a secret until she got the green light. Otherwise, some other operative might take credit for her idea. If she could capture Jennifer, she could bargain a trade. Perhaps fifty years of freedom from the Family, from being an operative. A chance for her to live away from Jormungant's control.

Surprisingly, Gourdy didn't disagree.

"I can reward faithfulness. But first, you have to collect the girl," Gourdy said.

Nodding, she said, "It plays on Jennifer's and Matt's weaknesses. Just like my dragon guide plays on mine."

"I'm listening," Roland said.

She didn't think Roland would necessarily take credit for her idea, but Johan would if he found out about it. She needed him removed from the picture before she told Roland more. "Not until Johan is pulled from the case."

"That might be awhile." He sighed. "You're concerned that Johan will take credit?"

"Yes."

"Send me a file of your plan, explaining in detail why your plan will work. Father will never agree to anything without first considering the plan and its potential consequences."

"And you can guarantee I'll get the credit? In exchange, I want fifty years of freedom."

"If it captures Jennifer, I'm sure Father will give you credit." He paused. "We will have to find Johan to pull him off the case. If that's what Father decides is best."

"I thought you said he didn't report in, and that Father wasn't worried. That sounds like they know how to find him."

"He didn't, and Father's not worried."

She chewed on her manicured nails. When she realized

what she had done, she forced her hand back to her side. "Then why did you say you needed to find him?"

"He planned to pull out this weekend. Early this morning at the latest. Of course, if he failed, he would regroup. But so far, he's not called, and he's not here. All we know is his phone is disconnected, and we expected him to pick up his new cell this morning. He could just be delayed. We've sent operators to track down his car and visit his apartment."

"By visit, do you mean empty the apartment?" she asked. When a job was finished, the Family erased all traces of her ever visiting a city. A group cleaned out her housing arrangements and a company removed any digital trails. As far as people remembering her, at each job, she intentionally stayed in the background, a side character few even noticed. She kept the people who recognized her at a distance, not having many, if any, close relationships. She reckoned some physical papers, such as photographs that weren't online, probably had her picture. Still, she wouldn't put it past the Family to break in and steal or destroy proofs—even in the stalking cases, documentation changed from showing her photos to someone else's. It was like she just disappeared.

Gourdy laughed, drawing her attention. "Just imagine if Jennifer killed him. If we could prove it, picture her in jail. She'd be a sitting duck."

"If he's dead, Dr. Smith did it. You don't eat a dragon's heart without being a killer. Plus, Jennifer doesn't have the backbone to —" Did it matter? If Dr. Smith or one of the other people murdered Johan, could Jennifer be blamed? That would be even easier than her plan. Amy could frame Jennifer, and the Family could extradite Jennifer to Wing It Laboratories.

"Wait, don't clean out his apartment," she shouted, and out of a suspicious reflex, stared around the room, searching for someone who could hear her.

"You're alone, Shanna. No one can hear you," Gourdy said sarcastically.

"Why? What are you thinking, Amy?" Roland asked.

"May I have fifty years away from Family? Fifty years to be free if I bring in Jennifer?" she asked.

Roland exhaled. "Usually, when Father awards an operative, he forces them to marry and have children. Are you willing to take that step?"

Marriage? Children? Did she want that? She had with Jared, but the desire for marriage and children died with him. "Can I have fifty years without marriage?"

"Listen, I'll talk with Father and ask him to give you fifty years to do what you want, without requiring you to marry, if you bring in Jennifer. But why are you requesting us not to clear out Johan's apartment?"

"What if we frame Jennifer for killing Johan, even though he's not dead? Leave his place alone, and place evidence that she killed him."

"You're saying to fake a murder and blame Jennifer for the murder?"

"Yes. And Johan missing is the perfect opportunity. Pull him to headquarters and hide him there... Or send him to another part of the world. I'm sure the Family can arrange to plant bloody clothes or mess up her phone so that Johan and Jennifer are at the same place, right before he is missing. It can't be—"

"I'll explain your idea to Father and ask him not to clean the apartment. I'll even request for them to leave traces of Johan's murder behind. But I can't guarantee Father will agree to any of it."

"Please try. I know it will work. It has to work," she said. "I'll go to the police department tomorrow. If there has been any foul play, I'll make sure they blame Jenn—"

"Do you have any idea how old Johan is?"

"No. Only older than me. But if the Family can erase someone, they can create someone. Plant information that makes his story hold true in a court of law. When Johan shows up because he skipped town, the Family can create a crime scene and make Jennifer look like the guilty party. The Family can get her from there."

"Is that your plan? Fake a crime scene to get Jennifer?"

"No, but—"

"Send me the other idea. I'll pass the plans on to Father. He might like them. Especially the first one. It's a twist on erasing. But, Amy, until then, Johan is the operative with the job of bringing in Jennifer."

Her nails had found their way back into her mouth. *Stupid nervous tic,* she thought, forcing her hand away. Lowering her voice, she asked, "What did Johan get if he delivered Jennifer?"

He huffed. "I'm not sure. Usually, Father gave him money for harvesting a dragon."

"He didn't have to pose as a different person?"

"No."

"Then why do I?"

"Because, Shanna, you are young. Johan didn't start with that much freedom. Freedom has to be earned."

"Good. Then, if I bring in Jennifer, if I make it possible to capture her, I want fifty years of freedom," she said.

The phone went dead.

Yet her mind raced. For almost twenty years, the Family had treated her like she didn't matter. After living through a fate worse than death, she'd been sent from location to location. One decision from Father could give her a chance at freedom. If he didn't agree, she'd lose it.

Moving beside Gourdy, she grabbed her pillow, pushed it against her face, and screamed.

CHAPTER 10

JENNIFER

THE CONCENTRATION LINES ACROSS PETR'S FOREHEAD CAUSED Jennifer to pause before distracting him. There was something fascinating about a man who focused so much attention on one task. She could love this man if she didn't already.

She decided enough time had passed. Reaching up, she tapped on his open door, causing it to move slightly inward.

When he glanced up, a tight smile cracked his lips. He leaned back and grunted as he exhaled. "Jennifer." Did he sound relieved or stressed at seeing her?

"How are you?" she asked, resting a shoulder against the metal doorframe.

"I've been better," he said, touching his wound. "You?"

… Water surrounded her ankles…

No. She refused to dwell on the past weekend. "Getting there."

Dark circles had formed under Petr's eyes since this morning. What was bothering him? Was it pain, her being hunted by other people, or something else? She trusted him enough that she knew he would tell her in his own time, so she ignored her concerns for now.

"I'm done with classes," she admitted. "Want to go for a run?"

Both arms started to come up like he was prepared to talk with his hands, but he grimaced as he lowered the one resting in a sling. "Can't. I have to finish this before we leave."

"Okay. What if I went to the gym without you?"

His lips pinched together. Any second, she expected a refute. Before he could, she continued. "Campus is still crowded at this hour. I'll stay out in the open. Do you mind if I go back to my dorm, change clothes, and jog on a treadmill?" Shaking her fingers loose and rolling her neck to demonstrate, she added, "I need to move. Get some energy out. You know, add some good feeling dopamine."

Petr's face didn't relax. "I do mind." He huffed. "Tonight, when I finish, I'll take you to my gym and wait while you run." He pointed to the seat across from his desk with an unspoken request for her to sit.

Staying near the door, she whispered, "I can't live in fear. This is my way of pushing past this. I'll stop as soon as you arrive."

"Jennifer, I—"

She cut him off, begging him to understand, "Petr, I hate treadmills. If I wasn't desperate…"

"I can't lose you," he said, sounding distraught.

"You're not. I'm not going to be alone. There will be other students everywhere. I get that someone wants to take me to their leader or whatever."

…Johan stood in front of her…

"I just, I need to get back to living," she pleaded.

"My life has been spent waiting for you," he said, switching to Dragon, speaking like a native.

85

She responded in Dragon, "Not me, Petr. You've been waiting for your nephew."

"And you, Jennifer," he said in English.

Glancing in the halls, she saw students still scattered from one side to the other. Continuing the conversation in Dragon, she said, "I killed"—*Johan fell into the water, a hole in his chest*—"one threat. I can do it again." She clenched her jaw, summoning determination.

"And so you did... You will stay among the herd, in plain sight?" he asked in Dragon.

"Yes," she replied in English. How it happened, she wasn't sure, maybe because she was almost always with Petr for the last week, but she just realized she didn't have his cell number, only the office landline that was listed on his syllabus. Taking a few steps, she stopped in front of his desk. "If I didn't need the exercise, I wouldn't be asking." She held out her hand. "May I have your phone?"

Reaching out, he gripped the device and didn't release it. "If you think you are being followed, call and return here to me. Do you understand?"

Something akin to pride raised its ugly head. She wanted to snap at and remind him she was a ferocious dragon that spit fire. *Assume innocence. He cares for you and doesn't want you to get hurt*, she coaxed herself. "Of course."

"I'm serious, Jennifer. I know you can defend yourself. If you sense danger, you come back to me." His hold loosened, and he relinquished his cell.

She held it in front of his face to unlock the screen with his biometrics. Quickly, she texted herself. "My number. Later, I'll add you to the app my parents use to track me. If something scary happens, I'll call you."

He took the phone back with his left hand. "Do that," he said, still talking softly. "I'll come by the student gym to get you when I'm finished."

"I'm leaving my bookbag here," she said, placing it on the

ground after retrieving her phone and sticking it in her pocket. She turned and walked out of his office.

As she passed people, she sniffed. She didn't detect any strange odors, only the new normal of people full of gossip— the smell of buttery popcorn. The silly young adults around her college wagged their tongues with stories, but there were no dragons or people who consumed the orange smelling life-fruit of the City of Giants.

She used the back entrance to enter her dorm building. Taking two stairs at a time, she climbed to the second floor and unlocked her door. Belinda's rose perfume that she seemed to pour on herself overwhelmed Jennifer's senses, and she blinked to clear her tears as she adjusted.

Before last week, her room didn't feel so lonely, but without Petr, it did. Years appeared to have passed since she was here. Yet the blue comforter on the bed hadn't even collected dust. Only the dents from the milk crates she used to move out of the dorm last week showed she had left.

She had left a few clothes as a farce to keep people from guessing the truth. Based on the gossip she overheard all day, it hadn't done any good. The rumors were much worse than the reality.

Sighing, she retrieved an outfit from her closet. She would have only two sets of clean clothes left in her dorm after today. She debated taking them to Petr's house as well. "I like having outfits here, like a locker," she said to Barry, coming to a decision.

"You're acting like you don't have a choice on where you want to live. You can pick, Jennifer. You're the dragon. If you want to move back to the dorms, we can move back to the dorms. You might burn the place down, but..." Barry thought.

She'd almost forgotten about that—last week, when she turned into a dragon while sleeping, flames licked her skin and caught the bed on fire. With everything that happened over the weekend, that seemed like years ago and it had slipped her mind. Such a minor thing compared to taking a life. The reality of potentially hurting so many people reminded her of why she sought out Petr in the first place. "Yeah. Petr's it is. My choice."

Placing her clothes on the bed, she began to remove her shirt.

The door opened. Belinda jumped when she recognized Jennifer, grabbing her chest as she closed her eyes. "Oh my gosh, Jennifer. You scared the bad juju out of me."

Frowning, Jennifer responded, "Sorry."

Closing the door, Belinda, with her hand still over her heart, said, "Are you back? Please tell me you had that cretin arrested."

...Johan fell, a hole in his torso...

Shaking her head to clear the image, she said, "No. No. Not back. I'm still hiding from anyone who wishes to harm me. While there are people still outside to witness if I'm kidnapped, I'm going to change clothes and run at the gym."

"You hate treadmills," she said. "Wait, do you have time to go to the cafeteria to catch up and eat? I can walk you to the gym after if you're concerned about being left alone."

I can't continue to be afraid. Plus, Petr giving her orders as if she didn't have a mind or will of her own wasn't going to work. Would he be angry? Probably. But he did say to call if she felt like she was in danger. She'd be safe with Belinda, and the area would be crowded with other students. That should deter someone from attacking or kidnapping her. "Sure. Let me get dressed, okay?"

Belinda squealed while dancing. She threw her books onto her bed and said, "Awesome. Finally, some roommate stuff."

As Jennifer took her top off, Belinda said, "Guess who we saw this morning?"

After pulling the cold fabric of the clean shirt over her head, Jennifer asked, "Who?"

The room filled with rose-flavored buttery popcorn, and Jennifer hesitated while unbuttoning her jeans.

"Matt," Belinda announced.

By the smell, there had to be more. Jennifer said, "Not unusual. Amy lives in the room a few doors down."

"You want to know why Matt broke up with you? Because that is the question I found the answer to."

Did Jennifer even want to know? Not really. She was more worried about why Petr seemed to be pulling back. A question she really wanted answered would be what did Petr have planned for their date night on Wednesday.

"Oh, I want to know," Barry interjected.

"Does it matter if I care? It sounds like you want to tell me," Jennifer said, sitting on the bed and pulling on sweatpants.

"Matt thought you were dating Johan behind his back. Thought you kissed him," she said.

...As if in slow motion, she could hear Johan's breath. The fireball released in a roar, sizzling as it cauterized while slicing through Johan's chest...

"Jennifer?" Belinda said.

"Yeah," she responded, blinking.

"Did Johan kiss you? Is that why you turned all white and pasty?"

Thinking about Johan and what she had to him, made her sick to her stomach. She, Jennifer, had taken his life. "No. Sorry, Belinda. I wish I would have never met him."

Belinda sat on the bed beside Jennifer and placed her hand on her leg. "He hurt you that bad?"

"He did a lot of mental damage, that's for sure."

"Hopefully, moving out has caused that to stop. Did he find your new hiding spot?"

"If he has, I haven't seen him standing outside," Jennifer said.

"Good… I'm changing the subject, well, a little. Because it's something you need to know. Amy started the rumor that you were dating Johan behind Matt's back."

"Why would she do that?" Jennifer asked Barry.

"The rumor is she did it to break up you and Matt," Belinda answered.

"Well, it worked," Jennifer said. She picked up her running shoes that she had worn to class and put them on.

"But Matt found out and broke it off with Amy," Belinda continued.

No words came to her mind. Jennifer's relationship with Matt was in the past and no longer mattered. Because of everything that happened over the weekend, Jennifer could almost believe she and Matt had never been a couple. But Belinda was waiting for an answer. "Poor Matt."

"What? That's it? That's all you have to say?"

"Ready to go eat?" Jennifer asked, raising her eyebrows.

"Yes. But you should be like, glory be."

"Okay, what does that mean?"

"Glory be, you got what you deserved. Come on." She stood and offered Jennifer her hand. "Let's grab some food."

"Okay."

They walked in silence until they stepped outside. Belinda zipped up her jacket. "Brr. Where's your coat?"

She'd unintentionally left it again. As a dragon, she could self-regulate her temperature and never felt cold or hot. But if she wanted to appear wholly human, she needed to remember her coat. She couldn't tell Belinda that. "I forgot it." She wrapped her arms around her elbows and pretended to be cold.

"Do you like the place you're living?"

"Yes."

"Is it with Dr. Smith?" she teased.

Glancing shyly over at Belinda, Jennifer answered honestly, "Yes."

"Wow. Are you, I mean, have you—"

Jennifer knew where the conversation was going. "Milked that cow?" When Belinda nodded, Jennifer said, "No. Not even close. I've been friend-zoned. He's like an overprotective parent."

"But you like him. I see it in your eyes," Belinda accused.

"Yes. I like him... Something in me is drawn to him. When he enters the room, I know it. When he talks, I hover in anticipation at each word. Yes. I like him, and I like him in every way."

At the cafeteria, Belinda held the door wide open to let Jennifer pass. Once inside, Belinda grabbed Jennifer's arm, forcing Jennifer to look her in the eyes. "Be careful, Jen. Men much older than us are typically after only one thing. I could handle a one-night relationship... Well, that is, before I met Rob. I know you. You're not a one night only type of girl."

"I'll be careful. See you at the table," Jennifer said. Her mouth watered at the thought of biting into a hamburger. She made her way to the right line, filling her plate to the top.

After Jennifer paid, she joined Belinda. With both hands holding her tray, Jennifer watched as the door swung open. Matt Davis walked in, locked eyes with her, and headed straight toward her.

CHAPTER 11

MATT

MATT'S MOTHER TAUGHT HIM THAT SOMETIMES, WHEN YOU worked hard for something you needed, you had to trade it for something you loved. Step one of repairing his relationship with Jennifer involved such a barter.

At South Holt, every freshman knew calculus-based statistics was a weed-out course designed to remove students who couldn't hack complex math. They had also all heard of the golden exam guide, the test key that had been leaked from the professor's office and held all the answers to that course.

According to legend, whoever possessed the paper, aced the class. Most students believed the document was only a fable. But Matt knew it existed; he had won the mythical piece of paper from a senior during a card game last semester. The answer sheet came with an oath to only share it with his successor and to never make a copy—lest the college find out and change the key, not to mention possibly expelling the student.

Bidding with Belinda started with the golden ticket to pass statistics, but as Jennifer's friend, Belinda wanted more.

In exchange for Belinda's help, Matt gave Belinda two

promises: he would never misuse the information she gave him about Jennifer and actively work toward Jennifer's best. For collateral, he gave Belinda a picture and a video where Matt admitted he wore nothing but black, including a cowboy hat, and wrote fan fiction on a furry community as a pre-teen. If he screwed up, Belinda would show the campus his photo and some of the fan fic.

He guessed he should be happy that Belinda's support only cost him his guaranteed A in a class and confessing his darkest secret. For her part of the agreement, Belinda texted to let him know they, Jennifer and Belinda, were getting dinner.

Matt bolted from the library to the cafeteria. Entering the dining hall, it didn't take long to find Jennifer sitting at her normal table, shoving a hamburger into her mouth, cheeks spread out like a squirrel gathering nuts in the fall.

Despite her face crammed full of food, she looked beautiful—radiant, even. Swallowing his pride, he studied the room. Students sat everywhere. He searched for familiar faces and found a few from the Pi house. Good. The more who witnessed his humiliation, the better the penitence.

While walking toward Jennifer's table, he clapped three times. "May I have your attention!" he demanded.

The room quieted. Catching Jennifer's eyes, he raised his voice. "I've done something evil to an innocent person. I falsely accused Jennifer Wright of cheating on me with Johan. I am here to not only embarrass myself but also to beg for her forgiveness."

"Please stop, Matt," Jennifer said. Her normal smile was missing from her lips, and she placed the hamburger on her plate.

"No, Jennifer. I need to do this," he whispered.

She breathed out. "Fine," she said, crossing her arms in front of her chest, dinner forgotten.

Clearing his throat, he sang in an off-key voice, "I was

wrong. Jennifer never kissed Johan. She never cheated on me. I was wrong, and I'm sorry."

People clapped despite it being some of the worst-sounding clatter anyone had ever heard. One of his poker buddies stood, whistling. He bowed to his audience, and the room broke back into everyday conversation.

He held out his hands toward Jennifer. "Please wait," he requested. "I'll grab something to eat and join you and Belinda for dinner."

Shoving her plate away and tossing her napkin on top, Jennifer said, "No. Matt, that's okay. I'm done eating." To Belinda, Jennifer said, "When you're finished, can you walk me to the gym?"

Somehow, he had screwed up again. Staring at her disregarded meal, he said, "I'm sorry, Jen. I didn't mean to bother you during dinner."

The lights caught the green in her irises before she closed her eyelids for a second longer than a blink, like she was thinking about how to respond. "It's fine, Matt. I wasn't as hungry as I thought. I'm done."

Taking the seat across from Jennifer, he put his hands on the table, fidgeting with his fingers. "Look, Jen, I'm truly sorry for what I did to you. I should have never broken up with you, by text or otherwise. I should have taken all my concerns directly to you and not made assumptions. I should have been there to protect you from Johan. Do you forgive me?"

Looking everywhere but at him, she shook her head. "It's not like that. I didn't feel anger, but I did feel shocked and surprised. I didn't think you were the type to... I didn't expect you to end things. I thought we were fine. Matt, I thought you were faithful and on my team. That hurt."

Her words stung more than he thought possible, and they struck him right in his sense of honor. He could make excuses

—he thought she cheated, he was lied to, Amy led him astray —but none of that would own his mistake. "I'm sorry."

She locked eyes with him, and sadness rested somewhere deep in her, almost like the depth of her soul had grown vaster—that he couldn't fathom whatever she had gone through. It was the most beautiful, torturous thing he'd ever seen. *She* was the most beautiful thing he had ever seen, even though he partly caused the pain he now saw in her.

"You're forgiven," she said.

She forgave him! Now, he had to quench his guilt.

The smile she gave him didn't take away the hard edges of hurt.

How had he forgotten her incredible natural beauty? Golden blond hair pulled back in a ponytail directed attention to her high cheekbones. A dab of ketchup at the corner of her lip reminded him of her adorable, awkward cuteness. There had to be a way to spend more time together, to heal the damage he had caused.

Seeing that Belinda wore a decorative sweater, he bet she had matched it with a skirt. This could be his way back into Jennifer's good graces. "Belinda, are you working out too?" he asked.

Quickly, Belinda looked between Matt and Jennifer, settling her gaze on Matt. "I was just walking her there. She has a stalker, remember?"

Once again, his fault. "I remember." Pleading, he said, "I'm not hungry, Jen. The least I can do is walk you to the gym. That's if you don't mind." Folding his hands together as if praying, he added, "Plus, it would make me feel better to see that you're safe."

She hesitated. He opened his mouth to say he understood, but before he could, she said, "Okay. Are you ready?"

Jubilant, his stomach did a little flip. "Yes," he said, kicking the chair back in a hurry to stand. "Let me take that for you." He took her tray, waiting until she released it, and nodded before standing. As he turned toward the door, he caught her biting her lower lip in that oh-so-sexy gesture. His dreams were filled with that exact expression.

Jennifer followed him to the door, and he opened it after he dumped her uneaten food in the trash. Outside, he watched as her breath came out in white billowy puffs. "Where's your coat, Jen?" he asked.

She shrugged. "I forgot it." Wrapping her arms around herself, she asked, "Thanks for walking me, but don't you have B-Movie Monday?"

To spend a few minutes with you, to say sorry, is worth missing any and all parties, he thought, but he said, "It'll be okay for me to miss one." He paused, trying to think of the right words before he spoke again. "I can't tell you how sorry I am for breaking up with you, for doing it over text, for not trusting you. It was wrong."

"You're forgiven. Let's forget about it, okay? Let's act like it didn't happen."

He did a double take to study her face. What did she mean by *act like it didn't happen*? Could she be suggesting they could get back together? *Surely not, but wouldn't it be wonderful if that's what she meant?* Her expression gave nothing away. Regardless, because of how it ended, he'd let her make the first move—by holding his hand, asking him on a date, kissing his cheek. Whatever she did, he hoped it was soon.

But that reminded him. He asked, "What were you going to tell me? You said you had something you wanted to share with me last week, some big secret. But I..." But he sent the text ending their relationship. "But I screwed up."

She sighed. "Well, it was more like I had something important, life-altering, I wanted to show you. But that was... Then, and this is... Now." She glanced over at him. "Now it's not important."

How idiotic could he be, thinking she wanted to get back

together? Of course, she didn't. But what could she have wanted to show him? Could life-changing mean something else, be an innuendo? It wasn't his place to ask. Yet, he had to know. "Jen, were you planning…" How could he ask an innocent woman if she had planned to make him her first? He swung his arms between the two of them, back and forth. "Something to deepen *our* relationship?"

She missed a step, and her cheeks reddened. It was true. She had intended for them to have their first time together. How could he have been such an idiot?

Taking two steps, she caught up with him. She said, "It's all good, Matt. Let's not discuss it anymore… How're classes going?"

Not talk about it? It was all he could think about. Jennifer had wanted him to be her first. How could he have been so blind? The one event that topped all others should have happened. Instead, he would regret what he'd done last week for the rest of his life. He needed this woman. He couldn't be the only one to blame for the messed-up wreck of a perfect relationship. Frustrated, he remembered everything from the time he left her apartment fall semester until last weekend.

He owned the responsibility but wasn't alone in the events that led to the text message. Most of the responsibility belonged to Amy and her lies. But Jennifer was partially to blame.

When he flew back to the States, Jennifer could have met him at the airport, but she didn't. Before they had left their homes for college this semester, she could have driven to his house and spent a day or two with him. Jennifer could have studied at his apartment. Instead, she had made a few quick phone calls promising to meet up later. If Jennifer had been around more, Amy's lies would have never stuck. Jennifer could have been more aggressive and defended their relationship better.

Her lack of enthusiasm helped him believe Amy's lie

about Johan. His aggravation at missing his opportunity, at losing his dream girl, leaked out. He asked, "Why did you spend so much time away from me?"

She glared at him. "How couldn't I? I would ask you on dates to get coffee, to see movies, just to hang out, but you were always busy. Remember the library? What was that, last week or the week before? I asked you to spend time with me then, but you had to be at your apartment for the Monday night B-movie. I accepted your words at face value, as if they were the truth. I thought you were hanging out with your friends. We agreed not to be a couple that always needed to be together, but instead, you were with Amy. Do you know how much your betrayal hurt? The thought that I had planned to make you my first, to share my darkest secrets with you, while you were bedding—"

"Stop! I was a fool. Okay? An absolute fool." He never had sex with Amy, but he didn't correct Jennifer. Technically, he only dated Amy for a week, but would Jennifer believe him? How could he have been so easily fooled by Amy?

The whole thing frustrated him— Amy, Jennifer's reserved attitude before the text—but there was nothing he could do now but move forward. Agreeing they needed to change subjects, he said, "Classes are going well. How about yours?"

He opened the door to the gym, and she walked in under his arm. "I'm still making A's," she said.

He followed her inside. "No Johan on the way here," he commented nonchalantly.

Instantly, her body trembled. He let go of the door and moved in front of her. She didn't seem to notice him, her face turning paler and her eyes glossing over.

Did she see Johan? He turned in the direction she was looking and searched the area for the blond man but didn't see him.

If only hearing Johan's name caused her this much distress... And he had accused her of cheating on him with Johan!

Placing his hands on her shoulders, he stepped closer to disrupt whatever her mind's eye was envisioning. "I'm right here, Jen. You're safe." He hugged her, and she wrapped her arms around his waist. "I'm sorry, Jen. I should have been there for you. Even as a friend, I should have been there for you. Has it been that bad?"

"Yes," she whispered.

Eventually, she gently shoved his chest, turned on her heels, and headed to the first free treadmill. Pushing the button on the machine, she switched the television channel. While the motor warmed up, she said, "Thanks for walking me over here, Matt. Dr. Smith is picking me up a little later and returning me to my hideout."

"That's nice of him to find you a place to stay."

"Just the type of guy he is," she said, climbing on the treadmill. She kept hitting the speed button until her legs looked like a blur. Still, he was positive she could run faster outside.

"I know it's not true, but I heard you were sleeping with him as well," he commented.

"I've heard those rumors too. I wonder who I'll be sleeping with next week?"

The gym was empty. With a stalker running around, she shouldn't be left alone, and he wasn't ready to go. "Do you mind if I walk on the machine beside you?" he asked.

"Sure. It's the university's equipment."

Taking the treadmill beside her, he trekked to nowhere while trying to think of a topic for conversation. He said, "You really should run track. I bet you could be in the Olympics."

She smiled. "Nah. I've got other goals."

Well, Matt had read that building a new bridge after epically burning one took time. By the cold shoulder she gave him, it might take this whole semester. But she was worth the price. When Dr. Smith arrived, he'd thank him, glad someone was around to keep Jen safe when he went through his stupid phase.

CHAPTER 12

JENNIFER

Forcing her eyes forward, Jennifer regretted eating with Belinda. Not because of nausea or from Matt embarrassing her, but because she could smell Matt's desire, and that was not how she felt toward him. Unintentionally, she'd misled Matt, and she wasn't sure how to correct her mistake.

None of this would have happened if she had gone straight to the gym.

"You remember our first date?" Matt asked.

She turned to glance at him. He'd removed his coat and thrown it on the bicycle seat beside him, revealing a tight-fitting T-shirt over hard muscles. His black hair and dark chocolate eyes could ground a woman so that he became her gravity.

Yet he wasn't for her.

"Sure," she said, forcing her sight forward. The aerobic machines overlooked the weight room. On the bench in front of her, wearing a black sleeveless shirt, sat Barry, a bag of popcorn sitting in his lap. He grinned and winked. "I'm loving this. I can smell his pheromones from here." He threw a kernel up, catching it with his teeth.

"*Oh yeah. Me too. So much fun,*" she thought, pushing the

up arrow and pounding the machine with every thrust of her legs.

Earlier, she knew she crossed a line. When he hugged her for comfort, his natural odor filled the area with the musk of lust. She'd hoped they'd move on as friends. When Matt found out the truth, when Petr permanently came around and announced they were a couple... She shook her head... When they declared they were a twosome, it would hurt Matt.

Hopefully, he would be over her by then.

"Remember how we went to the basement, and it was locked?" Matt asked.

"I do." On the lowest level of this building sat an indoor track. During regular school hours, the doors were unlocked. At night, only an honor's key would allow students in, and she had such a key as a scholarship holder. They talked all that night, her heart fluttering with each word, sure Matt was the last guy she would ever want.

"I'm curious. Knowing how much you hate treadmills, why aren't you in the basement right now, running on the indoor track?" he asked.

Honestly, because she had hoped Petr would walk on the treadmill beside hers, or if he couldn't with his hurt shoulder, stand alongside her, like Matt was doing now. They could only talk once a lap if she ran on a track. Next time, she'd ride with Petr to his gym. "Dr. Smith. He's already made sure I'm safe. When he picks me up, I thought this would be an easier location to meet up," she fibbed.

Nodding, he stared up at the row of ceiling-mounted televisions. "You know, this is kind of like that, us on the treadmill talking."

It was a leading comment. Matt wanted her to agree. She didn't need her dragon skills to deduce that.

"You're going to have to confess the truth," Barry said.

"And what's the truth, Barry? I went out with Petr once. We've

not kissed. We've not declared our relationship. I've claimed him. He is aware of that. I'm not sure that counts as a relationship."

"Oh, it counts," Barry said. "Intent is what counts. You're taken because you gave your heart to someone else."

She knew Matt waited for her to say something, to pick up where they had left off. She couldn't. So much had happened.

…Johan splashed in the water, his hair fanning out in the waves…

She wasn't the Jennifer he had dated. What did they have in common now? She couldn't share with him that she was a dragon shifter, or that she had claimed a man who was thousands of years old. She tried to remember what it was like before she recognized or became a dragon shifter, but those days were gone.

"Matt—"

The door beside the weight area swung open. Despite wearing unattractive, mismatched professor clothing, Petr strolled in as if he owned the university. His untamed curls and beard kept his true, powerful beauty from escaping, and his hideous clothes disguised his thin, muscular build. He appeared to be in his early thirties tonight, especially with the dark worry circles under his eyes. After locking eyes with her, his hands in his pockets, he sauntered toward her.

Not once did he acknowledge Matt. She sniffed the air. When she exercised, she could detect odors better. She could smell his usual scent—cashmere and sandalwood with a moldy hint of brewing beer—but there was more that she couldn't distinguish. *"Explain what I'm smelling, Barry."*

"A little lemon, maybe lime, barbeque… Hm." Barry moved from the weight bench and stood beside Petr at the end of her treadmill.

"About done?" Petr asked her, his deep, throaty voice resonating through her whole body.

"Something is bothering him. It's the same level as earlier, though. Perhaps slightly jealous of Matt, but not like before. I don't sense any lust from him. You, on the other hand. The second he said something, you spiked lavender fields... Oh, wait. I smell pain from him. I taste copper. He's bleeding."

"Yes," she answered Petr while slowing the treadmill to coax down her speed and trying to keep her face relaxed. She might not be in love with Matt, but she cared about him. She wasn't ready for Matt to know about Petr out of fear it would hurt Matt.

"Did you get in enough miles to destress from school? What did you call it, building an endorphins reserve?" Petr asked.

If she stared him in the face, she'd be drawn to him like a magnet. Instead, she focused on Barry. "Yes. Oh, wait. May we go by your office and get my bookbag?"

Matt slowed and stepped off the treadmill. "Dr. Smith," he said. Grinning, he offered Petr his hand.

It was the first time Petr acknowledged Matt and looked away from her. Her heart flipped at knowing she was the center of his attention.

Awkwardly, Petr switched to his left after pointing at his wound. Matt compensated, using his other hand, and they greeted one another.

"What happened to your shoulder?" Matt asked.

"An accident while camping this weekend with Jennifer."

Why did that comment make her feel guilty? Both men's faces trained on her. Jennifer sniffed the air. Yes, Matt was jealous. He could be jealous all he wanted. She was more concerned for Petr. Only a little flavor of barbeque, and she glanced at the man she claimed. *"Why isn't Petr jealous?"* she asked Barry, her inner voice panicking. On the outside, she maintained her calm exterior.

"I thought you hated camping?" Matt asked, sounding wounded.

"Matt, things change," she admitted. "I went camping

with a group of people this weekend. Dr. Smith included." She tucked a hair behind her ear and bit her bottom lip.

"Would you like to go this weekend? Camping, that is, with me?" Matt asked.

Barry laughed, holding his belly. "Tell the poor boy the truth."

"How can I? I don't have a defined human term for what Petr and I are. I can't tell Matt I claimed him as my mate." Well, she could, but that would sound out there.

Petr shook his head no, answering Matt for her. "I'm sorry, Jennifer, but I have to remind you—I'm taking you to your parents this weekend."

That's right. She was introducing Petr as a friend to her family. "Sorry, Matt. I can't. He's right. I'm going home this weekend."

Petr reached inside his coat and pulled out a handkerchief. After licking a corner of the white material, he dabbed the outside of her mouth. "You had something red there," he commented.

The action reminded her so much of something her parents would do. It made her feel like a child, and her cheeks heated.

"At least Matt assumes your relationship with Petr is harmless. That is, if that's what you want," Barry said.

Great. She felt immature beside Petr. His heart wasn't accelerating. No woodsy scent of lust. No lumberjack waiting to toss her over his shoulder and take her back to their cabin.

"It's fine, Jennifer. You're not producing your regular amount of pheromones either. You can't expect to be all lovey-dovey when you're talking with him and Matt," Barry interjected.

"Are you ready, Jennifer?" Petr asked again. "I have your bookbag in the car."

Nodding, she said to Matt, "Talk to you later. Thanks again for walking me to the gym."

"No problem," Matt said. "I'll call you soon."

"Okay," she said.

Petr acted the gentleman at every opportunity, opening all the doors for her. At the sedan, he waited while she got in, then closed it as she put on her seatbelt. The most handsome man she'd ever seen, even though he was buried under a layer of hideous clothing, walked around the automobile and sat in the driver's seat with a grunt of pain.

"So, Matt escorted you to the gym?" he asked, putting the key into the ignition. The car's heat blasted once it started, and she noticed he wasn't wearing a jacket.

Sniffing the air, she didn't sense any hostility or jealousy. Still, she felt like she needed to explain. Quickly, she said, "Belinda was in the dorm room when I went to change clothes and asked if I wanted to eat. Matt found us in the school's cafeteria and apologized for breaking up with me... And for accusing me of dating Johan."

...Johan's blond hair and blood touched her leg....

"He walked me to the gym."

"Good. Hopefully, this means the two of you will be friends again. But next time, I'll take you to the gym."

"You don't seem jealous." *Controlling, yes, but not jealous,* she thought.

"I'm not."

"Why?"

He sighed. "Jennifer, do me a favor." He glanced over at her for a second. "Put your hand on my leg."

Cautiously, she touched him. Instantly, the smooth electric tingles of the claiming vibrated up her arm as peaceful, happy dopamine flooded her senses. *Mine,* her body screamed.

"Jennifer Wright, once I knew you claimed me, you were mine. Matt can't have you back, and you don't want to leave me either."

Finally, she smelled the lust, but it was muted. She wanted to know why. "What's bothering you?"

"A lot. Kamar came across a person who ate a dragon's heart at the mall today," he said.

"He did?" she asked.

"Yes."

It dawned on her. "That's why you were so upset."

"Yes. It's making me question your safety while staying in school."

"But—"

"I know. I know. You want to finish school."

"More than that. My brother is growing up. I want to be there for my parents, my grandparents. My family."

"But if you're dead, you won't be there for them at all. At least in Dernogard, there's a chance you'll see them again."

"What about you? What about your teaching job?" she asked.

"It doesn't matter. I'll find another occupation when it's safe. I'll have to create a new identity, but I've done it before. You, however, do matter."

All of it made sense. His fear, his distance. Everything but treating her like a child. "Why did you clean the side of my mouth like a parent?"

He chuckled. "Didn't like that, did you?"

"Not particularly."

He shrugged, which brought on another moan. He said, "With how you acted, I assumed you weren't prepared for Matt to know about us."

"I don't want to hurt him, and I think it could," she confessed.

"Then we'll tell him when he's ready. By treating you like a child, Matt doesn't know or even suspect. He thinks I'm protecting you."

"That doesn't bother you, me keeping you a secret?"

Glancing down at her hand resting on his leg, she closed her eyes, focusing on the smooth vibrations.

"Does it bother you?" he asked.

"Some." She thought about it, needing to better explain what she meant. "I mean, I don't want to hurt Matt, but yeah, I want others to know you're mine."

She opened her eyes and caught him smiling at her.

"I am yours, and you are mine. Jennifer, names that people use to label a relationship are empty words. Besides, this separation is temporary. If everything in our lives keeps progressing like it has been, everyone will know soon enough. We can enjoy the trip and the destination."

"Yeah." She sat back against the seat but wondered if he was referring to the sparks between them or being forced to leave sooner than planned for Dernogard. "About that. Is our date this Wednesday?"

"No. Not this week." He sighed as he swiped on the blinker to turn into his neighborhood. His lips turned up in a lopsided grin, and she did a double take. She had memories of Petr giving her ancestor River that thin-lined smile before he did something unexpected. "We have plans tomorrow evening."

Glancing out the window, she wondered what mischievous ploys he had contrived.

CHAPTER 13

SHANNA

To concoct a beautiful lie, a convincing deceit, the scene must be set. Creating Amy, Shanna removed her makeup, cried for an hour, and left her hair in its natural state. She rolled her shoulders forward, slouching, and pretended to be distraught. "May I have a tissue?" she asked the investigator, pointing to the blue and white box on the desk's corner.

The officer with dark brown, almost black hair pulled into a tight bun wore a crisp uniform that was either dry-cleaned or iron-starched based on the sharp angles in the material. Without looking up, the policewoman said, "Have at it."

The surface lacked any pictures or mess, kept impersonal and clean. From all the observable facts, Shanna concluded the professional Clair Windham would do the investigation by the book.

"For the record, please restate your name," she said.

The chair they offered her wasn't much of a seat, just a folding chair like people used for parties. Shanna had dusted it off like she thought Amy would and gracefully crossed her legs at her ankles after sitting. Taking a tissue from Clair's table, Shanna said, "I'm Amy Poland."

"What brings you here today?" she asked.

"My friend, Johan, is missing. I've called him, and it goes to a message saying I dialed the wrong number, but his number was programmed into my phone, so I know it's the one I called him from before. I've gone by his apartment, and he's not there either."

The woman wrote in a handheld wire-bound notebook—so very retro. "Is it common for Johan Rogers to disappear?"

"No. He's never done it before."

The officer glanced up from her notes. "May I have his number, Miss Poland?"

"Sure." Shanna gestured for her to hand her the notepad. Clair reluctantly forfeited it. Shanna pulled out her cell phone and copied Amy's and Johan's numbers. She handed the information back to the investigator. "I gave you mine as well."

"I noticed you had to look yours up. Don't you have your phone number memorized?" the policewoman asked with a raised eyebrow.

Without missing a beat, Shanna explained, "Why memorize what you can look up?"

"Okay." She sounded doubtful. "Have you had this number long?" Clair asked.

She realized that Clair Windham was throwing Amy onto a list of suspicious characters. Ignoring the implication that Amy did something wrong, Shanna said, "No. Back to my friend. It's not like him not to call or visit. We meet almost every night for coffee, and now no one seems to know where he is," she said, looking at the ceiling. She didn't need to do this but wanted it to seem like she was thinking. In truth, Roland had sent her a text yesterday telling her that Johan's car's tracking mechanism had disappeared in the mountains. Which meant it might be foul play. Then again, Johan could have lost control, and the vehicle careened into a tree. As long as he didn't lose his head, he should survive. People who ate a dragon's heart were hard to kill.

"Miss Poland, when was the last time you saw your friend?" she asked, drawing Shanna's eyes back to the investigator.

Sniffing, she let a single tear slide down her face. "Friday. After class, he stood by the fountain, and we talked before he left for his apartment."

"When did you expect to either hear from or see him again?"

"Saturday morning. We were supposed to grab coffee. Usually, he would be waiting outside when I got up."

"Miss Poland, are you dating Johan?"

Finally, the opportunity to plant a seed of suspicion about Jennifer. "No, ma'am. He claimed he was dating a girl in my dorm, Jennifer Wright." Shanna dabbed at her eyes. "I went to his apartment and knocked. He never answered the door. It's just not like him to not answer his phone. He didn't go to classes either."

"Good job, soldier," Gourdy said.

"Since you often visited Mr. Roger, do you have an address?"

"Yes." Shanna gave all the details of Johan's pseudo information—both addresses, the fake back story, and a description of his fancy car.

The officer stood from her desk. "Thank you for bringing your concern to us. Hopefully, your friend just went out of town for a vacation and nothing more, but I will do a preliminary search and will be in touch with you with anything I discover. Please call us if he returns." Clair held out her hand, offering a business card.

"Thank you." Shanna took the card. She turned and headed toward the exit through the maze of scattered desks, fantasizing about trapping Jennifer in prison.

She walked out to the VW bug assigned to her for this job. It was cute, white, and curvy, with a grinning solar toy flower that bobbed back and forth. She watched it for two beats before pulling out her phone and opening her messages.

Only one new text, a message from Roland.

Father agreed if you bring in the package, with only one catch. Congratulations are in order for your upcoming wedding with the man of your choosing.

She swallowed. If she brought Jennifer in, Father consented to her having a lifetime away from the Family, provided she married and had a child—the price of freedom. At least she would be allowed to choose her husband.

He'd have tan skin, a long waist, luscious black hair and eyes—a contrast to her pale features.

If they had a son, she'd have to bring him up in the way of the Family. He'd be trained to fight and indoctrinated to believe the Family's taking-over-the-world-supremacy bull crap. However, she wouldn't be alone. She'd have her son in her life.

Starting the car, the radio station defaulted to a generic broadcast. It was the way she avoided anyone discovering the truth about Amy. Amy liked different music than Shanna, and Shanna hated Amy's taste. The local station was a compromise to protect Shanna's secret identity.

This morning, a talk show played between songs. She turned up the volume, ignoring everything around her, and drove to the nearby English tearoom.

"Guess what?" the female radio host spoke up. Shanna believed the hostess went by Ginger, or Red, something to do with her hair color. "We have unconfirmed rumors that I'm trying to verify—"

"What rumors?" Paul, the main announcer, asked. Shanna guessed him to be in his late forties and a smoker by his rasp.

"Well, hold on, and I'll tell you," Ginger sassed. "Okay, the rumor is that a famous comedian will be performing an unpromoted booking at The Fillmore this weekend for a televised comedy show."

In the plans that Shanna submitted at Roland's request, she requested Knuckles perform a show in the area. Matt's roommate, Lauren, loved Knuckles and wouldn't miss a show if he came to town. An impromptu skit in Charlotte on such short order by Knuckles would mean that Father agreed to her plan. It also meant, while Matt's roommates were out, she could isolate Matt at his apartment.

"Really, which comedian?" Paul asked.

"Please say Knuckles," Shanna said.

"Knuckles," Ginger squealed.

Elated, Shanna wanted to dance and do a jig. Kidnapping Matt was the key to her plan. Jennifer didn't let many people into her inner circle, but the ones she did, she protected. Matt had a similar weakness. He didn't want to be the cause of anyone's pain. With the Family's help, she planned to use their shortcomings against them.

Amy's publicly hurt emotions would lure Matt into talking with her, and then the Family would kidnap him. Once Jennifer found out what happened with Matt, she would voluntarily give herself up trying to save a friend. Not trade her freedom, more like meet up with Shanna to help find Matt.

Excitement welled up. She was so close to temporary independence.

Instead, she forced tears after turning down the radio station. She needed to be believable for what she was going to do next. Pulling into the English Rose Tea Room, Amy parked in the back of the lot, away from onlookers. She glanced in the mirror, needing more color, and pinched her cheeks.

She liked Matt's mother, Maria Davis. When the Family sent her to the Bahamas, the two of them bonded over alcoholic drinks and random trivia. The relationship developed so quickly that Maria encouraged her to meet her friends before they separated, yet this was the first time she'd been able to join the threesome in person. Shanna used college classwork as an excuse not to meet up with them.

Running her fingers through her hair, she plastered a smile on her face, one that screamed *I'm not happy, but I'm pretending to be*, and left the comfort of the car.

The tea house opened to a storefront lobby where different British treats, tea sets, teas, and other random things, all lacy and delicate, waited to be purchased. Above her head, intertwined flowers and fairy lights ran along the beams. The walls were painted pink. The smell of roses and cooking food, like shepherd's pie, filled the atmosphere.

It all felt feminine.

"May I help you?" a woman slightly taller than Shanna and wearing a floral-patterned apron asked.

Searching the table area past the storefront, Shanna hunted for her group. "Yes, I'm meeting Maria—"

"Over here, Amy," Maria said, standing and waving a napkin in the air.

"I see my table. Thank you," Shanna said to the hostess.

Shanna made her way through the sea of mainly women, avoiding the red hats that stuck out into the slim pathways between tables. Her mouth watered when she saw the multi-tiered trays with finger foods and English biscuits. Cucumber sandwiches were one of Shanna's favorites.

Two of Maria's friends flanked either side of her, a steaming pot of water in the middle. As Shanna sat, she noticed each party had a different themed fine china set. Her table had begonia teacups with gold rims and matching saucers. Everyone in her group had their glasses turned over, tea diffusers inside the cups with empty individual bags of sugar or artificial sweeteners ripped open and on the saucers.

"I ordered a collection of teas. Grab one, Amy," Maria offered. "The finger food tray will be out in a second. I've also ordered a salad for us."

Nervously, she hung her purse over the back of the chair and studied the new women.

The overweight woman to her right, with chubby cheeks and thinning hair, almost looked like she was tsking at Shanna's appearance.

The woman to her left had ridges of wrinkles and gray locks parted in the middle, with wide eyes focused on her as she tapped the tea bag in and out of her cup.

Only Maria Davis, wearing a neutral expression, seemed unaffected by Shanna's Amy-in-mourning look.

Turning over the teacup in front of her, Shanna grabbed a packet without identifying the flavor. With the awful *Ode de Dragonne* perfume blocking out most smells, she barely smelled orange as she poured water into the cup. "Thank you," Shanna said shyly, staring at the brown liquid taking over the clear, but she knew the others' eyes were on her.

"Amy, this is Elaine," Maria said, pointing to her friend with a critical stare. The woman nodded; her multiple chins waved with her.

"And this is Diana," Maria said, glancing at the salt-and-pepper woman.

"Hi," Diana said, then smiled.

"My best friends, this is Amy, Matt's girlfriend—"

"I take it Matt didn't tell you," Shanna said, starting her lie with the truth. "He broke up with me yesterday."

"What?" Maria sounded upset, and her eyebrows rose. "He didn't tell me. That explains your... It explains your state of disarray. I told the girls how incredible your sense of style is, and now I know why... What did my son do?"

"Oh, no," Shanna said. She knew never to blame someone's child for anything wrong. Mommas defended their babies. "It was my fault. Johan, a guy at school, told me he and Jennif—"

"The girl that Matt dated before you? The one that cheated on him?" Elaine asked.

"Yes. But she didn't cheat—"

"Regardless, she wasn't good for my son," Maria said. "Are you saying that my son broke up with you because someone accused Jennifer of cheating on him?"

"Me. I accused Jennifer of cheating on him with Johan. Because Johan said he and Jennifer were dating," Shanna confessed.

"Well," Elaine said, her voice matching the accusatory face. "If there is smoke, there is fire."

The other two women nodded and gave each other knowing looks. It was too easy. They believed Jennifer cheated, even though Shanna made it all up.

"Now, which one of the girls that drooled over Matt is Jennifer?" Diane asked.

"The one he met at college who he liked so much. She's a cute girl. A straight-A student, according to Matt. But..." Maria glanced at Shanna. "You tell them, Amy. Tell my friends what you saw. My friends knew my first husband. I bet they'll see some of his traits in Jennifer as well."

"Well, it's not right for me to tell you this. It feels like gossip..."

"Go on, sweetie. We know you don't mean any harm," Elaine encouraged, placing her hand on top of Shanna's that was holding the teacup.

"Well, Jennifer is obsessed with making good grades no matter what it takes. Do you know what Adderall is?" Shanna asked, staring at each of the women before continuing.

"I haven't heard of it. Is that something like speed or that rave party drug?" Diane asked.

"Not like Molly," Elaine answered. She stared at her friend across the table. "What? Diane, Molly is the rave party drug." She patted Shanna's hand. "My son is a police officer. I've heard all about raves and parties. Please continue." She placed her hand back in her lap.

"It's like a performance drug for college students who

want good grades. It makes them study harder and focus better." She glanced at the table. "A lot of the kids at South Holt use it. Especially those who are in the honors program... I don't blame her. I would hate to have that much pressure on me. Anyway, when you first start using it, it can cause visions or hallucinations... I caught her outside at four in the morning, searching for something or someone named Buttercup." Shanna enlarged her eyes like she was shocked.

There were some facts in the story. She had found Jennifer hunting for a horse on the campus sidewalks before daylight. The dreams of your ancestors messed with your sense of reality. Shanna had a few similar stories herself. But that truth fit so well with Adderall's overuse that it made for a believable lie.

"Oh, my," Diana said.

"Adderall can cause people to hallucinate," Eliane agreed. "I saw an article recently while I waited at the doctor's office. It's rare, but it can happen."

"So, you think—" Diana said but stopped when the server placed the food tray between them.

Shanna moved her hand under the table. The cucumber sandwiches were calling her name, but Amy was mourning over Matt, too upset to eat. She reminded herself she had a part to play.

The conversation picked back up after the server left. "I don't need to think. College students use Adderall to study. Jennifer needs good grades," Maria said, grabbing a rather yummy-looking sandwich. "I don't need Matt involved with a girl who abuses drugs, no matter what excuse she uses."

"I so agree," Diana said. "Don't worry, Amy," she added. "Matt will come back around. He's a smart boy. Trust me." She grabbed another delightful treat, leaving one more.

"Doesn't Jennifer remind you of him?" Maria asked her friends.

"Your ex-husband?" Diane asked.

"Very much like him," Elaine agreed. "I see why you don't want Matt with Jennifer."

"Matt's old enough to make his own decisions. I just want to take Jennifer out of the equation," Maria said matter-of-factly.

"I agree. Having Amy around can keep Jennifer from coming back," Elaine said.

"I'll make sure you're invited to all our family socials," Maria said to Shanna. "My son will see reason. Don't you worry, Amy."

"Thank you." And with that, Shanna had planted the seeds of discord. Maria loved Amy but hated Jennifer. Shanna snatched the last cucumber yumminess. After all, she earned it. Plus, now that Matt's mother would help her win Matt back, she felt good enough to eat something small as a reward.

CHAPTER 14

JENNIFER

COLLAPSING IN THE SPARE CHAIR IN PETR'S OFFICE, JENNIFER allowed her backpack to slide off her arm and rest on the floor. *"I'm exhausted."*

The room filled with the odor of wood and fall leaves as Barry materialized, sitting at Petr's desk.

She closed her eyes and leaned against the wall.

...The fireball zoomed through Johan. He fell into the lake...

She opened her eyes. Eventually, her body would just shut off, and she'd sleep.

"Oh my," Barry said, grabbing her attention. "These are love letters to Professor Smith. Oh my!" He bent over, close to the desk's surface.

"Barry, you can't read," Jennifer said, ignoring him.

"You mean, the real me couldn't read. The real-me is dead, so there's no way that version can read. But the me-you has all your abilities." He smiled mischievously, and instead of human teeth, he sported his dragon teeth.

He tried to pick up the letter. The paper lifted in the air

about a foot, gliding back to the desk, landing on the stack of documents.

"I've never seen him leave things on his desk. Not that you've lived with him long, but he seems… organized," Barry commented.

"Me either," she said out loud, not caring if she was overheard.

Leaning over the desk, he whistled. "I was just joking. But, oh, oh, oh, what have I found? This is so interesting. Let me read it to you…" He cleared his throat and raised his voice a few octaves, imitating a woman. "I missed seeing you this Friday, so I thought I would turn in this paper anyway. I try to live my life without regrets, so here goes everything. I graduate this spring, and I want to know you better before then. I find your lectures fascinating, your personality amazing, and know we'd make a great team. And I've seen the way you gaze at me during lectures. But, other than our hours together each week, it's just not enough. I guess what I'm saying is, would you like to go to dinner with me this—"

Jennifer grabbed the document from underneath him, cutting him off. She flipped the homework over and found the note on a yellow sticky tab from the woman who sat beside her in anthropology—Cali.

"That's the cheesy girl who sits near you. The one who wrote *I love you* on the backs of her eyes." Barry laughed.

She huffed. *"The one you used to make me shift."* Barry had sent images of Petr kissing Cali when she struggled to turn into a dragon.

"My method worked, didn't it? But you're not jealous anymore, and it wouldn't work now."

"No need to be jealous. He's mine."

"True. While we wait, why don't you try and get some sleep?" Barry asked.

"Every time I close my eyes, something wakes me," she thought. Then she said in frustration, "I'm done."

"Done with what?" Petr asked, strolling into his office, carrying several books in his one working arm. Despite the mismatched clothing, he owned the room like a multimillion-aire playboy.

"Apparently, his outfit is good enough for Cali," Barry said dryly.

"I'm not sure that girl has competent judgment if you consider the creative ways she's tried to obtain Petr's attention. She probably loves his crazy outfits," she thought. "With school for the day," she answered quickly. The real response was sleep, but he already worried about her. She didn't want to bother him any more than he already was.

Petr nodded, dropping the books on his desk. They fell with a thud, one tumbling over the edge. Jennifer caught it before it hit the floor.

"Thank you," Petr said. When she placed the book on the desk, he touched the back of her hand. Electricity crawled up her skin. It was such a pleasant sensation that her eyes wanted to roll into the back of her head as she slept. "Barry is in here, isn't he?" he asked, moving behind the desk.

"Yes," she answered.

"I can smell him," Petr said as he sat on top of Barry. Their features intermixed. "What's wrong?"

"You, ah… You're sitting on him." With laughter, Barry disappeared. "He's gone now," Jennifer announced.

He raised his eyebrows, but he stared everywhere but at her. "Let me clean up my office, and we'll head out."

"Do you want help?" she asked, stacking the books on the corner.

"Sure. Just, ah, make stacks for me. I'm not planning to work tonight, but I'll pick up where I left off tomorrow."

"Because of our date to—"

"There've been some… changes," Petr interrupted as he fiddled with the latch on the satchel he used as a briefcase.

"Something's up, Barry. He's not looking me in the eye."

"Oh, this man is good at hiding his secrets. I can barely smell his emotions. He's nervous. I can detect that, but he's making sure you can't discern his thoughts," Barry said.

"Well, I can stop that," she thought. She moved around the desk, placing herself in front of him. "What changes?"

Sighing, he held her bicep, his thumb gently rubbing it. She felt warm tingles through her body, and his heartbeat accelerated, exposing that he was having a similar experience. "Even with Kamar teaching me to hide my feelings, you know something is wrong."

"Yes," Jennifer said.

"That's why he's not looking you in the eye. A dragon taught him when and how to conceal his thoughts. That's brilliant. Petr avoiding your eyes and hiding his emotion is like playing a game of hide and seek. There is nothing a dragon likes better than a challenge," Barry said.

"Kamar found more people who ate dragon's hearts," Petr said in Dragon.

"Oh," she answered.

He let go of her arm and moved over to his desk, pulling out his cell phone. "I got this today."

The text message wasn't in a language she recognized. "What does it say?"

"I wondered if you could read it." He didn't elaborate as he took his phone back and put it in his briefcase. Still avoiding her eyes, he retrieved a small square box.

Every woman on the face of the world knew what it meant when a man kneeled. She gasped anyway as he went down on one knee, her hand coming to her mouth. He opened the container, revealing a princess-cut emerald about the size of a dime, surrounded by tiny diamonds set in a white gold or platinum setting.

"Jennifer Wright, will you marry me?" he asked in English.

At first, she could say nothing. She knew one day he

would propose. That one day, he would be down on a knee, but this was too soon. She glanced toward the door. The desk might block his head, but if anyone was close by, they might have heard his question.

It didn't matter. None of it mattered except him. She focused back on the pleading look in Petr's eyes.

"What happened?" she asked, placing the ring on the table. Reaching down, she helped him stand.

He touched his wound and rolled his shoulder as he peered out the door. "Our plans have been expedited. The text you couldn't read is from the White Jaguar. She told me to get you out of Charlotte and to Dernogard. The Immortals have laid a trap to capture you," he said in Dragon.

Last week, when she showed everyone the text she received from the White Jaguar, she smelled love and betrayal from the tall dragon Kamar. Jennifer guessed the White Jaguar was not only a woman but someone Kamar had had a relationship with or still loved. Evidently, either Kamar told Petr or Petr had come to the same conclusion.

Nodding, she stared at the ugly linoleum floor, digesting the information. Was the trap the one she had just avoided or a new one?

...Johan lying dead in the lake...

"Is your nod a yes?" Petr asked, bringing her out of her memory.

"No. Why should I say yes? We've not even had our first kiss, and we've only been on one date."

"In some cultures, marriages are arranged. The bride doesn't see the groom until the wedding day."

"Yeah, but I'm not from one of those cultures. And being hunted doesn't give you an out from taking me to dinners, movies, and everything else couples do. You still have to wine and dine me," she said, crossing her arms over her chest. Switching to Dragon, she asked, "Could she be on our side?"

"Maybe. Either way, taking you to Dernogard is the safest solution. There are enough dragons there to protect you that I won't have to worry about your wellbeing," Petr answered in Dragon.

Taking a small step, he entered her space. Sandalwood and cashmere swirled around, so close now that their noses touched. She didn't dare look away, but she wondered if anyone noticed a student was inches from a professor.

He positioned his left hand under her chin, and his eyes gazed into hers. "I desire you to be my wife and mate, Jennifer. I want to marry you," he said in Dragon. Leaning in, he placed his mouth lightly on her lips. Tingles electrified her skin. Every hair on Jennifer's body stood at attention, her mind fully alive.

The kiss wasn't long, but it left her wanting more. When he backed away, she missed his heat.

He raised an eyebrow. "Is the answer yes now?" he asked in English, then smiled.

"Why do I need to answer? Can't it wait until next week? *Mister-one-date-a-week*, you're going rather fast suddenly."

He reached behind him and retrieved the ring box. Opening it, he said, "The ring needs to be fitted. The sooner I get it to the jeweler, the quicker we get it back, and I'd like you to wear it this weekend." He shrugged, looking shy, and continued. "I'd like you to have the ring on when I meet with your parents."

Taking a step back, she realized his intent. He planned to tell her parents they were getting married. *Deal with one thing at a time. I can talk to him about surprising my parents later.* "Ring size?"

"Yes. That's all I really need for tonight."

"Easy enough. Do you have different rings, those ring measuring devices?"

"Yes," he said, reaching into his pocket. He passed her a keychain with bands of various widths.

Finding the right one, she handed the device back. "Size six, please."

"Are you accepting?" he asked.

"I'm not saying no."

"I'll take that as a yes," he said.

Did she mean yes? Eventually, sure, but this was too sudden; this was unromantic. Plus, did he consider she might be killed right after they consummated the marriage? And was he talking today, tomorrow, or in the far-off future? "What about the wining and dining? I'd like a few more romantic evenings before I get bound to a ball and chain."

"Absolutely. Are you ready for our date?"

"Sure," she said, throwing her bookbag over her shoulder.

Grabbing his briefcase with his good arm, he walked to the door. She followed, watching him shuffle his load to accommodate his wound.

She glanced in either direction. Had anyone seen him kiss her? Would there be new rumors about her and Dr. Smith tomorrow? Did she care? "So where are we going tonight—dinner, movies, gym?"

"Dinner, no movie, no gym," he said, moving his briefcase over to his other side.

"Where are we eating tonight?" She trailed him at least two paces out to the parking lot. Outside, he stopped and waited for her to catch up.

"Somewhere special," he answered, walking beside her and peeking over at her.

"Special?" That could mean anything with him, and since his proposal was anti-climactic, did he plan to make up for it later?

"Yes," he said. He popped the trunk, throwing his brief-case into it.

"Should I be nervous?" she asked when he opened her car door. She slid inside.

After she buckled, she watched him get situated in his seat. When he put the sedan into reverse, he said, "No. Not nervous. This is my best shot at treating you how I want to."

She meant her question almost as a joke to lighten up his mood. He seemed intense and overly worried. But his answer surprised her. Did he mean something more by his comment? "How should I be treated?"

"Like a princess," he said, pulling onto the road.

As they passed unfamiliar houses, Jennifer realized Petr was driving in the opposite direction from his home. She had only visited Charlotte while growing up and lacked familiarity with the potential restaurants. The structure of the buildings reminded her more of the downtown area. Fear and excitement gathered as she pondered their actual destination. Were they getting married tonight? That would be something, introducing her husband instead of her fiancé. She doubted her mom would be happy about that, but Jennifer could smooth it over by allowing her mom to plan a wedding later.

Quietly, she withdrew her phone and searched for where to obtain a marriage license in Charlotte. She gulped when she realized they would be there in less than thirty minutes if they continued on the same path.

A few blocks away, in a part of town under renovation, he turned right, away from the justice of the peace. Right past a wooden sign reading *Bently's Bed and Breakfast, Built in 1802, Historic District*, Petr turned into the driveway. As he proceeded down the cobblestone path, a white Southern mansion appeared, with columns, a large, covered porch, and balconies. The house reminded her of a scene in *Gone with the Wind*.

Jennifer frantically thought to herself, *What does the location mean? Are we having sex tonight?* She hadn't shaved this morning, but would he care? People didn't care about body hair when he bedded his last wife, did they?

Petr interrupted her inner contemplation. "I hope to continually surprise you like this in the future. You are a precious gift I didn't earn or deserve. Wining and dining you for the rest of our lives will be my pleasure."

He parked in front of the white marble stairs that led to the mansion's front doors. On the staircase, a group of individuals, similarly dressed in gray, headed toward them. She glanced back at Petr.

Rubbing his hurt shoulder, he stared ahead. "Before dinner, I want you to pick out an evening gown, makeup, and anything you need to wear to dinner. Cost doesn't matter." He winced as his hand dropped from his wound. "You'll be driven around town and have a woman attendant to help you make your choices. All of it will be put on my bill. Buy whatever you want."

The driver's side door opened, and a man in a gray suit stood behind it, his face out of view.

Petr ignored the valet and said, "Tonight, we will dine here, and we have two separate rooms if need be. My plan was to propose after we ate, but well, things are happening faster than I thought they would, and I needed the ring size sooner than I thought."

The two different beds wouldn't help her rest. If she turned into a human dragon, she could accidentally set the place ablaze. She wouldn't be able to sleep knowing she might kill everyone in the hotel, but she could mention that later.

Petr exited the vehicle, using his left hand on the roof to aid in his maneuver. When the attendant stretched out his arm in greeting, Petr pointed toward the sling, and they fist-bumped.

With a creak, the door beside her opened, and Jennifer jumped, surprised. A woman in a gray pantsuit uniform with brown hair pulled into a tight ponytail reached out her hand as she smiled. "I'm Sarah, Jennifer. I'm going to be your valet tonight."

After Jennifer exited the car, Petr tugged her into his personal space. He swung her around, his hand on her elbow. He stood close enough to her that she could see the tiny specks of other colors in his otherwise blue irises. "I'll see you in a few hours." This time, the kiss he drew her into wasn't a peck. His lips, tender and demanding, reserved yet desiring, held a sweet promise of their future together. The beard tickled her sensitive skin. When he let go, her body gyrated. She gawked at him as he ascended the stairs and then disappeared into the bed and breakfast.

"Are you okay?" Sarah asked.

"Yes. What just happened?" she asked, shaking as the tingles slowly vanished.

"That man paid a lot of money to take you to dinner. Come on, let's turn you from beautiful to stunning."

CHAPTER 15

JENNIFER

HOURS LATER, JENNIFER GAZED INTO A FULL-LENGTH MIRROR. The green evening dress fit snuggly against her body, enveloping her and pushing her breasts together, creating cleavage. The color exaggerated her eyes, making them pop like shiny gems framed by mascara.

Encouraged by Sarah and a team of makeover professionals, Jennifer wore new lacy undergarments, her nails had been manicured, and her hair was teased into long, large ringlets. Someone actually matched her to a perfume and forced her to have a complete facial.

Did the reflection match reality, or was it one of those high-tech specialty AI mirrors that smoothed your edges and perfected everything?

"Wow," Barry said, standing beside her, peering at the same piece of glass. "If I didn't live inside your head, I wouldn't recognize you."

"Don't know if I like that," she said, trying to adjust to the changes. She wanted Petr to like her for her, not what sat on the outside.

He sniffed the air and said, "That new fragrance only

heightens your lavender pheromones. You might be mated by the end of the night."

Well, she'd been waxed, so no more hair insecurities. She frowned at Barry and searched around the room for the key. *"What does that mean?"*

"Petr has no idea how much trouble you'll cause him tonight."

After glaring at him, she returned to her search. She ran her hands over the bedspread, hoping the busy pattern hid the misplaced key. The staff called this room the Flower Room, and it lived up to its name, the bouquet of white, pink, and yellow wallpaper stretching into the private bathroom.

Someone knocked on the door, and she froze.

"Yes," Jennifer answered.

"Are you ready?" Sarah asked.

"Yes. Well, sort of. I can't find the room key." She stood, straightened her dress in the mirror, and opened the door.

Sarah laughed. "I have it," she said, dangling the missing item on a lanyard. "I'll lock up your room and give the key to Nick."

A few seconds passed as Jennifer connected the name Nick to Petr. *"That's right. Nicholas Smith is Petr's legal name now,"* she thought to Barry but said to Sarah, "Thanks."

"You look dazzling," Sarah said. Stepping out of the doorway, she continued. "Let me show you to your dinner."

The three-inch-high heels completed the outfit. But as Jennifer stepped carefully across the carpet in the pointed shoes, she remembered why she didn't wear or even own anything this fancy—she lacked practice. Walking like a dignified, sexy woman wasn't happening. Her goal for the evening involved standing or sitting as much as possible. Oh, and not falling on her face. As she moved, she repeated a mantra in her head—*Heel first. Trust the heel.*

To her side, Barry laughed. She didn't turn to give him any dirty looks, keeping her eyes focused on the ground. He said, "Well, you're pretty when you stand still. When you move, though... You remind me of a green penguin. Wobble-wobble."

"Stop it, Barry! Heel-toe."

"What a facial expression. You have concentration wrinkles and a pout of misery. When you walk, you look like you're in pain." He chuckled.

At a set of French doors, Sarah stopped. The doors opened to a second-floor balcony enclosed in glass. White LED lights were strung across the ceiling. Lit candles sat on a table that held food and wine. Soft music played in the background. Jennifer swallowed.

"When Petr wants to be romantic, he goes all out," she thought.

"Yeah. Relax your face and lose the scowl, then look over there," Barry said and pointed.

She followed his finger to find Petr standing in a darkened corner, one arm in a sling and the other to his side, dressed in a form-fitting black suit.

How had she missed him? Like a bug drawn to a light, her eyes couldn't look away if she tried.

The man had changed so much in the hours since he had left her. He'd lost the untamed locks that blended into an unkempt beard. His lack of scruff revealed his beautiful, thin lips, unique pointed nose, and defined chin. Unexpectedly, his hair had been cut close to the scalp. Her prince charming no longer seemed to be in his thirties but appeared closer to twenty-five.

"Yummy," she thought to Barry. "Wow, you clean up nice... my prince who slays the dragon. Perfect in every way," she said.

Petr's eyes grew large and drank in her outfit, slowly crawling up her body with tantalizing precision. "I'm pretty sure I'd let the dragon do whatever she wanted and thank her later, meelaya."

"Me laya?" she asked.

"Mm, yes. Or would you prefer rypka," he asked.

"Um, what language is that?" she asked.

"Russian." He smiled.

"What do they each mean?"

"Meelaya is my loved one."

"And ribaka?" she asked.

"Rypka, my fishlet."

Scrunching her face, she said, "Fishlet doesn't sound... right."

He laughed. "Meelaya it is."

Heel-toe, she thought, stepping into the room and toward the table. *Be sexy*, she thought, placing one foot in front of the other. Her shoe caught on something, and the would-be charmer fell.

Before reaching the ground, Petr grabbed her, stopping her collapse. Warm chills spread from their contact. Her heart raced. When he stood her up, she came face to face with him, aware that her chest touched his. Every inch of her vibrated in peaceful harmony.

Someone cleared their throat. Petr's arm dropped as Jennifer turned to face Sarah, forgotten and standing near the door. She held up the key on the lanyard. "Jennifer's room key." She placed it on the table. "I'll leave you two to your dinner. Enjoy your meal and have a lovely night." But the mischievous smile on her lips, like a cat's that finally caught that pesky mouse, suggested she thought they would soon be busy doing things other than eating.

Would they? "Thank you," Jennifer said, but her gaze fell once again on Petr.

He ran his left hand through his hair and then took her elbow. "Let me help you to your seat." Using him as a support system, she navigated the short distance to the table. At the chair, he released her and, in one fluid motion, tucked the seat under her as she sat down.

"How's your shoulder?" Jennifer asked.

"Better. Che-non re-wrapped it," he said, taking the only other chair on the patio.

"Che-non is here?"

"No, he helped me get ready and do a few other things. He's already left to take the ring to the jewelers." He took the rolled silverware, grabbed the napkin, and put it in his lap. "Good news. The ring should be fitted and back by Friday afternoon."

"Wow, that's soon. When you proposed at your office, I thought maybe that was the idea… To tell my parents that we were getting married."

"Yes and no. It's been a progressive decision. When Kamar called yesterday after running into a group of Immortals, I decided it would be appropriate to introduce myself as your boyfriend. When he called today, that's when I left campus and picked out the ring. But tonight. This." He looked at the ceiling and raised his arm, indicating their surroundings. "I made the reservation last week with no intention of mentioning marriage. I'd have rather proposed here, but to pull off what I plan to tell your parents, I needed your ring size to have it back in time." He grabbed his glass of water and took a drink. Then he poured himself some wine or champagne. She wasn't sure of the difference between the two. He took a sip, taking his time to swallow. "Would you like some wine?" he asked.

If she did, would she keep her head, or would it lower her inhibitions? Make her do things she'd regret, such as tell Petr she loved him before he told her? If they had sex and she was drunk, would she remember it? "No. No, thank you. I'll stick to water."

He raised his eyebrows, almost like a challenge, but continued. "This morning, when Kamar found even more people… I think we're up to five Immortals in Charlotte now. Well, when I heard that, that's when I knew the right thing was to let your parents know my true intentions. It will give them a sense of peace if we leave quickly. I can tell them my work has called me away. Anyway, I left campus and bought your ring. I had hoped to do that with you—"

"It's perfect, beautiful."

"Good." He nodded, taking another sip.

While he had the wineglass to his lips, Jennifer said, "Then you saw the text message. Do you think she meant Johan?"

Placing the drink down, he said, "No. I don't. The Immortals have a sinister plan for you. I'm not sure what it is, or when it will happen, but a trap is planned. Their behavior, well, it's not normal for them. I wonder why they want you so badly that they'll go out of their way to capture you."

"I'm Jormungant's descendant. He wants me because I'm his, in his opinion. Without him, I wouldn't exist."

"Too bad for him, you are mine," Petr said.

With those words, something changed in the atmosphere. Her skin tingled, though they didn't touch. The air buzzed like the beat of hummingbird wings, and even the lights in the room seemed to sing.

"Okay, I'm out of here," Barry said. "This is disgusting." Magically, a headset covered his ears, and he started singing. He vanished for a second. When his harmonious chatter returned, it was muffled and distant. She glanced down past the balcony at a lighted path. Barry sat near a pond with a colored waterspout in the center, shouting lyrics at the top of his lungs. *Can you hear me?* she asked.

"No!" Barry yelled back. "Don't even think to me!"

After biting her lip to keep from smiling, she asked Petr, "Is this area part of the bed and breakfast?" She indicated the trail below them.

"Yes. It's sitting on thirty acres. I'd love to explore it with you. I'm told it's decorated and a sight to see at night. After we eat, we could go for a stroll?"

"I'd like that. But I didn't mean to interrupt you. Kamar found more Immortals, and you bought the ring. When did you decide to pop the question in your office? I mean, this place is awesome. But couldn't it have waited?"

"No." He reached up, taking her hand. Warmth and calm soothed their way up her skin to her heart. "Other than I had to get the ring to the jeweler's tonight to guarantee the ring was back by Saturday, I also had a call from Fritz."

"Who's Fritz?" she asked, trying to remember. She'd heard the name before.

"He lives near Dernogard. Owns a security company. I don't know him, and he's never called me until today."

"What did he say that has you on edge, Petr?" she asked.

"MiFeng and Lung, River's parents—"

River was another of her ancestors, and she'd experienced Lung's memories in a dream. "I know who they are. Go on," she encouraged, rubbing his rough knuckles.

"Lung cried. She already thinks of you as her grandchild, a part of her family. She wants you safe and tucked away in Dernogard."

Was he implying that they would leave before the end of the semester? What about finishing college? What about her dreams? Closing her eyes, she thought, *My safety first.* Opening them and gazing at her love, she said, "The way I remember it, they aren't the law. Dragons will do what dragons want to do."

"True. They aren't the law, just the council. But…"

The reason was written on the softening of his features. "But they feel like family, and you love them," she said.

"I do." He moved his hand upward, staring at where he touched her, and gently ran his nails down her arm without scratching her. "Hearing about the trap, hearing about Lung, I decided then our best approach was to tell your parents part of the truth…"

The truth! Tell her parents she was a dragon shifter?

"No!" he said. "I see it in your face. I didn't mean to tell them about the dragon world or the truth about us. I have every intent of marrying you when we get to Dernogard. Almost right away, in fact. I want them to know my level of commitment to you. What my plans are."

"What happened to waiting four years?" she asked.

He leaned back in his chair. "Did I ever tell you about Roz and Perun? How they met?"

She thought back to what he had told her. "The mermaid legend. Roz was sitting on a riverbank, bathing. He saw her—"

"And he waited. He waited for months, learning our language. When he came to the village in one of the harshest winters, he brought furs and dried meats... As her bride price, a gift to our family for Roz. Our clan's food supply was low. My parents had both recently died—"

"Roz was offered to him?" The idea of a poor maiden being offered to a beast, a sacrifice so her tribe could live, was both fascinating and horrible. She blinked several times to clear the image.

"No," he said, then laughed. "Let me finish. First, you have to understand Roz and I weren't like the other villagers. We had our own building while the rest of our tribe lived together."

"Your tribe lived in the same building?" she asked, wondering how that worked. Did people copulate in front of the children? Where did anyone go to be alone? Would her dreams ever go so far back that she'd see this type of lifestyle? So far, all her ancestors lived in buildings with individual rooms.

"Yes, a huge hut structure made with mammoth bones and hides."

"Did it smell?" she asked, wrinkling her nose.

"You got used to it... Anyway, my sister and I had our own, much smaller version of a round hut structure."

If they would have met at another time and they would have married… She imagined herself living in the village with Petr. What would it have been like? For some reason, she thought the location was near Saint Petersburg, long before it was a metropolis. She'd seen pictures of the lake that ran through the city, frozen in the winter.

"What is it?" he asked.

"Nothing, sorry. Just imagining the tribe. Please, go on."

"We had a different building because our father wasn't from the tribe and felt uncomfortable being so close to so many other people. I'm not even sure where he originated from, but he brought a zebra pelt with him, so I assume it was from somewhere warm. My mother's father found him injured and almost dead. My mother fell instantly in love with him—"

"It was insta love? I didn't think you believed in that." But maybe she had subconsciously superimposed one of her views onto her image of Petr and he never felt that way. Now, it sounded like he had always believed in love at first sight.

Before she met him, she didn't believe in destined or fated love. And even now, what she had with him wasn't instant love. Her ancestors knew Petr, were friends with him. Their strong feelings from their memories influenced her opinions of him. She couldn't help it. She had asked Barry not to give her any more details about Petr because until she had the dream about River, she wouldn't truly remember, but she understood enough to know she loved him. For Petr's part, he wanted to wait four years and take it slow, which, until this moment, had spoken volumes to her that he didn't believe in instant love either.

If he believed in love at first sight, though, she wondered why they were waiting for a more intimate relationship.

He refilled his wine glass, then took a long sip while looking up at the ceiling. "I believe in desire at first sight. I'm not sure about instant love. But if you decide to commit to someone forever, you stand by your word and fully commit. I believe love is a decision, not an emotion, though you can feel love as an emotion," he answered.

"Go on," she said, not ready to sway him off-topic. She desired to learn about where and how he grew up, about his parents, everything. These were things River never knew, that she didn't know. "You were saying your mom instantly fell in love with your dad?"

"Yes. She claims she did. What I know she did do was fully commit to my father and love him regardless of growing up in a different culture. They blended their cultures and gods. Roz and I didn't grow up like the other kids in our tribe because of that blending." He scooted his chair closer so their legs touched and took her hand with his good arm. His fingers parted hers. "We had a separate hut. The villagers feared us, twins born with odd hair."

He'd mentioned that before, that Roz had white hair with an auburn red spot at her crown, at the exact location he had his white patch. It was almost gone now with his cut being so short. With her unoccupied hand, she reached up and touched the white area. Soft, so soft. "You told me she had the opposite of your hair color."

He nodded. "When Perun offered for her hand, I asked Roz what she wanted. She agreed almost immediately to Perun's offer." He looked up to the ceiling, she guessed because he was remembering. "She was romantic about the idea, but her main concern was survival. She agreed to the marriage because the influx of goods in a hard winter meant we would live longer."

"Oh," she said, blinking. "I thought she loved Perun."

"With all her heart."

"But not at first?" she asked.

"With all her heart. That's what I'm trying to tell you, Jennifer. Love is a decision. Sometimes you feel love, and sometimes you don't—"

"You don't feel things when—"

"Stop. We aren't going there. I feel more with you than I have felt with anyone, ever. I never want to be away from you. I want to throw you down and watch you experience pleasure over and over. To see your face in ecstasy, to cause you to reach your release… Am I being too crass?"

With every word, she felt her cheeks warm. She didn't need a mirror to know they had reddened. "No. The opposite. While you talk, the room becomes saturated with"—she shrugged—"your essence." She closed her eyes, tasting the air, then continued. "Your musk. It's like cashmere, sandalwood, and passion."

His fingers left her hand, and she opened her eyes soon enough to catch him seconds before he traced the outline of her lips. "I choose to love you, Jennifer. I choose to live my life with you. I recognize that means I will die without you. My decision to pick you has nothing to do with the lust running through my veins."

"Then why are we waiting for years to become lovers?"

"Eager to share my bed?" he asked.

"Yes," she answered matter-of-factly.

"Only out of respect for MiFeng and Lung, and to get their blessing and nothing more. Though showing we can restrain ourselves will show the citizens of Dernogard that we have strength of character."

"Like having the fastest draw in a gun battle?" she asked.

He laughed. "Or having the biggest bear hide in front of the hearth."

She raised her eyebrows but didn't ask what exactly that meant.

"When we're living in Dernogard, I want to marry you and tie myself to you in every way possible. Do you accept?"

The claiming ran from his fingertips to her very core. "Petr, I choose to love you, to live my life with you. I accept that if you die, I will die too. But I'm not saying yes. At least not yet."

Removing his fingers, he stood and pressed his lips to her mouth. Opening it, she received his tongue as it danced with hers, his good hand finding its way to the back of her head, deepening the kiss. He tasted of mint and wine that was harvested in the early fall, of perfection and hope, of a future.

As he backed away, he said, "I love you, Jennifer Wright." And she knew he meant it.

CHAPTER 16

SHANNA

FOR EVERY QUESTION SHANNA ANSWERED ABOUT THE FAMILY, another emerged. She knew the Family had the power to create whole identities. She assumed their pockets were deep enough to bring a famous comedian into town to do a show. Still, the speed at which they threw her plan together overwhelmed her.

It was a complex plan too. It involved a way to isolate Matt, kidnapping the poor college student, purchasing a building to stash Matt in, and bringing in a slew of operatives. Her job, convincing the faithful Jennifer to join them in exchange for Matt's life, would be a cakewalk in comparison.

Where did the Family's influence end? If she wanted to escape, could she? Could she use today's meeting to navigate away from the Family?

The small coffee shop where she chose to meet Roland, catered to locals. Decorated with mismatched couches and pillows, families and couples made themselves comfortable at almost every table. If she knew how popular it was, she would have picked a different café.

She rested on a chaise lounge, a drink on the tiny colorful table in front of her and watched the door.

When Roland walked in, he surveyed the room until he locked eyes with her. He pulled off his gloves, shoving them in his pockets. The strong, icy wind that had moved into the area last night had given him red cheeks. He kept his light, mousey brown hair shaggy and cut in layers. Unlike Father, he wasn't handsome. He had a narrow nose, longer than most people's, sitting between itty bitty blue eyes. He reminded her of a mouse or a rat.

Nodding at her, he turned to the counter and ordered. She watched while the baristas poured him a black coffee. He waited, standing unnaturally still. When he had his cup, he sat in the chair across from hers, sipping his drink and observing her.

She imagined what he saw: Amy's vibrant red hair pulled up on top without running a brush through it and no product to calm the curls. Like Medusa's snakes, her locks stuck out and frizzed in every direction. Her makeup was long forgotten, her own face cherry colored and swollen from crying for days.

"Hi," she said, breaking the ice.

"Amy." He tipped his head. "You look—"

"I know. Like a disaster."

"No. Like the best actress the Family has ever had."

A compliment? "Thanks. Were you able to secure the location?" she asked.

"Yes, it's set up. The other operatives will show you the way after you obtain our target."

Over twenty years of working for the Family, and she was finally meeting others.

Like dating, an interview, or even the first day on a new job, her nerves and excitement warred with each other. She wondered how many felt trapped like her, and if some of them didn't believe all the Family's crazy ideas of taking over the world. Could one of them be another dragon, or was she it? The possibilities made her insecure—would they like her?

Want to kill her? Maybe even fear her? It also made her hopeful—maybe there were others who could share her experiences and who she could be herself around.

She swallowed. "Good," she answered about having the building.

"Did you place the cheese for the rodent?" Roland asked, referring to a game where cheese meant bait.

"The room is packed and clear. Amy left a dramatic note for her roommate. Any minute now, Matt will call," she said, confirming everything was in place. Before she abandoned campus, she'd boxed up her things and written a message explaining she couldn't handle the breakup with Matt and was dropping out of college. Then she drove to Greensboro, North Carolina, to meet with Roland.

"As an extra precaution, we have several additional operatives in the area, watching, and the tickets have been delivered."

She only briefly caught what he said. Her mind digested what more people from the world of dragons in the area meant. With more operatives, someone might be a Nose, a person who could smell dragons. The Family took pride in killing dragons and using dragon hearts to make more immortal operatives. She understood her heart gave the same long-life medical properties. An operative raised to believe in killing dragons would assuredly try to kill her in a second—ending her heartbeat. But she desperately wanted to wash off the overpowering perfume. If she washed the perfume off, would they hunt her? "Do they know about me?"

He took a sip of coffee. "Yes," he said, placing the cup on the counter. "All the operatives in town have been told of Father's special daughters."

Father's special daughters, meaning more than just her? Who was the other one? Did he mean Jennifer?

"Is it safe for me to stop wearing the perfume?" she asked.

"Yes," he answered.

143

Finally, in the next few hours, she'd scrub all the awful clove, cinnamon, and spices off her skin... Right after this meeting and she found the hotel. She sighed in relief.

An infant at the table beside theirs threw a teething ring on the floor. As the parent leaned over to retrieve the toy, the baby looked at her. Shanna forced herself to look away, but not before she noticed the curly, sandy blond hair and button nose—exact images of how she imagined her children with Jared, the love of her life, would have looked. Concentrating on Roland, at first, she fought the tears. But Amy hadn't cried in a minute or two, so she let the tears fall freely.

Roland pulled out a handkerchief because, of course, being as old as he was, he had one and handed it to her. "You have snot coming from your nose."

"Thanks," she said, taking the cloth. "I can't wait to stop crying. Just two more days, and it's back to acting like myself and dressing all in black."

"The red hair looks better on you. Black doesn't suit you at all."

"Still, you bought the black dye, right? I want to spend the next fifty years closer to who I really am, not this," she said, trying to remember what it was like to be able to express her opinions.

"It's purchased. Don't forget, you aren't completely free to do what you want. Father still expects you to marry. I suggest you meet someone you love, even if, in the end, they die. It will feel more meaningful that way."

"Will do. Are there any limitations to who I can wed?"

"Of course. We will always have rules."

Did that mean Roland had rules he had to follow as well? If so, what were they? Did he hate being controlled as much as she did? If he did, he could be a future ally. If not, she'd keep being guarded around him. But right now, she needed to know the rules of who she could pick. She'd ask her other questions at a future meeting.

Roland continued. "You can't settle down with anyone in the Family, especially a person who has eaten a dragon heart."

"Why?"

He crossed his legs. "Because Father won't allow it. I wouldn't challenge his authority, Shanna." She knew he had harnessed her real name to emphasize the importance of what he was saying.

"Is it because we would be too close genetically?"

He snorted. "Father doesn't care about that, but you are so far removed from most of us genetically that it's irrelevant. His rule has more to do with putting you back to work after fifty years. If you marry someone who has eaten a dragon's heart, an operative who will live as long as you, then you can't be placed in the field except with that person. Father doesn't like his operatives to get the dragon-love fever and focus so intently on you that he can't use that person freely ever again. Father likes to keep his options open."

Why would a human lifetime together matter if she didn't form an attachment with them? An operative who hadn't eaten a dragon's heart should be acceptable.

"One night with Greg, and he sat behind bars, waiting for either you or death," Gourdy thought.

"Thanks for the reminder," she thought. Her husband would be attached to her, unable to be free. Ending up in a grave from old age would be better than that kind of obsession.

But Father's reasoning could be more related to the consequences of falling in love. A person who understood the dragon world would be a friend and a partner—and two were stronger than one. Someone who would help her end the suffering.

She shook her head. No cult wanted their members to know freedom. To protect the Family, Father would never allow her to join with anyone who ate a dragon's heart. Still, if she didn't ask, she would never know. Maybe Father would allow a non-immortal Family member. She knew she would like someone she could share her secret life with. "What about if a Family member hasn't eaten—"

The phone in her purse rang. She held up a finger to Roland. "One second." Needing to play the mourner, she cried, allowing fresh tears and snot to run down her face. A few people stared.

"Hello," Amy said, dabbing her nose with the handkerchief.

"Ms. Poland?" the woman on the other side asked.

"Yes."

"This is Clair Windham with the police department. A Johan Roger lived at the apartments you indicated, but his landlord said he moved out this past week. I looked through the college records for a Johan Roger, and there isn't a student by that name listed this semester. The phone company tells me the cell phone you gave me will be deactivated in a couple days. It's a planned deactivation. The person paying the bill canceled the phone plan." Clair breathed in deeply. "I'm sorry, but it looks like Johan Roger has moved on, and I find no evidence of foul play. With nothing more to go on, I'm closing the case."

"I understand," Shanna responded. "Thank you." She confirmed the call had ended and placed her phone on the table. She glared at Roland. "The Family didn't care enough to search for Johan?"

"It was the opposite."

"What?" she asked, surprised.

"We looked for him but never found him. A team went to his last satellite location and searched the area. There's no sign of him, his car, or his cell. All have vanished into the mountains."

She swallowed. "Oh... What about his records at the school?"

He furrowed his eyebrows and said, "A crew removed

any sign of him at South Holt. He'd already canceled his cell phone and prepaid for his apartment. All we had to do was cancel that rental contract."

She didn't bother to mention her first plan, the one to get Jennifer arrested. Rehashing the idea would be met with resistance. What was done, was done, and the Family wouldn't recreate Johan for the *capture Jennifer in prison* idea. Bringing it up now would only cause unnecessary drama. At least they supported one of her methods. She'd take that as a win.

Her primary concern was how quickly they dropped Johan. Shouldn't they continue to search for him? What if he was hurt and needed help? Would they do this to her one day —cover up her disappearance as if she never existed? Squeezing her phone, she said, "We're expendable, all of us. What good does it do us to give Father what he wants when he could care less if his plans kill us?"

But there was a silver lining to Johan's absence. Could she fake her death and make a getaway?

Roland breathed out, sitting back in his chair. "We aren't expendable. You're not expendable," he whispered, almost like he had read her thoughts.

Did he know she wanted to escape from the Family?

"Fifty years?" she asked. She could come up with a getaway scheme during that time. Maybe even use Johan's idea, find an internet dead zone and disappear. Sweet sugar canes, she'd live in the forest if it meant freedom from being controlled.

"Yes," Roland confirmed again.

Sighing, she surveyed the room. It had cleared some, but it was still more crowded than she liked. *Get your mind in the game*, she chided herself. Focusing back on the plan to capture Jennifer, she asked, "Did you get the van?"

"Yes. I also have another car for you to drive off into the sunset."

He reached into his back pocket and retrieved a folded

paper from his wallet. Two pieces of plastic fell onto the table when he passed it to her—a credit card and a license.

Grabbing them, she unfolded the paper. It listed a hotel name, location, and room number on the outskirts of Charlotte. She looked at Roland over the edge of the note.

"Your room for the next week. You'll find clothes, luggage, and anything else you need in the closet."

"All the outfits are black?" she asked.

"So I've been told."

He reached over and grabbed the credit card and the license, putting them back in his wallet.

"Hey, I can't keep those?" she asked. She didn't even have time to see the name listed on the ID. Was she to be an Annie or a Zina?

"Not until it's time to change jobs. For now, it's best not to have… any misleading information that could ruin our plans."

"Okay," she said.

It was rare to meet with Roland in person. Now that she had all the information for her plan, she could take a few minutes and see if Roland would give her more details about his rules within the Family, because she didn't know when she'd have another chance. "You mentioned that Father let you marry for love?" she asked.

"It's a reward. Don't expect fifty years of freedom to come often."

"You make it sound like you're bound by the same rules I am. Do you have to do what Father says as well?"

He leaned forward and looked at her from beneath thick blond eyelashes. "All the Family has to obey him," he whispered.

Did she hear grit in his words? Did he feel trapped as well? "Is Roland your real name?"

"No. Just like Amy isn't yours."

Weighing the intense gaze he now locked on her, she

wondered what had caught his attention. Did he see her fear, her hate, or the walls of her mental cage? "Then I will enjoy my freedom while I have it," she said.

The phone on the table vibrated. Matt, according to Caller ID. She sighed before thinking of Jared and allowing the tears to pool in the corners of her eyes. Her act must have been believable because several people faced them, gawking at her. A few scowled at Roland. They likely thought the mean Roland had hurt the poor, sweet, innocent Amy. *Looks are so deceptive.*

"Matt," she said, hyperventilating.

"You didn't answer my text. Are you okay?" Matt's words lacked genuine warmth, sounding more irritated than anything.

Technically, she hadn't seen Matt's text, but she didn't care as long as he played his part in the plot she weaved. "No, I," she said and faked a sob. "I was busy."

"Please stop crying," he ordered. "Are you crying because of me?" In her opinion, the question had more to do with what others thought of him than about Amy's well-being.

"Does it matter?" she shot back.

"Yes, Amy. I don't want you to throw your life away because of me."

What an arrogant man, she thought. Hysterical weeping erupted. She dabbed her eyes with Roland's handkerchief before remembering the snot. Gross. She wanted a shower, a bath, to no longer cry...

Sniffing loudly, she said, "It just hurts too much. I just need some time." She blew her nose; she hated that part of the act. Clogged sinus passages were not fun at all. But she had a job to do. Clearing her throat, she said, "Can we discuss this Friday night? I think we should talk about it in person."

The other side of the line grew silent for a few seconds before he answered. "I'm not sure."

How many tears did she have to cry? The people who had

stared at her initially with pity now looked away, allowing her to be miserable. The ones who paid attention to her glared at her, like she'd ruined their calm, peaceful café' break with her emotional display. Some of the children even pointed with shocked expressions on their faces.

"Okay, okay. We'll talk Friday. Does eight sound good?" Matt relented.

"Can we do it earlier? I can be at your apartment at six." All the plans that she already had in place hinged around that time. He had to agree, or she would need to come up with another idea.

"Fine. I'll see you at my place at six." He huffed, obviously irritated.

She didn't hear any background noise, and she suspected he hung up, so she asked, "Matt?"

No response. She put the phone back into the shiny pink purse. She moved the red curls out of her eyes and tried to straighten up.

"It's arranged," she said.

"Good." He reached into his pocket and placed the change on the table.

Glancing at the counter, she saw the tip jar and figured most people left tips there, but she said nothing. She held out the snot-covered cloth and said, "Thank you."

Waving his hand, he refused to take it. He stood, scooting the chair away. "You keep it. I'll see you later, okay?"

She nodded.

Roland turned and exited the coffee shop. When the door closed, she again stared at the address and room number on the paper and smiled. Two more days at most, then no going back to Amy, only forward. Like a mousetrap, the cage sat, ready to be sprung.

CHAPTER 17

JENNIFER

AFTER TWO DAYS WITHOUT GETTING ENOUGH SLEEP, JENNIFER'S mind meandered in a dream-like state as she leisurely climbed the stairs. *"This is what it's like to be on cloud nine, isn't it?"* she asked Barry.

Not waiting for his response, she repositioned her backpack and sniffed Petr's T-shirt she wore. Cashmere and sandalwood mixed with her new perfume—a sugared vanilla and lavender blend. They smelled right together.

He'd forgotten to buy or bring her any clothes but had offered her his. Her jeans and his white shirt, joined into one outfit.

"We had 'the talk.'"

When Barry said nothing, she added, *"All relationships start with 'the talk.' Usually, it involves a lack of sleep and discussing dreams and hopes—a baring of one's soul, so to speak. The experience probably releases a hormone, like oxytocin."* After that milestone, a couple changed from being two to one. She guessed they were either Jentr or Petifer now.

No, neither sounded right.

But she was different, maybe even transformed, by the

escapade. For sure, she felt more secure with Petr. She'd had "the talk" with Matt, but this… This was incomparable.

"Lots of growth for you in the last month," Barry said, walking beside her, dressed like any other college student in jeans and a sweater. He focused more on the people they passed on their way to Dr. Smith's office than on her.

"I don't feel like the same person," she thought to Barry. She and Petr were closer, more integrated, like a cake. She was the egg, and he the flour.

"And I'm the sugar," Barry added, listening to her thoughts. "Imagine what it will be like after the two of you consummate your relationship."

At Barry's words, butterflies danced in her stomach.

Yesterday redefined her, almost like a baptism—two becoming one. Sex would be incredible. She smiled to herself, not caring about the ramifications of losing her independence.

In the hall, she beamed at the other students, who all gave her a double take.

"Is she high?" one whispered.

"No, man. At least, I don't think so," the other said.

Great, the next rumor to spread across campus would be that she was a stoner.

This morning, she'd finger brushed her hair and cleaned up any mascara from under her eyes. Her love, her boyfriend, her future fiancé had loaned her the T-shirt he wore underneath his sweater yesterday. And because he planned to change his outfits to be viewed as younger, he bought all new clothes that now sat in the trunk of his car. He changed this morning, wearing jeans and a form-fitting sweater.

"Cali liked his new digs as well," Barry observed.

The class reacted in ah's and whoo's when they saw Dr. Smith stroll down the aisle and stand at the podium. Girls giggled when he glanced their way. No doubt, more students would find time to stop by and ask the professor for help with their homework.

"That's right, you won't have just Cali chasing after Petr now," Barry said.

"*Noted,*" she remarked.

"Missing those ugly shirts and pants now?" Barry asked.

"*No. I have no doubt that I own his heart. They can look, but if they touch—*"

"You'll eat them!" he finished, letting his pride leak through.

… Johan stared at her, a shocked expression on his face as the fire-ball passed through his gut...

"*I thought I was over these visions.*"

"Memories, not visions. I don't know that you won't always remember what happened. Maybe after you've killed more people, it won't be so bad?"

"*More?*"

"You're a dragon of wyvern heritage. We eat people first and ask questions second. Falling in love won't change that."

She frowned and gave Barry a cross look but didn't deny it—part of what he said was right. If someone hurt Petr, she'd do it again. She knew that was true. No matter how much it would take from her soul.

At the door to Petr's office, she stopped. Barry slid by her, positioned behind Petr's shoulder, moving his mouth as he read.

"Boring," Barry announced. "He's grading papers." Barry moved to the chair across from him, flopping in the seat.

Crinkling his nose, Petr stared up from his work and smiled when he caught her leaning against the doorframe. "Barry's in here. I smelled him before I noticed you. That's really fascinating."

"Oddly and strangely fascinating," she agreed.

"I'm right here. He can talk to me," Barry said.

Ignoring Barry, she sighed because she dreaded the next couple of minutes. "Are you ready?"

"Yes, give me a second." He sorted his papers with one hand and stacked them to the best of his ability, shoving them into his briefcase.

While he prepared to leave, she stepped into his office and closed the door. "Let's call my mom now and avoid my dad."

Petr stopped and regarded her. "Your dad?"

"Yes, my dad. Petr, he loves me. I'm his princess. If I can avoid him by making a phone call and let my mom broach the subject to him, then by Saturday, things should go smoother."

"Oh."

"I'm not sure how you should pull my dad aside and ask for his permission, but I doubt he would give it. If we call, my mom can smooth our—"

"Call about visiting this weekend, now? You want to do it here and not at the house?" he asked, raising an eyebrow.

She sat atop Barry, who disappeared the second she touched his lap. "Yes. I thought about it earlier today. If I show up at their house with a friend, that's one thing. If I show up at their house with a fiancé, it's another. Then I considered how my parents will react. My mom will be upset. My dad will be furious." She glanced at her watch. "Dad's at work. If we call now, it will give him a few days to calm down. He typically gets home in about thirty minutes." She'd already decided not to answer their calls that would come after this call. She'd text them to let them know she was alright and studying.

As he settled back in his chair, she studied his face. He told her last night that he shaved and dressed differently for her so he could sell being closer to her age. Older or younger wouldn't matter to her parents, though. They'd be shocked, then angry.

When she had dated Matt, her parents did a background check on him. She wondered if Petr's history was buried so deep her parents wouldn't be able to find any information about him. She wouldn't put it past them to dig until they found the truth. Switching to Dragon, she asked, "Where did you live before here?"

"Why?"

"I'm sure my parents will hire a company to do a background check. Will they find anything?"

Smiling, he leaned back in his chair. In English, he said, "They will find I went to college in Colorado. They won't find anything suspicious."

"Wait, you—"

"Jennifer, time. Your dad," Barry said.

"Thank you," she thought to Barry. "Remind me later what I wanted to ask you." She wanted to know if he went through college when he changed names and careers. She assumed he had faked the degree as well. But that wasn't important.

She pulled out her phone and selected her parents' land-line. Her heart hammered with each unanswered ring.

Finally, Randy picked up the phone. "Grand Central Station," he said, almost singing. She kept the cell by her ear, not needing to put it on speaker. Petr had dragon hearing; he'd be able to pick up everything.

"I take it the phone has been ringing a lot?" she asked.

"Oh yeah, off the hook. Let's see if I can summarize. The Grands are coming up with Grandfather Stewart. They'll be here this weekend—"

"Hold on for a second, Randy." She muted the phone. Last semester, Petr had met Randy, so she didn't need to tell him about her brother, but she needed to explain who the rest of her family members were. "The Grands are my grandmother and great-grandmother on my mom's side," she said. He nodded but didn't look surprised or ask about her grandfather, Stewart. Why was she astonished that Petr knew who her grandparents were? He likely made one of those family trees for her like he had for Matt.

She unmuted the phone. The Grands only visited during Thanksgiving. In the summer, her family—the Wrights—took a few weeks to see them in Florida. Her grandparents weren't ones to break their normal routine. Could something be wrong? "Go on. Why are they coming up this weekend?" She tried to keep the fear out of her voice.

"Someone with you?" Randy asked.

"Yes, sorry. I was explaining who the Grands are. Go on."

"I'm not sure Mom would like someone else knowing family stuff—"

"It's okay. Go on," she said, closing her eyes while she talked.

"Okay. But if Mom gets angry, you better get me out of being grounded."

"I will. And she won't ground you. Trust me. She'll be upset with me soon enough. What's happening, Randy? Are the Grands okay? Is Grandfather okay?"

"Yeah, they're fine. Just on their way up here."

"Why are they coming up?"

"Yesterday, Mom got this letter overnighted from a private investigator. Get this: he found some information on an ancestor of ours, Robert Sowards. Apparently, GG was kidnapped when she was little by her mom. The kidnapping and secret father swapping was one of those family secrets that no one shared with us. Robert Sowards is GG's biological father. So this Robert Sowards is our great-great-grandfather."

Last semester, Jennifer dreamed she was Robert Sowards. She knew he grew up in Kentucky, traveled to New York, and had made a fortune, only to lose it all in the stock market crash. Could Robert Sowards still be alive? She didn't think so. "What did the detective find that made the Grands decide to come up?"

"Oh, Robert Sowards remarried after GG disappeared. He had a son. Or was it a daughter? Anyway, we have two cousins, or whatever, living in Kentucky. The grandparents are on their way here because GG wants to meet them. Wild, right?"

Jennifer had already known that MaryAnn's mother, Mildred, had an affair and left Robert Sowards. Not only had she dreamed of him because he descended from Barry, her dragon guide, but Mildred descended from River. Jennifer also dreamed she was Mildred, except that dream felt more like a movie with Barry beside her.

Petr gave her an odd expression, like the news caught him off guard. She tried not to smile, enjoying that he didn't know everything about her. He shook his head as if clearing his thoughts, winced from the movement, then placed his hand over his shoulder. After the call, she'd ask what had surprised him.

She said, "Oh, wow. That's very wild, indeed." She paused to take a calming breath. "And it's about to get wilder."

"I'm not sure Mom can handle much more. She and Dad have been talking, and Mom's been cry—"

"Dad's there?" she asked, then swallowed.

Horrified, she locked eyes with Petr. He laid his hand on the table and mouthed, "It will be okay."

Meanwhile, Randy continued. "Yeah, he stayed home from work. I've heard some serious emotions coming out of their room. I think Dad is going to take a few days off to go with Mom to Kentucky." Randy paused. "And I get the house to myself," he whispered giddily. "I have this friend, Crystal. She plans to come over, and, well, it's going to be... fun, Jen."

"Things I didn't want to know, little brother." Boosting her courage, she thought, *Pain only lasts for a second; it will be okay. Be brave.* "Get Mom or Dad, or both."

"That big, huh? It can't wait?"

Jennifer glanced at Petr, his eyebrows furrowed, and he nodded. She placed her hand on top of his. Calm vibrations crawled up her skin, encouraging her to continue. "Nope, I need to talk to Mom and Dad." Giving her parents a few days to calm down and digest the news was better than springing it on them Saturday.

"Fine," he said. The phone clattered on something, and she imagined him dropping it, leaving it hanging by the cord. Randy's muffled voice screamed, "Mom or Dad!"

All sound died away. A few seconds later, there was a clip from someone picking up the phone. "Jennifer?" her mother asked.

"Mom." Her heart thundered in her chest.

"Honey, this is a bad time. Can I call you back?"

Before she brought up her news that might not get a positive reaction, she had a question she didn't understand and wanted an answer. "No, I need to talk to you. But why is it a bad time? I heard about GG, but why is something that happened to GG sixty years ago bothering you so much?"

She sighed. "It's your grandmother. She's set on meeting her cousins now. It's all a mess. I asked them to wait to come up, but no one listens to me. And now I have to make sure everything is safe. Your dad and I aren't even sure if the information the investigator provided is still right. The address exists on a map, but we couldn't verify who owned the land or who might live there. Your dad and—"

"I don't understand. It happened to great-grandmommy. Why does grand mommy care?"

"Lausy me. GG would drive blindfolded if she didn't think the police would pull her over, and Mom follows suit like a dog on a leash," her mom whispered quickly, though not to Jennifer. The first part, *Lausy me*, translated to *Lord have mercy on me*. Jennifer imagined her mother with a sponge in her hands, cleaning in a mad, frustrated frenzy, something Jennifer's mom did whenever GG had a whim.

"I don't know why there's such a rush, dear," her mom said, her normal volume and speaking pattern returned. "But your dad is helping me set up the hotels and confirming the cousin's residence. We've called the number for your GG's nephew that was given to us by the detective, but no one answers, and it doesn't go to voicemail. It just rings. It seems suspicious to me, and I just want them to wait until we confirm who they are and where they live." Her mother sounded upset. "Why are you calling?"

"I'm coming home this weekend."

"I know you want to meet your cousins—"

"No, Mom. I'm coming home to introduce you to my fiancé."

"Fiancé? What?" On the other end, her mother fell silent, but someone else breathed into the receiver.

"Randy, are you on the line?" Jennifer asked.

"Yes. This is classic, Jennifer. You're getting married?"

"What?" her father said, muffled from somewhere close by. She swallowed.

A few seconds later, her dad asked, "Jennifer, explain what your brother just said?"

"Hi, Dad," she said, then bit her lip.

Petr turned his hand over so his fingertips caressed hers. "Go on, Meelaya."

"Dad, Mom, I'm getting married and need to bring my fiancé home."

"Matt?" her dad asked.

"Why this weekend?" her mother asked at the same time.

She sighed. She had never told her parents about the breakup. Then again, it had only been a little over a week ago. "Matt and I are no longer together... I'm sorry this is such bad timing, and that I didn't tell you about Matt, but I have to introduce you to my fiancé." Trying her pleading voice, she added some truth. "It's because I might have to leave any day with him. I want you to meet him before then. Please don't go until we visit."

"What's this man's name?" her mom asked, her words clipped. She could imagine her mom with a pen and paper, ready to start the background check.

Should he be Petr or Nick? "Nick Smith," she said, deciding on his modern pseudonym. "Doctor Nicholas Smith. He was a professor of mine. Well, still is. Weirdly, Matt introduced us."

This time, Petr winced.

"My gosh! How old is this *man*?"

How old should Petr be? Definitely not his real age. "Stop, Mom. He's nowhere near yours and Dad's age... He's not too old for me."

"How long have you known this man?" her mom asked in her neutral voice. Which meant she was anything but calm. Any minute, Jennifer's mother would explode, revealing her momma bear side. Jennifer needed to get off the phone with her parents as soon as possible. If she gave them time to process, she wouldn't be on the receiving end of her mom's temper at all.

She couldn't tell her mom that she had memories of Petr from dreams of her ancestor, River. Or that River had been his good friend. "I've not known him very long. Six months." It was how long Petr had known Jennifer, so it was true enough.

No one spoke. Petr massaged her hand while they waited.

"I guess he'll have to meet your grandparents sometime. And if we're going to dig out all the family dirt, we should do it now, in front of this stranger"—her mom said, showing that she didn't believe Petr would stay in Jennifer's life, that he was an outsider—"But Jennifer, it wouldn't surprise me if you change your mind and don't marry this professor. You haven't known him long enough to have a deep connection," her mother said.

Her father stayed silent.

"Thank you, Mom and Dad. We'll be at your house on Saturday."

"Jennifer," her mother said quickly, using the voice Jennifer hated the most. Angry dad was one thing. Angry mom was a scary, horrible monster who lacked sanity or mercy.

"Yes."

"Be at the house at nine a.m. I want to be on the road early."

"Yes, ma'am."

After Jennifer hung up, she bit her bottom lip and glanced up at Petr. "This isn't me saying yes," she whispered.

"Technically, when you said you would be my wife, that was a yes. But I'm all for trying to convince you," he said, raising his eyebrows.

When she let go and the tingles died, she got to her feet. "Ready to go home?"

"Meelaya, I love hearing you call my home yours." He smiled, stood, and grabbed his jacket and briefcase. He walked over to Jennifer, standing in front of her so their chests touched. His lips gently grazed hers. "I don't expect your parents to give up their daughter to a perfect stranger. It will take a while before they accept me... us. Plus..." He kissed her head. "We met three months ago."

"We did? It seems like I've known you forever," Jennifer replied, burying her head into Petr's shoulder, breathing in his musk for comfort, and sighed. "Why did you look surprised about my great-grandmother not being raised by her father?"

"She had siblings."

"Meredith couldn't have children after GG. Her brother and sister were adopted. You did research on my family," she accused.

He shrugged. "Of course. When I researched your family, I found she wasn't an only child. I'm surprised that she was one of your dragon lines, is all." He walked around her, opening the door.

She followed. "I have a request. Could you hold me while I rest, please?"

"I will," he said, nodding. "Do you feel extra pyro tonight?" he asked.

"It's been two days since I've had a good four hours of sleep."

"You slept on me for at least an hour last night," he commented.

"Exactly. It's the claiming. It's comforting."

"I would be honored to be your pillow." He opened the door to head outside.

"Let me ask you something else. What did you mean when you said you went to college in Colorado? Did you really get a degree?"

"All eight years. Yes. I have a Ph.D. in biology. Whenever I create a new persona, I earn the credentials for my position. In the case of Nicholas Smith, I went to college to be vetted," he said in Dragon.

"Oh," she said. This meant that even if she didn't finish her four years now, eventually, she could return. It also sounded like she could earn several diplomas if she copied Petr.

He opened the car door for her, and she sat inside. As he walked around and got situated, her phone dinged.

"Who is it?" Petr asked.

She pulled it out of her backpack and unlocked the screen. "It's from Belinda. They're meeting in the library tomorrow night. May I go? Or would that make you uncomfortable?"

He laughed and said, "It makes me relieved. I'm trying to think of something to outdo our last date. Now that it's not on Thursday, I get an extra day to come up with something special. If saying you'll be my wife wasn't a yes, then I've got to convince you to say yes before we go to Dernogard."

She yawned. "Yesterday will be hard to top, but I wish you luck." She placed her hand on his leg, closing her eyes as the warm tingles gyrated through her body, relaxing the tension away.

CHAPTER 18

MATT

WHEN MATT DATED JENNIFER, SHE HAD TOLD HIM THE LIBRARY'S third floor was for talkers. To be honest, he didn't see any change in activity between the second and third floors other than the furniture arrangements. Green couches, lots of book-shelves, balconies, and computers—a different layout, but all there. This floor included tutoring rooms used by stoners and copulating couples, but he never cared enough to find where the rooms were located.

His heart rate sped up as he climbed the staircase. Studying with Belinda, Jennifer's blond hair created a halo that framed her work. "Hi," he said, pulling out the chair across from Belinda and Rob. Glancing at Jennifer, he asked, "You don't mind if I join you, do you?"

Jennifer surveyed the area, possibly looking at all the empty tables. "Sit away."

He pulled out his math homework. Across from him, Belinda and Rob sat close together and shared a book. To Matt's surprise, Belinda was left-handed, her paper pad sitting between her and Jennifer.

Jennifer looked radiant, like a star that fell from the sky

and now occupied the building. No one had the right to appear so alive, so unearthly.

How had he let her go?

Belinda leaned forward conspiratorially. "Guess what?"

"Shh," Rob whispered in her ear.

"Stop that, baby," she said. "We're studying up here because this is the talking floor. I haven't gossiped with my best roommate since Monday. If she doesn't hear the rumors from me, who will she hear them from?"

Jennifer glanced up from her book and said, "We're almost the only ones on this floor, so we're not bothering anyone. If I knew how quiet it was up here last semester..." She shook her head and frowned like she mourned not visiting this part of the building sooner. "That's what I get for trusting a senior's blog."

"True, it's quiet now," Matt said, sympathetic to Jennifer's dilemma. "But that's because it's still early in the semester. The slackers—sorry, efficient thinkers and those with a healthy life-school balance—are at the pool halls and bowling alleys."

"Or the Pi house," Belinda spoke up. "There's a cranking party tonight."

Belinda gave Matt a pointed stare. "Why aren't you there?"

Belinda knew the answer because they had talked earlier. Not only that, but she suggested he show up at the library. He had asked for an opportunity to make things right with Jennifer... if there was a chance. Belinda offered him tonight but said to expect complications—whatever that meant.

Blinking, Jennifer put her pen down and glared at Belinda. "Because he cares about his grades." He guessed Jennifer understood the truth and realized he desired to discuss their relationship but was giving him an out so he didn't have to admit it. "Matt, I have a question I've wanted to ask you."

"What would you like to know?" For her, he was an open book.

"I know last year you said you weren't ready to pledge, and you joked about it, but I never understood why. I mean, you were always over at the Pi house. So why didn't you pledge?"

When he first came to campus, he thought about it. His dad had been in a big shot fraternity at his college and claimed the connections he formed jump-started his career. Matt had met his dad's friends. All his life he'd listened as they discussed his future, not asking Matt what he wanted. Though Matt didn't consider himself rebellious, in this, he was. He needed to do things his own way, to make his path his own. He shrugged. "I don't know, Jennifer. Before joining a fraternity, I wanted to get familiar with the campus and make friends. Get settled before I make any commitments."

After he said his words, they repeated in his mind. Did Jennifer think he didn't want a long-lasting relationship with her? "Not that I'm against commitment, that's not it. I—"

Belinda giggled sarcastically. "We get it, Matt." She scooted up in her chair and peered at Jennifer. "Jennifer gets it too. If she gives you another chance, you will completely commit," she said in a deeper voice, like she was imitating him.

Heat consumed his cheeks, and he glanced at Jennifer through his eyelashes. He wasn't the only one who was embarrassed. She stared beyond the table, her skin flushed. Licking her lips, she returned to her books, her eyebrows furrowed.

What did her silence mean?

He retrieved his math book from his backpack, flipping over the pages to problem thirty-four, an integration of a natural log, and frowned. His mind couldn't concentrate on schoolwork today.

"Matt," Belinda said.

"Yeah?"

"I heard that Amy left campus because she was pregnant. Is that true?"

That got Jennifer's attention. Her head snapped up and her eyes locked on him.

"If she is, it's not mine, Belinda. We were only together for a week," he refuted.

"Isn't that what all the guys say?" Belinda asked, tilting her head to the side. She was supposed to be helping him, not destroying every chance he had of getting Jennifer back.

"It's not mine if she is, okay," he said, his irritation giving his words a sharp edge.

He took a gander at Jennifer. She turned her head, focusing on a guy who moved into the room and sat in a chair less than two table lengths away. Her face visibly paled. Her hands trembled as she pulled out her phone.

Matt reached over and touched her hand. "Are you okay?" he asked.

"Fine," she said, but she didn't look up, fingers flying over the cell.

Whispering, his hand still on her wrist, he said, "Jennifer, please don't be upset. I never had sex with her."

She glanced at him and said, "Matt, it's okay. We're not a couple anymore. You can have sex with whoever you want."

Ouch. Her words stung. "Listen, Jennifer, I don't want to be with anyone else. I want to make us right."

Shaking, she pulled her hand away and fixated on her phone. It dinged. Her hands flew over the screen. When she finished reading her text, she placed it in her backpack. Glancing over her shoulder, she stared at the man in the corner. He looked up from his book and glared menacingly at Jennifer.

Until then, Matt hadn't paid much attention to the man.

With his ankles crossed and a full blond beard, he was built more like a bodybuilder than a college student. What stood out, though, was the scowl and the evil that radiated from him. Matt had never seen so much hate before, and it was all focused on the girl he loved. "Do you know him, Jennifer?"

She turned away, grabbing her study materials. "No," she whispered.

Belinda glanced behind her at the man. The stranger glared at Belinda with what looked like death wishes. "Oh. Wow. He's scary," she said.

Despite being far enough away that he shouldn't have heard Belinda, he smiled like he had.

Frantically, Jennifer packed her books into her backpack and stood. "Guys, as soon as Dr. Smith gets here, I'm going to leave. Do you want to study next week?" She caught his eyes, and Matt was sure she meant him too.

It wasn't what he wanted, but it was a start to recovering what they once had.

Another man with a lean build and a chiseled chin came up the stairs and approached Jennifer. When he stood beside Jennifer, Matt recognized the man but couldn't believe it. Dr. Smith didn't appear old anymore and had lost weight. How did anyone lose at least thirty-five pounds in two days? Even plastic surgery couldn't give someone abs like that in a few days. And why would any professor dress like a fashion model, anyway?

Jennifer placed her hand on Dr. Smith's shoulder. He groaned. "I'm sorry," she said, then leaned over and whispered something in his ear. Her voice was so low that Matt couldn't understand a single word. As she talked, Dr. Smith made a fist with his non-slinged hand and clenched his jaw. The guy across the room gave the professor the evil eye as they entered into a staring contest.

Awkward seconds went by before the man stood, slamming his book shut as he did so, and disappeared beyond the stairs. Jennifer breathed out and closed her eyes, her shoulders rolling forward. Did Jennifer have a new stalker?

"You scared him off, Dr. Smith," Belinda said. "Thank you."

"Hi, Dr. Smith." Matt grinned, remembering what his mother said—smile first, always smile first. "Did you do one of those makeover shows or something?" Matt asked.

"Hello, Belinda," Dr. Smith said, facing her. "Rob and Matt." He turned toward Matt. He made eye contact like the old Dr. Smith, but there was a confidence Matt had never noticed before. He stood straighter and seemed less absent-minded, more in control. "To answer your question, Matt, I shaved, had a haircut, and bought new clothes. I've done nothing extreme as a makeover show."

Jennifer placed her hand on Dr. Smith's elbow. "Are you ready to go?" she asked, close to his ear.

Matt didn't like the signs of attention, but after seeing such a scary guy, it made sense that she found some comfort in the older man.

"Wait," Belinda said. When Dr. Smith glanced at her, she added, "I heard you turned in your resignation."

Jennifer paled, and her mouth opened in surprise. Matt concluded she thought she was privy to Dr. Smith's plans and was shocked to find out she wasn't. What exactly was going on that Jennifer believed she should know about Dr. Smith's decisions? Was it because he found her housing?

"Rumors have already spread, have they? I've had a family emergency that involves a job offer in another country. The original goal was to wait until the end of this semester, but..." He faced Jennifer, searching her face. Something unspoken ran between them as they stared at one another. "I have a... I will be leaving campus earlier than expected," he answered Belinda, but he told Jennifer.

Matt swallowed, unwilling to believe what he saw. It wasn't possible. It'd only been two weeks.

Peering around the room, Dr. Smith seemed to be hunting for something. When he didn't find what he was looking for, he locked eyes with Matt. "When the three of you leave, why don't you leave together, just to be safe? And I'll alert security that some crazy guy is walking around campus." He pointed in the direction the man had just left. "He's up to no good."

Without a word, he held out his hand, and Jennifer gave him her bookbag.

"Please be careful," Dr. Smith said to them. To Jennifer, he said, "Ready, Meelaya?"

"Yes," she said. "I'll talk to you later," she said to the three of them as they walked toward the stairs.

As Matt watched them disappear down the open staircase, he realized he liked the old Dr. Smith better.

"Did that seem weird to you?" Matt asked after a minute.

"Which part? Dr. Smith changing his appearance? The rumor that he turned in his resignation? Or the story that he's dating Jen?"

He couldn't utter any words in response.

Leaning over the table, Belinda said, "That, Matt, is the complication. I asked Jennifer, and she said they weren't dating. Then he appears at school looking smoking hot. I'd say you have some competition."

Could one mistake cost him the only girl he had loved forever? He forced a confident grin, the one he practiced in front of the mirror. "Jennifer and I have history. What does she have in common with Dr. Smith?"

He glanced back in the direction Jennifer had just left. The next few weeks, he had to up his game to win her back. "Do you mind if I study with you next week?"

"I don't mind at all, but it might be a losing battle. I mean, you saw how Dr. Smith looked. They even have their own secret language."

He stood. "I lost this battle, but I'll win the war."

She smiled. "That's the spirit, Matt. Besides, you two look

cute together. I'll help you however I can. As long as you never break her heart, cowboy."

Now, all he had to do was convince Jennifer, and since Dr. Smith planned to leave the country, it was just a matter of time.

CHAPTER 19

JENNIFER

Every few minutes, Jennifer had to stop and take a breath. Not from exhaustion but anxiety. She glanced at the sunrise, studying the shades of orange that blended together. Normally, Petr would be driving her to school. They'd be chatting about her classes, not preparing to move to another country.

"Are you okay?" Petr asked, sitting his load down on the porch.

"Yeah. Fine," she said, but she wouldn't tell him how scared she felt. If she spoke the words out loud, she'd give the emotions more power. Already, her legs trembled.

Her mate gave her a long stare, placing his left hand on his hip. She wouldn't lie to him, but she could keep him from knowing the full extent. He heard her heart racing and knew she'd had several panic attacks since last night. But he nodded, letting her push through this on her own.

"Good," he said.

Standing outside in the open took more courage than she felt she had. Exposed to anyone who was hunting her, only protected by the roof on the porch.

Too much, too soon.

Barry manifested close to her, his body taking shape over a wood column on the porch so that she could no longer see the structure. He held her wrist. His comforting touch was solid, though he was just her figment. "You can do this. You can handle this. One step at a time; breathe between each movement. Not only are you a dragon, but you control the element of fire. They invaded your territory. Fine. You did the right thing, but if they come here, we will eat them."

"One of the dragon eaters was on campus."

He nodded. "We will eat them."

"He knew where to find me. Knew I was studying with my friends."

An apple appeared in Barry's hand. "You're making me hungry, Jen." He took a bite, and her tongue was coated with the tartness of a green Granny Smith. With chunks of the fruit in his mouth, he said, "We will eat them."

"I'm not some random target. They're following me," she thought.

"I know. You're thinking about this all wrong. It's great. It's like delivery for dragons. They come to us, and we eat them. Yum," he said before chomping into the fruit.

At least Petr took it seriously. He stood near her, waiting for her permission to continue loading the rented moving van.

If she moved out of the city, would her friends be okay? What about her family?

"Petr, tell me again. When we leave, will they leave the area? I need to know my family and friends will be safe."

If they would have caught the guy and interrogated him last night, she could have confronted her fear. But by the time they left, he had disappeared.

Petr sighed, twisting so the headboard, a load light enough he had been able to carry it with his good arm, rested against his side as he placed his hand on her shoulder. Warm zippies, something between an electrical charge and the tummy-pulling reaction from safely free falling, clawed up her skin, through her body, and calmed the tremors.

Her mate, her own personal drug.

"They'll be fine. But Kamar is staying behind to make sure the area clears out." He smiled, showing his teeth, his stubble standing to attention. His fingers left her shoulder and played with some loose locks that fell out of her ponytail. "Che-non and Kamar will mail the furniture to Fritz's house, and it will be there for us soon after we arrive. We'll need to buy more furniture, but we can figure that out when we get there."

Walking away, he repositioned the guest bedroom's twin headboard, struggling with its awkward size as he situated it under his good arm, and started down the sidewalk to the van.

With his citrus scent and slicked-back black hair, Che-non walked out the front door of Petr's house carrying the footboard. When he passed Petr, he asked, "Did you want your bedroom furniture too?"

"No. I'm leaving that for Kamar. But—" He glanced at Jennifer, asking her permission, but for what? "But go ahead and bring all the things on the shelves and surfaces from my bedroom."

He was inquiring about keeping the stuff he'd collected from his second wife and their daughter. She was no longer jealous. She understood that the man she chose had been married and loved before, but she wasn't sure she wanted reminders of them laying around.

"Take back your life, Jennifer. The dragon heart-eater guy surprised you. You couldn't have eaten him in front of everyone or set the place on fire. Maybe when you're trained, you'll be able to do something. Now, move one leg, then the other, and help Petr pack. Then your stuff as well," Barry said, tugging on her arm. She let him lead her back into the house.

Stopping in the guest bedroom, it appeared barren with

the bed missing. Petr planned to leave the desk. On his knees, Kamar pulled the last books off the bookshelf and placed them in a box.

After Kamar stood, dusting off his hands, he noticed her. "Your mate wants to keep the bookshelf."

She nodded, but other than because it looked handcrafted, she wasn't sure why. Compared with the Amish piece at the entrance, the bookshelf was simple. She'd have kept the Amish piece and left the bookcase.

"I guess he has an emotional connection to it," she said, grabbing a box of some of the hardbound books Petr planned to take. She sneezed from the dust. Most of them were in Russian and talked of his sister or brother-in-law, or at least the myths created about them. With her load, she headed out the door.

Petr stood on the steps. "When you put those in the van, come and sit with me."

"Okay," she answered, stepping out from underneath the porch's ceiling and searching the sky for drones.

"Paranoid?" Barry asked.

"Yes."

When she entered the covered truck bed, she felt more protected. Her fear, her suspicion, existed in her head because she knew that at any second, someone could ram their car into the truck, causing an explosion.

"No. I don't think they could," Barry said. "Explosions in movies wouldn't happen in reality."

Did it matter? She raised her eyebrow at Barry, dropped her load, and cautiously left the van, checking the clouds for eavesdropping drones as she moved along the ground.

Petr waited for her at the door. Wearing casual straight-leg slacks and a form-fitting, ribbed, long-sleeve shirt, he held out a steaming cup. "Come, sit with me."

Rooibos tea had a unique scent, floral yet earthy like bark.

When she sat, she inhaled more before tasting. The rose came from Petr—

"It means he loves you," Barry said, sitting in one of the other two empty chairs.

"Cinnamon, ginger, chamomile, and…" She frowned.

"Dandelion. It should help with stress and calm your stomach," Petr said.

Sighing, she studied the back door and its window that took up half the frame. Could someone stare into the room and spy on them while they talked at the table? "I feel like the whole world is watching me."

"It's not," Petr said.

"Maybe. But Petr… I don't feel safe. I feel violated." She glanced out the window again.

Barry manifested at the door. "I'll watch for predators."

Had someone tapped her phone or Belinda's? If so, how long had they followed her? Recently? If they had tracked her, where would it stop? "How did they know I was at the library?"

Petr shrugged. "I'm not sure they did."

"Do you think they've followed me my whole life?" she asked. After last night, she suspected they had followed her since she was born. The idea destroyed her image of her perfect upbringing. Up until last night, she'd felt safe and secure—now she felt… violated. She wanted to get into a small cave and hide, never show her face outside again, and she wanted to bring her family with her.

"I've considered the possibility that they have followed your family for generations. Tracked them and their lives," he said.

Nodding, she said, "I've wondered the same thing. I keep remembering weird things that happened in my past, I kind of explained away. Such as, when I was around seven, I played soccer… I spent more time picking four leaf clovers than chasing the ball, or I might not have noticed this strange guy standing at the end of the field in a suit, regardless of the weather.

"One day, I left my water bottle on the field, and we went back to get it. The guy was gone. I figured he was there for one of the other kids, even though I never saw him with anyone. What if he was there to watch me?"

"Could be," Petr said nonchalantly.

"It's creepy, Petr. And you think they are watching my family."

"Very likely."

"Promise me, if my family needs to be saved, that we will save them." She took a sip of tea.

"No. I won't promise."

The cup at her lips, she sat it down in shock, hard enough that the liquid sloshed over the side. "Petr, if they need—"

"I won't promise, but we will move your family… if needed. We aren't sure the man at the library was there for you." He pointed to his face. "I was attacked before Christmas as well." Taking her hand, he sighed. "Jennifer, I want you to reframe last night's event. We're leaving and going to a place where you can train and learn to defend yourself and your family."

She liked the idea of being strong and taking on anything that threatened her world, but that didn't solve the issue immediately. "But what about right now?" she asked.

"Eat them," Barry said, shrugging.

Petr glanced around the room and grabbed his tea, taking a sip. She knew he did this to gather his thoughts on how to respond. "The tracking app your parents insist you have on your phone."

"What about it?"

"Where is your family?" he asked.

She pulled out her phone from her back pocket and opened the app. It showed a picture of each family member, their location, and their cellphones' percentage of power.

"Randy's at school. My dad is at work, and Mom is at the grocery store."

He nodded. "Is that unusual behavior for them?"

"No," she answered.

"And I heard you talk with them briefly last night," Petr said.

"Yes," she said, shrugging. "What does that prove?"

"That they are safe and unaware that someone is probably watching them... The Immortals seem concerned with dragons. In the past, when we've encountered them, they've intentionally left the humans alone, cornering the dragons and killing them when there were no witnesses."

"Are you sure?"

She didn't have an answer.

"It's really simple, Jennifer. Just eat them," Barry said.

Placing his cup down, he took her hands. "I don't want you to ever hurt, physically or emotionally. That includes worrying about your family. I don't believe the Immortals will change their ways. They will watch your family until they are considered a threat. If we hide your family or tell them about dragons, we increase the risk that the Immortals will move on them."

"So why don't we take them with us?" she asked.

"And tell them you're a dragon?" he asked.

"Yes," she said.

"I've thought about that. Your parents could refuse if we tell them you're a dragon and ask them to go with us. You can't make someone do something they don't want to do. And once they know the truth, there is no going back. They would be aware of the possible danger all around them."

"And if they decide to go?" she asked.

"I've seen it before, Meelaya, threats everywhere and yet people stay where they're comfortable. The people of Pompeii had seen the volcano smoke, felt the earthquakes, knew it could cover them in minutes, yet they stayed... Your dad has a career. Randy has school. More than likely, your parents wouldn't be willing to move because they would have too much to lose."

"Including their lives!" she insisted.

He rubbed her arm, smooth tingles gyrated up her arms. "Bottom line, if we tell them, they will see danger wherever they look. But you decide what we will tell them. It's a big decision. Would you like them to know someone could be watching them, tapping their phones, and waiting for another of your family members to become a dragon shifter?"

What he was saying made sense, and she sighed before taking another sip. If she told her parents, what would they do? Her mom was already panicking because her great-grandmother dropped everything to find a potential nephew. Would they force Randy to come straight home, quit his sports teams, and pick him up from every school event? It could stifle his independence, and Randy was at the age where he needed that. If someone wanted to kidnap them, was there anything her father could do to protect them? Maybe being blind to the world around them was the thing they needed most.

The front door opened. Che-non walked in, closing the door behind him. He exhaled and jumped up and down fast, his teeth chattering like it was cold outside and he was warming himself up. Quickly, he approached them. "It's packed. Do you want me to charge it to your credit card?" he asked.

"Yes," Petr said, like money didn't matter to him.

She'd never priced international shipping, but she guessed it would be costly. "Air or ground?" she asked.

"Great question," Che-non said. "Which would—"

"Air," Petr answered, glancing at Jennifer.

"Kamar!" Che-non yelled.

The giant man came out from the hall. "Are we ready to leave?"

"Yes," Che-non answered. Turning back to Jennifer and Petr, he added, "Be back soon." They moved to the entrance-way, closing the door as they exited. The lock clicked, but she stood, went to the door, and ensured the latch was secured.

Walking back to the table, she didn't make eye contact, but she felt Petr watching her every step. She sipped her tea before looking at him. "Is there honey in here?" she asked, tasting something sweet.

"Very little."

"What happens next? After Che-non and Kamar return?" she asked.

"They're getting us lunch and picking up your ring."

She gulped. "We're still talking to my parents in the morning?"

"Yes," he said. "But we're flying to China tomorrow night."

"Tomorrow?"

"Yes."

"So soon, and yet not soon enough," she absentmindedly said. She couldn't shake the feeling of being watched. If she was in China, she wouldn't feel watched, but she'd worry about her family. This wasn't an easy decision. Leave for China and leave her family vulnerable? "Kamar will be staying?"

"Yes," Petr confirmed.

"Can he move closer to my parents?" she asked.

"I don't see why not. We can ask him too."

She nodded. She had to believe the Immortals would leave them alone. After all, she didn't even know someone spied on her. They knew she was a dragon, and no one had bothered her parents or her brother. "Okay. We don't tell my family I'm a dragon tomorrow."

He nodded.

She glanced away from Petr toward the back window and Barry. "I think you made the right call," he said.

She allowed her worry about her family to ebb away. In its place, though, she had another worry. "How do you know they won't follow us?"

"I don't."

She glanced back at him. "And if they're on the plane, ready to kidnap me?"

"Eat them!" Barry shouted.

"Then I guess it's a good thing you can breathe fire and fly," Petr said. He leaned back and smiled, appearing unconcerned or unaffected that people were always watching her.

"How can you stay so calm? Why aren't you worried?"

"What has changed, Meelaya?" When she didn't answer, he continued. "Only that you are aware that someone has followed you a lot longer than you knew." He pointed to his head with his uninjured hand. "Those fears are in here. And if you aren't careful, the horrors you can imagine will be worse than the ones you face." He waved his hand around the room. "Right now, there is nothing to worry about."

His fingers gently landed on her lip as he leaned forward, tracing her mouth. He whispered, "When I am worried, I've trained my mind to plan. The plan is for you to train in Dernogard, to learn to defend yourself. To stay calm, I prepare. The Immortals are always planning evil." His hand dropped to her chin, pushing her face toward him. He gently kissed her lips. "Using my brain instead of allowing it to run rabid keeps me from being paranoid."

"I've been paranoid for the both of us." She sighed and closed her eyes. *Calm. Focus on something other than being hunted,* she encouraged herself.

He laughed, and the atmosphere lightened some. "I never thought I would be telling a dragon who has proven to me she can defend herself not to worry, yet here I am. You are strong, Jennifer. That I do not doubt. If you can control your mind, you can control the fear."

She opened her eyes, searching his face. He had such a

warm glow to his smile—friendly, inviting, intoxicating, desirable.

"How about I distract you?" He reached over, grabbed her hand, and brought her fingers up to his lips, kissing each fingertip. "You've still not said yes, only that you will be my wife, but not when you will be my wife?"

"Okay, stepping outside… Gross," Barry said.

She heard a door close but didn't turn away from Petr. She knew Barry had left the room. "Do you need an answer now?"

"It would be nice to know before I see MiFeng."

"When I say I will be your wife, I want it to be romantic, Petr," she said, but she knew the truth. It wouldn't be long from now.

Two months ago, she was human. A week ago, she killed her first person. In a month, she will be a wife. Her heart felt like it was on a roller coaster—scared someone hunted her, lost in lust, and afraid for her friends and family.

"Only one thing you can do," Barry said. "Enemy buffet, here we come!" She tasted a tart apple and knew he had conjured one.

Agreeing with Barry, she closed her eyes and kissed Petr, losing herself in the emotion of chaos.

CHAPTER 20

SHANNA

"Last performance," Shanna said to the air, staring at her tear-streaked face in the mirror of Amy's white VW bug. She looked awful, perfect for her ending scene. However, without the dragon hiding perfume, she could smell everything but smelled nothing like Amy.

Inhaling deeply, she got back into the Amy role—how she'd feel and react. Right now, Amy felt hurt but bubbly with anticipation. Confidence brought on by strong parents fed into her belief that she was flawless. She enjoyed boys, parties, watching sports, and drinking copious amounts of alcohol.

She took off her mother's necklace and opened the door. "Ready as I'll ever be." She sighed.

Bending over, she placed the gold chain with Jared's ring on the front seat where she could see it and grabbed the sunglasses, putting them on.

She parked beside the van advertising "The Laughing Painter" with a giant, smiling paintbrush. Inside sat two men, both operatives for the Family.

She hadn't officially met them, but they confirmed who

they were by holding up two fingers—bunny ears—then used their other hands to simulate a gun blowing up the poor rabbit's head, Roland's signal idea. It worked. She'd never seen anyone else make that symbol.

When she passed, she nodded at them. She walked until she faced Matt's apartment door and prepared to knock.

"Let Amy ruin her life. It's her choice," she heard Doug, Matt's roommate, say through the door.

Wait, their comedy show started at six. Why were they still at the house?

"Get over it, Matt. You're not the reason she's having a mental breakdown. She was crazy before you met her," Lauren, Matt's other roommate and Doug's fiancée, said.

Shanna smiled at the truth of the statement. But she understood Matt's conscience wouldn't allow him to oppress anyone. She was counting on it. If Matt could do something to heal Amy, he would.

Footsteps approached the door. She estimated at least two people were headed in her direction. As Amy would, she stood up straight, her fist ready to knock, and allowed water to gush from her eyes.

"It's your life," Doug said. The doorknob rattled like someone had their hand on the other side. "Listen, Matt, Lauren scored tickets to go watch Knuckles tonight. Don't do anything stupid, like take the crazy girl back, but if you need us, call us. We'll come rescue you."

A lopsided smile crossed Shanna's lips. When Amy visited the apartment last, Lauren confided she loved Knuckles.

"You'll be my rescuer?" Matt asked. There was a pause. "Thanks, man… You guys are late if that show started at six."

"Yeah, but Lauren had to put on makeup, just in case the rumor of it being filmed panned out."

More movement. "You look nice," Matt said, slowing the last word down to emphasize it. How he drawled out "look nice" made Shanna think something had changed. She wondered what that meant.

Another set of feet headed toward her. "I graduate this spring, so it's time to look the part of a grownup. I might even bleach my hair back to its natural color," Lauren said from close by.

"Which is?" Matt asked.

"Dark blond," she answered as the door swung open. Doug took a step backward to keep from running into Shanna. Lauren bumped gently into his back.

Shanna dropped her hand. Allowing herself only a few seconds to grasp the changes in Lauren's appearance before she moved her gaze to Matt, she noted the lack of the usual black or white clothing. Instead, Lauren wore warm makeup, a short red dress, and loose curls in her black, shoulder-length hair. Nothing like the goth, emo girl she'd met a few weeks ago.

Inwardly, she sighed and welcomed the warning of his roommate's startling change. Without it, she might have gaped too long, which would be a misstep in portraying Amy's personality. Amy cared more for herself than others and wouldn't be the type to notice even a drastic change.

"Hi, Amy," Doug said, sounding friendly but devoid of the cover-up perfume, Shanna smelled the lie. "We were just leaving. Have a fun night, you two."

She didn't wave or say any byes, focusing on Matt and breathing in, collecting the flavors on her tongue. Matt reeked of fear, disgust, and zero attraction.

Opening the door wider, he gestured for her to move inside. "Come on in," Matt said.

She turned her head and watched Doug open Lauren's car door.

It was going to work. It had to work.

"No," Shanna said, sniffling. "I'm sorry for being such a

baby about us breaking up. I need you to see something, and then if you don't want to see me again, I understand… May I show you?"

He blinked while looking at the ceiling and said, "Sure."

Almost there! So close. "It's in my car."

Turning, she took a step toward the VW.

Matt didn't budge.

"Please?" She steadily took off her sunglasses and gazed into Matt's eyes. She knew he saw a defenseless, tiny-framed girl with tears streaming down her swollen face.

Shaking his head, he said, "Whatever, sure." He shut the door to the apartment, and she realized he left it unlocked. Oh well. She wasn't going to go back and lock it for him.

The two operatives were unloading their vehicle staging the area with tools as if they had an actual painting job. They strung white drip tarp between two ladders, creating a fake wall that would block Matt from the apartment building's view.

Matt didn't even pay attention to the others as she led him to the car. The little VW appeared tiny amongst the blue King-Cab F-150 and the industrial van. She walked between the two vehicles, crying as she moved. For this to work, Matt needed to focus on her.

When she unlocked the car door, she opened it to create a barrier between her and Matt. "It's in my seat." As she bent over and picked up the necklace, there was a loud crack, followed closely by Matt slouching over the doorframe.

Did the blond brute murder Matt?

As she stood, she kept her emotions in check. If the Family were like sharks, would they sense her concern for Matt and kill her, too? Blood ran down the VW's window and pooled on the ground, but the men had put up the white barrier around the vehicles. No one could see them move Matt.

She placed her hand under his nose while she listened to his heartbeat. She found a smooth, rhythmic heartbeat pattern and that he was breathing. Matt should be okay and only have a horrible headache if nothing else happened to him.

"Hurry, move him. We need this mess cleaned up. Please tell me there's a clean-up crew on the way?" Shanna demanded and arranged the necklace so the ring nestled between her breasts.

Meanwhile, behind her, more tarp walls were constructed so that they were surrounded. She had gotten this idea from her dad. When he painted cars in their front yard, he surrounded the car with tarps before he spray-painted the vehicle. She didn't know what people would think if they saw the white fort. But if they hurried, it wouldn't matter.

The tall, blond, bearded brute attempted to sling Matt onto his shoulder, but the unconscious Matt slipped out of his grasp, landing on the ground with a slap.

She blinked, placing all her fears in a deep box. *This is my freedom. I have to look strong.*

She ignored the struggling operative and surveyed the area, looking for heat signatures of people who might have witnessed the kidnapping. The zone was clear. She walked outside of the makeshift tent and glanced at every forward-facing window, checking for silhouettes. All the windows were void of bystanders, but they needed to hurry.

Entering behind the curtain, she turned back to the man pulling Matt by his shoulders. Matt's feet dragged on the ground between the two vehicles. "Gloss, grab his legs, man!" the tall brute said, the muscles in his neck straining and the veins popping out.

Another operative ran awkwardly toward Matt's legs, stopping in front and bending down. She hadn't seen this operative yet. While tall like Jormungant, this man, Gloss, had dark, almost black hair and brown skin. It was such a contrast to the other operatives running around, she stopped for a second just to watch him. Like most of the Family, he was handsome, but his was wilder and had more of an exotic appeal.

Shanna stopped ogling. She had a job to do, so she turned away from staring and focused on the next task—changing cars. Roland had explained that the Family had secured three parking spots, only vacating the middle one so Amy could park there. Two days ago, one man had parked the blue F150. Yesterday, the white van claimed its current spot. And finally, a fourth car, a blue Miata, which moved for Amy to park, took the center location to secure the turf where the VW sat.

When Shanna parked, the Miata began making rounds around the apartment parking lot, spying for witnesses.

It surprised her when she saw a woman behind the wheel of the Miata. Not only had her dreams shown her the Family was composed of men, but Roland had told her only men worked for the Family. Was the woman part of the Family or a hired hand? And if she was on the payroll, how did they know she wouldn't go to the police? After all, snatching a person was a crime. But Shanna decided that was the Family's issue. If they wanted to get rid of the other woman, they could.

Shanna moved outside the tent in time to see the strange woman driving the Miata as it passed in front of her. The woman slowed down and gave her an all-clear thumbs up before traversing off for another loop. So far, no one had witnessed the kidnapping.

"He's heavier than he looks," Shanna heard one of the operatives say on the other side of the fabric. She walked back inside the fort to find the tall brute of a man straining under Matt's weight, despite help from Gloss.

Considering Gloss, she started at his toes and worked her way up to his face—a very worthy specimen. She wondered about the origins of his coloring. Roland had mentioned Father met his last wife in Colombia, so perhaps this was their son?

"Wait," Shanna ordered. The tall man released Matt's shoulders and scowled at her. Gloss slowly lowered Matt's legs and peered at her curiously.

She needed to retrieve Matt's phone in case his family could use it to locate him. Each dragon was different, she'd been told. Not every dragon kept their strength when human, but she did. Showing off and to keep the men afraid of her, she tapped into her dragon strength, and with one hand, she shoved Matt's body at an angle, allowing her to search his pockets and take possession of his cell phone. She didn't locate his wallet, so it must still be in the apartment.

As she stood, she let go of Matt, and he thumped to the ground. *Please be okay, Matt,* she thought. Within the VW, a plastic bag rested on the car floor. Placing the device into the bag, she walked back to the concrete walkway.

If the phone had been rubber, the force she used to slam it to the ground would have bounced it above the three-story apartment. Instead, the internal electronics crunched as the screen shattered. Her heel crushed the remaining parts to ensure the tracking mechanism inside was utterly broken. She picked up the fragments and threw the bag away in the nearby trashcan.

By the time she finished, the men had Matt's body dangling out the van door. Both men were in the vehicle, one to the left of him and the other on the right, pulling Matt up with their hands braced under his armpits, grunting to hoist his weight. She shook her head and wrapped her arms around Matt's feet. "Pull," she said. She pushed from below as they did as she directed. Matt's limp figure moved upward until he rested in a seat.

"So," Gloss said, panting. He wiped his brow and jumped out of the vehicle, landing beside her. The other man secured Matt to the seat with wire ties. At first, Shanna didn't acknowledge Gloss, but his chocolate-brown eyes penetrated her skin, and she had to glance at him.

A smile, innocent and sweet, displayed his perfectly white teeth. "Father said you were one of them. Is that true?" His accent reminded her of someone from Puerto Rico, as if he grew up speaking both Spanish and English. Without saying the word *dragon,* he asked her if she was a dragon.

The brute stopped, peeking up to watch her. She glared at him, and he returned to his job.

What harm could there be in answering Gloss's question? She wanted to meet the other operatives, anyway. "Does it matter? Will you kill me and eat my heart if I am?" she asked.

She tasted the air. He was appalled at the thought, which made him interesting. She tasted nothing yeasty—he hadn't had a dragon heart himself. Shouldn't he want her dead so he could live forever?

"No. On both accounts. Father said to treat you with respect and not to hurt you," Gloss answered, his accent making her girl parts feel like goo. Could his delay in answering be because the idea of eating a dragon's heart disgusted him?

"Father, you say? Did you talk to Jormungant himself?" Shanna scrutinized his appearance. The tall, skinny man had Jormungant's nose, mouth, and eye shape. On the outside, he appeared innocent and young, possibly in his late twenties or early thirties. She tasted the surrounding air. A scrumptious, spicy clover danced with white almond and it intrigued her. But there was something else, something dark, maybe even dangerous, and she liked it.

"Yes." Gloss's cheeks flushed, as if he read her lustful thoughts.

Even more interesting. What skills did he get from being born from a dragon father? She knew he couldn't transform. In the Family's extensive history, no one who was half human and half dragon could shapeshift between the two forms. But, from time to time, someone was born with extra gifts. Did Gloss have unique talents he'd inherited from Jormungant?

Gourdy appeared in the van, directly where she looked when she wasn't studying Gloss. "You're flirting. Father said not to take a Family member as a spouse."

"Are you his youngest son?" she asked Gloss. She didn't care how bold and incorrect it sounded or if Gourdy approved. *"If he is Father's son, all the more reason to take him. Technically, he hasn't eaten a dragon's heart, and Roland never said I couldn't take a Family member who would someday die."*

"It was implied," Gourdy said.

"It wasn't. I asked, and he didn't answer. Plus, think about it, Gourdy. Out of all the things you want to do, you want to keep us alive most of all. By having a relationship with a Family member, we have that extra layer of strength, someone who knows how to protect us from harm. Someone who knows what we're up against. We'll have a partner." It didn't hurt that Gloss was her type of poison—dreamy body, face, and darker than her.

"You can't escape the Family, Shanna," Gourdy said.

"Gloss might make staying in the Family worthwhile," she answered.

"Fine," her figment said, then disappeared.

Through his luscious, thick black eyelashes, Gloss considered her. "I am." The handsome man was Father's son, his direct descendant.

"So, you've never killed someone like me?" She knew the answer. His scent didn't reek of murdered dragon. At the same time, she confirmed his suspicions that she was indeed a dragon.

The brute moved to the driver's seat and distracted her from her thoughts. "Shut the door, Gloss. You and the dragon get out of my way."

Gloss obeyed while Shanna thought of eating all six feet six inches of the man. Once the door closed, Gloss delicately took her arm and led her to the sidewalk. The white van pulled out and revealed the curtain had shrunk to surround only the VW, with "Do not cross" written across it in bold green letters. The workers behind the tent maintained utter silence, surprising her. With dragon hearing, she expected to hear at least a little of whatever cleaning they were doing, but she couldn't.

Taking a risk, she turned to face Gloss. Moving into his personal space, close enough that her breasts slightly touched his chest, she searched his black eyes. *"If I take him as a lover, he will be mine, and because he is Father's youngest, he will be more inclined to actually fulfill his word of giving us the fifty years of freedom."*

"Only if Father doesn't kill you both," Gourdy thought.

"We should live a little, and we can." She said, "There are two ways to live forever, and both involve a dragon's heart. Would you care to try one of those methods?" She didn't have to tell Gloss she couldn't love him and that choosing her meant death. But she didn't lie either. For most dragons, a coupling meant they'd be bound together forever.

Around her, the air became thick with the musk of arousal mixing with his white-almond aroma. The Miata pulled into the spot vacated by the van. The engine stayed on as the other woman stepped out.

Shanna took a step away from Gloss, though he did not move, and his eyes remained trained on her.

The woman ignored that she'd caught two operatives close together. "Caitlyn," the woman said with a gravelly, husky voice.

"I guess that's me?" Shanna asked.

"Caitlyn is who the documentation in the car says you are. Nice to meet you. I'm Father's daughter, Maxine."

Did she mean she was Father's daughter, as in his biological child, or another of his normal cult weirdos? Shanna didn't ask.

The tropical scent of sugared mangos wrapped around Shanna as she approached Maxine. Shanna surveyed the woman, looking for signs she might be Jormungant's daughter. Maxine either wore a wig or dyed her hair black, because the color clashed with her extremely pale skin. She had bangs, a bowl cut, observant blue eyes, and a skinny build with large breasts. Other than her coloring, Shanna didn't notice anything that reminded her of Jormungant.

"Roland said this is your new car, and I am to take the VW to another town and sell it. Are all the legal documents in the glove box to unload the vehicle?"

"It's waiting for its next owner once they remove the blood," Shanna answered.

"Good. I placed your makeup in the car. I've been ordered to stay with the clean-up crew. When they're done, I will ensure the car is sold." Maxine made eye contact with Gloss, and they nodded to each other. "Caitlyn," Maxine said, still blocking the door to the Miata. "I've got a team," she said, pointing to a small device in her ear that looked like a hearing aid. She continued. "They are searching the web for any missed surveillance video. They've wiped your photo from the school directories and destroyed all the closed-circuit video or security footage. You're in the clear." She held out the keys.

When Shanna reached to take them, Maxine pulled her hand back. "Be careful and enjoy your Family vacation." She tossed the keys, and Shanna caught them. Maxine disappeared behind the white parameter around the VW bug.

Gloss's eyes trained on her. He neither smiled nor frowned. "I must go," he whispered. With that slight Spanish accent, she'd need more than one night with him to feel satisfied. As he sauntered away, the sway of his hips screamed sex. He vanished from view beyond the cleaning crew's white tent.

Alone, she gave the crime scene one last review and saw nothing that needed to be done that wasn't already being handled.

She clicked to unlock her car when the truck parked

behind the blue Miata blocked her exit. The window rolled down. "But I will see you tonight?" Gloss asked.

"Hold on," she said and jumped inside the vehicle, smelling its newness. She grabbed the bag of cosmetics and dug out the pencil eyeliner. Walking over to Gloss, she said, "Hold out your hand."

He did, but he was too far away for her to reach him. She opened the passenger side. A step popped out. She stepped up and leaned over the seat. She wrote her hotel number on his arm. "I'll be there shortly," she said. Hopping back down out of the truck, she shut the passenger door and stepped away.

Through the window, she watched his lips parted in a smile, his eyes at half-mast. She recognized the look, had seen a similar expression with other men in her bedroom. Her cold black heart thumped, inspired by her hormones. "Until then," he said and drove away.

"You've done it now," Gourdy thought.

"Yes, I have. I've found a way for us to survive."

Gourdy stayed silent.

Noticing that the Miata was a bona fide convertible, she perched in the front seat and rubbed her fingers down the leather surface. Smiling, she shut the door.

Amy's pink purse sat in the VW. She had only kept Amy's cell phone to lead Jennifer away from the flock. The Family would destroy the contents of Amy's wallet.

On the passenger side of the Miata rested a new bag with a red Native American dreamcatcher symbol woven on the side. She dumped the handbag out and inspected the contents —hand sanitizer in a scent called Groovy Love, a mood ring, a magnetic nose ring, a new cell phone, and a wallet. Quickly, she added the nose ring and put on the mood ring. It turned a vibrant blue. She opened the wallet. So her name was Caitlyn Hatcher. She had long, wavy black hair in the picture. It must have been from when the Family first collected her. She wasn't sure why, but she felt she had come full circle.

Fifty years free of the Family. Fifty years to find her way out. Without being constantly observed, she could decidedly be more of who she really was, and if she played this right, she would have one of Jormungant's army members in love with her forever—not just any Family member but Tom Johnson's son.

CHAPTER 21

MATT

"Smile," Matt's mom said. She had her straw hat on with a red ribbon tied around the middle, her hand resting on top to keep it from blowing off in the sea breeze.

"Mom. I was just stung by a jellyfish," Matt screamed, his left side partially numb and partially in sheer pain. When he studied his chest, he found tiny crystalline needles jutting out. "I need a doctor, not lessons on how to behave in public."

"No, dear. Even when we are in pain, we hide it. Others don't care, and they will use our weakness against us. Bottle up your grief, fear, and any negative thoughts by adding a smile. It works as a shield. Do it with me, my son; open your lips and give me one of those famous Davis smiles."

Angry, he tried to move, the sting at his wrist and ankles so sharp he opened his eyes. Gone were the white beaches and the blue sunny sky of a warm day. He sat in a dark, damp, cold room. The throbbing he felt in the dream was still present. His head leaned on his right shoulder with his arms behind him, his body sitting in an uncomfortable position. When he moved, his neck was stiff. It ached and combined with the pounding in his skull. The abruptness of the action made him want to vomit, but he fought the urge.

He jerked his limbs to try and escape the chair. Something cut into his wrists and ankles. He tried again. When that didn't work, he floundered around, pulling and tugging with every muscle that he'd earned from his time in the gym.

Who had tied him to the seat and why?

Panic set in, and he rocked and kicked to free himself.

A car passed by, temporarily lighting up the room. While he had light, he grabbed as many of its details as possible— shiny metal, high windows, white walls. That light also brought with it shooting pain. Sick, he jutted out over his body as much as possible, losing the contents of his stomach. Some landed on his shoulder, and the stench drowned out the room's chemical odor. He leaned his head back and breathed through his mouth.

Think! What happened? How did I get here?

A crying Amy had wanted to show him something in her car. Despite the bad vibes and the foreboding he sensed, he followed her to her vehicle. Several painters had gathered their things nearby. One of them, unusually tall, moved behind him. He didn't recognize the man then, but now, thinking back, that man reminded him of the bodybuilder from the library. Could they have been the same person? If so, why did he hit Matt? And why tie him up? Was this a prank, like a hazing? Did someone think his parents were wealthy and he had been kidnapped for ransom?

Matt struggled with his ties again. He had to free himself.

When he calmed down, he thought about Amy. *Was she safe? Did they hurt her?*

If they bashed him on top of the head, what had they done with her? She was standing right there, with only the car door between them.

Hopefully, she ran off and found the police. But there was more than one painter in the area collecting cans. He wasn't sure she got away. If she didn't, why wasn't she in here with him? Did they kill her?

In the distance, he heard a dog barking, the noise echoing off the walls. Was this a basement? If he shouted, would his capturers be aware he was awake and then torture or murder him? Regardless, he tried opening his mouth. His jaw ached.

Briefly, he remembered hitting the VW's door, which jarred his teeth, pushing them back toward his skull.

"Help," he screamed. "Help me!" Hearing his scratchy voice did something to him, generating an anxiety he hadn't felt before.

He wasn't sure how long he struggled and yelled to get free, but during that time, a fear grabbed his soul to the point he ignored the pain and fought against his restraints. His energy spent, he slouched as much as possible, relieving some of the burn from the tension in the straps that bound him.

Whoever captured him and tied him up had left him there to rot. If they hadn't, they would have investigated all the noise he made.

A car passed by, lighting up the room again. Beside him, a metal worktable glistened in the low gleam. He sat in a room of painted cinderblock walls and stained gray concrete floors. In the center, he noticed a drain. Under the reek of throw-up, there was a hint of a cleaning product, like the stuff used at hospitals, not the lemon-fresh scented spray sanitizing his parents' home.

The chilliness of the room helped his head, though his body shivered. He needed to move, run, escape. Again, he tried to stand. For all the energy he expended, all he accomplished was scooting the chair and cutting his skin. From the way the abrasions burned, the restraints were skinnier than rope.

Were they plastic ties?

A third car passed, which illuminated the outline of a window set high into the wall. This time, the light from the headlights ran along the top of the ceiling as gravel crunched underneath the wheels. It stopped somewhere close by. He debated the wisdom of screaming again. If they were his capturers, would they hurt him if they knew he was awake? But what if they were just parking and not involved in his kidnapping? Could they help him?

Did it matter? He had to get out of here... No, he would escape.

"Help," he said. "Help me!" he yelled.

The sound of a car door opening was followed closely by a second. Two people exited the vehicle.

"Help! Please, help!" he screamed, re-challenging the bindings.

He recognized the sound of a latch turning, then clicking. Someone used a key to unlock the door. His brain engaged him to stop screaming. How did they unlock the door if they weren't the people who had put him there?

Their footsteps grew louder until, with blinding, painful clarity, the light came on in the room.

He was in some kind of surgical room. A medical tray, resembling one of those foldable tables to set TV dinners on, held sharp, pointed, torture-type devices. He turned quickly away, hoping they wouldn't cause him any more pain. Instead of a decorative light fixture, a single bulb dangled from a chain. Whips and leashes hung from a coat rack. Restraints were built into one wall. He saw ways of breaking the truth out of him everywhere he looked.

A woman with the same fashion sense as Lauren, everything black from hair to shoes except for her pale, ashen skin, stood with her hand on the switch. In the doorway positioned beside her was a tall, dark-haired man with olive-toned skin and dark-brown eyes.

Fear heightened his senses, and Matt remembered the man was one of the painters.

Smile, he heard his mom say. So he gave them his bright, toothy, all-American grin that was like the one he witnessed in all the toothpaste commercials. "What do you want from me? Are you after my parents' money?"

They said nothing. The man walked with confidence to the torture tray. He picked up a syringe with one hand and pulled a small white labeled bottle out of his coat pocket with the other.

"What are you doing?" Matt asked the man. But Matt understood what happened next. He'd seen enough horror movies. The man stuck the needle into the bottle, turning it over. He filled the syringe with something clear.

"Come on, Matt, do you honestly think we're after money?" the woman said.

"What did you do with Amy?" Matt demanded.

"I was Amy," the woman said. Her voice had a similar pitch to Amy's, but it was harsher somehow. The room still spun, and he squinted to make out her facial details. Amy's blue eyes, her tiny, freckled button nose, her round face—it was Amy!

"Amy? What have you done? And why? This is, this is..."

"Crazy?" she finished. The man circled him, the medical needle in his hand. Something oozed from the tip—just like in a horror movie.

As useless as it proved earlier, out of desperation, he struggled against the restraints, wanting to shove the man away.

Amy sighed. "You know one thing I really hated about you?"

He didn't answer, his eyes on the sharp object in the man's hand.

"No. I guess you don't."

Matt glanced away from the needle back to Amy. She scrunched her nose, squinting.

She continued. "I'll tell you anyway. You believe everything that happens is about you." She flung her hands around her as she talked. "A party at the Pi house... That was so someone could take your poker title away. A girl smiled at you... That was because she found you attractive. A teacher handed out a pop quiz... They were out to test your knowledge. No one else's in the class, just Matt Davis's. It got so freaking old."

As she talked, the man disappeared behind him.

"Are you watching my lips?" She pointed to her mouth with her long, black, manicured fingernail. He said nothing. "This. Is. Not. About. You." A wicked grin graced her lips, something Amy never did. She brought her fist up in the air while looking at the guy beyond him.

The needle slid into his neck with a sharp sting, followed by heat as the chemical spilled into his blood system. He tasted copper or something metallic. "If this isn't about me, then why have you captured me?" he asked.

She laughed. "You'll think it's crazy."

"I already think you're crazy," he protested.

"Fine. Not that it will do you any good. This is all about Jennifer."

Jennifer! Why would anyone want to hurt Jennifer? Boring and innocent were things he loved, but there was nothing special about her.

She walked to the wall behind her, where all the whips and chains were lined up. Grabbing a hand whip, like the kind used by equestrians, she smacked it against her hand. "I know what you're thinking. Straight-A Jennifer is dull, doesn't have any secrets. Why would an organization want someone so pure?" She hit her leg with the whip. "Stings nicely," she said to the man. Turning back to Matt, she said, "But you're wrong. She's nothing like what you think." She moved to the door, standing there. "I intentionally lied to you to end your romantic relationship with her. Not so I could have you, like I would ever want you." She tilted her head to stare down at him. "They ordered Johan to kidnap Jennifer, and he failed." She tapped the metal table with long black fingernails, making a *dong* noise that echoed off the cinderblock wall. "They sent me to watch Jennifer, and now my plan is to capture her."

He knew things from his love of B horror and all the many superhero movies—if the bad guy told you their plans, they planned to kill you. Whatever was going on, they didn't intend to let Matt live.

He couldn't fight the tiredness that washed over his limbs just then.

The man finished, tossing the needle into the trash can, and rejoined Amy.

"Hopefully, she cares enough about you to save your life." But Matt sensed the truth. He'd wake up again, or Amy would have said goodbye. Tomorrow, he would hurt more than he did now. And, though Jennifer did care for him enough to sacrifice herself for him, Amy would kill him anyway.

As Matt dozed off again, he smiled. He wasn't dead yet, so he still had hope that he would escape.

CHAPTER 22

JENNIFER

TOO MUCH, TOO SOON.

Parking behind her grandfather's dark gray Cadillac with its Florida tags, the sun caught the emerald engagement ring. Her stomach flipped, and she wasn't sure if excitement or dread that led to her unsettled nerves.

"My grandparents are here," she announced to Petr.

"We knew they would be." He paused. "Let me see if I can remember. Stewart is your dad's father. He likes history, base-ball, golf, and, like your father, was an architect," Petr recalled from their earlier conversation.

"And the Grands?" she asked.

"Your mother's mother and grandmother. Both are from Cherryville. Well, your great-grandmother is from Kentucky, but that secret just came out and varies from what's listed on her birth certificate. They both kept house."

"Stay-at-home-moms, yes. Try to keep with modern terms," she answered.

What would they make of her bringing home a college professor? The fiancé part was bad enough. "Wait, Petr, before we get out, even though Randy's met you, he saw you when…" She stared at her mate, wearing a tight-ribbed black sweater and jeans. She doubted Randy would make the connection. Petr looked different than he had that night at the restaurant, and Randy was fifteen. He'd likely not paid attention or at least not to Petr.

"Don't be too worried if he recognizes me. He'll have to re-meet me, regardless. After all, I'm going to be his brother-in-law."

She swallowed. "Right."

She hurried around the car and moved to his side. Petr had twisted and used his left hand to open the door, but she didn't want him straining his hurt shoulder more than necessary. "Let me help you out," she said, offering him her hand. He took it, clumsily getting out.

Standing, he faced her, close to her nose. They were about the same height, so losing herself in his eyes was easy. Especially when she desired to escape. With his good hand, he rubbed the side of her face. "Ready?" he asked.

"Like an unarmed gladiator preparing to face a den of hungry lions," she said. Her dreams were taking place in Athens at the end of the Byzantine Empire. Though they didn't have gladiators since they preferred chariot races, it was a common phrase to hear her ancestors say.

A corner of his mouth turned up. "Let's go, Meelaya." He grabbed her hand, leading her to the door.

She debated knocking but pulled out her key to open the door. Inside, she retook her mate's left hand. Warm tingles tried to calm her nerves.

To her left, the stairs jutted upward. To her right, her family had moved all the furniture. The long couch, the armchair, and the loveseat faced the door and blocked the TV. Her family—parents, brother, and her grandparents— occupied most of the available seating. The loveseat was piled high with suitcases. Meaning they were being directed to sit in the two empty folding metal chairs that faced where her parents were sitting, like an intervention or an interrogation.

Sighing, she breathed out—the placement of the seating arrangement had been made on purpose, readying for the trial of her and Petr's relationship.

Leaning over, she whispered in Dragon, "Make that two dozen hungry lions."

"It doesn't matter, my love," he replied in Dragon.

Glancing at their faces, she saw only two that looked friendly, the Grands. Her brother held a smirk: her father and mother, pure hostility. And Grandfather stood near the window, expressionless.

She fought to keep her stomach inside her body.

It felt like forever as the two of them, holding hands, watched her relatives as they studied them. She knew she should introduce him, but like an opossum facing danger, she couldn't budge.

Her father broke the standoff, though he didn't smile as he stretched out his hand to Petr, so she didn't relax. "I'm Jacob Wright," he said.

Petr touched his wound apologetically, arm still resting in a sling. "Sorry, injury." Releasing Jennifer's hand, he offered his left instead. "Nick Smith," Petr said.

Typically, her dad would have insisted on introducing the guest to each individual in the room by having the family member move to where the newcomer waited. Uncharacteristically, Jennifer's dad pointed them out, starting with Jennifer's grandfather. "My father, Stewart Wright." Beside him, Randy casually rested in the armchair. "My son, Randy." Randy nodded, his blond hair bouncing, a smirk on his face. Next, he directed his attention to the couch where Jennifer's grandmother and great-grandmother sat. "My mother-in-law, Josephine Lee."

"Hello." Josephine waved and smiled. Jennifer made a note to thank her grandmother for the first warm welcome.

Her father continued. "Beside her is Josephine's mother, MaryAnn English." At the very end, her mother stood, approaching them. Her father added, "And this is Jennifer's mother, Pauline."

"How do you do?" MaryAnn grinned with a mischievous twinkle in her eye.

Gratefully sighing, Jennifer knew she could count on the Grands' support no matter what. If the Grands accepted him everyone would approve in time.

"Jennifer, is this the one from your dream, dear?" MaryAnn asked while squinting.

The dream? Then she remembered telling both Grands about Petr at Thanksgiving, how when she slept, she saw him lead Spring down the aisle. "Yes. You remember about the prince?"

"Yes, dear, I remember," MaryAnn said as she used her hands to push herself off the couch and stand. As she approached Petr, she continued. "After you had your vision…" She stared Petr up and down, and Petr uncomfortably shifted. "You said you met him a few days later at a restaurant." Beside Jennifer's father, she leaned in and cupped her mouth like she was sharing a secret with Jennifer, even though everyone could hear her. "You were right. He is a handsome man."

Glancing at Petr, Jennifer remembered how he looked when he walked Spring to marry Che-non, like he had stepped out of a historical romance. He inspected her as well, then smiled.

"Oh," Josephine commented, her eyes enlarged and voice energized. "Help me up, Randy." Before Randy could get out of the armchair, Josephine maneuvered to her mother's side. "The dream about the man…" She trailed off. "Oh dear, he does look like a fairytale prince."

"Surprised you told them," he said in a low voice close to her ear.

"It was just odd because I dreamed of you right before I met you," Jennifer whispered.

"Well, we told you, Pauline, dear. Your daughter is…" Josephine scrunched up her features. "What's the word—"

"Clairvoyant." MaryAnn finished. "Jennifer seems to have a gift. She also dreamed of my biological father. It's nice to meet you, Prince Nick, and I happen to believe in fate, so welcome to the family."

"Why am I always the last to find out about these things? I was the last to find out about my daughter's current boyfriend, that my grandfather wasn't my grandfather, and now…" her mother said, her expression the same as when Jennifer shattered one of her fine china pieces. "I was the last to know about Matt too."

Mom paused awkwardly, glancing between Jennifer and Petr. Jennifer understood her mother's pause was from a social misstep. Mentioning Jennifer's ex-boyfriend to her fiancé broke an unspoken taboo or rule. Mom recovered and said, "And I'm the last to know about you, Nick."

With a toothy grin, Mom finally greeted him with a friendly hug. "Nick, I'm Pauline."

When Mom leaned away, Petr returned the warmth and said, "Oh, so you're the one my bride gets her beauty from." He glanced at Jennifer.

Patting him on the back, Josephine said, "Welcome to the family."

Her grandfather stayed by the window but smiled.

"Come and sit," Mom said, grabbing Petr's arm and leading him to one of the metal chairs. "I, for one, would like to know why you're rushing to get engaged."

Everyone who was standing moved back to their seats, while ushering Petr and Jennifer to the metal chairs. They had welcoming smiles on their faces. She glared at the stack of suitcases on the comfortable sofa. Message received. They accepted Nick Smith on the surface, but this battle was far from over.

Right after he sat, Petr said, "I have a job offer in China."

He turned toward Jennifer and said, "I can't imagine my life without your daughter."

"Do you plan on marrying her before you leave?" Dad asked.

"I plan to marry her as soon as possible," Petr answered. "I don't want to—"

"Disrespect her," Grandfather suggested.

Petr studied Grandfather. "Exactly."

"We don't know you," Dad said, shaking his head. "And she hasn't finished college."

"I, for one, would rather the two of you live together than for Jennifer to marry you," Mom said.

"What?" Randy and Jennifer said at the same time. Randy sat up straighter.

"Alright," Petr agreed.

"What?" Jennifer turned to face Petr and crossed her arms.

"My love. We will get married at Dernogard, but we can have a wedding later for your family," he said to her in Dragon. "It's perfect." She must not have seemed convinced. "Having sex is more binding for us anyway, whether or not your family knows it," he continued in Dragon.

She sighed and faced her family.

"When did you start talking clickety clap? You sound like those guys in the bar in that movie—" Randy said.

"Not now, Randy," Mom chided.

Dad crossed his arms. "You've agreed too fast. Did you deflower my daughter?"

Randy laughed. "Or Matt did," Randy said under his breath.

"What?" Jennifer said, glaring between Dad and Randy.

"No," Petr said.

"Not yet," Randy whispered.

All eyes focused on Randy. "It's not like it won't happen if it hasn't happened yet. No one waits until marriage anymore."

"Precisely, Jacob," Mom pleaded with Dad. "We can't expect our daughter to live by our generation's beliefs. Our children won't wait until marriage like we did."

Jennifer raised her eyebrows while staring at her mother; she knew her parents had had sex before marriage. She'd dreamed of her mother's life. What self-righteous banter was her mom on, claiming she and dad never had premarital sex?

Dad frowned at Mom. "Pauline…" He paused, then turned toward Petr. "Fine. I'd rather her know for sure if she wants to marry you than pay for a horrible divorce. Why can't she wait until after she finishes college?"

"I can't wait that long, Dad," she said. Facing Petr, she added, "I'll go where he goes. Isn't that what a spouse does? They live together?"

"I want you to finish school. If you drop out, you'll have to pay for college yourself when you decide to go back," Dad said.

She wanted to remind him that her scholarship paid for everything already. "Fine." She gripped the bottom of the metal chair.

"When she's ready to go back to college, I'll pay for it," Petr said, taking her hand in his. Her father opened his mouth and leaned forward like he was about to say something. Petr spoke first and added, "I'll even put it on paper that should she wish to leave me, I will still pay for her to go to college. I'll have my lawyer set up the legal documentation and create a trust fund for her with your name on it," Petr said.

"And who said chivalry is dead?" MaryAnn said, then smiled.

"Okay, now that that's settled, what happened to your arm?" Randy asked, interjecting into the conversation.

"Shoulder injury, not arm. I went camping with Jennifer—"

"Jennifer Louisa Wright! You went camping after what

happened last time?" Mom fussed, giving her the *don't touch the cookies* eyes.

"I did, and I like camping." She peered around the room, then looked at the clock. Their plane would be leaving in five more hours. She swallowed.

"You're running out of time, Jennifer. Now that your parents have given you permission to live in sin, you should get your passport," Barry told her.

"Right." She glanced at Mom. "I'm sure you're eager to get on the road to Kentucky, and well, we should be going soon." She glanced at all the friendly faces and felt confident that Petr could handle her relatives now that all the important decisions had been made, if not accepted. She stood. "I'll grab my passport, and then we'll be heading out," she announced to her family.

"So, you teach college?" Grandfather asked Petr, changing the subject. "History, by chance?"

"Biology and anthropology," Petr answered.

At the stairs, she heard her dad ask, "How much education have you had? You look too young to have a doctorate."

She stopped listening when she reached the second floor. The scent of the house she grew up in had changed to fresh paint and burned wood from a vanilla carpet cleaner. There were hardwood floors instead of carpet. The walls were painted with a fresh eggshell white. The ceiling's popcorn paint was missing and buffed to a flat surface. All the pictures that once lined the hall had vanished.

"Mom and Dad have been busy," Jennifer thought to Barry. It made her sad to think that the next time she came home, more things would change. Would Randy be married, maybe a father? Would the Grands still be alive?

Suddenly, a high-pitched screech that reminded her of a scream, an airplane landing, or a bomb going off forced her to cover her ears. She lost control of the dragon, shifting to a demon-dragon girl. Her hair became flames, her skin covered in scales, her legs thick as tree trunks with sharp, nailed talons. All her clothes burned in the heat wave's blast.

The ringing disappeared, and she could hear again. Something or someone stood behind her. When she turned, she found her brother. Not a second later, the horrible shrieking returned. The pain at the base of her skull was so intense that she closed her eyes.

As rapidly as it came, it vanished. When she dared to look, in the spot Randy had occupied was a four-legged dark blue dragon, who looked like the kind drawn in the Chinese Zodiac, not like a wyvern at all. On the sides of his body, he had bright yellow stripes, with fins by the ears.

Randy whipped his tail, and the newly painted wall that joined to his bedroom caved in.

"Jennifer," Petr shouted, followed by the thumping of his feet on the stairs.

"What's going on?" Dad said, terror lacing his voice.

She blocked out the panicked familiar voices from the first floor as they came closer and focused on Randy. Despite every instinct telling her to stay a dragon, she forced herself to turn into her human form, ignoring that she stood there naked. Still, she used caution and stayed a safe distance away from her brother.

Over Randy's shoulder, at the top of the stairs, she saw Petr staring in shock.

Taking control of the situation, she whispered as calmly as she could, "I got this, Petr. Please go back downstairs and keep my parents calm. They can't come up here."

Randy's giant head snapped toward Petr.

"No, Randy," she yelled and clapped her hands. Like a snake, his snout trained on her. He took a step forward. In his dark green lizard irises, she saw her reflection. She waited to move until after Petr disappeared down the steps.

"Randy, it's me, your sister. I know this is hard to believe, but we're dragons. Calm down, and you'll turn back into a human. Don't worry about how tired you are. It's perfectly normal, and it's going to be okay."

Approaching him slowly and with caution, she controlled her breathing until she stood close enough to rest her hand on his nose. "Love you, brother," she said, patting his scales.

When she was a dragon, she thought her scales felt warm. Randy felt wet, almost slimy like a slug, but when she pulled her hand away, it was dry and not sticky.

He licked her face, his tongue like a cat's, reminiscent of sandpaper. Then he rested his head on her shoulder. When his head went slack, and all its weight was placed on her back, she lowered him to the ground. He'd lost his battle to the dragon transformation and snored while he slept.

He didn't instantly change back as she expected, which allowed her to study him. With his dark-blue scales that turned all white on his belly, he differed from her in both color and form. In some locations, like around his eyes and on his sides, he sported yellow stripes, like a sports car. As a dragon, like as a human, he was handsome.

Guess I'm not alone anymore, she thought, unsure how to feel, and whether it should excite or scare her. How would Randy like being a dragon? How would it impact his schooling?

She didn't think about it long because of the grumbling on the first floor. "He's my son," Mom yelled.

Quickly, she grabbed a robe from her room, only briefly noticing the hardwood floors stopped at the threshold. She covered herself as she walked, carefully stepping over her brother and the debris from the collapsed wall. She took the stairs two at a time.

Petr had barricaded the staircase. Dad's face was red like a chili pepper, his fists at his sides, preparing to hit her mate. The rest of her family stood close by and looked almost as angry.

"Stop," Jennifer said.

"We need to tell them the truth," Petr said calmly without looking away from her father.

"What truth?!" Mom demanded. "All I know is Nick won't let me go upstairs!"

"Shh, Mom, Randy is asleep. Trust me, you don't want to wake him."

"What do you mean, we don't want to wake him?" Dad said.

Holding her hand palm down, she said, "Stay calm, and I'll explain everything. No screaming, okay? The truth is hard to understand. Petr, will my family all turn to dragons if I show them?"

"Who's Petr?" Mom demanded.

"Dragons?" Grandfather asked.

Petr shrugged. She could see the concern on his face and wasn't sure if she also recognized fear. Perhaps he thought the room was about to be filled with dragons.

"Barry, do you know?"

"No. I only know what you know. And I'm surprised at this one. Just putting one and one together. That first sound had to be someone shifting to a dragon. That means there's another human dragon close by in addition to Randy."

Swallowing, she begged, "Please stay calm, okay?" Jennifer made eye contact with each family member before showing them. *"Here goes nothing, Barry."* Jennifer turned her skin into red scales and threw off her robe. Moving forward, her family backed away, retreating to the walls. When she had enough space, she allowed her body to turn into her wyvern form.

Mom sat down. Dad and Grandfather had the same shocked looks on their faces. Josephine looked impressed, and MaryAnn said, "I knew we were special. I just knew it!"

CHAPTER 23

MATT

THE DRUGS WORE OFF, AND WITH EXCRUCIATING PAIN, MATT became conscious. Sunlight entered through the small window above the cabinets to his left. He was alone in a dusty, cold, and damp medical room with the scent of chemicals and his vomit.

He rolled his neck, trying to work out the kinks. *Count your blessings*, he encouraged himself in his mom's voice. *Things could be worse. After all, I'm still alive, and nothing is broken.*

Though if he didn't escape, he would be murdered. *Think, Matt Davis, think.*

Surveying the area around him, his eyes landed on the scalpel hanging off the edge of the medical tray. He might cut his fingers if he retrieved it, but if he could get it if he maneuvered the chair to right below, all he had to do was hop. Stitches were better than death any day.

With the way his hands were tied to the metal frame, the only thing he could reach was the lip of the seat. He grabbed it and pushed up with the balls of his feet.

He moved. It wasn't much, but it was toward the sharp,

pointy object. He tried again and doubled the distance from one to two inches. *Only two feet to go! I will do this!*

The echo of a door opening in another room caused him to freeze. Footsteps of at least two people headed in his direction. Grinding his teeth, his fingers dug into the underside of the chair. If only he could defend himself, then they would be sorry.

"Are you awake?" a masculine voice asked as they approached the room.

"Surely he's awake by now," another male said.

"Caitlyn wouldn't mind if we had a little fun, would she? After all, she had fun with Gloss last night."

"Wait, are you talking sexually?" the second male asked.

"Maybe," the first responded.

The door opened, and two men walked into the room. He recognized the tall one from the library and as one of the painters. Today, the man wore a plaid shirt that reminded Matt of a lumberjack. He didn't recognize the second man. This man stuck out; he was considerably shorter, with dark blond hair, and wore a blue golf polo tucked into jeans. He had an athletic build, like a long-distance runner.

Both men had non-lethal items that could be used as weapons. The lumberjack sported a baseball bat that he continually banged against his hand. The other, the distance runner, wielded a belt and made smacking noises with it.

"I'm not gay, man," the runner clarified.

"I'm not either," the lumberjack said, circling Matt.

"But you said... Well, what you said made me think you liked guys and all." The runner came to stand in front of Matt.

Behind him, the lumberjack answered, "No, I just like the fear. And he reeks of fear. Smell it?" He took a deep breath, sending chills up Matt's spine as he prepared to be swatted.

"I can see why you might consider him appealing. Sexually, that is. He is a looker." The runner smacked Matt's cheek with the belt. "Maybe we make him look uglier?"

"I like your idea." The lumberjack hit the baseball bat on the ground as if in answer. "Besides, I'm sure Father will want him dead when we have that girl, Jennifer."

His head already pounded, and the bat, smacking his side, jerked his neck sideways. A curse word slipped out as it felt like a thousand small fractures coated the impact site, but he stayed awake. Like a noise from a lion, a loud roar reverberated through his body. *"Enough!"* it screamed.

When Matt was ten, he and a friend had dared each other to hold their breath underwater for as long as possible. The winner would receive a pack of grape bubble gum. He had stationed himself at the pool's ladder and forced himself to stay under until he absolutely couldn't stand it. His lungs burned. He even saw spots. When he came up for air, he gulped in short, voluminous breaths. With his lungs filling up and knowing the victory gum belonged to him, a sense of elation filled him. He knew he could do anything.

A similar experience of gasping for air after holding it for so long overcame him now. He inhaled as the room shrank. No longer feeling any pain, his head smacked the ceiling. His mouth and nose extended, becoming a blue-green snout. Matt kept all five fingers on each hand, but they were thicker, colored like his nose, with sharp fingernails on the ends. His clothes shredded to pieces as the chair crumpled under his body.

The lumberjack cursed, and a sweet aroma, like brown-sugar barbeque rub, filled the room. "He's a dragon!"

"Remember Dragon 101? If we kill him, we can divide his heart," the runner answered, but fear came from him as well, and it tasted... edible.

Without thinking, he bit at the lumberjack, and the man disappeared inside his long snout, deep in his mouth, with only his legs and feet dangling out. The man's head twisted against his tongue. In response, Matt dug his teeth deeper into his flesh until he snapped the man in half.

True to the nickname Matt had given him, the runner bolted for the door. As Matt released the top part of the first man, he used his enormous tail to stab through the second man's chest and out the crest of his head. The runner died instantly.

Exhausted and with the danger over for now, he settled back down on the blood-soaked floor and fell asleep. As he drifted off, he heard another loud clang from somewhere close by.

༄

Matt dreamed of Professor Nick Smith at different times and places.

Professor Smith acted like a father to him and a little girl named Mesyats. He called him Uncle Petr. Uncle Petr gave him soup, while in the distance, a herd of gray mammoths stomped and ate from trees.

Next, Matt became a girl in Germany.

Peter Rosenberg, aka Professor Smith, was a neighbor who always had candy treats.

In a small village, a farmer visited a store owned by a crazy Russian, Dr. Nicolas Smirnov.

The dream continued, revealing image after image of the same person with a different name. He was always around somewhere, waiting.

"Find Petr! He will protect you!" a man shouted.

Lying in a pool of congealed blood, his hands stuck to the ground as he sat up. Frantically, he waved them, trying to remove the yuck, but the stuff stayed stuck to his fingers. The odor from disemboweled corpses caused his stomach to twist, and he dry heaved.

A phantom breeze made him realize he was naked. He needed clothes.

The lumberjack's clothing would fit. That is, if his dragon teeth hadn't punctured holes in the pants. Finding the man's bottom half, he inspected the material for any damage. The torso had snapped above the jeans, leaving them whole, and the crooked man's corpse still wore shoes.

Something to wear—check.

But... tennis shoes? Matt thought, trying not to think about what he was doing. *I would have worn cowboy boots with that plaid shirt, but I'm glad he didn't. It would have been hard to get them off.* Matt still struggled to pull off the man's footwear, flinging them through the air.

Without the top half, the bottom rotated, jerked, and made stinky fart noises; but eventually, he removed the jeans. He held his breath as he put the pants on, one leg at a time. The denim was a little too big, but not as much as he thought it would be. The lumberjack's height must have been in his waist and not his legs.

Done, Matt moved in the stiff jeans, searching for where the shoes landed after he tossed them. He detached his mind from the carnage.

Later, much later, Matt thought, *I will need therapy.*

Under one of the metal tables, the right shoe stuck upside down in a layer of guts. He glanced away as he retrieved it. He located the other near a door that he hadn't been able to see earlier because of the restraints. On his way, he slipped slightly on something, regained his footing, and refused to look down to see what it had been. Obtaining the sneaker, he noticed the door had a small window that sunlight poured through.

Cradling the footwear, he pushed open the door. The next room appeared more long than wide. On the right sat empty metal cages stacked on top of each other. On the left were cabinets and an oversized sink. A little further on the left was a tiled shower with no curtains. Placing the shoes near the shower drain, he wildly searched the cabinets, hunting for cleaning products. He didn't even find a bar of soap. As he turned the shower knob to the left, he prayed the building's water was still on. Clear liquid poured through the opening. Holding his hand under the stream, he waited a few seconds for the water to warm up.

Deciding he couldn't wait, he stepped into the frigid stream. He used the detachable spigot to hose off as much gunk as possible. He stood there, ignoring the cold, watching the water change slowly from bright red to clear.

After he stopped the flow, he slid his feet into the footwear. Orange-tinted liquid gushed out of the holes in the shoe's breathable material, and he swallowed his breath. The shoes were smaller on him than the jeans, and his toes curled at the tips. They would have to do.

A neon exit sign hung over a door at the end of the hall-like room. He approached cautiously, peering out the window while putting his hand on the knob.

Outside, the world went on as usual. He saw a road full of cars going in both directions under an overcast sky. After saying a silent prayer that his captors neither alarmed nor monitored the escape path, and none of the goons waited for him, he opened the exit, surprised to hear the sounds of the outdoors and not an alarm.

A cool breeze greeted him, and he grabbed his chest to maintain some warmth. He searched the empty back lot and observed some drivers gawking at his lack of a shirt in winter, but no one stopped, nor did he flag anyone down. Two dead men waited inside the building behind him, and he wasn't sure how to explain that. If he got help, someone might find the carnage and question him.

He walked around the side of the building to the front. A white four-door sedan sat near the entrance. Hoping the vehicle belonged to the criminals, he made his way to the car and tried the handle. The door opened, and he scented a mango cleaner. He couldn't help it; he stared in both directions before sitting in the seat, even though he thought it made him look guilty. Searching the console, he found the key fob in a cup holder. He pushed the button, and the car started.

"Good thugs," he said, patting the steering wheel. He checked all the indicators on the dashboard, pleasantly surprised to find a full gas tank. He set the heat on high, despite only cold air blowing out. It would warm eventually.

At first, Matt drove in large loops, searching for anything that appeared familiar. Finally, he recognized a gas station, and he turned right. Driving down the road, he glanced in his rearview mirror for anyone who might tail him. The path stayed clear. Matt considered himself a closet nerd and had proved it by spending hours watching horror and sci-fi movies. From those theatrical depictions, he ascertained there could be a tracking device on the vehicle.

Imagining men in a white van trailing his movements, he found Saint Maria's Eternal Episcopal Church and parked across the street in its overflow parking. A sign on the post indicated this area lacked video surveillance, so you parked at your own risk. He thanked his friend Tony, who had told him about his car being stolen from this lot last Sunday and how there was no recorded evidence of the criminal act.

Paranoid that someone would link his fingerprints to the dead men's vehicle, he searched for anything he could use to smudge or clean the interior. He found a set of disinfectant wipes in the glove compartment. Grabbing a few, he wiped everything down, including the sanitizer container.

The cold smacked into him as he exited the confines of the car. He ignored how chill bumps formed on his arms as he threw the key into the vehicle and left it unlocked. With any luck, someone would steal the sedan. He discarded the wipes in a nearby trashcan.

Dr. Smith's house sat in a newer neighborhood a couple of

miles from the church. Because he'd had to see that the love of his life had left him for Dr. Smith, he'd driven by the house early Friday morning before the stores opened. He was never more thankful for his curious ways as he jogged, still wet, toward the house. He wondered how odd he must look running down a busy street in soaked jeans and no shirt, but he ignored the honks and waves and pretended to be on a casual jog.

With the green road sign in view, Matt's energy ran out, and his limbs grew wobbly like jelly. He walked the last few steps with his hands on his hips.

When he had driven by the home, he saw two black sedans parked in the driveway, and Jennifer's new car parked parallel to the sidewalk. Now, only a black sedan was parked in the driveway.

He moved faster when he stepped onto Dr. Smith's land as some of his energy returned. Instead of going to the front door, he headed to the back of the house, hoping there was a second way in, like most homes. True enough, once he passed the corner, a small concrete porch with two tall dumpsters greeted him. The back door had a window. He knocked and screamed, "Jennifer! Petr!" When no one came, he searched the area. Finding a substantial rock, he busted out the window. Glass shattered everywhere.

In case the professor owned camera surveillance, he said into the surrounding air, "You'll have to forgive me. I was told to find you." He reached through the pane and opened the door without cutting his hand.

Inside, different scents surrounded him, some of which seemed familiar. One odor, though, a perfume really, caused him to drool. He wanted the person who wore that fantastic, fresh lavender scent. He headed in the fragrance's direction. It intensified as he went deeper into the home. The sight of the refrigerator redirected him to search first for food. Opening the door, he found the perfect thing for a college student:

pizza. He flung the boxes out, and they landed on the floor with a thud. He didn't bother with plates, pilling all the slices into one box to use it as a dish.

After eating half a person, I should be full, he thought for a second before he forced the thought away. He would worry about his soul another day.

Though hungry, he wasn't a barbarian. He took his mile-high meal to the table and sat. As he packed food into his mouth, he noticed a folder with his name on it. He glanced at the documents inside and smiled at his senior school picture of him dressed in his football uniform. Underneath the image, someone had drawn several symbols in red. He flipped the page and identified his genealogy tree. He disregarded that because exhaustion overcame him as his body digested the food.

Leaving everything on the counter, he followed the peaceful, erotic scent toward its source and found a bedroom. The perfume intertwined with the familiar musk of Uncle Petr. But, for now, he ignored that. He tore off the stinky clothes, dropped them in a pile on the floor, and climbed into bed.

As he drifted to sleep, he wondered if he had left the refrigerator door open.

CHAPTER 24

JENNIFER

If Jennifer had ever wondered how her family would react, well, she would have been completely wrong about everyone's response but her mother's. Mom sat on the couch, head between her legs, breathing in and out. Dad had his hand on her back.

"Mom, I'm still Jennifer," she said in her demonic voice.

Mom broke out crying, mumbling under her breath.

"That's enough," MaryAnn said, glancing at Jennifer and Mom. "Pauline, grow up! I'm so tired of all your worrying. After your dad died, you've tried to control everything. It's eating you away. You can't control the weather, and you can't control that your daughter is a magnificent creature." She placed her hands on her hips and moved in front of Jennifer's parents, blocking her view. "And now you have two children who are also magnificent creatures. Dry your tears and deal."

Jennifer couldn't see her father's expression, but Grandfather's stance shifted. "Son, Pauline is strong enough to handle this."

"Remember what the good book says. God won't give you more than you can handle," Josephine said to Jennifer's parents.

Who would have thought that the oldest in her family would be the most accepting? Shouldn't it have been the other way around?

As MaryAnn moved back to Josephine, Jennifer watched as Mom sniffed and wiped her nose on her oversized shirt. All eyes were on her as she leisurely sat back up.

Petr, standing beside Jennifer, leaned over. "I'll be back in a second." He looked at his wristwatch, then ran his hand through his hair. "Our plane leaves soon. I'm going to cancel our plane tickets. Then I'll call Che-non and let Che-non and Kamar know what's happening," he whispered in Dragon.

"Okay," she answered, and he stepped outside.

"What language is that?" Grandfather asked. "It almost sounds like birds, except when he said airplane."

"I call it Dragon, but I don't know that it has an official name. It's spoken in Dernogard, the city of dragons," she said, moving from the staircase to the metal chairs. "If you all sit, I'll tell you what happened." She glanced at Mom. "Even the stuff you aren't going to like."

Before beginning, Jennifer waited until everyone in her family found seats. The Grands made their own, shoving suit-cases off the loveseat. Even Grandfather, a firm believer in standing, sat.

"How do you know this isn't a virus?" Mom asked, her voice breaking as if she was fighting another round of tears.

"Because I remember, Mom. I remember our ancestors, their lives, their languages, their skills. Viruses don't store memories from other people."

MaryAnn huffed and pointed. "And she's sitting there all red and scaley. Last I checked, viruses didn't change your species."

No one said anything else, so she continued. "It started in the fall when I went camping with Matt." She glanced at Mom. She hadn't admitted this to her parents because they were so opposed to drinking, but she needed them to know the whole truth. "I was drunk."

Her mother covered her mouth. Jennifer imagined Mom biting her tongue to keep from making a negative comment. Dad patted Mom on the shoulder.

She continued. "I had to use the restroom. But I forgot the flashlight and walked into a bear—"

"A bear? Jennifer Louisa Wright, how could you do something so foolish?" Mom demanded; her brow wrinkled while her eyebrows drew together.

"I bet that scared you," MaryAnn said.

"Yes, very scary. And, well, if it makes you feel better, I killed the bear."

"No, it doesn't make me feel better," Mom said, her voice clipped.

"Sorry, Mom, but that's the way this started. That's when I turned into a dragon for the first time." She stood from the chair, collected her white robe, and threw it around her. She metamorphosized into a human.

"Remarkable," Grandfather said.

Glancing swiftly at him, she smiled and sat back down. "It really is. It feels… interesting to turn into a dragon. Like the pressure is so much, then poof, it's gone. I'm sure it creates dopa—"

"Lecture us another day on the anatomy of turning into a dragon. Go on, Jennifer," Dad demanded.

"Right." Jennifer nodded. "After I turned, I got tired." She glanced behind her at the staircase. Somewhere upstairs, her brother was sleeping, having dreams similar to hers. "I dreamed of Petr."

"That's the second time you've mentioned someone named Petr. Who is he?" Mom asked, throwing her hands up.

The front door opened, and Petr walked in. "I am. My name is Petr, no last name. They didn't have them when I was born."

"Wait," Grandfather said as Petr sat in the other metal chair. "Are you saying you're more than thousands of years old? I mean, from my studies, surnames started in the fourth century."

"Yes," Petr said, taking her hand in his.

Mom's eyes followed his movements and focused on their joined fingers. "And you want to marry my daughter?" Mom asked.

"It's impossible for anyone to be that old," Grandfather said. He stared at the ceiling, his eyes darting back and forth in thought.

"Yes, I want to marry your daughter," Petr answered.

"What's impossible changed when I turned into a dragon for the first time," Jennifer said. She glanced at Petr. "Grandfather, let me finish my story, and then you can ask Petr all the questions you would like."

Grandfather crossed his arms. "Finish your story."

"I fell asleep right after I transformed for the first time. I dreamed of Petr." She faced Petr, amazed he was hers. "I fell in love with him before I knew he was a real person," she admitted, not only to falling for him but the concept of instant love. It obviously existed for some people.

He squeezed her hand.

"That's my story simplified. Be back in a second. Mom, are you coming? I want to check on Randy."

"Yes," she said, wiping her eyes as she got to her feet.

"Good. Petr can answer your questions while I'm gone. He knows more of the dragon world than I do." She untangled their fingers and stood from the chair.

"We think it takes fear to cause the transformation. I'm not sure what scared Randy—" Petr said.

"I do," Jennifer interjected, stopping on the stairs. "I turned into a dragon, but not by choice. I heard someone else turn into a dragon. I heard an awakening."

He nodded, but that brought up other questions. Would she change into a dragon every time there was an awakening?

She'd have to save her questions for later because none of that mattered right then. She pushed upward to the landing and the still form of her sleeping brother.

"An awakening is what we call it when someone born human becomes a dragon," Petr explained from the first floor.

She stopped listening. A naked Randy lay on his side in the fetal position. His skin was slightly blue, and his face sported a snout, but the rest of him was human. Passing him, she entered his bedroom and pulled the comforter and pillow from the bed.

When she returned, her mother sat beside Randy, brushing his hair with steady fingers. If her mother cared that her son destroyed a freshly painted wall and possibly made claw prints on the wood floor, she didn't show it. Gently, she pushed the pillow under his head after covering him up.

"He has three choices, too," Barry said. He stood down the hall in her childhood room's doorframe.

"Three choices?" she asked, staring at Randy. It was like waiting for a plant to grow. She wished she had a time-lapse video camera. She wanted to see the changes on his face as he went from dragon to human.

"He could pick me to be his dragon guide as well," Barry said.

"Why is he a different color?" Mom asked.

"I don't know," she admitted to Mom, but she suspected it had something to do with having three dragon ancestors. *"That's scary, two of you,"* she answered Barry. With his nose still extended out, he reminded her of a hammerhead shark. Those never looked natural, either. *"Did I do that?"*

"You mean did your jaw extend out unnaturally?" he asked, joining her as she studied her brother.

"Yes," she thought.

"Yes." Barry moved closer so his head blocked her view.

"He's not acting any different than you did when you trans-formed for the first time." He stood back up. "You have a problem."

"I have so many already. What new problem do I have?" she asked.

"If the Immortals are after you, they'll also be after Randy."

He was right. Glancing at Mom, she said, "Mom."

She must have sounded afraid, because Mom snapped her head toward her. "There are some bad people after me because I'm a dragon. We have to talk to Petr and Dad. If they're after me, they'll be after Randy."

Without waiting to see if her mom followed her, she stomped with purpose to the first floor.

"Did you ever meet King James—" Grandfather was asking but cut himself off when he saw her standing at the base of the stairs. "Jennifer?" he asked.

All eyes in the room turned toward her. From somewhere close behind her, Mom asked, "Why would they come after Randy?"

"We have another problem." She locked gazes with Petr. Then to Mom, she said, "Last weekend, a man by the name of Johan tried to kidnap me because he knew what I was. Mom" —she faced forward—"Dad, there is a group of people that wants to harm or use me because of what I am. If they want me, they'll want Randy too."

Standing, Petr moved closer to her. "Hmm. We'll have to take Randy with us," Petr said.

"Where?" Mom asked. She crossed her arms and her shoulders stiffened.

"No," Dad interjected.

She imagined the face she used to convince her dad to buy her the expensive bike when she was eight and said, "Dad, these people have been following us, the Wrights, for a long time. Probably following you, and you, Grandfather. They seem to think they're responsible for you being alive and could kill you to get to us."

"We can take care of Randy. These people won't touch my son," Dad naively said.

"Dad. Johan would have killed me or forced me to go with him." She couldn't tell her dad that he would have raped her too. It felt wrong to say it to him, and then she'd have to explain why mating was permanent for dragons.

Moving beside her, Petr said to Dad, "If Jennifer wouldn't have killed the man, I have no doubt you would have never seen her again."

…A fireball passed through Johan. He collapsed to the ground…

Suddenly, Jennifer needed to sit. Sensing her distress, Petr wrapped his good arm around her and helped her to the chair. "Meelaya," he whispered.

"Too much, too soon," she said under her breath.

"What's wrong with her?" Dad demanded. He didn't ask her, but Petr.

Somewhere behind her, Mom cried. The Grands stayed silent, watching. Grandfather placed his hand on Dad's back, urging him to return to his seat.

After acknowledging Grandfather, Dad retrieved Mom. "Come, Pauline," he said, encouraging her to sit on the sofa.

Once everyone sat down, Petr said, "We went to the woods last weekend. Dragons need to practice to become efficient in their skills. Jennifer, more than most young dragons… She is very gifted. She can control fire. We call it an elemental."

"Fire?" MaryAnn asked, scooting forward on her chair.

Able to shift parts individually, Jennifer turned her hand into tiny red scales and extended the dragon's attributes to her stomach, esophagus, and mouth. If she didn't, what she did next would burn her. The fire built quickly, and she spit the fireball into her hand, much like spitting out gum.

When Jennifer snuffed it out, Josephine said, "Wow."

Human, she thought as her body obeyed and she morphed.

"And Jennifer killed the man? The man who wanted to harm her?" Dad asked.

...Blond hair circled her legs...

"Yes," Petr answered.

"Can Randy throw fire around?" Mom asked.

"No," Jennifer said.

At the same time, Petr said, "I don't know." He glanced at her, moving a fallen lock that was in front of her eye. "Why do you say that, Meelaya?"

"His coloring... His skin... I think he can control air. It's almost like it comes off him in waves and makes him feel like silk," she said. She looked at Dad and said, "Randy needs to go with us, Dad. He needs to train. In fact, you all need to come with us." She hoped they saw her panic as she looked from one family member to the next. "They will hurt you to get us. I'm sure of it."

The room stayed silent until her mom said, "And killing someone... Will my daughter be arrested for killing a man?" At least Mom believed Petr.

"No. His body will never be found," Petr answered. "But she won't be in the States. I'm taking her to Dernogard so she can learn to defend herself."

Mom nodded and said, "Come, Jennifer." Mom scooted, making a spot between her and Dad.

Like a child, Jennifer stood, moving to the middle seat. Her mom wrapped her arms around Jennifer and inhaled the top of her head. Mom always said that even blindfolded, she would know her children by the smell of their heads.

According to her mom, it made her feel more comfortable knowing they were alive, safe in her embrace.

"You've had a rough time, haven't you, my little sky angel?" Mom whispered into her hair.

"Yes, Momma," Jennifer said, shedding some tears. She closed her eyes and listened, not wanting Petr to watch her break down. It was silly. If she were to marry him, he'd have to know she wouldn't always be strong. After all, there was no strength without tears—right?

"When do you plan to leave for this dragon city?" Grandfather asked.

"I canceled our plane tickets for this afternoon, but I'll rebook them after we leave here. Sometime next week by the latest."

"Why so soon?" Father asked. His rough hands were on her shoulders, petting her.

"Dragon parts have an interesting side effect. They can give you incredible hearing, the ability to see for long distances and smell emotions, and even make it possible to live forever. Your daughter is a valuable asset to people who would like to use her body parts for those gifts. Recently, we've met others who want to kidnap or kill Jennifer. Otherwise, I'd want her to stay here and finish her degree. My original plan was to move to Dernogard in four years and slowly intertwine my life into hers. I apologize for taking her away so soon," Petr said.

"How do you know there's a new threat? It sounds like Jennifer handled the person who wanted to kidnap her," Josephine said.

Keeping her eyes closed and resting her head on her mom's shoulder while listening to her heartbeat, Jennifer said, "They smell... different. People who eat dragons smell dangerous."

"We have other friends here helping—a dragon named Kamar and Che-non, who ate a fruit from the giant's garden."

"Giant's garden?" Grandfather asked.

"It's a place with fruit that gives long life," Jennifer said. "But really, it's neither here nor there. If the Immortals, the bad guys, have been following me my whole life, they've been following all of the Wrights. Who knows for how long?"

"Why would they follow us?" Mom asked.

Jennifer sat up and stared around the room, locking eyes with Grandfather. "Just the Wrights. The man in charge of the Immortals, the people who hunt and kill dragons"— she paused for a dramatic reveal—"he is one of our dragon ancestors, still alive, and not a nice—"

Someone knocked on the door.

CHAPTER 25

SHANNA

THE GODS MADE GLOSS'S PHYSIQUE, ALL SIX FEET TWO INCHES OF him. Skinny, he had only a slight muscular build. He had a sprinkling of hair on his chest and a dark, seductive happy trail.

Three times in less than twenty-four hours wasn't bad for the Latino lover, not to mention all the numerous moments he brought Shanna's body to climax.

He would do nicely for the next fifty years, she thought.

His wavy, thick locks tickled her nose as he kissed her neck. Leisurely, he trailed the kisses lower until he cupped her right breast while sucking on her left—hunger pooled in her girl parts, visceral heat collecting between her limbs. But she needed to question him, desired him to accept and understand, to agree, that he would be her partner.

Who was she kidding? She'd had sex with him; of course he would want her for the rest of his natural life. But she had to enquire, anyway. "Gloss," she said, tugging on his hair gently. "I need to ask you something."

"Mmm."

He didn't budge, continuing his downward kisses,

spreading her legs with his hand while the other toyed with her nipple.

"No, seriously," she said, barely getting it out before his free hand and mouth found her nub, rubbing back and forth, his tongue joining the dance. His other digits were still teasing her boob.

She groaned, feeling the urgency beckon her deeper out of conscious thought. *Thank God for tall men with long arms who can entertain multiple places simultaneously.*

"No." She shoved him, having to use her dragon strength to escape his exploring. "I need to ask you something. This is important."

He stopped. "What is it, mi amor?" Sitting on his legs, he probed her face with his dark chocolate irises.

Already, he had succumbed to calling her his love. Even now, he was trapped.

"You and me." She moved her hand between their naked bodies. "I've been told once Jennifer is caught, I will be given fifty years of freedom."

"Ah," he said, his eyes searching the ceiling. "Oh," he leaned back on his elbows. "My father made you agree to marry and have a child." He scooted to the side of the bed, throwing his legs over.

"What are you doing?" she asked when he stood and gathered his clothes. "Are you leaving me?"

Stopping, he surveyed her face, his eyebrows pressed together. "Mi amor, I won't stop you. If Father gave you fifty years, I wish you the best," he said.

As they locked eyes, she wondered about Gloss. No one had ever left her once they'd had sex with her. It was impossible to fight the effects of her being a dragon. Her curse was an instant addiction to the point of self-harm. If it wasn't for the obsession that followed sex, her body count would be higher. Plus, why would he leave? Did he not want kids?

She chose Gloss on purpose. The benefit of taking a

Family member as a lover was because they understood the dragon world, her world. Apparently, in Gloss's case, it had worked against her. Roland did say that most of the time, Father decided on the partner. Perhaps Gloss thought Father had picked someone else for her, and she couldn't choose for herself. But first, she needed to understand how he hadn't fallen deeply and madly in love with her. "How are you able to leave? Aren't you obsessed with me?"

He grabbed his pants off the floor, going commando, like he didn't hear her question. Watching him reminded her of yesterday when he'd undressed himself. It was one of the sexiest things she'd ever witnessed; him taking off his jeans, his happy trail leading to the best proportioned, super hard penis she'd ever seen.

"Huh." He rolled his eyes. "I am very addicted to you, to the point that my body is trembling." He snarled. "But I'm in control," he said through clenched teeth. "I'm not going to ruin your chances of happiness, Caitlyn." He didn't know her real name yet. It felt so personal to use her given name, something only Roland and Gourdy knew.

"Wait, are you saying you're willing to be in pain for my happiness?"

His smile was easy and relaxed across his lips, lighting up his eyes. "I would never take your happiness from you."

But most dragons copulated for life. If she had mated with him, they should be addicted to each other. Somehow, he derived the truth. Knew she wasn't capable of mating. "You know." She sat up as the realization hit her. "You know I can't be mated. You know I've been with someone before."

"Yes," he said. "My dad bragged about how he had developed and successfully used a concoction on a mated dragon. That she survived the death of her mate."

Dryness crusted her eyes when she refused to blink, unable to form words. He understood the risk, and yet, he'd slept with her. "And we—" She indicated both of them. "We had sex. Dirty, amazing sex. Why?"

He buttoned and zipped his pants. "Stupid, I guess. I thought maybe I would be different and not get addicted."

"Then would you be willing to be my lover?" She couldn't say marriage or spouse. She was Southern, raised to believe the man asked the woman. And lover sounded more appropriate since she couldn't give him her heart. It had died with Jared. She had killed it herself.

Biting his bottom lip, he devoured her with his eyes. "It would honor me to be your lover for the rest of my life," he said, slowly unbuttoning his pants and sliding them back down his hips.

It was the best present she'd been given, ever, she thought, watching him undress. She slid on the bed, so she sat on the corner and took his length in her hand, running her hand along the base, preparing to take him into her mouth.

The clanging crashed into her body, throwing her head backward. She grabbed her ears, waiting for the transformation. Nothing happened other than the emergence of excruciating pain in her neck.

When it passed, she glanced at Gloss. His face had gone white. She straightened herself on the bed, no longer in the mood for anything except acetaminophen for her headache.

"It was an awakening," she explained to the horror-stricken Gloss. "Closer than Jennifer when she first changed," she admitted to him.

What was different this time from the last? Why hadn't she been forced to turn into a dragon?

Another loud crash came, like an elephant running through a kitchen, knocking off every glass, pan, whatever onto a concrete floor, or a tornado blowing through a wind chime store. It ran through her body as if she was part of the resonance, echoing within her. She waited to be shattered apart. To be destroyed.

The sound ended as quickly as it started. "Two awakenings," she said to whoever would listen.

"And they were close," Gourdy said, appearing beside Gloss but staring out the window. "You need to dress. You might not get those fifty years," he said, but the amazement on his face said it all. Gourdy was so pale he reminded her of white sand on a sunny day, so bright he was hard to look at.

"Calm down. All we know for sure is there are two more dragons close to Charlotte," she thought.

"Gloss, we need to put our clothes on and check on Matt." What if one of her brothers had transformed and killed Matt?

"Have you ever heard of two awakenings before?" Gloss asked.

"Not before today." She grabbed her phone off the charger and pulled up the text thread she had with Roland.

Two awakenings just now. I'm taking another operative with me, and we will ensure Matt is still tied up.

She hadn't told Roland she picked her partner for the next fifty years and didn't ask for permission to check on Matt. She needed to see for herself that Matt was okay and couldn't wait for Roland's approval. After all, Matt was the only leverage she had over Jennifer. If this didn't work—

"Then we'll have to hit her on the head and take her back," Gourdy said, sending an image of Matt's bloody body leaning over the car door.

She went to the closet to retrieve something to wear. Whoever her shopper was, they hadn't bought her many clothes, and definitely not anything she would enjoy wearing. She put on what she could find: a long-sleeved dress and high heels. At least it was black. Then she stared into the mirror.

With her hair and nails black, she no longer looked like Amy. How would she sneak up on Jennifer to capture her?

She didn't have a clue.

Gloss came up behind her, surrounding her waist with his hands, and pulled her into his chest. He kissed the top of her head before his hand found the general location of her left areola hidden under the layers of material. Tracing circles around it, he leaned over and nibbled her ear.

"It will be okay, mi amor. I promise you."

But how could he promise her anything? He was subject to the same hateful Father she was. If Jennifer got away, all her plans would evaporate until she discovered another way to escape.

"Mi amor, I know you are worried about my father giving us your freedom. Trust me, we will find a way," he whispered into her hair.

Fighting to not laugh, she finally understood what it was. She'd never realized the overprotective confidence was another side-effect before, but if she thought back, she saw the signs in past lovers. The chemical or hormone or whatever caused a man who she had sex with to fall in love with her also brought about a sick sense of greatness. He thought he could save her. *Poor, innocent man,* she thought, and enjoyed his comforting arms before she led him out the door to the car and into a possible den of dragons.

CHAPTER 26

JENNIFER

Two awakenings. One, Randy, still slept upstairs. *Who was the other awakening?* Jennifer wondered.

Kamar sat sandwiched between the Grands on the long couch. Che-non sat alone on the armchair, her grandfather standing near the window, Mom and Dad on the loveseat.

"Settled." Smiling tightly, Dad nodded at Mom.

"We've been talking about it for months." Mom grabbed Dad's hand in both of hers. "We even met with Jacob's company's retirement department. There's ample money for Jacob to leave his job. The question hasn't been can we, but when?"

"Only two things have held us back," Dad said, staring at Jennifer.

"Let me guess, me and Randy?" Jennifer asked.

"No. Not you. Randy, yes. And the other reason is health insurance. I won't be old enough for full benefits for a few more years, only because it's age-based. I'll reach that age when Randy leaves for college. The original plan was to retire in four years, when Randy graduated high school, but—"

"But now." Mom focused on Jennifer. "When you have kids, you want to watch them grow. Want to be there at their wedding"—she peeked at Petr—"spend time with your grandkids. We have the money for insurance." She inhaled and slowly exhaled. "Now is the best time for your dad to leave his job, and we'll move with you to this dragon city. We won't allow anyone to harm our family."

Patting Mom's leg, Dad stood. "I'll let my boss off as easy as I can. He won't like me retiring suddenly, but if my daughter is getting married and my son is moving, I'll have no choice but to retire this weekend." He headed toward his office, Grandfather following him.

"Do you remember Xander Richards, Jennifer?" Mom asked.

An image of a gray-haired man with a brown mustache that never seemed to match his olive-toned skin and who reminded her of a friendly clown entered her mind. Jennifer nodded.

"His son, what was his name? He mowed our yard one summer."

Mentioning him brought a smile to her face. He was four years older than her—he had brown locks, a quick laugh, and was always getting in trouble. "Richard," she said. "Richard Richards. The neighborhood kids teased him because his first name was the same as his last. He rolled with it, though."

"That's right. Anyway, Richard is a sweet boy. He married and moved to Australia when he graduated high school— met the girl online. Xander visits his son for months at a time to see his granddaughter. He has his house winterized, and we check on it when he's out of the country. I'll call him and ask for the person who winterized his house and have them do the same to ours while we're gone. I'm sure Xander will have no issue ensuring our home is buttoned up until we return."

"Wait, Mom. You and Dad have this too well planned out. This can't be the first time you've thought of leaving North Carolina. How long have you organized an extended trip...

Or are you planning to move? And you did this all behind my back?"

"Please, dear. This wasn't done in secret. We've been planning a vacation to Sweden next winter. Your father wants to see the Ice Hotel. You know how he is about architecture. It's a dream of his, that and the northern lights. I'm not sure if they're still there, but he wanted to visit the Dutch beaches and hunt for Theo Jansen's wind-powered walkers. Then there's the troll artist—"

"The what?" Jennifer asked.

"Thomas Dambo. They have some of his giant trolls here in the States, but your father is determined to go to a park with several of them and a magical tower. And well, they are pretty, so I'm willing to traverse all over Europe to visit all we can while there."

"Basically, you planned to leave Randy here while you spent months out of the country?" Jennifer asked.

"No, dear." She looked shocked, with her round eyes and a raised brow. "We were taking Randy with us. I've been talking to the principal about working with them and using the internet so he could have life experience and finish high school. On Monday, I'll contact the school and expedite our plans. No big deal."

"What!" she exclaimed. "You were going to take Randy and abandon me here?"

"You're in college, sky angel. You're a grown-up." She smiled as if she was proud. "You can even defend yourself with fire if need be." Something on Jennifer's face must have shown how upsetting it was to feel forgotten because her mother added, "But all that is off the plate now. We'll be going with you to this dragon city."

"It's why your parents are pliable, my love," Petr said in Dragon, placing his hand on her lap.

"Don't you use that mating bond stuff to calm me," she said but didn't move his hand.

"Well, now that that's settled, I'm going to whip up some snacks," Mom said, then plastered on a smile.

Standing, Jennifer said, "I can help."

"No," Che-non and Mom said simultaneously.

Mom stopped at the door. "Why did you say that?" She tilted her head while eyeing Che-non.

"I... Your daughter cooked for us once. Scrambled eggs... I had pieces of shell in mine." He stared at Jennifer. "I didn't think messing up such an easy dish was possible."

"It shouldn't be. But... I've had my daughter's cooking," Mom said. "I'll be right back." She disappeared through the kitchen door.

Jennifer sat back down in one of the uncomfortable metal chairs, ignoring their comments. They wouldn't discourage her culinary hopes. She leaned over to Petr's ear and asked, "That sound, the first awakening, it was nearby. Where do you think it was located?"

As he often did, he ran his left hand through his hair and glanced at Kamar. Kamar had made himself comfortable with the Grands, entertaining them with stories. "Kamar believes it was in Charlotte, close to my house. When you awoke, the sound was fainter, and I believe he is right. Somewhere in Charlotte, there is another dragon shifter."

She swallowed. "Maybe the reason we keep running into people around town is I wasn't the only one who had the potential to turn into a dragon in Charlotte."

"Matt. It could be Matt," he said, but he glanced at the ground, his lips a straight line and his brows drawn together. She smelled the bitterness of disappointment; he didn't think it was Matt. "It's probably someone else. Who knew that North Carolina would be a dragon pit?" He frowned. "I need to get you to safety, and I need to find the third dragon."

"I need you to be safe as well," she admitted, placing her hand on his lap. "We'll locate them, but as a team."

"And if we run out of time?" he asked.

"At least we can try," she answered. But would it bother her to know somewhere out there, another shifter died because she didn't stay in the States long enough to save them?

The hair on her arms stood as Kamar twitched his fingers. On the couch, Josephine and MaryAnn sat on either side of him. "Could you do that again?" MaryAnn asked. She held an empty cup, and her daughter, Josephine, gripped a full glass.

Kamar shrugged. "This is nothing. I can do this all day." The water in Josephine's glass bubbled over the rim as it twisted into the air, looking like moving artwork. It did a swirl and landed inside the cup on MaryAnn's lap.

"All the abilities you get from being a dragon are nice. Do you think I might turn?" MaryAnn asked Che-non.

"No," Che-non answered. "We don't know what causes someone to shift, but we have found no one who is over twenty-five making the transformation."

"I can hope," MaryAnn announced. "One more time, Kamar?"

Jennifer leaned over and whispered into Petr's ear, "I'm going to get my passport and make sure Randy is okay. Change clothes and see if I can find any shoes. Would you like to check on Randy with me?"

She still wore the robe she had snagged to transform into a dragon.

"Yes," he said to her, taking to his feet. When Che-non locked eyes with him, he said, "I'll be upstairs. I'll make our reservations as soon as we determine when everyone can leave the country."

"We're going too," MaryAnn announced.

"Do you have your passport?" Petr asked.

"Not a problem," she said, crossing her arms. "When we come up here, we bring our passports with us, don't we?" She peered over at Josephine.

"I make them pack them every time we travel," Josephine said. "What, Mom? It makes me feel better to keep important documentation with me."

"And the other awakening?" Che-non asked. The water dropped on Kamar's lap.

"We'll do what we can, but I have to think of my mate," Petr said, taking a side glance at Jennifer.

"I'll stay," Kamar announced. "I'll stay behind and hunt the dragon-shifter."

"It will be risky. We don't know how many Immortals are in Charlotte," Petr said.

He shrugged. "I'll be fine... Besides, I have... unfinished business."

"The girl?" Jennifer asked before she thought about it. But now that the question floated in the atmosphere, she added, "The White Jaguar?"

An awkward pause settled in the room as Kamar studied Jennifer. His shoulders relaxed. "Yes. The girl."

Petr nodded. "It's decided then. We'll be back down in a bit," Petr said.

Then, as if the air wasn't thick with Kamar's rose scent and regret, Kamar said, "Watch this." He raised his arm, and the water dampening his pants rose and formed into droplets. They danced on nothing and landed in the cup being held by Josephine.

Jennifer ignored the conversation in the room, climbing the stairs with Petr in tow. At the top step, she heard a phone buzzing. Ignoring her sleeping, one hundred percent human brother, she searched upstairs. Her cell, laying among the debris of the collapsed wall, bounced around in a small circle.

"Huh, Barry. I thought it was destroyed when I shifted," she thought, bending over and picking it up. She didn't recognize the number and quickly sent it to voicemail. *"Glad I left my smart watch charging."*

"You know what else wasn't ripped into shreds?" Barry asked.

"No. What?" she thought back, but her brother, still on the floor, covered by a thin blanket, moaned as if in pain. She faced him in time to watch him sit up.

"Your ring. It turned into a silver and green color around your talon," Barry said.

"Why would it do that?" she asked, but watched as her brother's eyes opened.

"I don't know," he said.

"You stink," Randy said, his lip curled, nose shoved upward in a snarl.

"Thanks," Jennifer said. "What do I smell like?"

"Rotten flowers," he said. "And he"—he pointed to Petr—"smells like old gym socks."

"You turn into a dragon and become brutally honest?" Jennifer asked.

"Yes," he said. A few seconds later, he added, "That wasn't a dream?"

"Nope, brother. It was reality. You're a dragon."

"Cool, I guess." He stretched and yawned. "I'm still tired, Jen. How's Mom handling what I did to the wall?"

Jennifer shrugged. "Well. Better than I thought she would. We're moving. All of us. To Dernogard."

"Dernogard?" he asked.

"Yeah. It's a city—"

"I know what it is. I dreamed I lived in Dernogard," Randy answered.

Petr kneeled on his other side. "Maybe this means your guide will be River? He lived in Dernorgard."

"My first dream was in Dernogard, and my guide is Barry," Jennifer admitted. "What was your dream?"

"Oh. I wanted to make a present for my wife for our…" His cheeks flushed. "Anniversary. Let's go with that. At the foot of the mountain, there was a village… Oxie? Moxie?"

"We called the town Oxly. I know it," Petr said.

"Yes! That's the one. I went to barter for soap. This boy, a small boy, handed me a parchment made from this"—he pinched his fingers together and rubbed them, much like making a sign for money—"ivory-colored material that felt stiff but thin. On it were weird words. Like the alphabet resembled pictures, not letters."

"There is a scroll written on several whalebones in an old room at Dernogard. It's that prophecy that Kamar mentioned last week," Barry thought.

It sounded like something an ancestor did while sailing, like whittling. "Randy, was it a scrimshaw, like whalebone?" Jennifer asked. "The same stuff that was once used to make the bones for women's corsets."

Petr huffed. "Sailors would give their girlfriends small engraved baleen to wear close to their hearts, inside their… huh-hum"—he cleared his throat—"clothing. On it, they poured out their romantic souls in pillow talk. But can you remember what the document you saw said? What was carved onto the surface?" Petr asked.

She comprehended what Petr was asking since she knew enough of the prophecy to know its words wouldn't be remembered until the Mark of Redemption walked the Earth. They told her last week that red represented the color of change. Petr implied she could be this dragon that ushered in a new golden age of dragons.

"Yes. I do. I remember all of it." Randy stopped moving and searched her face. "Jen, you're a red dragon."

Petr's eyes swept over to her, staring at her like this was his first time seeing her.

Her phone, resting in her robe, vibrated. She swatted it, forcing it to go to voicemail.

"The prophecy said the dragon would be red," Randy said.

"I'm not the mark," she protested.

"You are red," Barry thought accusatorially.

Randy smiled. "You couldn't be the person. There is no

way my sister is the mark. Have I told you what she did to dolls when she was little? She took—"

"Randy Luke Wright, you better not say a word." She moved to cover his mouth, but Randy dodged, twisting his head out of the way.

"Jen, it's okay. I was teasing. It's not you. The prophecy says he, and you're not a guy... And if you need more proof, he breathes fire. If we want to find the mark, we need to find the red dragon that breathes fire. He's the mark."

Her cell vibrated in a short pattern—a text message. She ignored it and allowed the world to glaze over.

CHAPTER 27

SHANNA

SHANNA'S ANCESTRAL DREAM OF JORMUNGANT WAS ODD. HER dreams started when her ancestors were toddlers, except for Jormungant's. That nightmare began in his adulthood as he stared out of a cave entrance at an expansive tundra. The sun hung on the horizon's edge; the sky was cast in the oranges of a continuous sunrise or sunset. She knew nothing of where dragons came from or why they existed in a world of humans.

Something in the air reminded her of that dream, on the day when Jormungant stood observing all of creation, contemplating killing those he once loved. A stirring in the atmosphere, the icy wind blowing against her face, the crisp odor of ozone, like after a lightning storm, inspired the remembrance. Whatever it was, it felt ominous, as if the universe had sent her a warning. She pulled on the door to the vet clinic. It opened. Someone had left it unlocked.

Shanna knew she locked it last night.

She glanced behind her at Gloss. He surveyed their surroundings, checking for anyone who might be watching them. He nodded that the vicinity appeared clear. She entered.

Stepping through the door, she flicked the lights on, studying the waiting room where concerned pet parents sat on the benches until their names were announced. Everything remained calm, but not peaceful, more like anticipation... but for what? It gave her the heebie-jeebies.

Gloss stepped in after her and conducted his own survey. He covered his nose with his shirt like he smelled something terrible. "This is not right," he said.

She nodded and went to the back area, where surgeries were once done and where Matt should be tied to a chair.

The scene in front of her was more gory than she anticipated. She'd killed before, but when she killed, she didn't leave a mess. However, Jormungant did and created a similar revolting scene. She owned those memories as if she had lived them herself. She suspected that was why she knew something was amiss when she stood at the entrance to the abandoned vet clinic—death, like the kind Jormungant created, waited for her in this building.

She licked her lips, keeping the disgust to a minimum and doing her best not to breathe in the horrible, wretched decay. But she couldn't block all the pungent odors. The rosemary scent of a dragon, mixed with ozone, reached her nose. Walking into the room, the blood from the floor adhered to Shanna's two-inch heels, making each footfall tacky, like trotting through dried soda pop. She counted two bodies on the ground. One she recognized as a member of the Family; the other lacked a torso, including a head.

Gloss ran outside, leaving all the doors open. His footsteps stopped, followed closely by gagging and the sound of sick landing on the concrete.

Sighing, she knew she had to report the scene to Roland like a good Family operative.

"I scented a dragon when we arrived, but not Jennifer, so she's not responsible for this destruction," she said to the empty room.

The ancient, bearded Gourdy appeared beside her, surveying the damage. "Oh, I won't be happy about this."

"The rest of the Family will be. It's their chance for immortality." She glanced over at him. "And to gain the real Jormungant's favor."

The comment made her dragon guide stand taller, thus proving Gourdy was an egotistical sociopath. Then again, perhaps nothing changed in his posture, and the difference she noted was an illusion caused by her emotions.

Gourdy turned to her. "I can hear all your thoughts."

"And so you can, figment of my imagination." She kicked at a shredded piece of shoe. "These have to be Matt's. Who knew that Matt could go all dragon?" She raised an eyebrow at Gourdy.

"That odor, so familiar," Gourdy said. An image of a tall, very blond man, alike but not identical to Gourdy, appeared in her mind. Before she evaluated the subtle differences, the picture disappeared. The dragon guide sniffed the air, walking in a circle. The vision of the man returned: similar pale eyes, thinner yet shorter than Gourdy. He had a round, smiling, radiant face.

The corners of her mouth rose in a mischievous, wicked grin when she realized she didn't dream about this part of Jormungant's life. This memory came from earlier than the cave entrance. "You revealed something I didn't know—how the brother you hated smelled." From the nightmare of Jormungant's life, she remembered the brother's name— Perun. "Perun. The sibling you considered more untrustworthy than the others. He did something to you. Something horrible. You smell him! The brother you hated the most, the brother you killed before he mated... or so you thought... or you would have destroyed his family." She smiled at Gourdy. "I scent failure."

"Impossible. He was unmated, and my children killed

him," Gourdy said. She had a quick shared memory of a messenger telling Jormungant he had watched Perun die.

She huffed. "Yet no one brought you proof he was killed. Other than that runner, none of the other warriors returned." She glared at Gourdy. "You thought they took the body parts for themselves and left the Family for good." She mocked him. "I guess you should have asked for his head to prove he was dead. For all you know, he's still alive."

"He's dead, or he would have visited the real Jormungant. The hate was mutual."

"Apparently, his son or daughter survived. You have a great-great-great-nephew—Matt."

Gourdy bent down into the muck, the corners of his mouth slanted downward, puffing up his cheeks like a chipmunk. While he appeared occupied, Shanna pushed on to discover what had happened before he stood at the cave entrance.

If she managed to gain some knowledge by smelling Jormungant's brother, then perhaps she could uncover why her dreams started so late in Jormungant's life. What was he hiding? And how was he able to hide it?

The sensation ached, reminding her of seeing someone she knew but couldn't remember from where or their name. Maybe a minute passed before she captured a memory from a TV show or a history book. "Ah, Perun," Shanna mocked. "The Russian god of thunder. Thor in the Norse legends." She laughed. "Or at least the person the stories are based on. My uncle is better looking than I thought. So why did they call him the god of thunder?"

This caused him to pause and slowly rise, his eyes boring into hers. At his full height, the man towered over her. "He was an air dragon and an elemental. He could control the weather and make it storm, snow, or be sunny."

"The ozone. That must be what the ozone smell means."

Gourdy intensely stared at her. She ignored him. Unlike

usual, his emotions bled over to her. Overwhelming enmity burned more in the remnants of his soul than anything she had ever felt, even more than she hated herself.

While he stood, unstable, she drilled into the part of her mind she shared with Gourdy, seeking more information. How fiercely Gourdy blocked these memories testified to how hurtful they were to him. It made her want them even more. She needed another boost of sensory detail to help make that neural pathway. Leaning down, she picked up a piece of Matt's jeans and inhaled deeply—gore, death, ozone —hoping the scent would trigger more stolen recollections. She returned Gourdy's intense attention while he focused on her, digging and drilling into long-suppressed ancestral histories.

She whiffed more of the story; blurry, but there. Her head pounded from the effort, but there, just out of reach, there was more to the account of Perun, the god of thunder.

"You hate Perun the most because he caused you to kill your mate. It was his fault she died."

At this revelation, his face turned scarlet. She had struck a nerve, and it cost her as tiny fibers of pain exploded in her head.

"Call Roland now, young child. If you do not do this soon, the real me will be angry at you," he said.

"So you think. But the truth is, you no longer resemble Jormungant, who has lived for centuries. For one thing, his beard is gone." She stared at Gourdy, remembering the few pictures she had seen of the modern-day man. "He's slimmed down. I'm guessing his personality is also different."

"Don't underestimate betrayal, Shanna. My brother's betrayal left a deep scar on my mind." He moved closer to her. At this distance, he could kiss her or push her. He challenged her with his very stance.

"As you have betrayed me, dragon guide," she whispered between tight lips.

"Mi amor," Gloss said as he walked into the room. "What's wrong?"

She maintained her eye-lock with Gourdy, not glancing at Gloss. Gloss couldn't see her dragon guide, since he existed only in her imagination. "Nothing," she snapped, though she knew her posture screamed differently. She was on edge, prepared to fight. The piece of torn jeans she had been holding dropped to the floor.

When she turned toward Gloss, all the anger melted away in a second. The innocence of his sweet smile reminded her of a faithful puppy.

Using a gentle voice, she said, "I'll call Roland and report the deaths of the operatives. And the existence of a new dragon." She sighed. Drawn to Gloss, she glided through the sea of ruin and caressed his back. Their fifty years had evaporated... but maybe they could salvage it by catching the new dragon.

"All right, the Family will want to cover this up. I'll guard the outside and wait for the cleanup crew," he said, his eyes surveying the damage.

As he moved away, she reached for him and snatched his hand, causing him to turn back toward her. When their eyes made contact and their chests touched, she noticed a thin sheen on his pale forehead. Jormungant's son was not a killer. "I want you to know something before you go and before I call Roland."

He seemed intrigued, head tilting to the side. "What?"

"I want a pact. You declare I am your love. And I want something from you."

"Anything. I am yours, and you know it."

"Your name." A name, a forbidden truth, something that the Family expressly kept hidden by having operatives use pseudonyms. She assumed they did this to separate people from the real world, to indoctrinate the members into the cult. If Gloss's real name hadn't been wiped from the internet, she could look it up on the Family's pharmaceutical public profile. But for this assignment, the Family gave him a fake name, like they did her. She wanted Gloss to give her his birth name willingly. A trade for something the Family used as a tool of subterfuge.

Without hesitation, he said, "Romeo Johnson. And yours, will you give me yours?"

A Shakespearean character that sounded more made up than Gloss, but she liked it. Wasn't Romeo a lover, after all? "Shanna White," she said, revealing her hidden gem. Somehow, this act of giving names was more intimate than sharing her body.

He kissed her among the filth, and she was happy to find he at least used a mint to cover up being sick earlier. He demanded her attention with his mouth. Though it was not deep or long, it left her wanting. She watched him leave. When the door closed, she glanced at where Gourdy had been only seconds ago. Not even footprints were left on the sticky, bloody floor.

She took out her phone and pressed Roland's number. He answered on the second ring. Shanna heard cars and people talking in the background.

"All complete?" Roland asked.

"There has been a complication. Matt's escaped." She sighed. "I'll need a cleanup crew and an investigation team."

"How?" Roland asked.

"Tell him!" Gourdy screamed in her head, but she ignored him. Knowing that Matt was Perun's descendant gave her power over both Gourdy and Jormungant. The power that she might be able to wield to gain her freedom.

"It looks like a dragon killed his guards and freed him." She told the truth, just not the whole truth.

"Does it smell like Jennifer?" Roland asked.

"No."

"Does it smell like the other dragon, the one with Dr. Smith?" Roland asked.

Shanna sniffed the air, thinking, *What other dragon was with Dr. Smith?* Her life could have been in danger because she'd worn that perfume that clogged her senses. Roland should've divulged there was another long before now. Calming her rage, she answered, "No, doesn't smell like him."

"TELL HIM!"

"No!" she thought, keeping the anger from her voice by smiling first. "Smells like we have another dragon."

"I wonder if that is one of the two awakenings." He sighed. "Matt's missing. He possibly is now a dragon, and there are bodies at the vet clinic. Correct?"

"Yes. Correct," she said.

"I'm calling Father after I send a cleanup crew," Roland said.

"I'll wait for them." Her finger was raised to hang up the phone call.

"Tell him Matt is Perun's descendant. Please, tell him," Gourdy pleaded.

"Wait," Roland said, and he sounded upset. She'd never even heard him sound concerned; he was always calm and levelheaded.

She brought the cell back up to her ear. "What?" she asked.

"The operative with you, is it Ro- sorry, Gloss?"

"Yes," she answered.

"Is Gloss okay?"

"He is mine," she thought to Gourdy. "Yes. He's outside keeping guard, perfectly fine."

"I'll talk to you soon." Roland hung up.

"You withheld information," Gourdy said, using slurs and curse words in different languages.

"Gourdy, we're talking about fifty years." If Matt didn't go to

247

Jennifer, she could still use the kidnapping to get Jennifer to meet up with her and bonk her on the head then.

Gourdy stayed quiet, anger rolling out from the part of her brain that she thought he resided in.

"I didn't lie. I'm protecting us," she thought but dialed a number she had never used and had programmed into her phone since the summer when she prepared for her South Holt job—the number for Jennifer Wright. The first ring went to voicemail.

She tried again with the same results—this time, she texted.

Jennifer, please help! Last night, Matt and I were on a date. He's been kidnapped. The kidnappers let me go so I would tell you. They said they need to talk to you. Please call me, Amy.

But what if that wasn't enough?

If Gourdy's response meant anything, Perun's descendant would be worth more than Jennifer. Would Father give her a hundred years with no kids if she brought in Matt? If she brought in Matt *and* Jennifer, maybe she'd been given a few lifetimes free from the Family. If Matt went to Jennifer, there would be more dragons on Jennifer's side, but she could use the lies she'd already weaved. If it didn't work, it didn't work, but if it did…

She pulled up her text thread with Maria Davis, Matt's mom.

Oh, Maria, I've screwed up. Jennifer wants Matt back and has told him she can shift into a dragon. She's confused Matt. He believes he was kidnapped and is now a dragon too. She must be using some kind of illusion because Matt believes her! I'm afraid he is doing drugs with her. Don't believe her, and do what you can to help Matt. I'm so sorry.

"And now those secrets you are keeping from me will keep me alive longer and free me. Gourdy, we will get at least fifty years," Shanna said.

He didn't respond.

CHAPTER 28

JENNIFER

"WHY DID THAT DRAGON PROPHECY BOTHER ME?" JENNIFER thought, throwing on a pair of jeans. *"Most of my life, I've been living up to high expectations. It's nothing new. Plus, it's not like it matters. I can't do anything to ruin a prophecy, can I? Inside, I'm the same person I was last..."*

But she wasn't the same person. She'd lived many different lives in her dreams. How could you experience multiple lifetimes without changing?

Reaching into her drawer, she pulled out the only bra left —something bright pink and lacy that screamed danger and fun in one loud color. When she sought to finish strong in high school, she bought the frilly undergarment as encouragement. She'd imagined her partner's phantom hands removing it every time she said no to a date. It was symbolic, much like skinny jeans for a dieter. If she waited for a relationship, she could experience a passionate affair later. She'd sacrificed teenage experiences in order to make incredible grades—to push herself to excel.

Had that part of her changed, the desire for success?

No. She still wanted to do her best. But her idea of accomplishment, the bar by which she measured her achievements, differed from then but not her desire to dominate anything she tried.

"The prophecy doesn't matter, Barry," she said.

"How so?" he asked while she pulled a T-shirt over her head.

"Well, I'm still me. If it's a destined future, I can't do anything to change it. But I can still be me. Right?" she asked.

"What, predestination when it comes to a scroll written by a crazy guy before even I was born? Be yourself. Sounds reasonable," he answered.

She peeked into her closet and found the only pair of shoes left, old, grass-stained Nike runners she used to mow the yard. "Geez. Being a dragon is hard on shoes."

"You could go barefoot, turn your feet into scales."

Ignoring him, she tried to remember the dragon prophecy. "Can you see the prophecy?" she asked Barry as she pulled up her knee socks.

"Nope, all squiggly and nothing I can remember," Barry said.

"So, it can't be true since everyone will remember it," she commented as she wiggled into the footwear. "Ready?" she asked.

"Thought the prophecy didn't matter. Grab your phone from the pocket of your robe," Barry said.

"Thanks." She slid it into her back pocket and headed downstairs.

The living room felt thick with tension, plus a bitter scent greeted her on the stairs. No one said anything. Mom had her hand on Dad's back, patting it. Grandfather stood behind them. Randy rested in the armchair, legs kicked back, sound asleep. Kamar comfortably reclined in the middle of the Grands. Che-non was planted in the metal chair beside Petr.

"I can't believe it," Dad said.

The bitterness wafted off her dad.

"What can't you believe, Dad?" Jennifer asked, deciding to sit cross-legged on the floor.

The reek of dust from years past reminded her why she liked hardwood—dragon noses were too sensitive for carpet. She moved to lean against the wall.

"Your dad's boss asked him about you and Randy," Mom said, but that answered nothing.

Dad sat up, making eye contact with Petr. "It's not that he asked about Randy and Jennifer. When I told him I was retiring for medical reasons, he asked me to stay on."

"I would expect a company to want to keep you," Jennifer said. "You've worked there for years. I'm sure they don't want to lose your knowledge."

"No, Jennifer. I trained AJ to do my job. He's had two years of shadowing me. I'm convinced he'll be a better architect than me."

She'd met AJ a few times. Her father had invited him to dinner twice when she was in high school.

"AJ is a smart guy, Dad, but—"

"Do you remember Dan?" Dad asked.

"Yeah." When she was young, her parents socialized with Dan. He had twin daughters around her age who were named Brooke and Stone.

"He had a heart attack," Dad said.

"Oh no. Are Brooke and Stone okay?" she asked. She hadn't called the twins since before they moved. One was in New York, and the other was in California, pursuing their dreams. But she saw their social media postings.

Dad shook his head. "He's fine, as far as I know. But that's my point, Jennifer. I brought up Dan's heart attack and how it scared his daughters. My boss didn't remember their names, not at all. You hear their father's name and recall them right away, but I don't remember you being particularly close to Dan's daughters."

"I liked them, don't get me wrong, but they were homeschooled. Not that homeschooling is bad. It's not. Just, our school would have never allowed... your coworker let them express their creativity. At ten, Brooke had pink hair, and Stone dressed goth. Hard to forget them. They're very memorable." She'd wanted to dye her hair blue like a mermaid in fifth grade, but her school required natural-colored locks.

"That's my point. Dan brought his kids to work. Said it was to teach them responsibility. He'd give them assignments like sharpening his pencils or drawing their bedroom layouts on paper with dimensions. You and Randy stayed at home. I didn't put pictures on my desk because sometimes visitors use my office if I'm at a job site. Plus, I kept my personal life from my boss. Yet my boss couldn't remember Dan's kids' names, that sounded like a stony brook. Their hair color, the frequency of their visits, even their names should have stuck. Dan, who started when I did, and we've had the same supervisor for over twenty years. Yet my boss remembered both your names."

"You think he's a spy?" Che-non asked.

"Yes, after how he talked to me. He asked to come to my house, not to say goodbye or congratulations, but to check on Randy and Jennifer. He's not even a smart spy. He kept asking how Randy and Jennifer were doing and if there was anything he could do to help... When Dan had his heart attack, he could have cared less. Something is not right about this, not at all." Her father looked at Petr. "I'm ready to leave. Now. Today. Get my children safe into this dragon city. The only one of us not packed is Randy."

Petr nodded.

"Sir," MaryAnn said, leaning forward.

Jennifer watched her mate's head swivel slightly to face GG. "Yes," he said.

"Are these cannibals going to come in here with machine guns and serve up my great-grandchildren for dinner?"

"Cannibals?" he asked.

"The ones that eat dragons," she clarified.

"No. I suspect they are grouping right now," he answered, not correcting her term for the Immortals.

"If we took a detour tomorrow and left from another state later next week... say we visited Kentucky... Would they pursue us to Kentucky?" she asked, a tilt to her chin and a calculating twinkle in her eyes.

"Huh," he said, turning his head toward Jennifer. "Mee-laya, that's not a bad idea. They're probably expecting us to fly out of the Charlotte airport. If we leave town and fly out of another airport—"

"I see. The other team wouldn't be anticipating us flying from another international hub," Dad agreed.

"Good. We can go to Kentucky and meet our family," MaryAnn said, folding her arms. "Otherwise, I might not live long enough to meet my nephew. Especially if I go trotting around here and there. This is my opportunity to find out what happened to my father after my mother whisked me away to North Carolina. I'd like to have my questions answered before the good lord takes me home." When no one said anything, MaryAnn continued. "Now that that's settled, when can we leave?"

"It will take us some time to return to Charlotte and gather our suitcases, and I left my passport there... Unless you gathered it, Che-non," Petr said.

"No. It didn't occur to me. I threw my things in the car in case I needed to spend the night here, helping with Randy. My passport is with my stuff," Che-non answered.

"Why don't we divide, half go to Kentucky and the other half to Charlotte? That way, we can all leave the country sooner," Jennifer suggested.

"Sounds like a plan. All of us Wrights to Kentucky. Petr and his group to Charlotte," Dad said.

"No," Jennifer and Petr said together.

"Jennifer will stay with me," Petr said.

"But she's my daugh—"

"Nope, Dad, staying with him."

"I'll go with the Wrights," Kamar announced. "With Randy"—he pointed to her sleeping brother—"you will need the help of a dragon."

Che-non stood, walking over to the pile of suitcases that were shoved off the loveseat earlier. "I'll go as well. Which cars will we take?" He put his hand on a handle.

"So, just Petr and I are returning to Charlotte? Is that wise?" She glanced at Kamar.

"You can breathe fire, little dragon. You've already killed a man. I am confident you will protect your mate," Kamar said.

…Johan pointed the gun at Petr and pulled the trigger. Her mate's blood coated her tongue…

The memory was different, but she didn't have time to ponder why before Petr stood in her space. He whispered, "We'll get our bags and flee from Charlotte."

"What about the awakening? Someone needs to be hunting for the new dragon shifter," Jennifer said.

Looking at Petr, Kamar added, "When you leave for Dernogard, I'll drive back to your house and hunt the little dragon. Hopefully, they will stay out of trouble for a weekend."

The room erupted in noise as the group moved off the couches and became busy, as if they had received their marching orders.

"Wait! Where will we meet? We can't meet here or at Petr's," Jennifer asked.

"Great point." Petr raised his voice. "Listen." Everyone froze. He glanced toward MaryAnn, who stood near the luggage. "If we meet on Tuesday afternoon, is that enough time for you to pack and introduce yourself to your family?"

Blinking, MaryAnn said, "Let's see. Packing won't take

any time. We can be in Kentucky by tomorrow if we drive through the night. Sunday, we find where my relative lives and rest. Yes, I think Tuesday will be ample time to rendezvous."

"I know which airport we are all familiar with and can meet at." Mom waved her arm in the air. "What do you say, sky angel?"

"Do they have an international airport?" Jennifer asked as she remembered sitting in the cockpit of a two-seater plane at the Bluegrass Airport.

"If they don't, we can catch a connecting flight, dear." Josephine stopped at the front door, rolling a carry-on case behind her. "That sounds perfect, Pauline. What a smart idea."

Her stomach tossed and turned from the sense of urgency. "Come, Petr," Jennifer said, grabbing his good hand. Fighting the panic that crawled at her throat, she said, "Let's go."

Petr moved with Jennifer, but he tilted his head. "You know where we're going?" he asked.

"Yes." Jennifer waited at the door, watching her family move around. "I'll see all of you Tuesday afternoon, around lunch, at the airport." It was a command to her family and newfound friends. "Be safe!"

"Wait!" Mom screamed, dashing over to her. Mom embraced Jennifer, squeezing, only to hand her off to her dad. "I love you, Jennifer Louisa Wright, my sky angel. Please be careful."

"I love you too, Mom, Dad. All of you," Jennifer said, glancing over to where her brother turned sideways on the chair, snoring away. "In two days, I'll call you to make sure everything is okay and that you're ready to go."

Outside, she passed Grandfather's car. The trunk was open, and Che-non placed things into the back. She glanced around at the other houses. She didn't see anyone, but it was a frigid January day. "Petr, this would be better in the dark.

Every one of my parents' neighbors will know they're leaving."

"They'll pack and be out of here before the Immortals catch on," he said, sitting in the passenger side.

Once he buckled, she shut his door. When she climbed in, she asked, "How's your shoulder?"

"Fine. I'll rewrap it when we get to our house," Petr said.

Our house. She liked the sound of that.

When she leaned back, the pressure of her phone reminded her to take it out. She placed it on the car charger. The green light blinked. She'd forgotten about the message earlier in all the chaos. She read the message from Amy and froze, her eyes repeatedly landing on *Matt* and *kidnapped*.

"Petr," she said, hands trembling.

"What?" he asked, facing her. "Your heart sped up. What else is wrong, Jennifer?"

"It's Matt. He's been kidnapped," she said.

CHAPTER 29

JENNIFER

Driving down the interstate, the air thick with worry, Jennifer touched the call button on her phone, automatically cutting off the tunes over the speaker.

"Who are you calling?" Petr asked.

She held up her finger for him to be quiet.

"Hello." When she answered, Amy's voice cracked as if she'd been crying.

"Amy?" she asked for confirmation.

"Is this Jennifer?"

"Yes. Please explain your text. What do you mean that Matt has been kidnapped and that they want to talk with me?" Jennifer asked.

Amy panted like she was hyperventilating, but because the transformation happened so quickly, it felt forced, like she realized who was on the phone and started acting.

"It was awful, Jennifer. Friday night, we were leaving Matt's apartment to go out to eat... Somewhere private where we could talk. I had opened my car door to get something. I heard a thump... Someone had hit Matt on the head."

A blue vehicle on Jennifer's right passed her, pulled in front, and slowed down. After Jennifer readjusted her speed, she asked, "What do you mean someone hit Matt on the back of the head? What did they hit him with?"

"I don't know. I had bent over to retrieve my necklace out of my car since it had fallen off earlier, and when I looked up, Matt was slumped over my door."

"What? Was he breathing?"

"Yes. That's all I checked before I ran off, searching for help."

"Wow." Jennifer had too many questions at once. She glanced at Petr, his mouth pressed into a hard line. "Did you see the person who did it? Could you describe them?"

"I wasn't going to stand around and take their picture. They were tall, taller than Matt, blond, and built." Though the description of the bad guy lacked detail, it reminded her of the heart-eating predator that appeared in the library when they studied Thursday night. Only because Matt stood at six-foot-four and the heart-eating predator in the library was taller.

She assumed the Immortal followed her. But what if the Immortal had the ability to smell emotions? He would have known how important her friends were to her. Petr had joined her that night. If he could smell emotions, he would have known that Petr had also eaten a dragon's heart. Could he have determined that Petr was worried about her and her friends?

The eerie feeling of being watched returned, and she searched the surrounding cars for someone following them.

"The blond Immortal might have been following Petr, Jennifer. Remember, someone gave Petr his black eyes," Barry said. When school had started this semester, Petr had been sporting bruises from a fight. Later he told her it was a battle to the death.

Barry made a good point. *"It could be ransom, someone thinking Matt's family is rich,"* she thought.

"Or a prank. Matt's been very familiar with you. Maybe she is

jealous. It would explain her voice not sounding like she cried at all," Barry added.

"True. We'll call Matt when we are done talking with Amy," she thought.

If Matt had been kidnapped, Jennifer needed as much information as she could get from Amy if she was going to help him. "Where did you say this happened?"

"Matt's apartment," she answered.

Jennifer glanced at Petr, his left hand in a fist. "What time of day?"

"Around six."

"Six this morning. That means—"

"No, six last night. Friday night," Amy said. Instead of sounding concerned, she sounded irritated.

It was a busy place with people returning to work and school after a hard week. A passerby should have seen it transpire.

"Who do the police think did it?" Jennifer asked.

"I don't know. I didn't call the police."

A chill of apprehension ran up Jennifer's spine. She didn't call the police? That would be the first thing that Jennifer did. She caught her face in the review mirror; her eyes were so wide open they should hurt.

"Even more suspicious. If that happened last night... Dragon girl, that was almost twenty-four hours ago. I think she's lying and has a prank planned for you," Barry said.

She agreed; Amy's reactions were strange. "Why didn't you call the police?" Jennifer asked Amy.

"I didn't... I didn't want to get you in trouble," she said, stuttering as if she was crying.

"As much as she's crying, I would have expected her to sound more upset when she answered the phone. Her not calling the police... It's not adding up," Barry said.

Jennifer put her blinker on to pass the slower car in front of her, having already decided not to go to Petr's but to Matt's apartment. Hopefully, she'd find Matt sitting on his couch watching TV. If not, there had to be a witness or a clue.

"How would going to the police get me in trouble?"

"I had a text from one of them. A message to call you. They said they want a word with you if you want to see Matt alive again."

"If you ran away, how do you know they wanted to talk to me?"

"And how did they get her number?" Barry asked.

Amy paused momentarily, as if she was creating the story as she talked. "I had a message. A text message from them. They claimed to be the kidnappers and mentioned you by name."

"Why did they text you and not me?" Jennifer asked. If they were able to get Amy's number, they could get Jennifer's too.

"How would I know?" Amy asked. "Listen, they said that unless you showed up on Wednesday alone at the bridge, they would kill him."

"Oh, see, no crying. Why did she stop crying?" Barry asked. *"It's a prank."*

"Show up where and when?" Jennifer asked Amy.

"Amphitheater close to the arts building on campus at six p.m. Wednesday. Do you know where it is?" Jennifer peeked at Petr. He stared straight forward, smelling of a spicy barbeque.

"Anger," Barry said.

"Yes." Musicians played under the bridge in the small theater at odd hours. Before she became a dragon, she loved to study while listening to them. "May I have their number?" Jennifer asked.

"If Matt's really been kidnapped, I'll get him back," Jennifer promised Barry and herself.

"Sure. I'll text it to you," Amy said.

"Amy?" Jennifer hoped she hadn't ended the call.

Whether a prank or real, she needed to treat this situation as if Amy was telling the truth.

"Yeah," she answered.

"Call the police. I'm boring, Amy. I'm hiding nothing. Please call the police. I'll answer any and all questions they have." She put on her blinker to return to the right lane. "What about Matt's parents? Did you call them?"

"Yes," she said and started crying again.

"*I don't believe her,*" Barry said. "*She switches emotions too fast. It's a prank.*"

Jennifer agreed; Amy wasn't telling the truth.

Amy continued, speaking over Barry, but Jennifer was able to follow both conversations. "I'm so worried about him. Please do what you can."

"I will. Send me the number, and I'll contact them."

Music played over the car's speaker again on autoplay, showing Amy had hung up. "Something is wrong," Jennifer said to Petr.

"You caught that too?" he asked.

"Hard not to. Who wouldn't call the police first? Why didn't she do that on Friday when he was kidnapped?" Jennifer asked. "I think Amy is an Immortal." But she couldn't remember smelling anything over her perfume.

Shock bled over from Barry. "*In my defense, Jennifer, it's really strange to wake up in someone else's head.*"

"*What are you talking about, Barry?*" she asked.

"*I want you to know, I'm not God, and I don't know all your memories. I have to search them, just like I search your ancestors' memories,*" he said.

"*What? Tell me, Barry,*" she thought.

He sent her an image similar to daydreaming. One that didn't interrupt her ability to drive but allowed her to see and understand what she hadn't a few months ago.

The vision was right after her transformation, and in it, Jennifer walked down the hall of her dorm, passing

Amy. The clear, distinct scent, like baked rosemary chicken, wafted around her and, at that time, made her queasy. Then, she thought a hangover combined with someone making dinner had caused her stomach to be upset. Now, she knew and understood the smell. Amy was a dragon.

"Jennifer, she probably knows you're a dragon and has for several months," Barry thought.

How had Amy hidden the truth for so long? After the chance encounter in the dorm's hallway, Amy always smelled like cinnamon and spice.

"You didn't remember?" Jennifer asked Barry.

"No. When I told you to awaken, it was to myself as well. My awareness slowly grew with your dreams, Jennifer. It didn't occur to me to check your memories of Amy until now."

It took effort not to look over to Petr and tell him everything. Knowing that Amy was a dragon changed Matt's situation. And that Amy and Johan were friends meant there was a good chance that Amy had helped Johan with his attempt last weekend.

Did Amy kidnap Matt, and that was why she hadn't called the police?

New emotions wafted off from Petr and overwhelmed the car.

"He's concerned about the concentration lines on your forehead. If you want to keep the truth from him until you have more facts, you better do something to stop him from asking about it. Call Matt's cell," Barry said.

On the dash, she had a button shaped like a cell phone. She pushed it.

"Car's menu—" the automated voice said before she hit the button again.

"Call. Matt. Home," she said, thankful that she had added his name and number back to her friend's list, or she'd be searching while driving.

There wasn't a ringtone. "Hey, this is Matt. Leave your name and number."

It beeped. "I'm sorry. This mailbox is full. Goodbye." The music resumed playing.

Not accepting that as an answer, she hit redial. Nothing changed.

"Jennifer, I've had another thought," Barry said.

"What is it?"

"Amy knows that you're friends with Belinda. She could hurt Belinda as well."

"True. But Amy would have mentioned Belinda if she had hurt her or had her," Jennifer reasoned, but she pushed the button again. She didn't wait for the automated voice. "Call Belinda," she ordered and stepped on the gas, exceeding the speed limit by more than her normal ten.

Belinda answered on the first ring. "Hey, Jennifer. I was just thinking about you. We're talking about heading to the beach next weekend. Do you want to go?"

Jennifer exhaled now that she knew that Belinda was all right. She glanced at Petr. They would be gone soon, but before they left, she'd also ask Kamar to watch over Belinda while he searched for the other dragon shifter. Answering Belinda, she said, "I don't think I will be able to."

Petr touched her leg and rubbed small circles in her jeans. Warm vibrations crawled up her spine, generating a peace she didn't feel.

"Is Rob with you?" Jennifer asked.

"Yes, and surprise—I'm studying," she said. "I haven't had anything to drink in a week. I can't remember being sober for this long... I kind of like it."

"Good," she said. It helped knowing that Rob was safe too. Should she tell Belinda about Matt?

"Are you ready to let the campus catch fire with Matt's disappearance before the police find out? Cause if you tell Belinda, everyone will know. At least tell the authorities first," Barry said.

"There is one truth I can give her," she thought to Barry. "I'm leaving the country." She felt Petr's hand stop moving on her leg, then it resumed.

"That's awesome. Are you going with the professor? The rumor around campus is that he's quit."

"Yes. I'm moving to Europe with the professor and not coming back." Not only would that help everyone who cared know she was safe, but if Amy heard the rumors, maybe she would leave everyone at South Holt alone. "I wanted you to know. I'm not sure how long it will be before I can call again."

"Wow. Talk about role reversal. I grow up to be an adult and you grow up to be a reckless college kid."

"Love will do that to you... Anyway, that's all I called to tell you," Jennifer said. "I need to get off the phone."

"Love?" she whispered like she was thinking to herself. "Wait... Are you with the professor right now?" Belinda asked.

"Yes. And I better go. He didn't expect me to call anyone, and I'm sure he'll have questions as to why I'm telling you. I wanted to tell you that I love you, roommate, and to take care."

"No, Jennifer. That sounds like a goodbye. I don't do *good-byes*. When you get settled, call me, Jennifer... That's a demand, not a request. And if he breaks your heart, I'm here for you... Oh, and don't get pregnant."

"Okay, but aren't you going to ask me if I tasted the milk?" Normally, Belinda asked her if she milked the cow as a code for having sex with someone.

"No... Not this time. You wouldn't be willing to leave your dreams to be with him if you hadn't tasted something you like and wanted more of. Call me when you're settled and have a wild. Safe. Ride."

"I will," Jennifer said, hanging up.

The music in the background started, announcing the end

of the phone call. "You told Belinda you were leaving with me… I didn't expect the confession," Petr said.

"Me either," she admitted. "Hopefully, the rumor will spread, and the Immortals will ignore South Holt."

Drawing another pattern on her leg, he whispered. "I needed to touch you, Meelaya. Yesterday, when we talked about worry and fear, and I said that I plan and control my thoughts… I still feel fear and anger. I know we have a plan… but touching you, feeling the claiming, helps. I'm glad I have you."

For as long as she dared to look away from the road, she studied his facial expression to understand what caused his rose-tinted barbeque smell. Petr almost looked peaceful.

Would touching her still give him comfort if he knew the truth about Amy being a dragon? If she had never dated Matt, chances were that Amy would have never paid attention to Petr's sister's descendant.

Would Petr be thankful for Jennifer if he knew that she was the reason Matt had been captured, or would he hate her?

She had to tell him the truth, even knowing Petr might hate her for it. A partnership as deep as marriage and the deeper commitment mating had to be built on trust. "It's my fault, Petr. It's my fault they have Matt. They're after me, so they're going after people I care about."

She turned toward him for a few seconds to see his reaction. He appeared no different than the last time she glanced at him. But Petr didn't yet understand the connections she'd made to Matt's kidnapping and herself. Knowing the next few minutes were crucial in their relationship, she savored what she found in Petr. Her heart swelled at how incredibly handsome he was, and not just his looks but who he was as a person—strong, carrying, loyal. "If they knew how I felt about you…"

Taking her right hand off the wheel temporarily, she swiveled the rearview mirror to watch him as she drove.

"They could be after me. It could be a—" he said.

"A prank?" she finished.

He nodded.

"Amy's a dragon," she said, watching his face carefully for any changes, but his expression did not change, nor did he ask her how she knew. "Barry didn't remember until now, but when I first changed, I walked by her, and she smelled of rosemary chicken. I don't know how she was able to hide it from me weeks after—"

"Kamar met her two weeks ago. He didn't smell dragon."

It didn't surprise her that Kamar had sniffed around campus. "Right, of course you would know," she whispered, but she didn't expect him to answer. "She smells so strongly of her perfume that I didn't notice dragon."

The hand on her lap had stopped moving, and he glanced forward, his brows pressed together. She knew his mind was running through the different scenarios. Jennifer added, "Amy and Johan were friends."

He looked out the window, his skin a little paler, and ran his left hand through his hair. By his reaction, he seemed to understand the implications. Johan and Amy planned her kidnapping, and when that failed, they took Matt. Did Amy know that she killed Johan, and was Matt's kidnapping retribution?

CHAPTER 30

JENNIFER

Minutes later, his hand landed back on her leg, and his fingers slowly danced up it, closer to her torso.

She couldn't smell the musk of lust. "Are you trying to distract me?" she asked, placing her hand on his.

"And myself. Knowing Matt is in danger… or dead… I need a diversion because there is nothing else I can do… Will you offer my mind something else to think about? What's the story about the airport? Why is it so memorable?"

She thought he'd be angry with her and blame her, but instead, he had forced his thoughts away from the fact that his sister's line, that Matt might have died. It was the only reason he still lived, his one life goal.

"He did tell you the way he dealt with fear was to plan and move his thoughts away from things he couldn't control. He's focusing on what he can control," Barry said.

She obliged Petr's request, and asked, "Oh, that. Did you hear my parents' nickname for me?"

"Sky angel, yes. I heard," he said, his thumb tracing circles on her hand now.

"At my elementary school, we were learning about American history. Each person in the room had at least one state to write a report on. Some kids had two. I had Kentucky. My grandparents thought driving to the state would be more educational than to just research it. Can you imagine? Both Grands, Mom, Randy, and me crammed into a sedan. I mean, really cramped. I remember going through Nashville, singing out the window, hoping to be discovered as the next famous star.

"Anyway, there was an air show at the Bluegrass Airport, and my mom thought I would enjoy seeing the planes. I had expressed an interest in being a pilot. Or maybe the suggestion came from one of the Grands. I snuck off while they were trying to calm Randy. I don't think he liked all the noise. So, while my brother distracted them, I explored."

"Where did you go?" he asked, bringing her hand to his mouth and kissing her fingertips.

"I climbed into a plane. My grandfather could tell you what model. I don't know."

Petr smirked before asking, "You found an empty plane and climbed into it?"

"Well, no one notices little kids when they're busy, and the planes look like rides at amusement parks."

"Did you go into the air, Meelaya?"

"No, the pilot found me."

"Did he fuss?" he asked.

"No. The pilot gave me a behind-the-scenes tour. Apparently, he had a daughter about my age, and I reminded him of her. He introduced me to the other people at the airport. His name was David Schmuler, Schuler, something like that." Jennifer grinned. "For me, it was a great day."

"I can imagine. That's definitely memorable... and not very boring."

"Boring came after I had mono in seventh grade. That was the last adventure learning we ever did."

"Yes, if our child did something similar, I would have a hard time letting them out of the house."

Their child. Both fear and excitement coursed through her heart. "A journalist was there doing a story, and I caught his eye. He titled the article 'The Red Baron.' It fit since the plane had an open cockpit, like in the World War II movies. After that, my family called me sky angel.

"My family was introduced to all the pilots and the air controllers. I remember the event as entertaining. My parents told me it was stressful. You don't think the Immortals or the crazy dragon-eating people know about it, do you?"

"Yes. If they're as meticulous as I am, they know about it."

"Meticulous?" she asked.

"Very meticulous. I like to cover each"—he sucked on her index finger, sending chills up her spine—"and every base." He kissed the palm of her hand. "I'll show you in a few weeks."

With everything going on, was he flirting? In the air, she sniffed a little musk, but not much. He was mainly still worried.

"Assuming I say yes," she said.

"You will say yes, Meelaya."

"Well, then, I'm looking forward to finding out," she said, squeezing his hand and letting him go. She redialed Matt's number, and it went straight to voicemail.

But finally, she arrived at their exit. "I'm stopping at Matt's place." She glanced at Petr for a second while she waited for the traffic to clear so she could turn left.

"Good idea," Petr said.

"I could at least ask Doug and Lauren if they've seen him," she said. "If he isn't there, we check the Pi house, then his parents'? Those are the only two places I can think of other than his apartment where he might be."

"I like your plan," Petr said, returning his hand to her leg.

She made eye contact with her mate. "I can't leave until I know he's safe."

"Thank you for caring about Matt, Meelaya," he whispered.

As she turned left onto the street that led to Matt's building, she hit dial. The call was unsuccessful for a fourth time.

At the sight of the complex's pool, her stomach bubbled with dread. Would he be there? His vehicle sat in a spot in front of his place. If he were kidnapped at this location, she'd expect his car to be here. Finding it meant he could have been kidnapped from here.

She backed into the parking place beside Matt's F-150. "His truck is here," she said, filling the silence. Petr nodded. He knew it belonged to Matt, probably had the license tag memorized.

After she came to a complete stop, she checked the window behind Matt's balcony on the second floor. Movement beyond the curtain caught her eye. Everything in her hoped Matt was up there playing video games or idly watching a movie. She put her hand on the door handle. "Wait here. I'll see if he's home."

Barry and Petr were right; action felt better than fear.

Petr reached over, placing his left hand across her lap to halt her. "I'm going with you. If the Immortals are involved, they potentially have someone watching the door. I can't lose you."

She glanced over at him. The fierce expression on his face surprised her, and she no longer wondered if he would hate her if something happened to Matt. His eyes told the truth; he loved her unconditionally. She gulped.

They met in front of the car. The connection between them sizzled. She wasn't surprised when Petr led the charge to Matt's door. After all, he had a folder with Matt's lineage at his house and ensured Matt would be given a scholarship to the college where Petr taught.

She insisted on tapping three times on Matt's door. While they waited, she stared at the concrete landing. Odd thoughts distracted her from panicking, like, wasn't there a welcome mat last time?

The door opened. The dark blond woman in a peach suit who greeted them resembled Lauren, Matt's roommate, but Lauren had dyed black hair. "Lauren?" she asked in a questioning tone.

The woman glared at Jennifer, then at Petr. Over her shoulder, she said to someone in the apartment, "It's Jennifer." Then she stepped out of the way, letting them enter the apartment.

The voice confirmed it was Lauren. However, Jennifer wondered at the dry inflection she used to say her name. Was it an answer to who was at the door to another person in the unit or sarcasm?

Because she let her into the room, Jennifer assumed the tone was an innocent way of calling someone. Holding Dr. Smith's hand, she led him into the apartment.

The last time she had visited Matt's apartment, the place was picked up. Now, an open box of uneaten pizza sat on the kitchen table. She smelled coffee that gave the room a coffee-house odor. Funny, she'd never seen Lauren drink coffee this late, but things changed. On Jennifer's left, someone had scattered a bunch of index cards with phone numbers. The one on top said *Matt's Emergency Numbers*.

Soon, Doug joined them in the living room. He, at least, had not changed. Like Petr had a few days ago, Doug wore a full beard. The beer belly he had earned and the plaid clothing screamed nineties grunge bands, as usual.

"I like your hair," Jennifer said to Lauren. In acknowledgment, Lauren touched her head. "This is Dr. Smith," Jennifer said, still holding his hand, and pointed toward Petr. "Is Matt home?"

"Um, no. Matt went out with Amy last night and never returned," Lauren volunteered.

"We wouldn't be so worried," Doug said as he put his arm

around Lauren. "Except Amy has been acting strangely. And"
—Doug indicated the table behind him, where a wallet sat
beside the scattered index cards—"Matt left his identification
and the door unlocked. That's not like him."

"Did you call Amy?" Jennifer asked.

"Nope. We don't have Amy's number. I wish one of us
did. Matt's not answering his cell phone. It goes straight to
voicemail," Lauren answered. "We would have called you to
see if you've seen him, but we didn't have your number
either. Are you here because you know he's missing? Or have
you seen him?" She stared down at where Jennifer's fingers
were intertwined with Petr's.

"I'm moving out of the country," Jennifer admitted,
thinking quickly because she couldn't tell them the truth. The
less they knew about the dragon world, the better chance they
had of not being sucked into it. She glanced at Petr and
moved closer to him so they got the idea without hearing the
whole story. "Despite ending our relationship painfully, I still
care about Matt as a friend. I hoped he'd be here so I could
say goodbye."

Jennifer glanced over at the brown wallet and the blue
index card with his parents' number. She thought about
calling them directly but didn't want them sucked in either. If
she could find Matt, she wouldn't need to get them involved.
"Barry, remember the number," she thought. "Did you call his
parents?"

Doug said, "Yes. I've called his parents. They're not
worried even though they haven't heard from him. They said
that Amy called them and said Matt was fine."

Jennifer fought not to look over to Petr. Amy the dragon
calling Matt's parents couldn't be a good thing.

"Do you mind asking him to call me when he comes
home? I would rather him hear about me dating Dr. Smith
from me than from rumors around campus," Jennifer said.

"Sure. But he still likes you, and he won't be happy about this," Doug said.

Jennifer nodded; she knew Matt would get over her... if he survived this.

Petr led her to the door. "Thank you for your time," Petr said.

The Pi house would be the next logical location.

"Stop by the house first," Petr said as she opened the car door. "We can grab our stuff for our trip and find a hotel tonight. I imagine my house has been watched, and I can't lose both of you."

"After we go to your house, I want to search campus, including the Pi house."

He nodded. "All right."

The cloud of oppression, with its bitter vinegar scent, settled inside the vehicle on the ride to Petr's house. What could she say to Petr? What could she say to herself? Occasionally, she glanced at him. More than before, his face appeared hollow, like when a flashlight was placed under someone's chin, casting hard shadows.

Though she feared for Matt, her most significant concern lay with her mate. What would it be like to believe you lost the one thing you had been focused on for years? The guilt for causing Matt to be involved in the triad affair awaited, lurking for her in the future, she was sure.

She pulled into the driveway and opened her door. Immediately, rosemary and danger swirled from an unknown dragon. She placed her hand on Petr's, stopping him from getting out of the car.

"Dragon," she whispered.

"Are you sure?" he asked.

She nodded. "It's not Kamar. Kamar smells like the sea. This one is closer to..." She sniffed. "Concrete after a thunderstorm."

Standing beside the vehicle door, Barry said, "I'm going into the house. You stay here."

"Barry is going into the house," Jennifer repeated. She breathed out.

"He can do that?" Petr asked.

"Yes. He can split from me and go into buildings as long as I'm close by."

A few seconds later, Barry's laughter reverberated in her mind.

"What's so funny?" she asked.

Barry appeared in the same place he had disappeared from, all smiles. "The dragon is Matt. He's in Petr's bed."

She leaned back in the seat and exhaled in relief. "It's Matt!" she announced. "Matt's here, and he's in your bed."

Petr's shoulders relaxed; his features softened as the tension flowed out of his body. He grabbed his hurt shoulder. "Wait. Why is Matt here?"

"He's the dragon, silly boy." She couldn't help the smile that threatened to tear her face in two. "The one you've waited for. Your sister's dragon-shifting son."

"Let's go check on him," Petr said, unlocking the door and hopping out with more energy than she had seen from him all day.

The house keys slipped from Petr's hands as he hastily unlocked the door. He flung it open and didn't pause for Jennifer to catch up as he stormed down the hall.

Jennifer froze in the entranceway. "Great," she said. The back door stood ajar, its window shattered, and the glass fanned out underneath. She secured the front door and shut the refrigerator on her way to the mess. She closed the back door and locked it, but a lot of good it did with a person-sized hole in it.

When she made it to the back room, she found Matt sprawled on the bed. His frame was much larger than she remembered; the king bed appeared tiny. He lay face down, his head turned toward the wall, his hair matted and stuck to his skin. The sheet covered his body except for his bare shoulders.

A cold sensation filled her tennis shoes, and she glanced down to find wet, dirty jeans that reeked of blood beside an equally disgusting pair of sneakers.

Standing by the discarded clothing, Barry pinched his nose and said, "Even for a wyvern, this is gross."

She sat on a vacant corner of the bed, reaching over to brush his hair off his face. The act woke him, though his eyes stayed closed. He snatched her, slinging her around and then under him—their chests touching. It was such a fast motion she couldn't react in time.

"Mmm," he said. "You smell so good." Somehow, as she went to shove him off her, he grabbed her wrist with one hand and pinned it above her head. Gently, he kissed each of her cheeks before finding her mouth.

With her body trapped, she couldn't push him off. Her face flushed as she realized he was completely naked. "Matt, get off!"

CHAPTER 31

MATT

It wasn't Matt's fault that he trapped Jennifer, not completely.

He had been his mother, spending special time with his father... Both gross and, well, strangely fascinating. The part that most piqued his interest was the swirl of emotions that coursed through his libido. When he found Jennifer combing his hair with her fingers, the mood carried through him, and he acted impulsively.

Dreams couldn't do that, could they—carry their atmosphere into the real world? He'd never experienced such intense sensations that lasted after he woke. And his mom wasn't capable of feelings. At least, that's what he thought. Honestly, he wasn't accustomed to this many emotions all at once and didn't think it was possible for anyone till right then.

Overrun with unfamiliar stirrings and an awfully scrumptious smelling Jennifer Wright who pushed his hair away from his forehead, he acted like any predator with an appetizing meal and bit that bait.

The second reason he couldn't be blamed was he'd

dreamed of this very fantasy thousands of times… waking to find her at the foot of his bed. Naturally, he assumed this was his imagination. Until he'd flung her over, trapping her under him, her hands above her head.

Unlike his dreams, this Jennifer fought him. Imaginary Jennifer begged for him to strip her and didn't try to escape.

He blinked to clear the fog in his mind. The living, breathing Jennifer Wright lay underneath his naked body.

And they weren't alone.

He might have done things differently if they were alone, such as encouraging her to snuggle and never leave his arms again. As he removed his hands and leaned away, he said, "I'm sorry, Jennifer."

She scooted away from him, standing close to the end of the bed beside Dr. Smith… or was his name really Petr? "I broke your window," Matt said.

"You did," Dr. Smith answered.

While sitting on the edge of the bed, Matt rearranged the sheets around his nakedness. He studied the man. The eyes never changed, not even as Dr. Smith. His clothing, his hair, his weight all fluctuated, but not his eyes. "This will sound crazy, but I was told by this voice to come and find you. They said your name was Petr."

"My name is Petr." He smiled this radiant, over-the-top, bright grin. The kind Matt had witnessed on TV shows when long-lost families reunited. "I've waited for centuries to meet you." Tears formed in the corners of his eyes.

But Matt had had enough feelings for one day, so he didn't react right away. "I need to sort this out." He peered down at the stinky clothes on the floor. He'd washed them with water until the red turned white, yet he could smell the metallic zing of blood. Then he tightened the bedding wrapped around his torso. He glanced over at Jennifer. "I… This is going to sound crazy… I was being held prisoner. This"—he raised his hand, the material slipping, and he grabbed it back to cover himself. "This man took a baseball bat." He touched where his head should be caved in, but it felt normal. "He hit me upside my head—"

"Did the voice say *awaken*?" Jennifer asked.

Matt blinked several times, his brows drawing together. Did Jennifer have a similar experience? "No. It said *enough*."

Searching her with new intent, he noticed differences he hadn't seen before. It wasn't in her appearance; it was in the way she stood—taller, like if you put her in a room of a thousand people, you would be able to find her because of the strength that emanated from her and demanded your attention. That she might understand gave him the courage to speak the impossible. "I grew and became a dragon."

He waited to see her reaction, yet there wasn't one. Jennifer Wright didn't look surprised. She knew he was a dragon, but how? "You're a dragon too, aren't you?"

"Yes." She smiled.

"When?" he asked.

"Thanksgiving, the bear."

Puzzle pieces snapped into place. All the clues had been around him. He thought back to that trip. She'd lost her way, stumbling through the forest, and tripped on... "The dead bear. You killed the bear?"

Her cheeks flushed some, and she took on that faraway stare she had earlier that week. Quickly, she recovered and nodded.

He thought her crazy at the time. Wait. Her dreams. "Remember when you dreamed you were your grandmother?"

"Yes."

"I... I was my moth—" Another piece found its home. "Was the dream real? It felt like I was my mom."

Jennifer shrugged. "It's what she experienced. Her

emotions. Her life. But it's not real. You own her memories now. If you need to recall something that happened to her, you can think about it, and it would be like you lived through it."

"Oh." His becoming a dragon didn't seem unnatural, and he wasn't sure why. His mom having emotions, though, that bothered him. She wasn't the cold, heartless, uncaring woman he knew and loved. Instead, she felt everything more intensely than the burning sun. How could she stand waking up every morning? Even knowing now what she'd undergone—his grandmother strapped to a chair, kidnapped like Matt. Her face was bloody, swollen, and bruised. One last *I love you* before the gunman splattered her brains all over his mother's face.

She'd been young when her mother died. He knew that. But he had never learned how or why. It wasn't discussed. Nothing unpleasant was ever mentioned.

Smile, don't let them see your fear.

Matt couldn't smile. He understood the thick wall she placed around her passionate heart. He glanced up at Petr. "You've followed my family for…"

"Centuries," Petr finished.

"Why?" Matt asked.

"I had a twin sister, Roz. She's who you descended from."

"That explains why so many people called you uncle."

He nodded.

"And Jennifer. How do you know her?" he asked Petr.

"My ancestor, River, came from the city of dragons, Dernogard. River and Petr were friends," Jennifer answered.

When he had thought about a plan to win Jennifer back, he decided he would be a rebound. The older college professor would dump her eventually because they had little in common. But now, knowing she knew Petr from a dream, he assumed it wouldn't end the way he thought.

Smile so everyone thinks you're all right.

Ignoring his Jennifer problem, Matt pulled the sheet tight about his waist and held it with his right hand, pointing to the dirty clothes. "I, ah…I killed the guy who hit me with the baseball bat. I'm pretty sure I swallowed half of him."

"You have a bruise around your eye. That's all I can see," Jennifer said. She moved out of the way. Above the dresser and almost across from him was a mirror. He looked at the dark yellows and purples on his face. It appeared weeks old, yet he didn't think a day had gone by.

"What day is it?" he asked.

"Saturday. From what we can tell, you were kidnapped last night," Petr said.

"Amy sent me a text this morning. She says they're demanding—" Jennifer said, then she froze, sniffing the air.

She glanced at him like he had said something. Matt had kept his face well-guarded, as his mother had taught him. How could Jennifer know Matt felt disgusted at hearing Amy's name?

"What did Amy do?" Jennifer asked.

Even Petr turned toward her, like he was surprised as well.

She pointed to her nose. "I assumed every dragon could smell emotions, but maybe it will take some time for you to adjust. Regret, fear, anger, emotions that are negative, taste bitter. Well, not fear. It tastes delicious, frankly." She glanced at Petr. "Sorry. It sounds so inhuman."

"You're not human, Meelaya," Petr said.

"She was the one who arranged for them to kidnap me. But they're after you," Matt said.

Jennifer just nodded. "Thought so. When I talked to her, her responses weren't normal, and she's a dragon." She sighed, looking between Petr and him. "Well, speaking of smells, I'm going to remove those disgusting clothes. I'm assuming they're covered with the Immortal's blood," Jennifer said. She pinched her nose and acted like she might gag. "While I do that, you two can talk."

Before Matt could confirm that the Immortals were the bad guys, Petr asked Jennifer, "Are you going to burn them?"

"Yeah. Can I take them to the sink and set fire to them there? Would that be better?"

"They're wet, Jen. They'll be—"

Jennifer's hand rose as she pulled back her sleeve and flexed her biceps. As she wickedly smiled, red scales, shiny like rubies but tiny like a lizard's, formed on her arm, and black fingernails grew long from her fingertips.

Huh, that's sexy, he thought. Then she coughed, expanding her mouth, reaching in, and hacking until she spit out a flame ball.

"I can breathe fire," she said, waggling her eyebrows.

"I'd think that was cool if it didn't look like you were a cat spitting up a hairball," he admitted.

"It's still cool," she said, scowling. When the flames died out, she leaned over and picked up the clothes with her scaled hand. "Talk, get to know one another," she said as she left the room.

It was awkward standing in front of an ancient man who knew everything there was to know about him but who Matt knew very little about. It was made worse by the I've-conquered-the-world smile Petr wore.

"I'm sorry about your window," Matt said again. "You weren't home. It was cold, and I just wanted to sleep."

"I can buy another, but you... I can never have another you. You are the fulfillment of the promise I gave to my sister. Almost like karma understood I would find Jennifer right when my sister's hopes were fulfilled."

Was Uncle Petr saying Jennifer belonged to him romantically? But he had found her first. Years of his mother's training kept his muscles taut, so his thoughts stayed hidden. "What do you mean I'm your sister's fulfillment?"

"I promised my sister I would wait until the dragon blood ran true and she had her dragon ancestor. She died right after giving birth to your ancestor. It broke my heart," Petr admitted. He shook his head. "Let me help you. You need clothes." Petr sized him up for a second and frowned. "You're taller than me."

That's right. That's why Jennifer will prefer me. I'm a better specimen. He stuck his chest out a little more, knowing he was the superior choice, but kept his expression neutral.

Petr moved to the closet, digging on the top shelf. Jennifer's green meanie, her duffel bag, stuck out, though it was buried under piles of Petr's clothing. Matt's confidence deflated some.

"I bought some clothes for Kamar that are too small for him and are around here somewhere. They might be in the living room." He walked past him and stopped at the door. "I'll get those for you, but first, where's your passport?"

"My passport?" Matt asked.

Petr sighed and sat on the bed. "There's at least one group, maybe more, that we call the Immortals. They hunt dragons to eat their... body parts. I'm afraid you're included, even if you are just a shifter." He looked at Matt's chest. "If they eat your heart, they can live forever. It makes you... worth hunting."

That explained why those guys he killed earlier talked about an award. If they murdered him, someone else could use his corpse. Gross, and yet fascinating. "Oh." The last time he used his passport was this past December when he went to the Bahamas. He left it in his carry-on, in his closet at his parents' house. "My mom and dad's place."

"Maria," Petr said, then sighed, then blinked.

"What about my mother?" Matt asked.

"If the Immortals discovered you're a dragon..." He

trailed off. Petr ran his hand through his hair, then put his hand on his right shoulder.

"What really happened? With your shoulder."

"Do you remember Johan?" Petr asked.

"Yes."

"He shot me."

When was the last time Matt saw Johan? He searched his memories and couldn't recall—a week ago? "Did you kill him?"

"No," Petr said and glanced toward the kitchen. "I'm not sure why they're so interested in capturing Jennifer, but I'm thankful, nonetheless. It kept them from killing her when she was alone and vulnerable."

By breaking up with her when he did, he left her vulnerable. At the time, she needed his protection and stability, but he betrayed her. Those thoughts stabbed at a deep part of his ideals on what a man should be—on what *he* wanted to be as a man. She was his girlfriend then and his job was to ensure her safety, but he wasn't there for her. He had failed.

Petr continued. "It's also why we not only need to get our hands on your passport, but somehow, we must convince your parents to leave the country."

"Why?"

"If they kidnapped you to capture Jennifer, they would kidnap your parents to catch you. You are now more valuable to them dead than alive."

"I can ask Gung-Gung—"

"Gung-Gung, your grandfather? He's here in the States? I thought he moved to Germany when your grandmother died." Petr sat up straighter.

"He lives with my parents."

"That's great!" Petr stood. "I'll call him."

"Great? How so?"

Petr smiled warmly. "We were close friends. He'll remember me. After I bring you some clothes, I'll call him."

"Why would he believe it's you from talking over the phone?" Matt asked, tugging the sheet closer together.

"Because I know things about him no one else does."

At the door, he stopped and held the doorframe but didn't make eye contact. "Matt, I love you like a son, so I'll let you off this time. But don't kiss my fiancée again."

And Petr left him alone with all his emotions.

CHAPTER 32

JENNIFER

WHEN JENNIFER HAD HER TONSILS OUT IN MIDDLE SCHOOL, SHE initially put a calendar on her wall and circled August third, the day the doctor said she should be out of pain. Every morning, she glanced at the marked date until one day, she no longer hurt. She learned she could go through anything if she focused on the now, surviving one minute at a time.

Taking Petr's advice to cope with transitioning from human to dragon, possibly being a prophetic mark, her first kill, and discovering she had a soul mate, Jennifer concentrated on the next step. In three more days, Jennifer would be on a plane to a safer location. Once there, she'd uncoil the tension in her shoulders and deal with the suddenness of all the events in her life. Preparation to leave took on a new energy for Jennifer because keeping busy was part of her cure.

Drinking mint with honey tea, she completed things that must be done before they left. She'd swept up the broken glass, check. Petr ordered a replacement door online, called Kamar and asked him to install it, and covered the gaping hole with cardboard, check. What else needed to be finished before they left?

"You could change the sheets on the bed and wash the dirty ones," Barry suggested.

"Okay," she thought, placing her empty cup near the sink.

Numb, she didn't pay attention to the scents or sounds. If she had, she wouldn't have walked into a bedroom where Matt, wearing only a towel around his waist, stood over the bed, looking at a stack of clothing.

She turned to leave before he noticed her.

"Jennifer," Matt said.

"Yeah." She faced him. Her eyes raked over his wet, dark, curling hair that dripped water slowly down his toned muscles. For someone other than her, he would make a fine partner one day.

"I've been thinking," Matt said. If he caught her checking him out, he didn't let on, continuing to study the red shirt. Red wasn't a color she saw him in often. Perhaps the only clothes Petr could find weren't Matt's style.

"About?" she asked, folding her arms and leaning against the doorframe. She didn't need him to tell her. She could smell the musk and barbeque from where she stood; he was slightly aroused at finding her in the doorway and also fearful of something.

"Us."

"What about us?" she asked.

"I was wrong. About everything. I should have—"

"You've already said sorry, and I've already forgiven you."

He glanced at her. "I'd like to start again."

Appearing near the window with a bag of popcorn, Barry said, "And the saga of Matt and Jennifer continues."

Playing stupid, she said, "Start… again?"

He touched his chest, with the same hand he pointed to her, then placed it back on his chest. "Us. I'd like us back."

There was something there. She was attracted to him.

"Memories," Barry spoke up, his hand digging through

popped kernels. "You remember what it's like to be seduced by him. The spark, at least physically, is only a memory. Emotionally, you like who he is, his personality, and at one time, that was enough."

"Will it go away?" she thought.

"It's a phantom already. It wouldn't be so strong if you hadn't chosen Matt at one time," Barry said.

Briefly, she'd decided to mate with Matt and forget she claimed Petr.

Barry continued. "But I like Matt. So, I'm going to enjoy the game."

Buttery popcorn filled her mouth as Barry took his first bite. She wasn't sure why this reminded her and not the tea, but she realized she'd not eaten all day. Answering Matt, she said, "I'm with Petr now; you know that."

"I know. But I'm not done trying. Not yet." He unhooked his towel, and it dropped to the ground. She couldn't help but notice his gifted proportions and the way his hips narrowed around a firm bottom. As he grabbed the sweatpants off the bed, she turned her head.

"Man, I actually like this guy," Barry said.

She closed her eyes, but it was too late. Behind her lids, the image of Matt's physical perfection seemed to burn into her retinas, and she couldn't stop seeing it. Her mouth filled with Barry's buttery popcorn as she forced her eyes to stay shut.

"Really, Matt," she said.

"You're not even the same species as Petr, but we're both dragons." She heard some shuffling. "It's safe now," he said sarcastically, mimicking a higher-pitched voice. "Seriously, Jen, I imagine we'll see each other naked, unless you have a way to keep your clothes on when you transform."

She hadn't thought about transforming in front of Matt. Would she have to be nude around him? Exposed to other people? Her cheeks grew warm. She glanced over at Barry, hoping he had an answer. He shrugged.

"I'll do my best to respect your modesty if you don't mind doing the same for me," she said.

"Well, I had an alternative reason. You needed to see what you were passing up. I'd kiss you again," Matt said as he stared at the wall that connected to the rest of the house. "But Petr asked me not to kiss his fiancée."

So, Petr had told him. Though he was bound to find out sooner or later.

"There've been a lot of changes in the last few weeks," she said.

Matt sat on the bed and studied the sweatpants he wore. "This dragon, Kamar, he's taller and bigger than me. It's like wearing my dad's clothes."

"You're just as tall as Kamar," she said. "At least, I think you are."

"Nah, his clothes are bigger," he said, pulling on a pant leg.

"It doesn't look like something you would wear," she commented. Matt's sense of style was something she liked about him.

"All good. Sweats work until I can get to a store. Hopefully, Gung-Gung will bring me clothes."

According to Petr, Matt's family could arrive at any moment.

"That reminds me." She walked to the closet, sorting through the racks until she found a blue robe. She pulled it out. "I'll need to put this on to show your parents because I doubt you have the control to change to a dragon whenever you want."

"Ah, you could change outfits in front of me if you want to practice losing your modesty," Matt said.

She searched his face and sniffed the air but didn't detect a hint of flirting.

"It will give you a rehearsal for being nude in front of people," Matt said.

"No, that's all right." She folded the robe over her arm. "I'll go to the spare bedroom."

"I can go," he said and stood. "Where's Uncle Petr?"

"In his office. Ordering plane tickets," Jennifer said

"The office that's the spare bedroom?" Matt raised his eyebrows. "Oh."

"No," she said, shaking her head. "It's not like that…" She trailed off. "At least not yet."

"I take that as a maybe for us if there's a not yet," Matt said.

"It's a no, Matt."

"It's a maybe, Jennifer. You're not married. There's still a chance."

She turned to leave and said, "I'll go to the bathroom to change clothes."

"No," Matt said. "I'll go."

She stopped and waited.

Matt got to his feet. Standing in front of her, he searched her face. "Do you know how old he is?" She didn't respond, and he continued. "My first dream was of him. His sister's son watched him hunt mammoths. That makes him ancient in my book. Have you looked up how long ago the last mammoth roamed the earth? He's older than that."

She kept that part of their relationship separate from her working mind. Petr was old. She knew that. But not how old. She figured the myriad lives she'd lived each night made up for their age gap. But did it? Now that she had a clue to how old he was, should she try to determine how old he might be compared to how many dreams she'd had?

"Do it," Barry said. "See if you can narrow down his age."

Pulling her phone out of her back pocket, she searched for mammoths. The screen showed a picture of a mammoth on a snow-covered tundra and the number four thousand B.C.

She needed to sit and moved to the bed, flopping down. The love of her life, the man of her heart, was over four thousand years old. *"Barry, I feel like I'm in an urban fantasy novel,"* she thought to him. *"The back of the book says something like 'What happens when a dragon shifter falls in love with a four-thousand-year-old—'"*

"He hunted mammoths... That means he's older than four thousand years old. Let's go with six and not a day over."

She glared at Barry. *"I'm in love with a six-thousand-year-old man."*

Too much, too soon...

"Three days," Barry said. "Three days. Make it to Dernogard, and then we'll start digesting all this." He laughed. "Then we can eat the mammoth one bite at a time."

"Not funny," she thought.

"You didn't know?" Matt said. "He should have told you so you could have made up your mind and not let your emotions decide for you."

"I knew he was old, Matt. Just not..."

"Old enough to have survived the flood?" Matt asked.

When she said nothing, he sat on the bed beside her and placed his hand on her leg. "I do have one question, but if you aren't having sex, then you can't answer it."

"What?"

"Are his privates, you know, all shriveled up and stuff? I mean, living that long has to have some kind of impact... Effect... Whatever."

Did body parts age? She read somewhere that ears never stopped growing. It might be an urban myth, but still, did things change, or was she permanently frozen in a nineteen-year-old girl's body? Was it different for people who ate dragon hearts? She didn't know. She looked up at Barry. *"Do you know?"*

"I know we slow down. We age, but it's so unhurried that

no one notices. And look at Petr. Does he look thirty to you?" Barry asked.

"No, not at all," she thought. "None of your business, Matt. That's between Petr and me, all of it."

Squeezing her leg, Matt said, "I didn't mean to cross a line. I just care for you. You don't have to go with your emotions or nature… or even because your ancestor knew him. You have me. I'm here, born when you were, and we have more in common than we do with anyone else either of us knows." He stood and kissed her on her head. "You have me, Jen." He closed the door on his way out.

"Don't think. Don't react. Let it percolate, Jennifer. Three days. Think about this in three days," Barry encouraged.

CHAPTER 33

JENNIFER

THE DOORBELL RANG. BARRY, WHO'D BEEN HUMMING, STOPPED. "Show time, dragon girl," he said. Jennifer stood from the reclining armchair and turned toward the entrance as Petr bolted out of the living room with Matt.

"Want to see?" Barry asked. "I can spy on the new arrivals while you wait."

"Yes. Please go."

"It will be easier with your eyes closed," Barry said, disappearing.

She closed her eyes and was instantly transported to the entranceway. She found herself staring at Petr as he greeted Matt's family. Matt, to her left, nervously paced on the balls of his feet.

Petr offered his hand to Matt's tall, bald, muscular dad. They shook left hands once Petr pointed to his shoulder. "Come in," Petr said, giving the group more room to enter.

Tall and thin, Maria came through the door wearing an elegant wrap around her neck that she tugged. She smiled, but it didn't reach her eyes. Instead of touching Petr, she nodded and then moved into the home. Closer to the kitchen, her eyes roamed from the walls to the table to the cardboard covering the windowless back door as she judged Petr's house, a sneer on her perfect features.

The last one inside, Gung-Gung, dressed in jeans and a polo shirt, cleaned his feet on the welcome mat before entering the house. He hugged Petr as if they were long-lost friends. His eyes were bright as he released Petr and embraced his grandson warmly. He took Matt's hands and glanced up at his much taller descendant. "Matt." He patted his arms. "You smell even more like a dragon."

Jennifer swallowed.

Now that everyone stood just inside, Petr stepped onto the porch. His head swiveled in both directions. Then he came back into the room.

"I think he's looking to see if any spies are outside. Possibly following Matt's parents," Barry reported.

After Petr closed the door, he held out his arm. "May I take your coats," Petr offered.

Gung-Gung removed his and handed it to Petr as he sniffed the air. "Smells like smoke in here," he said.

"He can smell me," Barry said.

Gung-Gung continued. "Matt, my grandson." He patted Matt. "I'm always glad to see you... Dr. Cook asked me to bring your passport, but I'm not sure why. I left it in the car."

"Gung-Gung, I'm glad to see you too. I thought... Never mind," Matt said, then glanced up at his mother. "I'll tell you all in a second."

"That's odd, Barry. Why wouldn't Matt greet his parents?"

"Better yet," Barry responded. *"Why didn't his parents greet him?"*

Still holding Matt's hand, Gung-Gung stared between Matt and Petr. "See, I told you, magic is real. Our Matt and our Dr. Peter Cook. He introduced me to your mother," he said, looking at Matt's mom.

"That's how he did it, Barry. He reminded Gung-Gung about introducing him to his wife, Matt's grandmother." In those few

seconds, she wondered what life he had before this one. Was it as Dr. Peter Cook, or had there been others? Did he do the same work each time or venture into other positions? If she wasn't murdered and turned into an elixir, what would she do in a hundred years or even more?

As Matt's family rounded the corner, she opened her eyes, blinking several times to adjust to the height difference between her five-foot-nine and Barry's six-foot-one. When Matt's mother entered the room, taller than Jennifer in heels, she stared down at Jennifer, moving to the opposite side. There was such hostility in that look that Jennifer feared the woman would take off a shoe and beat her with it.

"What did I do to her?" she asked.

Barry materialized beside her. "I haven't got a clue. But that scent—"

Jennifer inhaled a giant whiff of burning plastic.

"That's hate," he finished.

Matt moved to Jennifer's left, their shoulders touching, almost like he knew he needed to defend her. Appearing unaware of the tension, Petr chose to be near her but stood closer to Matt's father.

Everyone awkwardly stood, staring around the room.

Matt leaned into her and spoke to Petr, who was on her other side. He said, "I get it. You knew my family."

"Yes. In India. Before I moved to the States. I was a doctor and delivered Maria," he said.

That answered her earlier question—he didn't have the same job every lifetime.

"You left when Maria was little," Gung-Gung said. "Do you remember him?" he asked his daughter.

"No," Maria said harshly, but she focused on Jennifer.

"Once again, Barry, what did I do?"

Her mate smiled, unaware. "Yes. In this life, I've been Matt's teacher." He raised his left hand in invitation. "Please, take a seat."

Petr moved to the loveseat with her as they sat. Matt went to sit beside her, but without any room left, Matt was forced to join Gung-Gung on the long couch. Maria noticed the awkward moment. She barely looked away as she occupied one armchair and Matt's dad the other.

The seating arrangements put Maria across from Jennifer, a perfect opportunity for Maria to kill her with deadly glares.

Straightening the robe, Jennifer greeted Matt's family. "Hello, Gung-Gung, Mrs. and Mr. Davis." She smiled and leaned into Petr for strength. Where they touched, she vibrated, and she took as much calming energy as possible.

"It makes even more sense," Maria said. "Amy said that Jennifer was a conniving, vindictive b—"

"Mom!" Matt said.

Confused, Jennifer tried to understand how Amy convinced anyone of anything.

"Let me guess." Maria turned her evil stare to Matt. The putrid burning plastic concentrated in the room, and Jennifer wasn't sure how the ones without dragon senses didn't smell it. "Jennifer's persuaded you to believe you are a dragon. Is that it, Matt?"

"I *am* a dragon," Matt answered.

"Do you hear that, Drew?" Maria said, using her hands to talk in a heated debate. She sighed. "Matt, I'm sorry, son." She got to her feet, her husband standing with her. "Let's go home. In the morning, I'll phone the doctor and get you admitted."

"What are you talking about?" Matt asked. "First, I'm a legal adult. I don't have to go anywhere with you. Second, Amy is the one who kidnapped me. Third—" He raised his voice. "I am a dragon. Show them, Jennifer." He looked over at her.

"You harlot," Maria accused, pointing her finger like a gun at Jennifer.

Petr stood. "Enough. You will not come into my house and call my fiancée names."

"Mom," Matt pleaded, moving to his feet. "Listen to me. If we don't leave the country, the same people who abducted me will take you. Don't you see? If they kidnapped me to get to Jennifer, they'll kidnap you to get to me. These people aren't playing. They're serious, and I'm worth more to them dead than alive."

Maria snarled as she talked, "Kill you? No one tried to hurt you. You don't even have a bruise. Other than that horrible outfit, you look fine." She took a step toward Matt. "Son, Jennifer wants you back and is making Amy look bad. She devised this elaborate plan." She pointed at Jennifer. "She's so manipulative, she's hired an actor to play one of my dad's friends. Let's go home, and I'll get you mental help."

Barry, between Jennifer and Matt, shrugged. "Perhaps she likes Amy better than you."

"Nothing I can do about that." Standing, Jennifer allowed the pressure of the shift to come over her. Red scales crawled down her skin. She took off the robe, placing it over the chair's arm. "I'm a dragon," she said in her demonic voice — multiple octaves, multiple people speaking at once. "So is Matt. If we don't leave, they'll kill Matt and harvest him for his body parts."

A sarcastic, evil laugh erupted from Maria. When she stopped, she raised her head and stared down her nose at Jennifer. She crossed her arms and said, "Maybe instead of college, you should move to Hollywood. With your acting and make-up skills, you could make movies. Demons aren't dragons, though," she teased.

"Fine. Scoot. Give me room," Jennifer huffed.

Not waiting, the pressure built, and Jennifer swelled, dropping to her clawed feet into her wyvern dragon form. This form reminded Jennifer of a cute and cuddly stuffed dragon—a round body, little wings, a long neck, and a salamander face. In order to appear mean, Jennifer roared like a dying bird directly into Maria's face. She willed saliva to drop down her pointed teeth while she breathed. Maria's hair blew in and out of Jennifer's mouth, tickling Jennifer's throat. She fought a sneeze. Yet the burnt plastic scent increased to the point of making Jennifer feel nauseous. *"Fear me, you little tiny human. What do you have to say about that?"* Jennifer thought toward Maria, though Maria would never hear her in this form.

A broad, authentic smile spread across Gung-Gung's face. "I knew it. See, I told you, daughter, we come from dragons! Futz-Lung, just like my father shared with me, and my grandmother, and as far back as..." He paused and looked at Petr. "When did our dragon ancestor exist?"

"Futz-Lung? Your ancestor's name was Perun. He was Nordic. And so far back, I can't even tell you the length of time," Petr answered.

"Can you make her change back?" Maria asked, her eyes locked on Jennifer.

"Eat her," Barry suggested.

"Remember when we went to the Bahamas?" Matt asked. When she nodded, he continued. "It was a setup. Amy was there intentionally, planning on breaking up Jennifer and me."

"I like Amy better than I thought, then. Smart of her to fly to another country to get the man she desires. Make her"—she pointed at Jennifer—"change back."

"Amy hates me, Mom. What about *she kidnapped me*, do you not understand?" Matt asked.

"Where is the proof, son? You look fine and unharmed to me." Maria breathed out audibly, raising her hand to her forehead. Her husband moved quickly, helping her to her seat. Despite Jennifer being a dragon, he glared at her while maintaining physical contact with Maria's elbow.

"Make the creature become human again," Maria said,

fanning her face and leaning against the back of the chair. Andrew kneeled beside his wife and focused his attention on rubbing her arm.

"Seriously, Barry, no fear, no oh wow, nothing," Jennifer thought. *"I told you. I'm stuffed animal adorable! In Dernogard, we need to find a giant mirror and practice snarling."*

"Meelaya, I'm sorry. Would you please morph back into a human?" Petr asked.

"Fine." She turned back into the human-shaped dragon, red and scaley. *"But not fully human. I'm not doing what that woman wants, Barry."*

"That's it, my dragon girl. Fight the system," Barry said, standing beside Matt, his arms crossed, giving the evil eye to Maria. Undoubtedly, if Barry still lived, he would eat Maria. He thought, *"You should have eaten her."*

She leaned over to Petr. "I'm going to go to our bedroom. Good luck."

"I'm staying here, Jennifer. If anything interesting is said, I'll let you know," Barry thought.

As she walked out the door, Gung-Gung waved. "You pretty dragon," he said. "I like you best for my grandson."

She smiled at the compliment but kept walking until she entered the bedroom.

"That's rude to walk out of here. Amy would have stayed. Matt, don't date her..." Maria said, but Jennifer didn't care about anything Maria had to say, so she stopped listening.

"You should have eaten her," Barry said. *"Maybe no one thinks of wyverns as cuddly because we ate them first. No time to claim you're soft and snuggly when they're being digested."*

Once in the room, she closed the door and locked it. The bed looked so inviting with its fresh, clean sheets. The old bedding was in the washer.

In Dernogard, she'd have to purchase machines with steam cycles to remove all fragrances. The scented beads were nice at covering up odors, but they didn't eliminate them, at least not for a dragon.

She stretched like a cat, arms up in the air, and morphed into a human. Naked, she crawled underneath the clean linen. Finally, she had some peace, and despite not eating all day, she discovered she wasn't as hungry as much as she just wanted to nap. She closed her eyes. After a long day filled with so many events, stillness overcame her limbs for the first time in a week. She allowed it to relax her core. *"I'm going to rest my eyes,"* she thought to Barry.

"You sure?" he asked, sending an image of him pinching Maria's nose, blocking her air passages.

"Are you doing this right now, or is that what you want to do?" Jennifer asked.

"I'm doing this now."

The woman rubbed and opened her mouth.

"I've found ways to entertain myself."

"Do I have a choice on resting or watching?" she asked.

"No."

A vision started.

…Matt placed his hands on his mother's shoulders and said, "I asked that they save you. I asked that they bring you here. The same people who tried to kill me will try to kill you. I need you safe…"

"See, that's a sexy dragon. Really, Jennifer, mate potential here," Barry thought.

"Let me sleep." She sighed and rolled over to her side. Another vision.

… Maria still sat in the chair. Andrew stood, his hand on his wife's back. "Don't be ridiculous. No one wants you dead," Maria answered. "Amy has already warned me about Jennifer and her dragon craziness. She called and said you would tell me you were kidnapped."

Petr asked, *"Did Amy tell you about me? That I would be so young? Because she didn't know about me."*

A second later, before Maria could respond, Petr added, "Did you tell Amy where you were going and that Matt was okay?"

"Why wouldn't I?" Maria tilted her chin upward in defiance. "Amy loves Matt, and she wanted to know where that she-devil Jennifer had taken him…"

"Ha! The she-devil would make a good name for you. But it sounds like Amy knows Matt is with you," Barry thought.

If Maria told Amy, could the group she was working for be on their way to capture Jennifer?

CHAPTER 34

JENNIFER

JENNIFER JUMPED OUT OF BED AND RAN TO THE WINDOW, SCALES forming as she moved. Her hair went from blond to golden flames. She pulled back the blinds and searched the street. The streetlights revealed other cars parked along the curb. What would someone on a stakeout look like? Would they have their vehicle lights on? Would they be in a car or on foot? Could they barge in at any second and take her away?

"Probably not," Barry hypothesized. *"They know you're a dragon, and they know you're here. If they were going to kidnap you, they could have done it by now."*

Matt's image shimmered in front of her as she returned to the bed. Simultaneously walking and watching caused her to be disorientated as she plopped down on top of the mattress. As she closed her eyes, Jennifer demanded, "Hook me up, Barry."

"As you wish."

"…Mom, you just told the person who tried to kill me where to find me?" Matt broke away from searching his mom's face to look toward the ground. His eyes glistened as his shoulders relaxed.

'*Poor Matt,*" Jennifer thought.

Her mate placed a hand on Matt's shoulder and seemed to wait. When Matt faced him, he said, "Matt, I have spent my life waiting for you, but I can't control you. Because of your mother, the rest of us are leaving tonight. Will you stay or go?"

"Well, at least Petr thinks it's serious, Barry. Maybe the dragon hunters have decided to take me by force since both Johan and the Matt trap failed."

"Son, you're staying with us. Amy is on her way here right now. Together, we are going to get you help," Maria said firmly.

Petr moved away from Matt. His face contorted into an expression of frustration, and he ran his left hand through his locks.

Although Matt's features also twisted, they displayed pain. "I'm sorry, Mother. I'm leaving with Petr and Jennifer. Gosh! I can't believe you don't believe me. When Amy gets here, if you don't recognize her, she's the goth girl with the black hair."

"Black hair?" Jennifer thought. *"We didn't know Amy at all."*

"I'm going with Matt," Gung-Gung announced, moving to his feet.

Petr searched the room. "Barry? Ask Jennifer to burn down the house," Petr yelled.

Opening her eyes, her sight became hers again. "I heard you," she shouted back.

"Quick, grab your duffel bag! The ugly green one we've taken everywhere," Barry said from near the closet.

She focused on the area. A large, oversized, imaginary fire appeared in front of the closet. Soon, the flames split in two, and Barry walked through them like they were curtains. Once Barry was in the room, the blaze vanished. "Well, my dragon girl, it's time to burn down the house. Snatch your duffel bag. Inside is what Petr needs_passports, identities, and money. Petr called it the go bag."

"You met with my mate without me?" she asked, both surprised and shocked.

"If you want to call it a meeting, then sure. He put a piece of paper on the table and asked me to pick it up. When I did, he told me what he placed within the bag. He said…" He changed into an identical version of Petr. "If we need to, burn down the building."

"Why?" she asked but rushed to the closet, grabbing the green meanie. "We took all the important things out yesterday. Why destroy the home?"

"Because, Jennifer, I have documentation still lying around. Plus, I used the computer to buy our tickets. If I destroy the evidence, it'll be harder for them to follow us." He returned to Barry. "Sorry, I couldn't add the *my love* crap he calls you. It's gross, don't you think?" He put his hands in his pockets.

"Sure. Gross." She stormed out of the room, meeting Petr in the hall. "You're getting Matt's family out?" she asked.

"Yes."

"Do you have the car keys?"

"I'll get them," he said.

"Get my passport. I left it in my car," she said.

"Okay."

"You're positive you want me to burn down the house?" she asked.

"Yes." He looked at her. "And get dressed after. You can't go like that."

She nodded and handed him the green meanie. Despite her red scales, Petr kissed her. When he leaned back, he said, "Hottest lips I've ever had the pleasure of kissing." He smiled, but she could smell the bitterness of nerves.

"Get everyone out," Jennifer warned. "It's about to heat up."

Although Petr was at the door ushering them out of the

house, Matt's mom sat on the loveseat with Matt, refusing to budge. "Amy is on her way," she repeated.

However, Amy was a threat to Jennifer's freedom. Jennifer sucked the heat from the room, trying to avoid the people, while she willed the pressure to increase. Chemistry lessons replayed in her head.

"We increase the pressure in a diesel engine, so the gas auto ignites," her teacher had said. Removing heat lowered pressure, yet somehow, she managed to both increase the pressure and steal the heat.

A ball of flame rested on the palm of her right hand. She smiled. *"I've upped my cool factor, Barry. I dare Matt to say I look like a cat throwing up a hairball now."*

"Yes, pyromaniac, I believe you've upped your scary game."

"What are you doing?" Maria's eyes grew larger.

"If you asked Amy, I'm sure she would say it's a magic trick, but I'm burning down the house. I'd leave if I were you, but honestly—no offense, Matt—I hope you stay."

Andrew, standing near the door, glared at Jennifer. While she appreciated Matt's dad's faithfulness and desire to protect his spouse when pushed against the wall, Jennifer could kill again. "Get out, now!" she said to Andrew, staring him down. "There is proof of dragons in this house and where you might find one. Personally, I don't want dragon hunters to eat me or force me to be their wife. Neither one is my idea of fun."

"This way," Petr directed. "We all need to evacuate."

They moved, more to escape the crazy flaming demon, but she'd take that as a win. She followed behind them, maintaining perfect control of the flame resting on her palm, feeding it with the heat in the house.

A proper host, Petr waited for the others to exit before turning toward Jennifer, and he said, "Don't make it too big of a fire. Fires spread. I don't want the neighbors hurt."

"I'll do my best," she said, wondering if she could put an inferno out with a thought. She'd try that later.

"Don't all house fires start with faulty wiring?" she asked Barry.

Walking back into the living room, she aimed the flaming ball at the television outlet. She only stayed in the room long enough to ensure the back wall lit up.

"Get dressed," Barry said. *"You can't flee from the fire naked or as a dragon."*

She ran back to the bedroom, glancing in the hallway to see a smoke cloud already forming under the ceiling. Her jeans were easy to find. She slid them on over her scales, ignoring underwear, as she pulled them over her hips.

"Bra. Where's my bra?" she asked.

"Just throw a shirt over your head," Barry said. *"If you can wear clothing while you're a dragon, why do you take your clothes off?"* he asked.

It was a good point she'd have to consider later, but not when she was trying to flee from the smoke. She tugged on a white T-shirt that bunched up at one side. "Shoes," she screamed over the roar of the approaching flames. She coughed when she breathed now.

"Hurry," he said.

She saw one and put it on, but not perfectly. She had to step on the heel part of the shoe. "Where's the other?"

"Leave it. Go outside and join the others! You're not smoke-proof," Barry demanded.

"I'm missing a shoe!" She broke into a choking fit, fumes stinging her eyes. *"How did my shoe get so far away from my other one?"*

"It doesn't matter. Leave, now!" Barry shouted.

She obeyed, sprinting down the hall, throwing a fireball at the computer sitting on the desk.

When she escaped outside, she collapsed on the ground, hacking. She shifted to her full human form, bending her knees into her chest and croaking. She coughed until her lungs burned. With each breath, she felt the branches of her bronchi sizzling. *"That was close,"* she thought.

Near the street, Matt said, "Look, Mom, I'm your son, and I'm not lying. Amy is not a good person. She will kill me." Matt gestured wildly as he yelled.

"Don't you think all this is a little eccentric?" Maria asked. "Andrew, let's go home before the police arrive. I don't want to be involved more than we already are." Maria pulled out her phone and tapped the screen. Matt grabbed the cell from his mother and threw it to the ground, crushing it.

Petr helped Jennifer stand. He threw his left arm around her, pulling her up to her feet, and drew her into his chest. She rasped into his neck, listening to the electronic crunching.

"Matt Davis, you get into this car this second," Andrew said.

"Meelaya," Petr said, kissing her head. He found her mouth, devouring it as if he was starving. When he pulled away, her lips tingled. He whispered into her hair, "You took longer than I thought you would. Please don't scare me like that again." He pulled back. The orange tint from the fire painted his face.

"No! Mom!" Matt yelled.

Leaving Jennifer, Petr ran over to Matt. "Calm down, Matt."

At the same time, Gung-Gung stepped in between his daughter and grandson. He turned to face Maria and placed his hand on her arm. His voice was firm as he said, "Enough. Matt is not human, and our world has once again changed."

Even from here, Jennifer spied tears falling down Maria's face. "Not again, Dad. I can't let it happen to Matt."

"It already has." Gung-Gung held his arms open, and she immediately fell into his grasp.

Andrew joined them, pressing the unlock button on his keys. "Maria, no more. Get in. Whatever is going on is deeper than we thought. I'm not taking us home."

Flames leaped and bounced on Petr's roof, making a roaring noise. "Fire!" Jennifer screamed, running to the house on the right. "Matt!" She needed his help to alert the neighbors in case that angry fire jumped between houses.

"Yes," Matt answered, but he had his back toward Jennifer as his mother broke into all-out sobs. She left her father's embrace and slammed herself into her husband's chest.

"Knock on the doors. Then crush all your family's cell phones, and I mean destroy them," Jennifer said. "Petr, stay where you are."

"Yes, ma'am," Petr responded.

"Fire," she repeated as she pounded on the door.

When the porch light came on, she ran back to the car. "Please tell me you got my keys and grabbed my passport," Jennifer said to Petr.

"I did," Petr said.

"We need to go before the police and the fire engines arrive. I don't want to be blocked off by them. We'd have to answer questions that could detain us. I'm afraid the Immortals will try to use this opportunity to catch us."

"Good thinking," Petr said.

Glancing across the yard, she saw the neighbors at the other house talking to Matt.

"Matt," Jennifer yelled. "We need to leave, now!" she demanded.

Matt trotted over to his parents. "No offense, Mom. I'm riding with Jennifer."

"I suggest," Petr said to Andrew, "that you follow us." Surprising Jennifer, Petr unlocked the sedan doors with the fob, not the keys. Since she'd met him, he'd always used the key.

"Where's the green duffel bag?" Jennifer asked as she searched the area.

"I put it in the trunk before you came out," Petr responded.

"Where are you going?" Gung-Gung asked.

"Can't tell you. I'm not sure whose side you're on," Petr answered.

"Oh yeah." Matt, who stood by the back passenger side of Petr's car, ran over to his dad. "Dad, Gung-Gung, I need your cell phones."

Reluctantly, Andrew handed Matt his mobile device. Matt dropped it to the ground and danced on it, breaking it into several pieces. Matt held out his hand to his grandfather.

"I left it at home," he responded. "Stupid thing anyway. But I did..." Gung-Gung opened the back door of the white Lexus, bending inside. When he came back out, he dangled a black leather-bound book from his hand. "I brought this," he said, giving it to Matt. "I would rather you have your passport right now."

Matt hugged him. "You're the best Gung-Gung ever! But I thought you were coming with me?"

"We will see what happens next, but your mother needs me. Matt, stay safe. Your safety is paramount."

"I love you, Gung-Gung," Matt said.

"And I love you," he responded.

"Mom, Dad, I love you, too."

Sitting in Petr's sedan, Jennifer inspected her foot. Gravel had dug into it, but there were no cuts or scrapes. Petr and Matt climbed in at the same time. Using his left hand to reach over the steering wheel, Petr started the vehicle, then leaned back, sighing. Before she glanced at him, she scented his blood in the air. Sure enough, dark red covered his shoulder.

"I can drive," she offered.

"Not right now." His features pressed together into an expression of concentration as he backed the car out and placed it in drive.

"Respect his space," Barry said from behind her. Leaning forward, she pulled down the visor, using the mirror on the back to search the back seat. For some reason, Matt chose to sit behind Petr, though Petr was taller than her. Matt would have more room if he sat behind her, but in their rush to jump into the car, maybe he just took the first seat available. Buckled in, Barry sat beside Matt, dressed as a cowboy, wearing a hat and spurs, and with guns at his sides.

"Sometimes a man needs to be a man." Barry tipped his hat.

"Later, I want an explanation of what the outfit is about, if there is one," she thought, but her eyes landed on her car, sitting in front of Petr's smoldering home. It felt symbolic, Petr's house burning, like she burned his path, changed it, and altered his life.

A fire engine passed them, lights and sirens blaring.

Glancing back, she lost sight of the building, only able to make out the smoke rising into the sky. In the mirror, she studied her reflection. Dark ash smudges covered her face. She opened the glove box and pulled out a brown napkin from a drive-through. Wetting it with spit, she did her best to remove the smears.

In the haste to leave, she'd abandoned her car, leaving it sitting there for the police to find. Would they go to her house and discover her parents had also moved to another country? Would they think that she'd been kidnapped? Place her face on milk cartons or make a TV show asking Americans if they'd seen her?

Leaning in her seat, she closed the visor and surveyed the man she had claimed. She studied Petr's nose and his perfect, sharp, angled chin. As much as her burning down Petr's house changed his life forever, he had also transformed hers. Without him, she'd likely be sitting across from Johan or dead. Because of Petr, she'd left her plans behind, her college career, her scholarship, and her humanity. Their path lay in Dernogard, and with it, the hopes of a bright new future.

EPILOGUE

MiFeng, in his human form, sat in the abandoned council room in the south tower of Dernogard. For days, he hadn't been able to take his eyes off the old whalebone document, still in perfect condition despite the centuries that had passed since its creation.

After River's death, he refused to become a human. Until now. One message from Che-non changed everything.

...River had a child, an heir. She's part wyvern and part Nordic. She's red, can control fire, and has the ability to morph into a human and a dragon at the same time...

MiFeng didn't need to check the prophecy to be reminded of what it said. He remembered every word.

River's descendant, the Mark of Redemption, Jennifer Wright, was on her way to Dernogard.

The End of Book 3
The Dragon Age Prophecy

ACKNOWLEDGMENTS

I have this amazing support group, that starts around my family. Thank you, husband, daughter, oldest, and youngest son for putting up with my continuous devotion to writing. I am blessed to have you in my life. I love you, all.

Mom and Dad, thank you for being a good role model and encouraging me to pursue my dreams.

Thank you, Vickie F. for reading each page of the first version. For saying you loved it and giving me your thoughts. Even though hardly a single word is left from that revision, the story is the same and you helped shape it.

Thank you, Xavier C, for helping with Spanish and Latino culture. Thank you, Yev for help with Russian.

I've been blessed to find several groups of like-minded individuals. The *Six A.M. Group* for listening to my success and my woes (Ali, Rae, Shanna, Zee, Erica, Karla, Katharine). The *2020 Finish Strong Group* put together by Dale L. Roberts (for advice on publishing, please visit: https://selfpublishing withdale.com). Five-years later and I'm still meeting with Andy, Guen, and Nick. YouTuber, artist, and writer H.K. Darkwood (https://hkdarkwood.com) and Melissa Eick, for being there, excited every time I mention what I'm working on.

I am blown away by the artwork from Neal at Elerfine - Etsy. Thank you for bringing Jennifer to life.

My first editor Vicki, thank you for your patience and for helping me learn along the way. Because of you, I improved so much I had to scrape the first version and update it. www.vickiedits.com.

If each time your ears tingle when you return a round of edits to me, Jennia, it's because I'm saying, "Wow. That's incredible. I love it." She went above and beyond to point out loops and mistakes, questioning the motivation of my characters. I appreciate every challenge she gave me to make the story stronger. Thank. You. Home | Jennia Edits

Roxana added the final touches to the work. Reading through it in record time and surprising me at how many mistakes were left. Her attention to detail is much appreciated. https://proofreadebooks.com

My editors are amazing. Each did their best to lead me to a powerful story. All the mistakes in this book are mine.

ABOUT THE AUTHOR

Let me share with you a secret. Well, it's not a secret to those that know me. I love math—believe it is God's language, perfect like he is—I adore math! My devotion is so strong that I've threatened to ground my three kids if they brought home anything less than A's in math. Math, to me, is natural, like breathing. Unlike grammar, where letters like to flip around and change positions, math stays faithful.

I thought grammar, like math, was something you understood from birth. And in college, I gave up my dream of sharing worlds with other people to go into engineering, because I had no clue what a passive sentence structure was or how to correct it. I wasn't one of those gifted with grammar.

Don't get me wrong, I love my day job. I love looking at data from machines and interpreting their language—Do they need maintenance? Is it failing? Is it behaving normally?

But I missed English and stories.

Then, one day, while cleaning my house, I listened to something I thought was an autobiography. It turned out to be a self-help book. In it, Scott Adams explained what a passive sentence structure was, and that grammar was learned.

What?!

Not only that, but the first time you write a story, it can be a draft that you change, manipulate, and update.

Oh my!

Finally, I could do things I never knew were possible. I could write a book. I love to make up stories and worlds.

Thank you for reading my story. I hope you enjoyed it, because I loved writing it.

-N. A. Hydes

Home | N. A. Hydes (nahydes.com)